Black Light

Michael O'Toole

Published in 2022 by Maverick House Publishers.
Maverick House, Unit 33,
The Business Centre, Stadium Business Park,
Ballycoolin, Dublin 11, Ireland.
info@maverickhouse.com
http://www.maverickhouse.com

ISBN 978-1-908518-71-2 (Print)
ISBN 978-1-908518-72-9 (Epub)

A CIP catalogue record for this book is available from the British Library.

This book is a work of fiction. Any resemblance to people or events in real life is purely coincidential.

To Olga, who is everything.

1

Dublin, Sunday, October 20, 2019

LAZARUS held his pistol up to the darkness.

He tapped the button beside the trigger. The magazine shot out of the stock. It landed in the palm of his hand. He closed his fist around the stainless-steel clip, so that only the top bullet was visible.

He placed the gun on his lap and eased the brass shell out of the magazine. He tried to examine the bullet, but the evening sky was covered by a blanket of heavy clouds that suffocated the light inside the speeding car. He lowered the sun visor and the vanity mirror lights came on.

He held the bullet between his finger and thumb and raised it to the light. He squinted to look for even the smallest speck of dirt, anything that could affect the shot. He knew he only had to check the first bullet, because that was all he needed.

One shot, one kill.

That's what his old army instructors had taught him.

And they had taught him well.

Lazarus was examining the bullet when he heard a loud snort from the driver's seat. He looked over and saw Detective Garda Harry McEvoy smirk.

'What's your problem, old man?' Lazarus asked.

'Your weird obsession is my problem,' McEvoy said.

'The piece is fine. You checked it a gazillion times back in the station. You always do this. Relax. Stop being so anal, *amigo*.'

Lazarus glared at him.

'Me being anal is why you and I go home in one piece every night. Remember that. And for the millionth time, amigo is Spanish. You know I'm Italian.'

McEvoy took a hand from the Toyota Camry's steering wheel and gave Lazarus a dismissive wave.

'Spanish, Italian, same thing,' he said.

Lazarus gritted his teeth, tried not to give him the pleasure of a reaction.

McEvoy winked at Detective Garda Rachel Winter in the rear-view mirror. She was sitting forward in the back seat, a hand on each headrest. It was as if she was watching her parents argue. Which wasn't too far off the mark.

'Don't mind Lazarus, Rachel,' McEvoy said.

'You're new, but he's quite nice when you get to know him. He just can't control his Latin blood when he's on a job. *Mamma mia!*'

That made Lazarus go full Italian.

He brought the fingers and thumb of one hand together, shook them angrily at McEvoy.

'*Porca Miseria. Basta, stronzo,*' he growled.

McEvoy looked at Winter in the mirror again.

'He's always saying that to me. I've no idea what it means, but it sounds nice.'

McEvoy and Winter laughed.

Lazarus shook his head, tutted at McEvoy, jutted his chin at him. He turned back to the bullet. He was always serious on a job and hated how his partner hid his own nerves by cracking jokes.

He lifted up the magazine and forced the bullet into it. Then he slid the magazine into the butt of the German-made Sig-Sauer P226. He snapped the slide back and heard the reassuring thwack of a 9mm shell entering the firing chamber.

Now the pistol was ready.

And so was he.

He swivelled in the passenger seat.

'You sure you're prepared for this?' he asked Winter.

'Yes, Sergeant.'

Lazarus's eyes tightened.

'Leave Sergeant for the parade room or the Super's office. It's either Lazarus or John.'

Winter blushed.

Then she thought for a beat.

'Okay...Lazarus,' she said.

Winter was the latest recruit to Lazarus's sex crimes team.

He considered her for a moment. She was barely 30. Her thick blonde hair was in a tight ponytail. Her mouth was narrow. Her eyes were pale blue and sharp. She had a soft face.

Lazarus eyed her.

'You look nervous,' he said.

She flushed.

'It's my first job with you. I don't want to mess up.'

Lazarus nodded.

'Nerves are good. They keep you alive.'

His dark eyes became even darker.

'And you need nerves when you're up against someone as dangerous as Sean Maloney.'

He felt his stomach tighten at the mention of that name.

Sean Maloney.

Killer.

Drug dealer.

Paedophile.

The team were driving on the M1 motorway out of Dublin to take Maloney down. Their destination was a hotel near the airport. It was 7.35pm. A heavy drizzle, that Irish rain that goes through your clothes and soaks your bones, fell from the sky. The wipers moved languidly across the windscreen of the team's black Toyota Camry saloon.

The simmering hatred Lazarus felt for Maloney – for all of the monsters he tracked down – boiled over. His fists balled, almost by themselves. He grimaced, stared into the night.

He sometimes found that hatred hard to contain.

It possessed him. Obsessed him.

Was close to destroying him.

McEvoy gave Lazarus a reassuring nod.

'We'll get him, Lazarus,' he said.

'We better,' Lazarus said.

'Maloney is an animal,' he said, more to himself than his colleagues.

'He once killed a woman over a ten grand debt. Blasted her face off in front of her son. Left the toddler alone with her. When the paramedics got there, he was hugging her corpse.'

Winter took in a sharp breath.

'Jesus Christ.'

'Another time he made a teenager lie on the road and ran over him on a motorbike because a kilo of coke he was minding was seized,' Lazarus said.

He stared hard at Winter.

'And he rapes teenage girls,' he said.

His eyes flared.

3

'No matter what happens, I'm taking him down tonight. He got away from me once. I won't let him escape again.'

'What happened?' Winter said. 'How did he escape?'

She didn't know the unit's cases yet. The job was so last minute that Lazarus hadn't had a chance to even brief her on their target.

'We had been investigating him for abusing a kid called Sarah Casey,' Lazarus said to Winter.

'She comes from a well-known family in the inner city. Her father and brothers are criminals, but that's irrelevant. She's a victim. Nothing less. She was only 14 when he groomed her. Then he raped her.

'She made a complaint and we were about to charge him-'

'But then he fucked off out of Dodge,' McEvoy said.

He clicked his fingers.

'Vanished just like that.'

'Jesus. Do you think he was tipped off?' Winter asked.

'No chance,' Lazarus snapped.

'Only Harry and I knew of the charges. These bastards have a sixth sense. We had arrested and questioned him. He probably knew charges were close.'

McEvoy sped along the road.

'We've been looking for him ever since,' Lazarus said.

'We have tried everything. Hounding the intelligence section at HQ, talking to informants on the street, checking if he had any social media accounts set up, the works. Nothing.'

Lazarus had repeatedly told his team they had to find Maloney for Sarah Casey. Because she counted. Like all the other victims.

But then Lazarus closed his eyes and thought once again of the woman who was the real reason why he faced down evil.

That one woman.

That one woman for whom he sat across from a monster as he tried to convince Lazarus the 86-year-old bedbound pensioner he raped was really into it.

That one woman for whom he kicked down the door of an apartment to rescue three teens trafficked into Ireland and beaten until they serviced the men who called to the same door.

That one woman for whom he watched hour after agonising hour of kids in Vietnam being tortured on camera so he could nail the Dublin solicitor who paid for the abuse on his company credit card and even tried to expense it.

That one precious woman.

McEvoy's voice dragged Lazarus back to the now.

'And then, thanks be to God, we got news on the fucker today,' he said.

A detective sergeant in Intelligence had called Lazarus at 4pm. An informant had seen Maloney check in at the Prestige Dublin Airport Hotel two hours earlier. That was the start of panicked arguments between Lazarus and his boss, Detective Inspector Mark Anderson.

Anderson had wanted to send in the National Surveillance Unit and then call in the ASU if the undercover operatives spotted Maloney in the hotel.

Lazarus patted his pistol.

He knew he didn't need the Armed Support.

Lazarus had gone above the D/I's head to the Superintendent and insisted on going in with his own team. He promised the Super he and his colleagues, who were always armed as detectives, had all the firepower they would need if the shit hit the fan.

He got his way. Just.

'I tell you this, Lazarus,' McEvoy said.

'You are fucked if Maloney isn't here. Anderson is waiting for a chance to shaft you. But that's what happens when you smack your D/I on a night out. They remember things like that.'

'He was lucky it was just one slap,' Lazarus said.

McEvoy laughed. He tailgated a van and flashed the blue lights. The vehicle lumbered out of their way. Lazarus was about to admonish McEvoy for his driving when he heard a beep in his pocket. Foreboding surged through him. He knew it was his wife; he had a special tone for her. He took out the iPhone XS and opened WhatsApp. His heart pounded in his chest. His mouth went dry. He grimaced and looked at the screen.

You said you would be back in time. They were waiting for you:(

He screwed his eyes closed.

'Everything okay, Lazarus?' McEvoy asked.

'I'm in the shit,' he said.

'With the D/I?'

'I wish,' he said.

'Jenna?'

Lazarus nodded.

'Oh fuck,' McEvoy said.

'What did you do this time?'

5

'Missed a play date with the boys. I was supposed to take them to their uncle Massimo for pizza and a movie.'

He went quiet.

'Bollix,' he said after a moment.

Then he shook his head.

'And Jenna was supposed to have the evening off. She planned to go out with a few friends.'

'Ouch,' McEvoy said.

He made a quick sign of the cross.

'Pray for Lazarus,' he said.

'Nothing I can't handle,' Lazarus said.

'Yeah right,' McEvoy said.

'You're shitting it. You're more afraid of Jenna than Maloney.'

Lazarus tapped on the phone keypad.

Sorry, carina, just at a meeting that ran on. I'll be home as soon as I can. Not much longer. I'll make it up to them. xxx

No way was he telling her the truth. He turned back to Winter.

'I'm nervous. You know why?'

She shrugged her shoulders.

'In case we miss Maloney?'

Lazarus shook his head.

'In case he kills us.'

Winter's eyes widened.

'Maloney will do anything to avoid jail,' he said.

'Even kill a cop. *Especially* kill a cop. Remember that. Be careful in there.'

'No problem, Lazarus,' Winter said.

Then after a beat: 'I won't mess up.'

'Don't,' Lazarus said.

He put the Sig in its holster and checked the rest of his gear. The pepper spray canister was on his left hip, the holster on his right. Handcuffs in a pouch in the small of his back. His baton beside the pistol.

A gust of wind swirled a knot of leaves into the autumn sky. McEvoy took an off ramp without signalling. Lazarus checked the passenger mirror. He saw three marked Garda vehicles close behind them.

Lazarus's stomach pitched.

The Camry sped across the link road from the M1 motorway to the hotel. Traffic was sparse and McEvoy, the best driver Lazarus had ever worked with, handled the Toyota with ease.

McEvoy slammed on the brakes and the car screeched to a halt at the entrance to a modern hotel. Lazarus was out of the police car before McEvoy cut the engine. He shivered as the late autumn chill bit at his olive cheeks. His Mediterranean blood was not made for this city. He always felt cold in Dublin, even though he had been born and bred there.

'Soft day,' McEvoy joked.

'I'm frozen,' Lazarus grumbled.

He zipped up his black overcoat. It reached down to his knees and had an internal fleece, which he also zipped to the max. He wore the collar up. He liked the look. He had bought it back home in Italy a few years ago. By rights, he should have worn the dark blue raid jacket with GARDA in bright yellow on the back and the force crest on the right chest, like McEvoy and Winter.

But he was the boss.

He did what he wanted.

McEvoy stood beside Winter. He was overweight and squat. He had joined before the Garda height requirement of five foot nine was abolished, and he just scraped though by half an inch. His belly strained at the buttons of a white shirt. He wore black shoes and dark blue cotton trousers that sagged around his arse.

McEvoy had a deep voice and had kept his strong southern accent, somewhere along the Cork and Kerry border, despite almost four decades in Dublin. He had a ruddy face, with a bulbous nose. Deep red veins stood out on his cheeks like rivers on a map. He had the wrinkled mouth of a smoker. He looked older than his 56 years. His grey hair was unkempt, and he had an oversized salt and pepper moustache. Two more chins than were necessary, too.

Winter was taller, almost six foot, and was in good shape. Lazarus knew she was into running and the gym. It showed. She wore black skinny jeans and hiking boots.

Their Garda jackets were open. Lazarus could see their body armour underneath. He tapped the ballistic vest hidden under his own coat. He found its hollow rap reassuring. The vests were supposed to stop a knife, or a 9mm bullet, or a shotgun blast. He hoped he never had to find out.

He examined the hotel. He counted six storeys on a glass-fronted block to the right. To its left and in front of him stood a smaller building. It housed the main entrance. It had long windows and concrete cladding. Both buildings were bathed in a soft pink light.

Lazarus strode to the entrance. McEvoy and Winter followed. The automatic doors slid open. He moved his hand closer to the gun on his hip as he scanned the lobby area for Maloney. He didn't see him. He breathed out.

He marched towards reception and singled out a woman who looked like a manager. She was in her mid thirties. Tall and thin. Perfectly brushed dark hair caressed her shoulders. A fringe skirted her eyeline. She wore a black trouser suit, high heels and a crisp white blouse.

She angled her head back to look at Lazarus coming towards her. Her blue eyes sparkled.

'Ms O'Donnell?' Lazarus said.

'That's me.'

She looked him up and down. Then she gave him a subtle smile.

Lazarus got that a lot. He knew he was handsome. He didn't abuse it, but many women, and some men, could not hide their admiration. He was tall and naturally athletic. His Italian looks – olive skin, dark eyes, strong nose, full lips – made him something of a catch. Better looking than most cops, as he kept reminding Jenna.

'Maeve O'Donnell. I'm the duty manager,' the woman said, her smile wider now.

'Detective Sergeant John Lazarus, Broadstone Garda Station. We spoke earlier.'

He showed her his Garda ID.

'I'd never have guessed. You undercover cops do a great job.'

Lazarus stared at her and her smile faltered.

That happened to him a lot, too.

'Where is he?' Lazarus asked.

He wasn't one for niceties.

O'Donnell bustled him a few paces to the side.

She looked around, lowered her voice.

'He's in his room,' the manager said. 'Room service was delivered 20 minutes ago at 7.20pm. Burger and chips and two Guinness.'

Two beers.

Lazarus frowned.

'Does he have company?' he asked.

Someone else in the room meant things could get messy. His stomach tightened at the prospect.

'No. He is alone,' she said.

Lazarus nodded.

The manager waved a hand towards a set of doors.

'The lifts are that way,' she said.

'Room 475. Fourth floor. Turn left when you leave the lift.'

She handed him a key.

'Thank you,' Lazarus said.

She winked at him.

'Try not to get any blood on the carpet. It's new.'

Lazarus ignored her.

He turned and nodded to McEvoy and Winter as he walked towards the doors. They fell in behind him. Three uniformed officers appeared in the lobby. Lazarus motioned for them to stay on the ground floor.

He opened one of the double doors and came into a hallway. Three lifts were on the right. One had its doors open. They stepped inside. Lazarus saw Winter stand apart from him and McEvoy. She bit her lower lip and pushed a lock of hair behind her ear.

McEvoy leant against a wall. He folded his arms and whistled.

The inside of the lift was covered in mirrors. Lazarus considered himself. He was six foot two, decent shoulders, good biceps, a thin waist hidden under all his police gear. Not too bad for a 39-year-old. He wore soft but sturdy boots and navy jeans. To help keep the Irish chill at bay, he wore a blue cotton shirt and white long-sleeved T-shirt underneath. None of it visible under his closed coat. Four layers, including the ballistic vest, and still he shivered. He wore his dark hair cropped tight. Dark stubble formed a shadow on his cheeks and chin. It accentuated his strong jaw line. He thought he looked okay.

More than okay.

Apart from his eyes. They betrayed him.

The eyes were dark and brooding. On the rare occasion Lazarus was happy, his eyes shone and softened his face.

But mostly they were sad. And angry.

And suddenly Lazarus felt fear grip his stomach.

He realised in that instant he was not afraid of facing Maloney, but of himself. He was frightened of what he saw in those eyes. The eyes told him what he was capable of, what he would do to Maloney if he had to.

If he got the chance.

The fury burning in his eyes was overwhelming. He had to turn away. He couldn't look at them. He couldn't look at himself.

The lift moved off and he closed those eyes that unnerved him so much.

Just for a second.

Just to enjoy that fleeting moment only hunters like him experience. That wonderful moment when the target is in your sights, powerless.

Lazarus pitied the normal people who went to work or to the pub or to a game and who would never experience that sacred moment. That moment when you know you have him. When you know it's over before it has even begun.

It's beautiful. It was better than the best sex, he once told McEvoy.

McEvoy told him he wasn't doing the sex right.

The lift stopped and the doors opened. Lazarus was first out. His mouth felt dry, his heart racing. He inched along the corridor, his hand on the soft holster, taking out the Sig, holding it up. He came to room 481. He kept moving.

Then 479. It was opposite a fire door and stairs leading to reception.

Room 477 appeared on his right.

He walked on.

Then he reached 475. Maloney's room.

It had a pine door with brass numerals. He put his ear to the wood. He heard no movement inside. He handed the swipe card to McEvoy. Lazarus stood on his right. Winter on his left. All three had their guns out now. Ready.

Lazarus nodded to McEvoy and watched him place the card in the slot.

There was a moment's stillness.

Then Lazarus heard a soft click.

The light on the door handle turned green.

McEvoy threw the door open and Lazarus bounded inside. He could feel Winter on his heels.

The room was pitch black. The heavy blackout curtains were closed tight.

Lazarus rushed towards the bed. His angry voice filled the room.

'Armed gardai! Armed police! Don't fucking move!'

He raised the Sig and pointed it to Maloney's head.

Winter was shouting, too.

McEvoy flicked a switch, artificial light filled the room.

And Lazarus felt his heart sink when he saw the bed was empty.

2

Lazarus was calm on the outside, like all good leaders.
But inside, he was in turmoil. His heart pounded. His mouth was dry.

He scanned the room. A patterned duvet had been thrown back and lay at an angle on the bed. Crumpled blue tracksuit bottoms were on the floor beside it. A black mobile phone was face up on a small pine bedside cabinet. It was connected to a charger in a wall socket. Wherever he was, Maloney had left here in a hurry.

Lazarus put his free hand to his forehead.

'*Bastardo.*'

He cursed whoever tipped off Maloney.

McEvoy came out of the bathroom. He looked at Lazarus and shook his head. It was beside the door they had barrelled through seconds earlier. McEvoy walked past Winter and Lazarus to the other end of the room. He checked behind the heavy mauve curtains.

'Nothing,' he said with another shake of his head.

Lazarus tried to think.

Maloney couldn't be far away.

'*Bastardo,*' he said again.

'Speak English, man,' McEvoy snapped.

His rebuke didn't register with Lazarus. He was zoned out, thinking of every possible scenario. Each worse than the one before.

He punched the mattress. He checked the time. 7.51pm. They had been in the hotel for just ten minutes.

'He has to be near,' he said, more to himself than the others. 'We'll search the whole hotel if we have to. Every floor. Every room.'

Sweat glistened on his brow. He started to feel the heat of the room. He unzipped his overcoat and fleece. They exposed his body armour.

'This is a clusterfuck,' McEvoy said.

'Anderson will go nuts when he hears we lost him. We're goosed.'

He shook his head again. The folds of skin wobbled on the back of his neck. His fat head was really starting to get on Lazarus's nerves. And the mention of Detective Inspector Mark Anderson aggravated his headache. His temples throbbed.

'I knew we should have waited for surveillance,' McEvoy grumbled. 'That's what Anderson wanted. He is going to fuck us from a height.'

'Listen,' Lazarus snapped. 'This is not your problem. Stay in your lane, Detective.'

McEvoy held his hands up.

'Fair enough, sergeant. You're the boss.'

'I am. And don't forget it,' Lazarus said.

'I made the decision to run this operation. If it goes wrong, it's me in the shit, not you. Don't worry, old man.'

McEvoy looked away. Lazarus examined the room. It was spacious, with a beige, deep-pile carpet and terracotta walls. The curtains McEvoy had checked moments earlier ran down to the floor. There were two lamps on the back wall on either side of the bed. Another light hung from the centre of the ceiling. It was covered by a plain lampshade. A large flat-screen television was attached to the wall opposite the bed. A narrow pine table sat underneath the screen, a wooden chair with leather upholstery tucked in underneath.

Lazarus saw the room service tray on the table. He walked over to it. The tray held a white plate with tomato ketchup smeared on it. The food was long eaten. An empty pint glass flecked with white foam from the stout sat beside the plate. Two half-crushed Guinness cans lay on their side.

Lazarus took the Tetra radio from its clip on his body armour and walked into the centre of the room. He got the uniformed sergeant downstairs. He told him to send back-up. While he was talking, Lazarus prepared himself for the nightmare search. It could take hours. But Maloney was still there. He knew it.

Lazarus finished speaking into the handset and looked up in time to see Winter walk towards a large wardrobe built into an alcove. It was on the other side of the bed. It had red pine double doors and was wide and long.

And suddenly he knew.

'Rachel, no!' he shouted.

He heard the panicked cry from his own throat and watched helpless as Winter threw him a puzzled glance. She wrapped a fist around a long handle of brushed steel on one of the doors. But before she could grip it, the door flew open and slammed into her.

The force threw her back. She crashed against the bed.

Maloney jumped out of the wardrobe.

He punched Winter on the side of her face with his left hand. Then he stood over her and kicked her in the stomach. He raised a pistol in his right hand, pointed it in her face.

Then he rammed the muzzle of the black semi-automatic into Winter's mouth. She was on her knees and raised her hands to the air as Maloney pressed down on the trigger.

The rest of the room fell away. Lazarus could only see the gun and Maloney and Winter cowering in front of him.

Lazarus inched his hand to the holster, but Maloney saw the movement. He bared his teeth.

'Move and I'll end this bitch! I swear to fuck!'

He motioned to McEvoy, who was still at the window.

'You, fat man, get back to your buddy.'

'Okay, Seanie, no problem. It's cool,' McEvoy said.

He put his hands out in a calming gesture and shuffled towards Lazarus. Maloney grabbed Winter's hair with his free hand and grinned at her.

'Do you like that? Do you like it inside you, bitch?'

He laughed in her face.

'Get up,' he growled.

Winter kept her hands up and used her thigh muscles to raise herself to her feet. Her angle changed as she got up. She was now side-on to Lazarus. He saw the muzzle of the gun was inside her mouth by at least two inches. Her lips were almost touching the trigger guard.

Maloney turned to Lazarus.

'Right, pig, I know you're in charge. I remember you. Here's what's happening. We're going out that fucken door.'

He gestured his head towards the hotel room exit.

'And you cunts are staying here.'

Winter kept her hands in the air. She was at her full height now and was inches taller than Maloney. He held the gun at an angle to keep it in her mouth.

Lazarus saw Winter's eyes bulging. Her cheek was blood red from Maloney's punch. Maloney grabbed Winter and began edging her to the door.

Maloney was just metres from freedom. Once he got through the door, stairs leading to reception would be within touching distance. There were only unarmed officers down there. Lazarus knew their batons would be no match for Maloney's pistol. He imagined Maloney commandeering a car and escaping. With Winter.

And then the memory of breaking the news to Sarah Casey and her parents that Maloney had escaped the last time flashed into his mind.

He wouldn't let it happen again.

He couldn't.

He moved forward, took his pistol from its holster in one fluid motion.

Maloney saw him and reacted.

'Get fucken back. I *will* kill her.'

Lazarus tightened his grip on the gun. He curled his index finger around the trigger.

He brought the pistol up, levelled it on Maloney.

Lazarus saw confusion on Maloney's face.

'What the fuck? I said I'd fucken kill her...'

Lazarus kept walking. He pressed the trigger, enough to move it a few millimetres, not enough to shoot.

His eyes were on fire.

'Wha..what?' Maloney stammered, a look of confusion on his face as he tried to figure out what the mad man opposite him was doing.

'John...' McEvoy said.

There was panic in his voice.

'Lazarus don't do this. Think ab-'

'Shut the fuck up, Harry,' Lazarus said, never taking his eyes off Maloney.

Lazarus held his Sig in a classic two-hand grip. He checked its sights. Maloney's head was in the centre of them. He took another step. He was less than two metres from Maloney.

Maloney's eyes were wide.

'I'll fucken do it.'

Lazarus didn't falter.

'I'll blow her head off!' Maloney hissed.

'John!' McEvoy shouted.

Lazarus took one final step towards Maloney.

The gun was almost touching his head.

One shot, one kill.

His finger applied a fraction more pressure on the trigger.

He could see the shock in Maloney's eyes.

'Get back you bastard or she gets it. This is your final warning,' Maloney said.

His voice was almost a croak.

When Lazarus spoke, his was calm and confident.

'I am going to end you,' he said.

Lazarus saw Maloney swallow hard. His Adam's apple bobbed against the skin.

Lazarus was so close now he could smell the Guinness on Maloney's breath. Winter was quiet. She was taking short breaths. Her mouth was wide open, the pistol still rammed inside it. Her eyes were swimming frantically in their sockets.

Lazarus put the Sig's muzzle hard against the centre of Maloney's forehead. He pressed the weapon into his flesh.

Maloney recoiled from the gun, but Lazarus moved forward to keep the business end of his pistol tight against his skull.

'You have five seconds,' Lazarus said.

'Get back. Move back.' Maloney shouted.

'Four.'

'Fuck off. I mean it.'

'John, stop this!' McEvoy shouted.

'Three.'

Maloney looked at Lazarus, then at McEvoy, then Lazarus again.

'Two.'

McEvoy tried again.

'Sergeant John Lazarus! Stop! Don't!'

Winter started screaming, the sound gagged by the gun in her mouth.

'One.'

Lazarus moved to pull the trigger.

And Maloney's shoulders sagged.

He withdrew the gun from Winter's mouth and raised his hands in the air.

3

Nothing happened for an instant.
Then everything did.

Lazarus waited until the muzzle of Maloney's pistol was away from Winter then sprang forward. She collapsed on to the bed as he reached Maloney.

He brought up a boot and slammed the toecap into Maloney's balls. Maloney howled, dropped the gun and crumpled to the floor. Lazarus gingerly moved the pistol out of the way with his foot and disarmed his own before holstering it.

'Jesus Christ,' Maloney gasped.

He lay on the ground and looked up at Lazarus.

'That Casey girl is a dirty slut. She led me on.'

Maloney grinned through the pain.

'And I've had better wanks.'

A picture appeared in Lazarus's mind.

A young woman. Half-naked. Destroyed. Black eyes, a broken nose, missing teeth. Clumps of her beautiful brown hair ripped out, exposing her pink scalp. Defensive injuries to her arms, cuts on her hands. Dumped in a ditch on the side of a cold mountain. Covered with leaves and shit and soil to hide her, but not enough to protect her from the rats and foxes and feral dogs that roamed the area.

Maloney was still in a foetal position on the carpet, his hands cupped around his balls. Lazarus was on him in an instant. A left, then a big right, then a left again. Another right hit the sweet spot on his chin. It was a flurry of punches. Lazarus knew he had lost it, but he didn't care. He must have landed half a dozen hits.

Maloney groaned and brought his hands up to protect his head. Lazarus countered by using his feet. He stamped on him twice, the sole of the boot connecting hard with his stomach.

Lazarus bent down. His breathing was laboured. He brought his mouth to Maloney's ear.

'This is for Gabriella,' he whispered.

Lazarus straightened. He was preparing to stamp on Maloney again, when he felt himself being yanked backwards.

'Enough, Lazarus. Enough!'

It was McEvoy. He was pulling on the collar of Lazarus's jacket.

'You'll kill the fucker,' he said. 'No more.'

Lazarus held his hands up.

'Okay, okay.'

He swallowed hard and went to say something else, but there was a blur of yellow at the door. Two uniforms burst in, one female, one male. The male ran towards Winter, while the female had her baton extended and made straight for Maloney.

'Stay down. Stay fucking down,' she shouted.

She landed her knees on the small of Maloney's back. She moved the asp up over head, then slammed it down on Maloney's bicep.

McEvoy went to Winter. She was struggling to get her breath. Lazarus moved back to Maloney's gun. He took a glove from his pocket, used it to lift up the weapon. He examined it and breathed a sigh of relief. It was a replica.

He took an evidence bag from his coat, placed the weapon inside.

Maloney had his hands around his head and screamed for the cop to stop, but she hit him again.

'Jesus! Please!'

Maloney's voice was high pitched and brittle.

The cop looked up at Lazarus and he nodded. Enough. Lazarus helped the uniform haul him to his feet. He grabbed Maloney, turned him around and slammed his face into the wall. His forehead banged off the hard surface. Lazarus heard him yelp. Then he saw blood on the wall. He took Maloney's right wrist and yanked it behind his back. He pushed the hand up Maloney's back until it was at a painful angle. Maloney screamed again. Lazarus looked to the female cop – he remembered her as Sinead Duffy, on the beat for two years – and she mouthed she had Maloney. Lazarus released one hand and reached around to the pouch on the back of his belt. He opened the clasp and took out the cuffs. The iron was cold in his hand. He opened one cuff and snapped it around Maloney's wrist. Then he pulled Maloney's other hand back and cuffed that wrist.

Maloney winced as the cuffs bit into his skin.

'Jesus fucken Christ! You're hurting me!'

Lazarus ignored him. He manhandled him around until he faced him. Lazarus could see blood and the beginning of bruising. His left eye was swollen. Blood trickled from a nostril. There was a deep cut on his right cheek.

Lazarus smiled. He always liked this bit. It made him feel alive.

Or maybe just less dead.

'Sean Maloney, I am arresting you for the rape of Sarah Casey. You are not obliged to say anything unless you wish to do so, but anything you say will be taken down in writing and may be given in evidence. Do you understand?'

Maloney said nothing. His eyes buzzed around the sockets.

'Do you understand?' Lazarus repeated.

'Fuck off,' Maloney gasped.

Maloney was small, around five foot eight, stocky and overweight, but with the cockiness of someone with power. He wore tight grey boxers and a pink T-shirt one size too small for his large paunch. His feet were bare. Four long gold chains hung in a bunch around his neck and over his top. He had a wide face, covered in a heavy ginger beard. His head was shaved. Lazarus thought back to the last time he saw him, in an interview room of Broadstone station two years earlier as he put the allegations of raping Sarah Casey to him. Maloney had folded his arms, looked to the ceiling and said no comment to every allegation. Back then, Maloney had a good head of dirty fair hair and his face was clean. Lazarus suspected the new look was an attempt to hide his identity. He grabbed Maloney's tracksuit bottoms from the floor and helped him put them on. Then he found a pair of runners under the table.

Lazarus laughed.

'You're not the hardman now, imagine cops having to dress you. And you won't be doing O'Hara's dirty work for a long time.'

Lazarus had forgotten the name Danny O'Hara during the drama of finding Maloney. But now, at the mention of him, Lazarus felt his stomach knot. The idea of that gangster getting involved in Sarah's case filled him with dread.

'Take him downstairs,' Lazarus told Duffy, trying to push O'Hara out of his mind. Duffy, who was holding one of Maloney's arms, was joined by the male uniform. They frogmarched him out of the room.

Lazarus turned to Winter.

'How are you doing?' he asked her.

She was on her feet. McEvoy had got her a glass of water and she was taking a slow gulp.

Winter rubbed the back of her head. She winced when she hit a tender spot.

'I'll survive. A bit sore. Nothing serious.'

Lazarus examined her. She was trembling. Her face was flushed. Her eyes were wide. Strands of hair had escaped from the bobbin keeping the ponytail in place. A bruise was forming on her cheek where Maloney's punch had landed.

'Do you need to go to hospital?'

'No. I'm fine, honest.' She spoke quickly. Lazarus knew she was trying to convince him she was okay.

He shrugged his shoulders. Her choice. He would have done the same.

He handed her the evidence bag with the pistol in it.

'Just in case you think your new sergeant is a mad man,' he said.

'I was a weapons specialist in the Army. The second I saw this' – he motioned to the bag – 'I knew it wasn't real. It is a replica. It's nothing more than a toy gun.'

Lazarus saw relief on Winter's face. McEvoy gave Lazarus a hard look.

'Let's go,' Lazarus said. He got up and walked to the door. He came into the hallway and saw Maloney with the uniforms. They had stopped to let him get a breath. He was trembling.

McEvoy and Winter came behind him.

Winter gave Maloney a cold, hard stare.

'By Christ, Seanie boy, you're in the shit now,' McEvoy said.

'Possession of a firearm with intent to endanger life, assaulting a garda and threats to kill. That's at least another five years inside – on top of what you'll get for riding that poor kid.'

Maloney sneered at him.

'Get fucked, you fat bastard.'

McEvoy laughed.

'I will be going home tonight to enjoy a nice steak and a few beers. I might even get the ride if I'm lucky. You, on the other hand, will be getting your arsehole opened by some big fella who wants a jail wife. His cock will go so far up you it will come out your mouth.'

Maloney looked away.

McEvoy smiled.

'You know what they do to paedophiles in prison? They've started cutting their mickeys off. They saw it off with a shiv.'

McEvoy brought his face close to Maloney. He made a sawing motion with his hand.

'Not too sharp. Nice and slowly.'

Maloney swallowed hard.

'And when they're done, they shove it in your mouth. You eat your own dick. If you're lucky, the screws get to you in time. If you're not, you bleed out.'

McEvoy flashed his fist towards Maloney's face. Maloney winced and closed his eyes, bracing himself for the punch. But McEvoy stopped millimetres away from him and grinned.

Maloney opened his eyes. Lazarus saw anger burn in them.

He began to say something, but the uniforms moved him towards the stairs.

They were on the fourth floor of the hotel and the view would normally have extended over north Dublin. But it was pitch black outside. Only streetlights and the glow from car headlights cut through the gloom.

They had descended two flights of stairs, Lazarus in the lead, when Maloney began talking. The shock of his arrest was wearing off. His natural cockiness came back.

'You wankers think O'Hara will let this happen? Not a fucken chance. I'll be getting my dick sucked in a club in Spain before you know it.'

'O'Hara won't do shit for you,' Lazarus said.

'He's already forgotten your name. You don't count anymore.'

Maloney began cursing. Lazarus pulled hard on his T-shirt and made Maloney lose his balance and almost fall.

'Fuck!' he shouted.

Maloney went silent.

Descending the staircase should have taken the team just a few minutes, but they navigated the stairs slowly. With his hands cuffed behind him, Maloney had no balance and they had to ease him down one step at a time. Lazarus walked backwards in front of Maloney, never taking his eyes off him.

It took them around ten minutes to get him to the ground floor. They came into the lobby just after 8.20pm. It was busy. A few guests looked in shock at the spectacle of a bloodied Maloney being manhandled by armed cops.

Lazarus saw O'Donnell, the manager, and left Maloney with Winter and McEvoy. He walked with her to the entrance. Lazarus had time to examine his surroundings. The foyer had polished green floor tiles. Cream wood panelling on the walls. Giant globes of orange lighting hung on long wires from the high ceiling. Topiary trees in oversized pots were dotted around.

A young family – mum, dad and two kids under ten – came towards them. They stopped when they saw Lazarus and all his hardware on display.

The mother's mouth tightened.

The younger child, a girl of no more than five, buried her face in the mother's dress. The mother, tall and graceful and blonde, put protective arms around her.

Lazarus walked past them and then stopped a few feet on. He bent down to pick up a cuddly toy on the floor. It was a blue and white cat, with orange eyes. He held it for a second and then went back to the family. He bent down to the young girl, who peered out from behind her mother's hands.

'*Signorina*,' Lazarus said in his best Italian accent.

He smiled.

'I think this is yours.'

He stood up and looked at the mother.

'We're here to check on the kitchens, ma'am. Just routine. They passed inspection. Everything is fine. It's a lovely spot. Enjoy your stay.'

The woman gave him a suspicious look, but then smiled. Lazarus winked at O'Donnell as they headed to the entrance.

The glass doors opened and they walked outside. Lazarus shivered at the cold. He zipped up his coat. They stood in silence, watching the uniforms place Maloney in a white Garda van.

O'Donnell saw the state of Maloney's face.

'Did he deserve it?'

'Yes.'

'Why was he arrested.?'

He told her. Her face went white.

Duffy approached them just as O'Donnell was about to say something.

The uniform was small, about five foot four, but sturdy. Sandy hair cut short, a round face with freckles and pale skin. Her face was intense, her blue eyes constantly looking for danger threats.

'Sergeant, there's a black SUV in the car park,' she said.

'The driver is dodgy. He keeps looking over to us and is doing a lot of talking. I think there is someone in the back.'

'Christ,' Lazarus said under his breath.

This was his worst fear. He went over to McEvoy and Winter.

'There are bogeys in that SUV,' he said.

He could see it now. It was a Volkswagen Touareg, black with 2016 plates.

McEvoy's eyes tightened,

'You think it's O'Hara's crew?' he said.

'Maybe. It could explain Maloney knowing we were on to him. They could have warned him.'

'Hold on,' McEvoy said. His brow furrowed.

'What if it's the Caseys? What if they're here to whack Maloney?'

Lazarus tensed. He hadn't thought of that.

He turned to Winter.

'Rachel, stay here with Maloney and the other uniforms. Harry, with me. You too, Garda Duffy.'

They moved off, Duffy a few paces behind the armed detectives. Lazarus took out his pistol. McEvoy did the same. Duffy extended her baton. They hid their weapons behind their backs as they walked towards the Touareg.

Lazarus could see the driver's mouth moving rapidly. As they got to about 15 metres from the SUV, he saw the man become more animated. He turned and started talking to someone in the back seat.

That movement changed the light dynamic inside the vehicle. Lazarus saw a glimpse of something long and black in the hands of the figure in the back seat.

'I don't like this,' he said.

He edged his finger towards the trigger of his pistol.

'There's something about the driver,' McEvoy said as he walked.

'I know him from somewhere.'

Lazarus eyed him. He had unkempt fair hair, stubble, and was wearing a black T-shirt.

McEvoy and Lazarus split up. Lazarus went towards the driver side, McEvoy to the rear passenger door. They were two metres away when the driver engaged the gears and pressed down on the accelerator.

The SUV moved forward.

Then Lazarus stepped out in front of it and brought his pistol up. He aimed right at the driver's head.

4

The driver's mouth fell open and he slammed on the brakes. The SUV shuddered to a halt.

He shouted, but the windows were closed and Lazarus heard only muffled yells.

He nodded to McEvoy and lowered his gun; McEvoy kept his trained on the SUV. Lazarus moved forward, his index finger on the trigger guard, ready.

He reached the driver's door and wrenched it open. Then he stepped back, brought the pistol up and aimed at the man's chest.

'Get out.' Lazarus said.

'Don't shoot!'

'Get out.'

'Jesus Man!'

'Out. Now.'

'All right!

'Nice and slowly. Keep your hands where I can see them. Same goes for your buddy in the back.'

'Are you fucking nuts?' the driver shouted.

'Get out of the car before I make you get out,' Lazarus said.

The driver raised his hands. Then he slowly emerged from the SUV. Lazarus saw him trembling. His face was pale.

Lazarus kept the Sig pointed at him. He looked over at McEvoy. He was at the rear passenger door. He saw him gesture with his pistol and the door opened. The man in the back edged out, his hands also in the air.

McEvoy told him to step away from the SUV. Then he edged forward and looked in the back seat. Lazarus saw him relax.

'It's a fuck-off camera,' McEvoy said.

Lazarus felt the tension drain from his own body. He had been worried they were gangsters trying to free Maloney. Or kill him if they were on the

other side, the Sarah Casey side. But now he knew exactly who they were.
And the fear on the driver's face told Lazarus they were no threat.

He nodded to McEvoy and they holstered their weapons.

'You can put your hands down,' he told them.

They did as instructed. Lazarus examined them.

They were of similar height and build. A few inches under six foot.
Slim, but not skinny. The driver had dirty fair hair that needed to be cut. It
was unkempt and verging on long. Lazarus guessed he was around 35. He
had a long and thin face, piercing blue eyes. He wore a plain black T-shirt,
dark blue combat trousers and black runners. A black Fitbit watch on his
left wrist. He hadn't shaved and his stubble had patches of grey whiskers
around the chin, but the rest of it was blond, lighter than the hair on his
head. His eyes darted around. He ran a bony hand up across his face.

Lazarus examined the other man. He was slightly younger. Maybe 30.
He had a harder face. His bushy hair was ginger. He had a ginger and grey
goatee and moustache. Like the driver, he wore a sober-coloured top – a
dark grey Under Armour long sleeved T-shirt with a zip from the collar to
chest. Black jeans and brown boots.

Lazarus suspected they chose their clothing on purpose so they would
not stand out. The second man was more muscular and his stomach was flat,
with broad shoulders and biceps that filled the top's sleeves. His eyes were
blue and calm. Lazarus noticed his intense stare. He looked unflappable.

'What paper are you with?' Lazarus asked.

The driver folded his arms.

'How do you know we're media?'

'My superb powers of deduction,' Lazarus said.

Neither man laughed.

'Your buddy has a camera,' Lazarus said. 'There is a notebook and pen
on the passenger seat. You're either reporters or private investigators. I know
most PIs in the city. So that leaves media.

'So, who are you with?'

The driver gave a sigh of resignation.

'*The Globe.*'

'That's an awful rag,' Lazarus said.

'I'll pass your comments on to the editor, I'm sure he'll be devastated.'

'What's your name?' Lazarus said.

The driver looked affronted.

'Surely you know who I am? All gardai know me.'

Lazarus shook his head.

'No idea.'

The driver's eyes tightened.

'Conor Sullivan,' he said. 'I'm a crime reporter.'

He gestured to the second man.

'And this is my partner Tony Gallagher. We're both multimedia jour-nalists. The days of reporters and photographers being separate are gone. Sometimes I write and he shoots, sometimes he writes and I shoot.'

'Never heard of either of you,' Lazarus said.

'That's fine. We know who you are,' Sullivan smirked. 'You're Detective Sergeant John Lazarus from Broadstone Garda Station's sex crimes unit. You chase rapists, wife beaters and kiddy fiddlers.'

He nodded towards the hotel.

'And you've just given us a great front page story. Maloney is O'Hara's man. And Danny O'Hara sells papers.'

He winked at Lazarus.

'Thanks, John.'

Lazarus got close to him.

'You can call me Detective Sergeant. Who told you about this?'

Sullivan smirked.

'We were just passing.'

Lazarus snorted.

'Funny guy. I like your style. But you weren't quite so funny a minute ago. In fact, you almost cried for your mamma.'

Sullivan's smirk vanished.

Lazarus tried again.

'Who told you about this?'

'I've nothing to say, garda.'

'I'm not a garda,' Lazarus said. 'I'm a detective sergeant. Now, who tol''

'*Garda*, I have nothing to say to you. This is a public area'

'This is a crime scene.'

Sullivan looked around theatrically.

'I don't see any tape. This is a public area. I am entitled to be here. Why are you harassing me?'

Lazarus suddenly felt on the back foot.

'How long have you been here?'

'I have no comment to make.'

Lazarus glowered at Sullivan.

'You fucking press. You're all the same. You're vultures.'

'Excuse me, *garda*,' Sullivan said.

'Drop the attitude. It's unbecoming of a member of the force, wouldn't you agree?'

Lazarus heard McEvoy stifle a laugh.

He felt his face flush.

'That's enough shit from you,' he said.

'I am directing you to leave this area. If you don't, I will arrest you.'

Sullivan's eyes widened.

'You're going to arrest me? *Me*? We'll see what the press office has to say about that.'

He jerked a phone from his jacket pocket. He began tapping furiously on it.

'I'll show you, Lazarus,' Sullivan said.

'HQ will have your badge over this.'

He put the phone to his ear and glared at Lazarus. Lazarus glared back. Just then he heard a voice from behind him.

'Whoa. Hold on here a second.'

Lazarus looked around. He saw Gallagher. His hands were out, like a referee coming between two boxers.

'Officers, we're just doing our job here,' Gallagher said. 'We'll get out of your hair right now. We don't want any trouble.'

'Show me what's on your camera,' Lazarus snapped.

'It's just pictures of you guys bringing him out. That's all we have.'

'Show me. Now.'

Gallagher sighed. He went to the SUV, took out the long-lens camera and gave it to Lazarus. Lazarus looked at it. It was a high-end version of a Canon SLR he had at home. He saw the controls were like his own camera. He pressed a button and the LCD screen on the back lit up. A photograph of Lazarus and McEvoy walking towards the lens. Their pistols quite obviously behind their backs. Not as subtle as Lazarus had hoped. He saw that familiar and angry look in his own eyes. Those fucking eyes, he thought.

The photo was good. Gallagher had framed them perfectly. Lazarus turned the wheel on the control panel and flicked through the rest of the images. The slideshow was in reverse, with the newest photographs coming on screen first. That meant McEvoy and Lazarus appeared to be walking backwards from the reporters' Touareg to the hotel entrance. Although taken from a distance in the dark, they were clear, thanks to the artificial lighting around the hotel grounds. Next came a sequence of Maloney being pulled out of the Garda van and reversed into the hotel.

Then, there was an almost comical series of images of Lazarus ascending the hotel stairs, with a shackled Maloney and the other cops moving up them backwards.

'It's like fucking Benny Hill,' McEvoy said.

'Who?' Lazarus said.

McEvoy frowned.

'Never mind.'

The last montage showed Lazarus, Winter and McEvoy walking backwards out of the building towards the Camry.

And that's when Lazarus knew he had a serious problem.

'*Cazzo,*' he said in a quiet voice.

Fuck.

Up until he saw the final sequence, Lazarus thought it was likely a hotel worker had tipped off Sullivan and Gallagher about the arrest operation. It had happened before. Lazarus remembered being at fresh scenes and the media arriving within minutes, thanks to nosey neighbours and busy bodies.

But these photographs showed the press were already there before Lazarus and his team hit the hotel.

And that meant Lazarus had a leak.

He frowned, foresaw shit back in the station.

He looked at Sullivan.

'I can seize this camera. This is evidence of a crime.'

'Evidence of a crime?' Sullivan's voice became shrill.

'The only people in it are you cops and some dirty paedo.'

Gallagher moved between him and Lazarus again.

'Can I have a word, Sergeant?'

Lazarus paused for moment.

Then he relented and walked a few metres to the side with Gallagher.

'This is all getting out of hand,' Gallagher said. Lazarus noticed he had a country lilt. He thought maybe Galway, or Mayo, somewhere out west. Not like Sullivan, who had a working-class Dublin accent.

'Let me tell you something: Sullivan is a bollix,' Gallagher said.

'He loves himself and is up his own arse. But we don't want any hassle. Let us go and we'll be on our way. I promise he won't go to the press office, or anyone else. I'll handle him. This row never happened. There won't be anything about it in the story. Just the job you did on that animal Maloney. And there definitely won't be any complaint.'

He paused.

'We're on the same side, you know. You arrest Maloney, we tell the world what a great job you did. Simple.'

Lazarus looked over at McEvoy and Sullivan. Sullivan's face still burned red. He was gesticulating at McEvoy as he ranted. McEvoy, hands in his pockets, was nodding as Sullivan vented.

'Why don't we just get out of your hair?' Gallagher said. 'None of us needs this grief. I know a few lads in the job. They'll vouch for me.'

Lazarus's face softened. Gallagher was right, Lazarus didn't need any more hassle. The last thing he wanted was the press office on his case over a stupid row with a reporter. He knew the communications team was part of the Commissioner's private office at Garda HQ in Dublin's Phoenix Park. He had been there once on an inquiry. A friend was a sergeant in the press office and the Commissioner was known to make unannounced visits, inquiring what stories the media had.

The more Lazarus stayed off the radar of Garda HQ, the better.

He let out a long breath.

'Fine. But you'll need to reel that man in. He gives me a pain.'

'Try working with him,' Gallagher said and raised his eyes to heaven.

'He'll be the death of me.'

They walked back to the SUV.

'Okay, Mr, eh, Sullivan, you and your colleague are free to go,' Lazarus said.

Sullivan demurred.

'Free to go? You pull a gun on *me* and you think that's the end of it? You could have shot me. Fuck that. I'm going to go to GSOC about this.'

Sullivan squared up to Lazarus. It was a mismatch. Lazarus towered over him. He smiled down at Sullivan, resisted the urge to pat him on the head.

'You talk to whoever you want,' Lazarus said.

'GSOC won't do shit.'

The Garda Síochána Ombudsman Commission was the independent body that investigated complaints against cops. It had investigated more than a dozen cases involving Lazarus, and he was always cleared. He was a straight cop. One complainant was jailed for six months for making a false allegation against him.

Lazarus knew he had done nothing wrong in the confrontation with the two men from the paper. But he also knew a GSOC inquiry took up a huge amount of time, and meant an unending conveyor belt of forms and interviews.

He decided attack was the best form of defence.

'You and Mr Gallagher were in my scene, and you were both acting suspiciously. I suspected you were armed criminals. I was entitled to produce my firearm. You're lucky I didn't shoot you.'

Sullivan looked at the ground.

'Do you know who we are dealing with here?' Lazarus said.

'Sean Maloney is part of Danny O'Hara's crew. One of the most dangerous gangs in Dublin. And you come to him in a blacked-out jeep. Are you nuts? Are you crazy? What if he had associates here? These people would kill you in a heartbeat. There are armed detectives here for a reason. Maloney is dangerous. O'Hara even more so.

'You got in the way of a sensitive arrest and you made me suspect you were criminals. I could have shot you when you tried to drive off. That was stupid. If this was America, you'd be Swiss cheese by now.'

Sullivan stood in silence, his eyes still on the ground, arms folded.

'Please feel free to go to the Commissioner, or GSOC, or the United Nations,' Lazarus said. 'I've no problem with anything I have done here. I'll defend my actions. The safety of my colleagues and of the public outweighs the needs of a piece of crap like your rag.'

Sullivan flared, said nothing.

'Now get out of here,' Lazarus said.

'Before I change my mind and arrest you for obstruction.'

The two journalists got back into their vehicle in silence. Gallagher winked at Lazarus.

Sullivan's face burned as he gunned the engine and engaged the gear.

The SUV edged out of its spot, moved off.

Lazarus held out his hand as it approached.

It stopped.

Lazarus ordered Sullivan to lower the window.

'What now?' Sullivan snapped.

'Just wanted to say have a nice evening, sir.'

Lazarus and McEvoy laughed as Sullivan drove off.

5

McEvoy led the Garda convoy back to Broadstone station.
He weaved from one lane to the other as gaps appeared in the
dual carriageway. He saw a space, dropped down a gear and gunned the
Toyota's powerful engine.

The drizzle had stopped, but the air was still damp, the roadway slick.
Lazarus looked over his shoulder and saw the Garda van carrying Maloney
struggling to keep up with them.

'There's no fire, Harry,' he said. 'Let Maloney stew.'

McEvoy glanced over at him.

'Do you not want to get back to tell Anderson what a great job we did?
I'm sure our glorious leader will be waiting at the station to praise us for
a job well done.'

Lazarus snorted, looked at his watch.

'It's almost 9pm on a Sunday. I don't think he has ever been in the
station at this time. He'd get a nosebleed.'

Winter laughed in the back seat. She had recovered from the incident
with Maloney in the hotel room. The colour on her face had returned to
normal, apart from a bruise on her left cheek.

'How you feeling?' Lazarus asked her.

'Living my best life,' she smiled.

'We can stop off at casualty,' he said.

Winter put up a hand.

'I'm fine.'

She paused.

'I've never had to face a gun before. Real or replica.'

Lazarus blinked, looked away.

'It'll put some hairs on your chest,' McEvoy said. 'You have a nice war
story for the grandkids now.'

Winter laughed again.

'Uh, thanks. I guess.'

She sat forward.

'Right. I think I need a crash course. What's the story with the Caseys? If I'm going to be dealing with Sarah, I need to know their background.'

Winter hadn't met Sarah or her family yet. She was still finding her feet in Lazarus's unit. They dealt with so many abuse victims that it would take months for her to get to know them all.

'They're gougers.' McEvoy said.

'Every single one of them.'

Lazarus punched his arm.

'Leave this to me, old man.'

He looked back to Winter.

'They're a family of five. Parents are Mick and Joanne. Sarah is the youngest. Two older boys, Josh and Rob. The mother is decent, works as a cleaner in a hospital. Sarah is quiet, probably because of what Maloney put her through. And very smart. She hopes to go to university.'

He frowned.

'The males, well that's another story. Harry's right. They're up to their neck in crime. Mick's nickname is Wheels. He was a top driver back in the day. A few crews used him for robberies. There is intel he did at least ten jobs. Only got caught once, though. Spent three years inside. He came out and told anyone who would listen he was determined to go straight. The truth was he was determined not to get caught again.'

'And he never did,' McEvoy said.

'He stopped driving, got involved in fencing stolen property instead. Now he has two sons, Rob and Josh. They are up to their bollix in drugs in the north inner city. Scum.'

'It doesn't matter that they're scum,' Lazarus said.

'Sarah Casey will get exactly the same care from us as any other victim.'

'Okay,' Winter said.

'And what about this Danny O'Hara fella?'

'He's the mother of all bastards,' McEvoy shouted.

He slowed behind a bus taking tourists from the airport to their hotel. It was full of pensioners wearing fluorescent green jackets and matching baseball caps. Have to be Yanks, Lazarus thought.

'O'Hara's major,' he said. 'You haven't heard of him?'

Winter blushed.

'Most of my service has been outside the city. I never came across him,' she said.

Winter had transferred to Lazarus's sex crimes unit a fortnight earlier. Her ten years' service had been in counties surrounding the capital.

Lazarus looked outside. They were at Whitehall Church, a major landmark on the road from the airport into the city, about ten minutes from their station.

The cross on top of the church was bathed in orange light from below. It stood out against the darkness.

'Danny O'Hara is one of the biggest drug dealers in Dublin,' Lazarus said.

'He brings in coke and heroin, bit of cannabis, too. He has strong links with European cartels. Makes a fortune. He controls most of the inner city drugs trade. And he guards it with other people's lives.

'Maloney is his main man. His enforcer, protector and confidante all rolled into one. There will be hell to pay when he finds out we have him. He'll have to do something.'

Winter leaned in.

'I've known O'Hara for more than a decade,' Lazarus said.

'I got him for possessing heroin with intent to supply back in 2008. I was in the drugs unit at the time. A tout tipped us off about a house being used to store gear. We did surveillance on it. After two days we saw O'Hara and one of his men going in. I never thought he'd be stupid enough to go there himself.'

'Why did he?' Winter asked.

'Paranoia,' Lazarus said.

'He didn't trust anyone. Turns out he was right.'

McEvoy snorted.

'We watched the house for a few minutes and next thing O'Hara and his pal come out,' Lazarus said.

'He was carrying a bag, so we decided to move in. They saw us coming and split. O'Hara went one way, his pal another. I went after O'Hara. I was younger and fitter then, but so was he. The chase lasted half a mile.'

He smiled at the memory.

'It was like a movie,' Lazarus said. 'It was before everyone had camera phones, but I wish someone had filmed it. I'd enjoy watching it. The buzz was incredible. He ran through traffic. Barged into an old man, sent him flying. Threw a fucking cabbage at me from a shop he ran past. Hit me right in the puss.'

Winter and McEvoy laughed.

'I got close and tripped him up. He tried to get up, but I smacked him. He went down. I made sure he stayed down.'

Winter was fascinated.

'And then I opened the bag,' Lazarus said.

'How much?'

Lazarus heard the excitement in Winter's voice.

'A kilo of pure heroin. It was worth €120,000 at the time.'

'Wow,' Winter said.

'It was the biggest seizure for the unit that year. I got a commendation and O'Hara was given a nice sentence. He pleaded, so a few years were taken off.'

Anyone caught with a significant amount of illegal drugs in Ireland is supposed to get a ten-year sentence, but judges take guilty pleas into account. O'Hara, who was then in his late twenties, received a seven-year term. He did his time in Mountjoy Prison, an austere Victorian jail close to the city centre.

'He met Maloney inside,' Lazarus said.

'He was doing five years for torturing an addict who owed him a few quid. O'Hara spotted him one day when he attacked another prisoner. It was ordered from outside by the inmate's own people. They thought he was touting. He probably was, but he didn't deserve what Maloney did to him.'

Lazarus looked at the city passing outside. He saw the wind shaking the branches on the trees that lined the Swords Road as it became Drumcondra Road.

'He went into the cell just after the evening meal, closed the door behind him,' he said.

'He spent 20 minutes with the poor bastard. By the time he was finished, the prisoner had a broken nose, fractured skull and a few smashed ribs. Two broken fingers, seriously swollen balls and a slash wound from his ear to his mouth. He told officers he fell.'

'Smart move,' McEvoy said.

'He'd be dead by now if he made a complaint.'

Lazarus nodded.

'O'Hara started to use Maloney as muscle inside. They were released around the same time and hooked up on the outside. And they haven't looked back since.'

'O'Hara is dependent on him now,' McEvoy said.

'He started off as a minder. But then O'Hara realised Maloney was good at more than just using his fists. Turns out he is excellent at logistics.

He sources the routes to get O'Hara's drugs into Ireland. He has a knack of finding the right lorry driver, or the right student who needs the money. Maloney has been helping O'Hara from abroad, even when he was on the run. He'd be fucked without him.'

'And that means we have a problem,' Lazarus said.

'If Maloney goes down for abusing Sarah, O'Hara is going to be in the shit. He'll have to try to get the charges dropped, for his own sake.'

'Why?' Winter asked.

They were on Dorset Street now, a busy thoroughfare leading to the heart of the city. It was dotted with shops, pubs, solicitors' offices and cafes.

'Maloney has claustrophobia,' Lazarus said.

'He developed it inside. He gets sick in an enclosed space. I thought of bringing him down to the hotel reception in a lift, because fuck him. But I didn't want him having a panic attack. His claustrophobia means he'll be easy pickings for the CHIS unit.'

The Garda Covert Human Intelligence Sources unit was always looking for fresh meat to act as informers. Maloney would be a top target for it – tout on O'Hara's drugs operation in return for a reduced sentence. That would be tempting for any criminal facing the next decade behind bars, never mind one who couldn't cope with enclosed spaces.

McEvoy saw a gap in the traffic. The Camry's tyres screeched as he did a hard right onto Eccles Street. He drove along it, past the Mater private and public hospitals that were 100 metres apart. Then he took a left onto Nelson Street and after a few seconds he came to Mountjoy Street. In less than a minute, he turned right on to Western Way. Broadstone Station was on the right, about 90 metres down. It was a squat three-storey modern building, with the pedestrian entrance on the main road. A blue Garda lamp hung over the porch. The station was red-brick with large windows dominating the three floors. It was square and imposing. Its modern architecture stood out on the street, which was largely Victorian.

He drove past the public entrance and took a right. It led to the small station car park at the rear. He drove inside, reversed into a space.

'Great bit of parking, that,' he said.

'What do you want? A medal?' Lazarus snapped.

He undid his seatbelt and got out of the car when its engine was still running. He wanted to be at the van when Maloney was taken out.

He stood by the side door. Duffy slid it back. She went inside. She emerged with Maloney seconds later. She winked at Lazarus and gave

Maloney's arm a yank as he stepped down from the van, causing him to stumble and nearly fall.

'Fuck's sake. You're hurting me,' Maloney shouted.

Duffy ignored him and gripped his arm as she walked him to the back entrance of the station, McEvoy by her side.

Maloney's head was down.

Then Lazarus heard a shout from Winter.

He looked over. She was staring at her phone.

'What is it?' he asked.

'*The Globe* has the story up online already.'

'Show me,' he said.

Winter handed over her Samsung Galaxy.

'It has everything.'

6

Lazarus looked at the *Globe* app and cursed himself for being so stupid. He forgot the paper had an online presence. He had expected the Maloney article to appear tomorrow, and thought he would have had time to break the news to the Casey family before it was published.

Sullivan and Gallagher had fucked him.

The article was the main story on the app. There was a large photograph over the piece. It showed Maloney being walked out to the Garda van by the uniforms, his hands behind his back, his face battered and bruised.

Lazarus saw himself in the background. He was out of focus, but sharp enough to be recognisable. He was talking to O'Donnell, the manager.

A smaller photograph showed Winter holding the evidence bag containing Maloney's gun. Lazarus thought back to the confrontation with Sullivan and Gallagher. He should have arrested them when he had the chance, he thought.

The headline was just one word: BUSTED. The strapline underneath read: *Moment armed gardai nab on the run "rapist" mobster in city hotel.*

Sullivan and Gallagher had a joint photo by-line.

Lazarus started reading.

This is the moment armed detectives swooped on one of Dublin's most dangerous gangsters – over the repeated rape of a young girl.

These exclusive Globe *photos show detectives from a Garda sex crimes unit with convicted criminal Sean Maloney at a hotel near Dublin Airport this evening.*

We have learned that the criminal – who is the right-hand man of an infamous Dublin drug dealer – is to be charged with more than 20 counts of raping a child. It's understood she was just 14 when Maloney (33) is alleged to have targeted her three years ago.

'Jesus Fucking Christ,' Lazarus said.

The Globe *has established that gardai have been hunting Maloney, from central Dublin, for almost two years after he fled Ireland just days before detectives were to charge him.*

Lazarus shook his head.

We can reveal that detectives from Broadstone station in central Dublin received intelligence that Maloney, who has more than 50 convictions including for drugs possession and serious assault, flew back from his foreign bolthole earlier today and was staying at the €100 a night Prestige Dublin Airport Hotel.

Officers mounted a special operation, led by Detective Sergeant John Lazarus, this evening to nab him. Sources say Maloney was arrested in his room after a brief, but violent, struggle.

'The sneaky shit,' Lazarus told Winter.

'He's trying to make it out that I'm his source.'

These exclusive Globe *photos show a bruised Maloney in handcuffs being led out of the hotel – and being walked under armed escort down a stairwell at the front of the building.*

Lazarus scrolled down and saw a photograph of him walking backwards down the stairs, facing Maloney and the other officers.

One officer is seen to carry an evidence bag, and it is believed detectives seized a knife from Maloney's room.

Lazarus snorted.

'They will just fill in the blanks as they go along.'

He went back to the story.

Sources say the girl's ordeal began in early 2016 when the child, who is now 17, was just 14 years old. It came to light when the girl, broke down and told her mother about the abuse. The mother went to gardai at the start of 2017 and met with Detective Sergeant Lazarus's sex crimes unit. The victim spoke to gardai despite close associates – who are heavily involved in crime – wanting to kill Maloney. "The mother and daughter held firm," a source said. "They were adamant Maloney should face the justice of the courts – not of the mob."

Lazarus cringed at the made-up quote.

'Is that true?' Winter asked.

She was reading the story as she stood beside Lazarus.

He nodded.

'Mick and her brothers wanted to take Maloney up the Dublin Mountains and leave him there as food for the foxes,' Lazarus said.

He scrolled down.

Detectives spent almost a year investigating the rape allegations, before sending a file to the Director of Public Prosecutions. The DPP had the complex file for six months then decided to charge Maloney in April 2018, but he fled the country before gardai could get their hands on him. That escape was 18 months ago and there has been no sign of Maloney since – until this evening's dramatic raid, caught on camera by The Globe.

We have also learned gardai searching for Maloney last year seized a laptop he owned – and the examination of it led to a decision to charge him with child abuse material offences.

Lazarus felt a stabbing sensation in his stomach. The family did not know about those charges yet.

Now sources say gardai fear Maloney's boss – one of the city's most dangerous criminals – will try to terrorise the victim into withdrawing her allegations. "Maloney is central to the operation. His boss will do everything he can to protect him. There have already been some threats and minor incidents, but now he is to be charged it will only get worse," a source told The Globe.

'Fuck,' Lazarus groaned.

He gave the phone back to Winter. He couldn't read any more.

'This is a disaster,' he said.

'How can they print all those details?' Winter asked. 'Surely the judge will go nuts?'

Lazarus shook his head. Jenna, his wife, was a solicitor before taking a career break to look after the kids and had told him the law.

'They can write what they want until Maloney appears in court,' he said. 'There is no question of it being sub judice before that.'

It's illegal to name a victim of sexual abuse, but *The Globe* had crafted the story so Sarah Casey would not be identified in it. Lazarus knew there was nothing the judge in Maloney's case would be able to do about the article. The paper was in the clear.

'That Sullivan shit is starting to annoy me,' Lazarus said.

He walked towards his office.

The detectives were housed on the ground floor at the rear of the station. Lazarus had his own office. It was small and cramped, with cheap grey carpet and a low ceiling and grey-blue paint on the walls. There was just enough space for a desk and chair, as well as four grey filing cabinets that bulged with paperwork.

His desk was standard issue public service; a steel frame and a wooden top. It had three steel drawers with silver handles. His black computer, with oversized headphones hanging from it, sat in the centre of the desk. There was a framed photograph of Lazarus, Jenna and their two boys, all of them smiling, on the corner. It had been taken the previous summer on a holiday back in Schio, a small town near Venice in the north-east of Italy where Lazarus called home.

He was born and raised in south Dublin, but Italy would always be his *real* home.

His parents came to Ireland young and broke in the early 1970s, looking for a fresh start. Italy was in even worse financial state than Ireland back then. His father Giacomo brought his young wife Maria to Dublin shortly after their marriage. He was a chef and worked in Italian restaurants in the city before he saved up enough to open his own in 1980, the year Lazarus was born. Lazarus was christened Giovanni Pietro, but growing up he always felt an outsider in the neighbourhood because of his name and dark looks. He could do nothing about his skin colour, but he could change his name, so started calling himself John. Only his parents called him Giovanni, even though it was the name on is official Garda ID.

The family restaurant, in Dundrum in south Dublin where Lazarus grew up, soon became a success and Giacomo opened two more outlets in the nearby suburbs. He used to say he had one restaurant for each of his three kids to inherit. But fate had intervened. Lazarus's older brother Massimo ended up taking over all three when their father retired to Italy, heartbroken and angry, almost five years ago.

After it all.

After the family's world ended.

The expectation had always been that Lazarus would follow Massimo into the family business, but he joined the Army instead, then became a cop. So Massimo had two.

The youngest child, a girl called Gabriella, wasn't in a position to do anything now. Her permanent home was a tidy graveyard in south Dublin.

And that meant Massimo had them all.

Lazarus felt the usual pang of hurt and anger when he thought about Gabriella and how she had died.

How she had died.

He had picked up some Irish traditions at least, he thought. Don't talk about her murder, even though it overshadowed every second of his life and was why he was now sergeant of a unit most detectives avoided like the plague.

He stood up and surveyed his office. It was half the size of his boss Superintendent Linda Fallon's office on the top floor of the station and was much less tidy. The cabinets stood against a wall. One contained threat assessments, intelligence and other paperwork. But the remaining three were packed with cases his team had worked in the previous two years.

There were dozens of them. Each bland folder hiding an individual horror story within its white A4 pages.

Each crime he investigated was different. Each crime was the same. The powerful swallowing up the weak, dehumanising them, robbing them of their dignity to satisfy their own depravity. Many detectives shied away from units that had been set up all over the country to deal with local cases of domestic violence, abuse, neglect, rape and paedophilia. But as soon as Lazarus heard a new team was being formed in Broadstone almost three years earlier, he was banging on Fallon's door demanding to lead the unit.

He had never wanted anything as much in his 15 years in the job. A chance to protect the defenceless. But the cases were horrendous. A toddler rescued from a flat after her addicted mother left her alone for 24 hours to go searching for heroin. A young man sexually assaulted after being drugged at a student party. A woman beaten and kicked and spat on by her fella as her kids looked on. A 14-year-old girl who went to meet a boy of the same age after talking to him on Snapchat, only for him to be a 50-year-old convicted sex offender who brought her to a city centre hotel and raped her for three days solid. A cop who had child abuse material on his phone, including videos of babies being water boarded.

The hairs stood up on the back of Lazarus's neck when he watched those videos. It was why he had the oversized headphones on his computer. He had to listen to the screams on the videos, but he didn't want to inflict them on anyone else.

He never forgot a single victim. He put faces to names as he ran a finger along the files crammed into one steel cabinet. The investigations may have been filed away, but the victims stayed in his head.

And he knew they always would.

Each case he investigated convinced Lazarus just a little bit more that there was an evil in some people. A badness that won out over good. A darkness that defeated the light.

He called it black light.

And that was why, above the cabinets and the horror stories, he hung a framed oil painting.

It was his protection against that black light.

The painting was of St Peter's Cathedral in Schio, the town where his parents were born and where he holidayed every year.

The cathedral dominated the town's main piazza. The Italian sun lit it up, making its white stone facade even more brilliant. The sky was bright and cloudless.

He always pictured sun and blue skies when he thought of home. He looked through the window into the Dublin night and reality hit him hard. It was raining, the drops meandering down the pane of glass. Cars moved along the road, heading out of town towards the suburbs. A few brave pedestrians struggled against the elements, hands clamped to the crown of their heads to secure their hoods and caps from the biting wind.

He opened a cabinet and put the Sarah Casey file that he had left on his desk on the scramble to the airport back with the others.

Just then his desk phone rang.

He walked back over and answered it.

'My office now, young man,' the woman on the other end said.

And then she hung up.

7

Lazarus bit a large chunk of a protein bar as he climbed the stairs. He was so hungry he barely chewed the chocolate fudge before swallowing it. The bar was his first food since he had wolfed down a salami and Cambozola cheese panini at 5pm, almost five hours earlier, before the move against Maloney. That was during a short break between getting the green light for the operation and briefing his troops.

He got to the final step and brought a silver travel mug with a black Juventus FC logo to his lips. He sipped some of the Americano inside. It was late, but he needed the caffeine. And, anyway, he and sleep were not friends.

They hadn't been for some time.

He came to a plain grey door with the word Superintendent on it. He ate the remnants of the bar, took another sip of the coffee and rapped the door.

'In you come,' a brisk voice said.

Lazarus opened the door and walked into a spacious office. Superintendent Fallon sat behind a large mahogany desk. An Irish flag hung from a pole at the wall behind her.

Lazarus noticed the office was ridiculously tidy compared to his own. The walls were off-white and were dotted with paintings and framed photographs of Fallon in uniform and in plain clothes. A black computer monitor dominated the desk, a small wireless keyboard in front of it. A white landline looked as if it had just been cleaned. It probably had, Lazarus thought. Four pens in a mug and a large blue notebook with the Garda crest on it. A framed photograph of a laughing Fallon with her husband Jim and their three adult kids. The room had a flat-screen television on the wall, two neat filing cabinets, a blue sofa and small coffee table with two armchairs.

Fallon smiled.

'Here comes trouble.'

She stood and walked to him. She was in her late fifties, with a gentle face. She had green eyes and a wide mouth. Her red hair was thick and parted on the right. She was in uniform – black shoes, navy trousers and a crisp white shirt and blue tie with gold tiepin. A red tab and diamond on her epaulettes signified her rank.

'You've had a busy day, young man. I can't wait to see your overtime claim this month.'

Lazarus laughed, but then sensed movement to his side.

His face hardened when he saw Anderson standing near the sofa. Lazarus stared at him. Anderson stared back.

'Inspector,' Lazarus said coldly.

'Detective Sergeant,' Anderson replied, just as icily.

Fallon ignored the tension.

'Have a seat, John.'

He picked one of two chairs across from Fallon's desk and far from Anderson. He placed his cup on the desk. Fallon shot him a withering look.

'Sorry, Super,' he said quickly and reached for the cup. He had forgotten how house proud she was. He held the cup on his lap. The heat became uncomfortable, but not as uncomfortable as a hard stare from Fallon.

'How are you?' Fallon asked.

'I'm fine.'

Lazarus looked at his watch. It was 9.33pm.

'We're just about to charge Maloney.'

'Great result,' Fallon said.

'And how is Detective Garda Winter?'

'Winter is fine, Super,' he said. 'She's just a bit sore.'

He went quiet for a second and thought of Winter's lucky escape.

'Could have been worse,' he said.

Fallon moved back to the desk and sat into her black leather chair. Anderson walked over and stood beside her, a sheet of paper in his hand.

He was around five foot ten and had a thin frame and oily short hair, dirty fair but greying at the temples. He had a sharp nose and beady brown eyes. His mouth was small and the lips were pursed together. He wore an expensive navy blazer, white shirt open at the neck, dark blue cords and brogues.

It was the outfit of a man who would never have to roll around on the ground with a burglar. Lazarus could smell expensive cologne. He wondered if Anderson was going out socialising with the important set again. He seemed eager to leave the office.

Anderson had made Detective Inspector because of his marriage to a senior officer's daughter. The pub talk was he had never made an arrest, but even Lazarus found that hard to believe. He must have arrested someone, even a drunk, in his 25 years' service. He joined Broadstone from Garda Headquarters 17 months earlier and had spent the previous seven years there as a sergeant in a back-office role, moving paper from one pile to another.

'Superintendent,' Anderson said, his gaze fixed on Lazarus.

'Here is my report on this evening. It's a bit short on detail, but I am waiting on a full report from Sergeant Lazarus.'

Lazarus bridled at the passive aggressive insult, but told himself not to bite. And then he bit.

'I am *so* sorry about that, Inspector,' he said.

He shrugged his shoulders, jutted his chin.

'I have been busy. Out in the field, you know? Paperwork is secondary.'

He stared at him.

'I'm not a desk jockey.'

Anderson went red. Lazarus smirked.

He thought back to a night in the pub a few weeks after the D/I joined the station. Alcohol consumed. A remark by Anderson to Lazarus in front of the team. Lazarus reacting and asking him outside. Anderson going pale, but then laughing it off and refusing to apologise.

And then.

And then.

Lazarus reaching across the rickety table, bottles and glasses flying. Grabbing Anderson by the throat, rushing his fist towards that annoying face and at the last possible second unclenching his fingers and slapping him hard on the cheek. McEvoy and the other detectives rushing to get between the pair, separating them, talking them both down. A muttered apology for any offence from inspector to sergeant in the office the next day. A grudging reciprocation from Lazarus. A handshake. No eye contact. Sixteen months of two fighters circling each other, knowing there would be a reckoning.

One day.

'There are some issues, Superintendent,' Anderson said. Fallon took the report from Anderson. The D/I hovered at her side.

'So, Inspector,' she said after she finished reading it.

'You believe Sergeant Lazarus should have waited for the NSU to scope the place and then send in the armed support unit before'

'I'm a detective. I'm armed. We all are,' Lazarus said.

Fallon glowered at him.

Lazarus looked at his feet.

'Sorry, ma'am.'

'You feel he was too hasty,' Fallon continued.

Anderson stared at Lazarus.

'Yes, Superintendent. While it was a good result to get Mallon'

'Maloney,' Lazarus interrupted.

Anderson flushed.

'Sorry. While it was a good result to get Maloney, resources would have been better used in having the specialist teams like the National Surveillance Unit deal with this. And what happened in the hotel room proved my point. Detective Garda Winter could have been killed. As you will remember from our conversations earlier today, I was opposed to Sergeant Lazarus moving so fast. My full report to the Chief Superintendent will reflect that.'

He smiled.

A senior officer was a friend of Anderson and had been instrumental in getting him the D/I gig, even though he was ill-suited for it. The cabal in HQ thought he needed time leading a unit of detectives before he went for superintendent and continued his rise up the ranks.

Lazarus shook his head.

'We got the bad guy. Took him off the streets. Protected other girls. That's our job.'

Anderson wasn't finished.

'I'm also concerned at the media being at the hotel. The leak must have come from this station. Not even this station, but the handful of people who knew about the arrest.'

Lazarus folded his arms and sighed.

'It was not me or anyone from my team,' he said.

'Are you suggesting someone in the hotel tipped them off?' Anderson smirked.

'I don't care who it was,' Lazarus said.

'Maloney deserves to be all over the papers. He's dirt. I did not brief my team until just before we left the station at 7.20pm. They couldn't have told the reporters in time for them to get there.'

'The leak came from your team and you know it, Sergeant,' Anderson snapped.

'It's a scandal.'

Lazarus jumped to his feet. He pointed an angry finger at Anderson.

'The only scandal is that you are my boss.'

Anderson turned red.

'How dare you!'

'Enough!' Fallon shouted.

Lazarus didn't think it was enough at all.

'I like to operate on evidence, Inspector. I'm funny like that. You're making allegations against my team with no proof.'

Anderson's eyes bulged and he was about to launch a broadside against Lazarus when Fallon stepped in again.

'I said enough.'

An angry silence descended on the room. Lazarus and Anderson looked away from each other. Both of them red in the face.

Fallon stared down at Anderson's report. And then her eyes hardened as she made up her mind.

'Right, Inspector. There is no basis for your complaint about the Sergeant's decision to hit the hotel.'

She opened her hardcover book.

'When you and I discussed this at 6.30pm, I agreed with the Sergeant. I noted your reservations then. But it was my decision to make.

'I made it. That's my job. Leadership is about being decisive. We have to strike when we see a chance.'

Anderson huffed.

'Yes, ma'am.'

Then Fallon turned to Lazarus.

'However, Sergeant, I am concerned about the press being at the hotel. It made a tense situation even worse. I run a tight ship. I don't like leaks. Find out who told *The Globe*.'

Anderson gave a self-satisfied nod. Lazarus sensed that was the complaint he really wanted taken on. Anything to damage me, he thought.

'That will be all, Inspector,' Fallon said.

Anderson went to the sofa.

'Whoever leaked this should be sacked,' he said, looking at Lazarus. 'It's a flagrant breach of discipline. You need to look at your team, Sergeant.

'If you don't, I will.'

He picked up a manila folder from the sofa and headed to the door, smoothing his oily hair as he moved.

The door closed. Fallon sat still for a long moment. Her head bowed in thought.

Then she looked up at Lazarus.

A smile appeared on her face.

'Jesus Christ almighty. What a fuckwit.'

8

Fallon used two fingertips to straighten her already straight notebook. 'Anderson is the most incompetent detective inspector I've ever worked with. And that's saying something. He couldn't investigate his way out of a paper bag. But, John, he can be all the fuckwit he wants when he is the son-in-law of a deputy commissioner. We're stuck with him until he gets the jump and heads back to the Depot to fly a desk there.'

Anderson was going for promotion to superintendent. He had the necessary pull to move up the ranks and would soon return to an office job in the Depot, the name most cops used for Garda HQ.

Fallon shook her head sadly.

'He'll be the same rank as me. Unfuckingbelievable. He shouldn't have got above the rank of sergeant. Do you know the station party calls him Ankles?'

Lazarus laughed.

'It's because he's so far up the chief's arse that only his feet are visible,' he said.

'It's working, anyway,' Fallon said.

'Word is he is going to be number one on the list. He won't be with us much longer.'

Inspectors going for promotion to superintendent were placed on a list if they were successful. They waited for a serving superintendent to get promotion or retire, before taking their spot. The lower your number on the list, the quicker you got promoted.

'I was 25 on my list,' Fallon said. 'I had to wait 11 months.'

'I'll be relieved when he goes,' Lazarus said.

'He's a disaster. If he had his way tonight, we'd have waited a week for the NSU to go into the hotel and scope the place out. Maybe do a risk assessment and sent a report in triplicate up to the Depot.'

And then, under his breath: 'Che stronzo.'

Fallon waved a dismissive hand.

'The National Surveillance Unit have more serious targets than one low life child rapist, no matter how serious a criminal he was.'

She looked down at her notebook.

'You did well this evening. That was a great result.'

'Thanks,' Lazarus said.

He wondered what Fallon's reaction would have been if she knew the truth of what really happened in the hotel room. It stayed between him, McEvoy and Winter, didn't go into any report. Lazarus had said he overpowered Maloney after he produced the gun. No mention of him placing the pistol in Winter's mouth. Or of Lazarus seeing red and being willing to sacrifice Winter to nail Maloney.

Fallon loosened the top button on her shirt.

'How are the Caseys?' she asked.

'They're happy he's caught,' Lazarus said.

'I rang them to tell them about the arrest, but they had already seen Sullivan's story. It's all over the internet now.'

'What about the CSAM charges? Have they made the connection?'

'No,' Lazarus said. 'I'm due to meet them tomorrow morning and fill them in.'

Sullivan's piece said Maloney was to face child sexual abuse material charges, as well as rape. But that was only half the story. Lazarus wanted to tell the Caseys in person tomorrow. He was not looking forward to it.

'And what about you?' Fallon said.

Her eyes bored into his.

Lazarus sensed danger.

'Come again?'

'You, Lazarus. How are things with you?'

He shifted in his chair.

'I'm fine, Super.'

'Everything okay at home?'

'Couldn't be better. A happy wife is a happy life.'

'What about the nightmares?'

'What about them?'

'Are you still having them?'

'Occasionally.'

By occasionally, Lazarus meant on the occasion of his sleeps.

She kept her unblinking gaze on Lazarus.

'Tell me, why have you been hassling Detective Sergeant Frankie Cochrane?'

She had him.

He partnered Fallon before she went up the ranks. She was the best interviewer he had ever seen. She would smile at a prisoner as she talked shite with them. Then, out of nowhere, she'd hammer them with a hard question. He loved watching it. Most suspects folded under her gaze. Now he knew what it was like to be on the receiving end. He suddenly felt like confessing to a murder. Any murder.

He swallowed hard and tried to think of a convincing answer. None came.

'Why are you hassling her?' Fallon said again.

'You know MIS a tough unit.'

Cochrane was a detective sergeant in the Major Investigations Squad, based in central Dublin. She and her team monitored the most dangerous rapists and paedophiles in the country. Men who had committed heinous crimes.

And who would again if they got a chance.

But she was also the detective who had the investigation into the murder of Lazarus's sister Gabriella, back in 2012. It was an unsolved sex killing.

It tormented Lazarus that the killer was still out there. He was a cop, a top investigator, a man who hunted predators. It was a personal affront to him that Gabriella's killer was on the loose.

Gabriella was Cochrane's case now. She got the leads, led the reviews, interviewed persons of interest. And had to deal with the phone calls and messages from Lazarus.

'Look, Super, I have rights,' Lazarus protested.

'Nobody is denying that,' Fallon said.

'But you have texted and called her every week for the last two months. Come on, man.'

Lazarus had never noticed the carpet in Fallon's office before. It was frayed. He empathised.

'It's been seven years,' he said. 'But it feels like yesterday to me. I just want to know if they have made any progress.'

He folded his arms, unfolded them.

Then balled a fist and slammed into his thigh.

'I don't want them to forget her,' he said.

'She was my little sister. I'm not going to stop until they catch him. If I have to step on a few toes, then that's just what'll happen.'

Fallon sighed.

'John, please. You can't keep messaging Frankie. Let her do her job. If there's a break, you'll be the first to know.'

Lazarus went silent.

'You're my top detective and my friend,' Fallon said.

'I need you here. Jenna needs you at home. Please take it easy. You look a bit stressed.'

Lazarus shifted in his seat, as he always did when Fallon tried to talk to him about feelings and emotions.

'I'm fine,' he said.

Fallon smiled.

'Go home, make sure the kids are in bed. Make your lovely wife Jenna some late food. Drink some of your lovely Italian wine.'

She paused.

'And then have some lovely sex. Either with Jenna or by yourself. Whatever works.'

Lazarus didn't know how to respond to that, so he changed the subject.

'I've got some paperwork to do on Maloney. We're taking him to court in the morning and he has more charges over the attack on Rachel Winter. And then I have a CSAM file to look at.'

'Jesus, it never ends. Is the CSAM case urgent?'

Lazarus frowned.

'The suspect had videos of kids being tortured and raped on his laptop. I'd say it's pretty urgent. It's a disgrace we've had to wait this long for the results of the examination of his laptop.'

'How long have the techies had the computer?' Fallon asked,

'A year,' Lazarus said. It sounded a long time, and it was, but he knew he was lucky to get it back so quickly. The Cyber Crime Bureau that examined seized computers was inundated with so many Child Sexual Abuse Material cases that there was a massive backlog.

'How many?' Fallon asked.

'Not that many,' Lazarus said. 'Just over 5,000 photos and 700 videos. He's into boys. None over the age of ten.'

Fallon put her head in her hands.

'Do you not see the problem here?' she asked.

'You think that many images of kids being abused and raped is' she brought her hands up and made the speech marks sign, '"not that many". It's obscene.'

'I've had cases where the man had half a million images and tens of thousands of videos,' Lazarus said.

'This one is small fry. I'm still going to enjoy ruining the bastard's life, though. I can't wait to knock on his door. He's a bank manager.'

Fallon laughed, but Lazarus didn't notice. He was too rapt by the idea of watching another paedophile collapse before him. He thought of the young lives the man had destroyed from the comfort of his house in Dublin, while his kids played in the next room.

'He deserves everything he gets,' he said.

'They all do.'

'You love taking paedophiles down,' Fallon said.

'There's no better feeling,' Lazarus said.

'Hunting them down, knocking on their door and ruining them.'

His eyes burned.

'What a shit job we have,' Fallon said.

'Men are bastards.'

She stood up and walked to the window. She stared into the night for a long moment.

'Forget about the bank manager for a while. Put him on the back burner. I want you to spend time on the inquiry into the media leak. We can't avoid it. Anderson will have already told his father-in-law the deputy commissioner about it. Just spend a few days on it, a week max. Keep the powers that be happy. Then you can go after the bank fella.'

'Yes, Super.'

Lazarus got up and walked to the door, the keep cup in his hand.

'John!'

He looked back to Fallon.

She was still at the window.

'Remember. Food and wine.'

She smiled.

'And sex.'

9

Lazarus sat into the driving seat of his 2017 Alfa Romeo Giulia. He hit the start button on the steering wheel. The engine came alive with a roar. He drove out of the station car park. It was a cold night and he was glad the leather seats were heated. He felt the warmth rising through him. The Giulia had a 2.2 litre engine, and 190 horsepower. It was a flying machine. Black bodywork, red leather interior.

The car was his pride and joy. Clichéd and Italian, of course, but so was he.

His olive skin, brown eyes and hair so dark it was almost black stood out from his colleagues. He revelled in his Italian heritage. He wore Italian clothes, holidayed there, supported Juventus, married an Irish-Italian woman. He played up on his Italianness, too. He had a south Dublin accent but sometimes he let out his Latin side. He often used exaggerated Italian gestures when he was a beat cop trying to talk sense to drunks. Lots of joining his hands in prayer, or putting the thumbs and fingers together and waving them like a maniac. He even used Italian curse words, uttered in a loud and exaggerated accent. *Cazzo…Porca Miseria…Stronzo…*

He quite liked hyping his Italian self.

He thought he came across as an Irish Al Pacino in that movie about him taking on the robbery gang. He used to tell Jenna that the only differences were he was taller, more handsome.

And a better shot.

Lazarus knew he straddled two worlds, always had. He felt Italian, felt Irish, too. When he holidayed back home in Italy, he was called *l'Irlandese*. The Irishman. And in Dublin, where he was born and bred, they called him the Italian. That night in the pub, Anderson had drunkenly called him a Wop.

He wouldn't do it again.

Lazarus glanced at the car's LED clock. It said 10.15pm. Maloney had been charged minutes earlier. He was for court in the morning. Lazarus's work was done for the night. He took Fallon's advice about the pervert bank manager. That was for another day.

He pressed down on the accelerator. The exhaust growled and he was pushed back in his seat as the Giulia shot forward. He drove along Western Way, where Broadstone Station was located. It was a new station, officially known as Y District in the job, and had only been opened a few years earlier. Western Way was a wide, tree-lined avenue that linked lower Phibsboro to the Dorset Street area of central Dublin. Lazarus guided the Giulia through the inner city streets. It was a Sunday night and there was little traffic. He was on Dorset Street now and stopped at traffic lights.

He pulled up to the white line, took the central lane, the one that led to his home in Malahide, to the north. It was only 20 minutes away. But as he waited for the red to turn green, he was filled with an urge he could not resist.

Lazarus had to see them.

He punched the steering wheel, gave into his desires.

'*Porco cane.*'

He took his phone from the cradle beside the steering wheel and sent his wife another lie.

Sorry. We got delayed again. I'll be home in an hour. Work's a pain, but it has to be done. Kiss the boys goodnight for me, carina. xxx

Lazarus put the phone back in the cradle without waiting for an answer. He knew she would be unhappy, but he had to go to them. The need to see them was an elemental one. Something he had to put before his wife and two boys.

He told himself it would be the last time. And he almost believed it.

He checked the rear-view mirror and quickly moved into the filter lane. Then, when the lights turned green, he took the left onto to the North Circular Road, heading out of town. He sped up the quiet road, past the Mater Hospital on his left and Mountjoy Prison on his right. He got the internet radio on his phone app, tuned into Rai 2, his favourite Italian music station. He heard Marco Masini on, singing his most famous song *Perché lo fai? Why are you doing this?* He laughed to himself. Even he saw the irony.

He kept up the speed as he drove through the suburb of Phibsboro, then skirted Phoenix Park and hit the Navan Road. Within ten minutes he was on the M50, the motorway that ringed the city. He took the southerly route. The limit was 100 kilometres per hour, but the speedometer on the Giulia flashed past 120. It took him 15 minutes to reach the cemetery. The clock said 10.35pm when he arrived.

He got out the car and looked around Bohernabreena Cemetery in the foot of the Dublin Mountains. He was alone.

Just him and the dead.

He pressed the button on the key fob and trudged through the gates. The hazard lights of his Giulia flashed once. The indicators bathed the headstones in a soft orange glow, before the light died into the darkness.

He shivered and lowered his head against the chill, then shoved his hands deep into the pockets of his coat. His hiking boots scrunched on the gravel. The boots and his shallow breathing were the only sounds that disturbed the dead air.

Lazarus was thankful the graveyard was open 24 hours a day. He liked it when he was alone with the spirits. He raised his sad eyes to the sky; it was covered by low hanging clouds. They were like a thick blanket, smothering all the light from the universe.

But he was used to the dark. He was comfortable in it and he did not need any light to guide him to his people. He knew where they were. They have been here too long and he has been here too many times. He could reach them blindfolded.

Their graves are 328 steps from the entrance. Lazarus knew that he eats up the ground faster than many men. Although he was used to bustling around in the world outside the cemetery, he always walked slowly when he moved through here. Maybe it's just habit. Or maybe it was death slowing him down.

He reached the row where they have lain together for almost five years. Then he stared at their grave. He felt overcome by sadness and remorse and guilt and grief. His eyes moistened and his mouth quivered. His heart became heavy.

He read the caption on the joint headstone, although he knew it by heart.

A loving wife and mother
Maria Lazarus
Died October 30, 2014
And her adored daughter, Gabriella
Taken from us on October 30, 2012
Che riposino in pace

His mother died two years to the day from Gabriella. And he blamed himself for both.

He blessed himself and prayed. He closed his eyes as he mouthed the prayers. But he said them in Italian, his people's language.

Lazarus opened his eyes and moved to the headstone. He knelt in front of the polished black marble. He caressed their names.

An uncontrollable anger seized him.

He punched the ground. His fist slammed into soil made hard by the cold. He didn't care. He punched it again.

He stood up and remained still, for a long time, lost in his thoughts.

Finally he snapped out of his trance. He blessed himself again and turned away from them and began a slow walk back to the car.

Then he stopped. A horrific image filled his mind's eye. The violated and beaten body of Gabriella in a ditch. He put a fist up to his mouth and screwed his eyes shut, but that just made the picture worse.

She was destroyed.

His stomach heaved the first time he saw the crime scene photographs of her body in the station. He had to run to the toilet. He just about made it before the vomit spewed out. It even came out his nose. Tears streamed from his eyes. He kept retching long after his stomach had been emptied.

He stood in the cubicle for ten minutes weeping before he composed himself and went back to his friend. And the photos. He looked at Gabriella again and found it hard to recognise her. She had two black eyes, a broken nose and several of her front teeth were missing. Both lips were cut and swollen. Clumps of her hair had been ripped out, from where she had been dragged. He saw injuries to her hands and arms. Most of her fingernails were either missing or broken. She was naked and had been strangled with her own bra. It was black and fine and was still around her neck when the photographs were taken. Her beautiful eyes bulged from the strangulation and the whites were blood red from the haemorrhaging she suffered in her last moments.

His friend on the investigation team had begged him not to look, but Lazarus insisted. He had lost count of the number of bodies he had seen. He thought in his grief he somehow needed to see what the animal had done to his beautiful Gabriella. Even now, years later, the image still haunted his sleep and came at him in flashes when he was awake.

Gabriella was 20 when she was taken. She was 12 years junior to Lazarus and the youngest in the family. She was tall and thin, with sallow skin like his own, brown eyes, high cheekbones, a delicate nose and full lips. She wore her chestnut hair short and usually dressed in ripped jeans, an old combat jacket, desert boots and a plain T-shirt. The age gap should have meant they were not close, but the opposite turned out to be the case, perhaps because of the sense of family many Italian immigrant families still have. Gabriella worshipped Lazarus, especially when he became a cop. He enjoyed watching his little sister grow into a fully-grown woman.

She was the apple of Lazarus's eye and he was always the protective big brother.

Until the night of October 29, 2012 when everything changed.

And everything went black.

He was on a surveillance job. Gabriella was in her final year at Trinity College Dublin, where she was studying Politics and French. She sent Lazarus a text at 8.35pm, telling him what student pub she was going to.

> *I'm out with the girls on the pull – make sure one of your*
> *hot colleagues arrests me later! #handcuffs*

It was the last time Lazarus ever heard from her.

At 11.57pm, she rang him, but he was processing a prisoner and couldn't take the call. He knew she wanted a lift home. She always did when she was out on the piss and Lazarus was working. She loved being driven in an unmarked Garda car. Sometimes, Lazarus and his partner would turn on the blue lights and speed to her flat as she sat in the back of the car squealing in delight.

Lazarus finished with the prisoner at nine minutes past midnight. He headed to the station car park and rang Gabriella. She was in one of the student pubs around Trinity College and Grafton Street. He was in Store Street station. Just five minutes away.

Her phone rang out. Lazarus disconnected the call when it went to voicemail. He didn't leave a message. He figured she was still in the pub and couldn't hear the phone. He waited four minutes and rang again. Still nothing. He sent her a message.

> *Buona sera! Tried ringing you. Meet you at the usual spot in 10 minutes.*

The usual spot was outside the Shelbourne Hotel on St. Stephen's Green. He left the station and drove there, arriving at 12.21am. She wasn't there. He rang again. This time her phone went straight to voicemail.

The takeaway she used was just a few hundred metres away. He went there. Nothing. An icy fear gripped his stomach. He tried ringing her again.

The phone was still dead. He left a voicemail. When it was played to him several weeks later, he could hear the controlled panic in his voice.

Ciao, it's me, sis. Where are you? I tried the chipper and nobody saw you there.
I'm heading to the boozer now. Gimme a call. Ci sentiamo.

He was at the pub four minutes later. A bouncer told him he had seen her walking down the road just before midnight – the time she called him. Lazarus got in his car and drove around the area looking for Gabriella.

Nothing.

It was as if she just vanished off the face of the earth. CCTV showed her leaving the pub by herself and heading to the rendezvous point at the Shelbourne. It was a distance of just over 700 metres, a ten-minute stroll for her.

But she never made it.

Her body was found three days later by a walker in the Dublin Mountains, about six miles south of the town of Tallaght. Her killer had tried to cover his tracks by burying her in a shallow grave in a ditch, but a bad storm uncovered the remains.

There had been a huge investigation, but no suspects were identified, let alone arrested. The theory was the killer had stopped in a vehicle and bundled her into it before escaping. Several cars and vans were spotted on CCTV in the area at the time, but back then cameras were analogue and poor quality, especially on a dark and rainy night. They weren't good enough to pick up registration plates.

The team got the make and model of each vehicle. They checked the national database and established there were 4,569 registered vehicles that matched those caught on camera. They tracked down every one of them, spoke to every owner. One by one, their alibis checked out.

All sex offenders had been checked too, but they also had alibis. The same went for lifers out on licence. Gabriella had scratched her killer, so his skin was under her fingernails. But the DNA profile raised from her did not match anyone on the Garda list.

Luckily, that also meant family and friends who had been under the microscope were ruled out. Lazarus and his father and brother all gave samples, as did her ex-boyfriends, neighbours, fellow students and even lecturers. Dozens of men who knew her were investigated. All were eliminated.

Gabriella's murder was sent to the cold case unit in 2015, three years later. There were numerous appeals on TV and in the press.

But there was nothing.

The investigation petered out, but it was an everyday unending nightmare for Lazarus and his family. He took it badly. He always felt responsible.

That she had been taken while he was on his way to collect her gnawed at him like a rat. It tortured him. Even now it was a constant dull ache in his heart. That pain became more acute at this time of the year, the anniversary of her murder.

Detective Sergeant Cochrane was now left with Gabriella's file. She bore the brunt of Lazarus's desperation to see the case solved. He texted regularly to see if there was any update. Cochrane was always polite even when, like the last few weeks, Lazarus had become manic.

But she had clearly had enough of the messages and had told Fallon. He thought of the bollocking the Superintendent had just given him.

And he knew she was right.

Lazarus reached his car. He sat in it for ten minutes. He felt grief at Gabriella's loss, but also guilt. Guilt that he hadn't been able to protect her. Guilt that he was at the grave in the middle of the night. Guilt that he was not at home with Jenna and the boys.

He drove off.

He was on the road heading home when his phone rang. He looked at the display and saw it was McEvoy. He pressed the green button to answer.

'Why the late call, Harry? What's up?'

Lazarus heard loud background noise and he knew were his partner was.

'HARRY?' He shouted it this time.

'Boss! Boss!' McEvoy shouted.

'I'm in a boozer. Gimme a sec.'

Lazarus heard McEvoy shout.

'Here, barman.'

'Yessir.'

'See that space at the top of the pint you just poured for me?'

'Yeah…?'

'Do you think you could fill it with water?'

'Water?'

'Yeah, water.'

'I don't see why not,' the barman said.

'Good,' McEvoy snapped.

'If you can do that, you can fill it with fucking beer. I'll be back in a minute. Make sure it's fucking fixed. Fuck's sake.'

McEvoy brough the phone back to his ear. Lazarus heard him walk out of the pub. He went somewhere quiet.

'Cheapskate bastard,' McEvoy grumbled.

'I see you're involved in a one-man public relations campaign for the cops, Harry,' Lazarus said.

'Good man, the Commissioner will be delighted.'

'Not half as delighted as he will be about us getting Maloney earlier,' McEvoy said.

Lazarus thought his voice was slurred. Not pissed, though. Harry knew how to drink.

'It was a great job, Lazarus, well done, *amigo*,' McEvoy said.

'Thanks, buddy.'

'Just one thing…'

Lazarus grimaced.

'Why did you lie to Winter?' McEvoy asked him.

'I don't know what you mean,' Lazarus said.

'Ah come on!'

Lazarus stayed silent.

'I'll spell it out for you,' McEvoy said.

'You told her you knew from the start that Maloney's piece was a replica. You did in your hole, *amigo*. Nobody can tell the difference between that replica and a real piece at the distance you were from him. No-fuck-ing-body. You only knew when you checked it afterwards.'

Lazarus didn't answer.

'What the fuck were you at?' McEvoy hissed.

More silence from Lazarus.

'You put our colleague at risk, *Sergeant*, and you know it. You're lucky I'm not making a complaint to Anderson.'

Lazarus felt his chest contract.

A complaint like that to Anderson and he was dead. He'd be sacked, at best.

'I couldn't let him go. I did what I had to do to end it,' Lazarus said after a long moment.

He glanced in the rear-view mirror. His eyes were manic. Just like in the hotel.

'I had to take him. I had to get justice for her,' he said.

'Who's her?' McEvoy asked.

'Watch your mouth,' Lazarus said.

Neither man spoke. The silence between them became heavy.

McEvoy broke first.

'I know you, John. I'm honoured to be your partner. You're my friend. You're the best investigator I've ever worked with. But by Christ you need to get your sister out of your head. I thought for a few years it was good that it made you tick, made you go after the sex offenders like I've never seen any other detective hunt them down. I know she's what drives you on'

'Putting animals behind bars is what drives me on,' Lazarus shouted.

'*Amigo*,' McEvoy said.

'How many of the boys' big days have you missed? How many of your anniversaries?'

Lazarus gripped the steering wheel, said nothing.

'You think I'm a fool, Lazarus,' McEvoy said.

'All this volunteering for overtime, taking on every new case, working all the hours God sends. I understand, I do. Gabriella's killer hasn't been caught. It must be a nightmare. But, fuck me, this is the first time your one man crusade has nearly caused the death of another cop.'

'I do what I do to get results,' Lazarus said.

'You need to cop the fuck on,' McEvoy said.

'I mean it. Sort yourself out. You deserve better. And so does your family.'

The phone went dead.

And all Lazarus could do was drive into the darkness.

By the time he pulled his car into the driveway, it was close to 11.30pm. The security light above the front door flashed on when it sensed the motion of his car.

He was still smarting from the dressing down by McEvoy. He sat in the Giulia for a few minutes to calm down. He checked the smartwatch on his wrist and it showed his pulse was 101. It was normally 59. He could hear his heart pounding in his ears. There was a sick feeling in his stomach.

And he did feel sickened. Sickened that he was in so deep he could even contemplate Maloney murdering Winter just so he could nail him.

He gritted his teeth.

'*Idiota!*' he said to himself.

He looked at the family home. It was a refuge from the evil he saw outside every day. A place where Jenna and the kids would be safe and secure. It was ten miles from the station, but may as well have been another world.

Lazarus got out of the car. He walked towards his semi-detached four-bedroom house. It was two-tone: red-brick on the ground floor, the upstairs façade painted magnolia. They had built a sunroom two years ago and had also installed triple glazed windows; their white frames stood out in the estate.

Lazarus reached the white front door, placed his fingers on the handle and noticed with satisfaction that it was locked. He put the key in the lock, opened the door and went into the hall. The house was quiet. Jenna and the kids were asleep.

The stairs had a deep pile blue carpet on them. The hall was narrow with polished oak flooring. The walls were painted a soft colour somewhere between light green and blue. Jenna said its name was Crystal Surprise, but Lazarus just called it turquoise. A small lamp on a radiator cover gave him enough light to make it to the kitchen.

The kitchen had large grey sandstone tiles on the floor, beige paint on the walls and white units, as well as an island. The counters were black granite.

He walked to the fridge-freezer. It was a brushed steel, American model. He opened it. He considered his alcohol options. He saw a bottle of Pinot Noir, but then opted for Moretti, his favourite Italian beer. He took out a brown bottle, brought it to the island and used an opener to take the top off. He sat on a high-backed stool and took a long, slow swallow. He felt the beer's coldness on his throat. It was so cold it almost burned him as it reached his stomach. He sat in the dark, drinking the beer, brooding about Winter and Gabriella, feeling guilty for lying to Jenna again.

He drained the bottle in less than two minutes. He wiped his mouth with the back of his hand. He went back to the fridge for a second. He downed it just as quickly.

When he was done, he realised he wanted something harder. He opened a cabinet. He looked inside and saw what he was after. He withdrew the thin green bottle of Grappa Bassana, a spirit from back home in northern Italy that made your eyes water.

He took a tumbler from a rack and poured in two fingers of the alcohol. He hesitated, then made it three.

He held the drink up to his mouth, paused for a beat, then knocked back the clear liquid. He started coughing as soon as he swallowed it. His mouth and throat were on fire. He felt the pungent liquid working its way into his system. He put his hand over his mouth to stifle the coughing.

His eyes began to water, so did his nose.

He forced himself to take another half glass.

He told himself for the millionth time he had to let Gabriella and his mother go. Realised, also for the millionth time, that he couldn't.

61

'Not a fucking chance,' he said to the empty kitchen.

Not while her killer was out there, walking the streets, mocking him. His hand gripped the bottle as he thought of the faceless animal who had taken his sister from him. The anger swelled up inside him. He held the bottle so tightly he thought it was about to smash.

He closed his eyes.

He sighed, put the glass and beer bottles in the sink and trudged upstairs. Their room was on the left at the top of the landing. He got to the top of the stairs and took a step towards it, then stopped. The boys' bedroom door was ajar. He eased it open.

The room was in darkness. But there was enough light from the landing to make out the boys. Although they each had a bunk, they were asleep together in the bottom bed.

They were in each other's arms. Pietro was on his back, his mouth open and snoring. Giovanni Junior was on his side, facing Pietro with an arm on his chest and his leg crooked over his brother's. The room was warm and they were both wearing pyjama bottoms and white vests. Their hair was matted with sweat and they had kicked off the duvet.

Lazarus saw they were breathing in unison. Long slow breaths in and out. In and out.

He kept watching them. The love he felt for them overwhelmed him. He often told himself he did what he did for them. To provide for them, of course, but more than that. He felt if he dived deep into the darkness of the world, embraced its evil, then they might be spared. The gods of evil would pass them by because their old man had already seen and done too much shit.

The ultimate taking one for the team.

He walked to his own bedroom door.

Jenna was on her back in the bed. She was breathing slowly. Her light coloured hair was splayed on the pillow. Her eyes were closed.

She looked at peace.

He let out a long sigh.

Then he undressed, got into bed, closed his eyes and waited for the nightmare to come.

10

Monday

Her eyes are begging Lazarus for help. They plead to him from the back window of the van. A heavy hand is clamped over her mouth, muffling her screams. But her eyes do enough talking.

The van speeds off. Lazarus runs after it, never taking his eyes off Gabriella. She is wearing a white T-shirt. Lazarus can already see the dirt and blood soiling it.

Her thin hands are banging on the window. Lazarus pumps his legs and swings his arms. He wrings every last bit of speed out of his body. But he is running through a sea a mud. He is slowing down and the van is speeding up. The distance widens by the second.

There is a puff of smoke from the exhaust pipe as the driver presses down on the accelerator.

Lazarus is running on the spot now and he sees the smoke, black and dense and threatening, waft through the air. It flows up and past Gabriella. It obscures his view of her. When it clears, most of the features on her beautiful face have disappeared.

The flesh is gone. The hair is gone. The lips are gone.

But her eyes remain.

They stare at him. He reaches for her. Gabriella's jawbone moves up and down. Even though there are no lips to form words, he knows what she is saying.

Save me.

She is a skeleton now. She brings up what was once her left hand. He sees the bones gripping a pink mobile phone. She presses a button on it. Lazarus hears his own phone ringing in the pocket of his jeans.

He fumbles for it with a sweaty hand. The display tells him it is her.

He stabs at the button to answer it.

But it continues its shrill ring.

He tries again.

The phone ignores his fingers.

He looks back to where the van was.
It's gone.
She's gone.
And still the phone rings.

*

Lazarus woke with a jolt. His mouth was sandpaper dry. His heart was pounding.

It took him an instant to realise his mobile was ringing in the real world. He clawed for the handset on top of the bedside locker. He saw Fallon's photograph on the display.

The fuck?

He hit answer just as Jenna began to stir. He leapt out of bed and scrambled to the bathroom. He held the phone to his chest as he entered the bathroom. He closed the door behind him.

'Superintendent?' he whispered.

'Sorry for the early call, John.'

'What time is it?' He must have been in a deep sleep. His brain still felt fuzzy.

'It's just after 12.40am,' Fallon said.

The fog in Lazarus's brain began to lift. He knew something major had happened for Fallon to be ringing now.

Something bad.

Something worse than bad.

'What have we got?' he said.

'A bad rape.'

The hairs on the back of his neck stood up.

'It's a woman in her twenties,' Fallon said.

'She was left for dead. She's in hospital now. Might not make it.'

'Where?'

'Griffith Park.'

Lazarus knew the location. It was a genteel park in Drumcondra, just off the main road leading from the city centre to Dublin Airport.

'Is anyone in for it?' he asked.

'Nope.'

Fallon went silent. Lazarus knew she was holding something back.

'And?'

'The 999 call was made at 11.53pm, our lads got there at 12.04am,' Fallon said.

'Jesus. Why am I only being told now?'

'Because, sunshine, it looked like a robbery at first,' Fallon said.

'She was found in bushes by some man going for a piss. Unconscious but fully clothed. Her bag is missing, so uniform thought she was mugged. It was only when she was taken to the Mater that she was examined and there were signs of sexual assault. And that means it's all yours.'

'What's her name?' Lazarus asked.

'We don't know yet. There was nothing to identify her on her clothing. It all must have been in her bag.'

'I'm on my way in,' Lazarus said.

'Not so fast. Did you have those drinks last night?'

Lazarus thought back to the beers and the Grappa.

'Yes,' he said.

'Okay,' Fallon said. 'There's a blue light taxi on its way. You have ten minutes.'

She rang off.

Lazarus stood in the blackness of the bathroom. He felt the adrenalin rush that comes with a new investigation surge through his body. And then he did what he always did at the start of an inquiry.

He closed his eyes and imagined himself sitting in a small interview room, the suspect across from him, about to break.

Snivelling.

Crying.

Pathetic.

He knew he would catch him. He knew the day would come.

Lazarus turned on the small light over the bathroom mirror and shaved. As he did, he considered himself in the mirror. He looked tired. His olive skin was pale. His face was set in its usual hardness. His eyes were as hard as ever.

He returned to the bedroom and got dressed in the dark. He cursed when he stubbed a big toe on the bedpost.

He went downstairs to the kitchen and heated up the coffee machine. It was a bean to cup model. He shuddered as he recalled the price. Worth every penny, he thought. He opened a unit door above it and took out a packet of Lavazza Rossa coffee beans. He filled the hopper at the top of the machine. Then he closed the lid, checked the water tank was full and pondered what drink to have. He went for a double espresso. It would be a long night. He placed a cup under the dispensing spout and hit a button. Almost immediately he heard gurgling as the espresso emerged from the spout.

He took a moment to marvel as the hot black liquid filled the cup. Then a thick brown crema settled on the surface of the espresso and he knew it was ready. Lazarus closed his eyes and inhaled the aroma of the arabica beans.

For a fleeting instant he wasn't in north Dublin, but in a café in Taormina with Jenna as they enjoyed a break in the town before the boys came along. He could almost feel the Sicilian sun beating down on his face as he sat opposite his woman and enjoyed an espresso under the blue sky. The aroma always did that to him. No matter where he was, it always brought him back to Italy. To his people.

He downed the coffee in one gulp and the smoke and heat struck him in the back of a throat like a punch. It was glorious. He felt the caffeine surge through his body.

Now he was ready for what the darkness would bring.

He heard a diesel engine outside. The driver of the Garda car switched on the blue lights for an instant to inform Lazarus of their arrival. He grabbed a banana from the fruit bowl and walked out of the kitchen.

He lifted his overcoat from the stand in the hall and went outside. He eased the front door closed. He hurried along his driveway to the waiting patrol car. He was glad he had put on a vest, shirt and jumper. But even then, the coldness bit through his clothing. He looked to the sky. He could see no light. Just a low base of dark clouds. He could see frost on the flowers and plants in his garden. The coast was 500 metres from his house. He could smell a pungent mixture of salt and gas drifting in from the estuary.

He got to the marked Hyundai and opened the rear door. The female driver nodded, but said nothing. Lazarus guessed she was in her late twenties. She was heavy set with short brown hair that had blonde streaks in it. She wore black stud earrings. She had a blue Garda fleece tunic over her uniform, and a yellow stab vest over that. She had intense green eyes. She drummed the steering wheel as she waited for him to sit in. The passenger, a male cop who was in his fifties with grey hair and a happy face, turned to Lazarus. He recognised him as one of the officers from Malahide, his local station.

'You in a hurry?' the officer asked.

'Command and Control just told us to pick you up. You want the sirens and lights on?'

Lazarus felt relief at the question. It meant details of the attack had so far been kept out of the groups.

Cops were notorious for spreading news of major incidents to each other on WhatsApp groups. Some had hundreds of members. Each station had one, some several. Incidents spread from one group to another like heroin through blood. Lazarus did not want the attack leaking from the groups out to the media. He knew the news would emerge, but he wanted to be ahead of it.

'Put the lights on, but only when you get on the main road,' he said.

'I don't want to give my neighbours any more reason to dislike me.'

The cop laughed. The car moved off.

Lazarus felt his phone buzz. He looked at the display. It was Harry McEvoy.

'I'm on scene,' McEvoy said when Lazarus answered. His voice was clear now, unlike their last conversation when he was in the pub. Lazarus marvelled at how quickly McEvoy could switch on.

'It's not good, John. I just spoke to the first uniforms to arrive on. They thought she was dead. But I don't understand why he dressed her after the rape. What the fuck was that all about? Some weird fantasy shit?'

'No idea,' Lazarus said. 'But it has put us on the back foot and has given him time to escape. Have you spoken to Winter?'

'She's on the way.'

'Ring her back and tell her to go straight to the hospital. I'll join her later.'

Lazarus glanced up and saw the driver examining him in the rear-view mirror. Their eyes met and she looked away. She flicked on the blue lights as soon as they reached the main road. Lazarus looked to his right and saw the estuary. It was still and black and deep.

Lazarus realised he had no idea what the uniforms had done at the park since the discovery of the woman. He took a notebook out of his pocket and started writing down a list of investigative tasks on a new page.

He looked up after a few minutes and saw the car speed past Whitehall Church. He had been on the same road hours earlier when the team was bringing Maloney to the station. Back then, the main road into the city from the airport was bustling. Now it was deserted.

The car's blue lights illuminated the buildings on the road and reflected on their windows. The pubs had long thrown out their patrons. The take-aways were closed. It had rained earlier and the road surface was slick. Lazarus craned his neck to look at the sky. He saw the thick clouds that hung over his home had made it to the city centre.

The car did a sharp right turn and sped along Botanic Avenue. Lazarus knew the entrance to Griffith Park was halfway up the road and on the right. As they approached, he saw a Garda car parked up, its engine running and blue lights blinking. The car stopped beside it.

The park entrance was a few metres away. It was a large park, made up of grassland with concrete paths, the River Tolka dividing it. There were knots of trees and bushes that, even in late October, still had their leaves.

Lazarus saw the park was enclosed by heavy iron railings. A small gate gave access to pedestrians. It was open, but white and blue Garda crime scene tape ran across it. Lazarus looked through the railings and saw activity deep in the park.

Three uniforms in yellow hi-vis gear stood on a path 100 metres in. He saw a dense wooded area just behind them. It was sealed off with more tape. The tape bobbled in the wind.

On the road outside the park, Lazarus counted four Garda cars. He also saw a van. It said Crime Scene Investigation Unit on the side. He was relieved the techies were already looking for clues.

A figure emerged from behind the van and walked towards him. McEvoy.

He pointed deep into the park.

'Along the path, Lazarus.'

McEvoy wore a Garda jacket and black trousers. His hair was uncombed. He wore a creased shirt under his jacket. But he was alert. He smelled of aftershave and mints.

A female and male officer stood just inside the tape at the gate. The female held a hard-backed A4 book. Lazarus and McEvoy ducked under the tape and nodded to her.

'Hello Chrissy,' McEvoy said.

Garda Chrissy Boyle grimaced, then started writing in the book. It was her job to log everyone who passed through the outer cordon.

'Bring these two up to the scene, Sam,' Boyle said to the male officer. Her eyes were fixed on the notebook as she spoke.

Lazarus did not know him. He was a rookie. He was short, about five foot six, and looked nervous. He was in his early twenties. His cheeks were red.

'What's your name? McEvoy asked.

'Garda Collins,' the rookie stammered. 'Sam Collins.'

'You cold?'

The rookie nodded.

'Baltic.'

McEvoy smiled. 'You'd want to get used to it, son. You've got a long 30 years ahead of you. This shithole is always freezing. Even in what passes for summer in Dublin.'

Lazarus walked on. He ate up the ground and closed the distance to the inner cordon. He was walking on the grass. He noticed it was wet from the rain. One of the uniforms looked up and saw him. She detached herself from the others. She walked towards him. Lazarus realised it was Linda Fallon.

She looked frazzled.

'Lazarus,' she said.

'Morning, Super,' Lazarus said. It was 1.10am.

'I'm glad you're here. I'm the only super on tonight in the entire DMR.'

She shook her head.

'The job's fucked.'

There should be two superintendents on at night in Dublin – one each side of the River Liffey that divided the city. But cuts meant Fallon was on her own. She was the most senior officer on duty right now in the Dublin Metropolitan Region, the area that covered the capital.

'Where are we with this?' Lazarus asked.

'The victim was taken to the Mater. When the doctor examined her, it became clear she had been sexually assaulted. So they contacted SATU in the Rotunda. The FCE is examining her now.'

That was a start at least, Lazarus thought. The Rotunda, beside O'Connell Street in the city centre, is best known as a maternity hospital. But it also houses the city's Sexual Assault Treatment Unit. A Forensic Clinical Examiner is on duty 24 hours a day to carry out examinations of men, women and kids who have been sexually assaulted.

'Has the examination started?' Lazarus said.

Fallon looked at her watch.

'Yes, about ten minutes ago.'

Fallon hesitated.

'You're on your own, buddy. There has just been a double fatal shooting over in the west. I should have been there 20 minutes ago.'

Lazarus nodded.

Fallon punched him on the arm.

'Don't fuck it up.'

She winked at him and walked away.

'The job *is* fucked,' he called after her.

She didn't hear him.

Lazarus took a deep breath.

He walked towards the inner cordon.

Towards the darkness.

11

Lazarus pulled a black torch from his coat pocket and flicked it on. Its bright yellow light cut through the night like a knife through flesh.

He looked at the area where the woman had been found. He could see a large forensics tent, white on the top half, dark blue on the bottom. Light from two torches inside shone through the translucent fabric. Lazarus knew they belonged to scenes of crime officers. They were searching for forensic clues.

Suddenly, the torches snuffed out.

Lazarus heard a voice behind him.

'Why have they done that?'

It was Collins, the rookie.

He and McEvoy were out of breath from the exertion of catching up with Lazarus.

'They're looking for body fluids,' McEvoy panted

'Without light?'

McEvoy went to answer, but Lazarus butted in.

'They have light,' he said.

'We just can't see it. They're using black light,' he said.

Lazarus kept his eyes on the tent.

'It's ultraviolet. It picks up blood or semen or saliva. Fluids that ordinary light can't see. They need the normal torches off so they can use the UV ones.'

'Get out of here, son,' McEvoy said to Collins.

'This is adults' work. You'll learn about this one day, but not now. Go on, scoot.'

Collins blanched. He turned away with his head down and trudged back to the outer cordon.

McEvoy and Lazarus watched the search in silence. After around 15 minutes, the ordinary torches lit up again. Then the tent flap opened.

A large, stocky man emerged. He wore a white forensics suit, its hood up. It was pulled tight around his face. He also wore a white mask. All Lazarus could see were glasses covering his eyes.

The man recognised Lazarus and waved a purple-gloved hand. He lumbered towards them. His white gear stood out against the night. He had a torch in each hand. One was on. It was large with a wide lens and its bright piercing light jerked along the ground as he walked. The second torch was smaller and was off.

He got to within a few feet of the inner cordon and took off his mask.

'Hello lads,' he said. He had a happy voice. Lazarus thought techies always seemed cheerful, despite the shit they saw up close.

'Ben,' Lazarus said.

Ben Flannery, the scenes of crime sergeant, lowered the hood and crouched under the tape. He did it with ease, even though he was in his late forties. Once on the other side of the cordon, he stood back to his normal height of six foot four. He had a ginger moustache and bushy eyebrows of the same colour. His hair was thick and grey. His blue eyes were magnified by the thick lenses of his silver-rimmed glasses.

'Anything?' Lazarus asked.

'No semen, some blood stains. We've marked them out already,' Flannery said. He held up the unlit torch. 'This showed them up on patches of grass.'

Most of the specialist search of the crime scene would be carried out in the daylight, but the black light test needed to be done at night.

'Anything else?' Lazarus asked.

'Not in the dark, no,' Flannery said.

'We'll do a fingertip search at first light. He might have left something behind. I need to head off to the Mater to take some photos of the victim.'

Lazarus thought of something.

'What about footprints?'

Flannery smiled. 'You're the only one who ever thinks forensics, Lazarus. It's quite muddy in there from the rain. We have stepping plates down so we don't disturb any ground. There might be something for you. We'll know in the morning.'

Flannery peeled off his white suit and walked to his van. Lazarus followed him and walked back towards the outer cordon. McEvoy was at his side. As they got closer, Lazarus noticed two uniforms talking to a young couple just beyond the tape. One of the uniforms was a sergeant called Liam Connolly. He stopped talking to the couple, made his excuses and came over to Lazarus.

'They found her,' Connolly murmured. He was a few years older than Lazarus. His head was bald and smooth. He was tall and well built. He had a thin face and sharp features, even sharper eyes.

Lazarus approached the couple and introduced himself. Both were in their late twenties. They gave their names as Adam and Debbie Sweeney. Lazarus eyed them. The woman was slim with blonde shoulder-length hair. She had black boots with a high heel, boot-cut green trousers and a cream trench coat tied tight around her waist. She sobbed into a handkerchief.

Her man was tall and broad and had a trimmed beard. His brown hair was short and well kept. His eyes were deep and blue. They darted around. He kept looking at cops and then away. He wore a black coat, zipped up to his neck, blue jeans and black shoes.

Lazarus was about to start talking when the man shook his head. He broke away and ran to the side of the main road. He bent over behind a parked car and vomited.

'He's very upset, like,' the woman said.

The man came back and apologised. Lazarus wondered was he upset, or putting on a front. The person who raised the alarm was always a potential suspect. Lazarus had seen too many men appear devastated on the surface only to be the culprit. The truth lay underneath. Always.

Lazarus smiled a false smile and shrugged his shoulders.

'No problem,' he said with a wave of his hand.

'Just a few routine questions.'

The couple looked at each other. Then at Lazarus.

The man nodded towards the uniforms.

'We've already told these officers.'

'I understand, sir. I'll just be a few minutes.'

'Whatever,' the man said.

Lazarus ignored the jibe.

'So tell me what happened tonight,' he said.

Debbie started talking.

'We live on the other side of the park.'

She gestured to the north.

'We were in a pub in Drumcondra tonight.'

'What pub?' Lazarus asked. His attention was fixed on the man.

'Fagan's.'

Lazarus knew it. Everyone in Dublin did. It was at the bottom of Botanic Avenue. He made a mental note to check its CCTV.

'What did you do after Fagan's?'

The man's eyes darted away. There was something about him.

'We went to the chipper up the road and then walked up Botanic Avenue and took the shortcut through the park. Everyone does, you know,' he said.

'Sure. What time did you leave the pub?'

'About half eleven.'

'Was anyone with you?'

'Just us.'

'What chipper did you go to?'

He named it.

'Did you eat in the chipper?'

'Yes.'

Lazarus thought of more CCTV that needed checking. If they were telling the truth, the cameras would back them up.

'What did you do after you left the chipper?'

'We walked down Drumcondra Road, over the bridge and turned right down there.'

He pointed to the bottom of Botanic Avenue.

'Walked to the park.'

'What time did you get to the park?'

'Uh, about ten to twelve, something like that.'

Lazarus knew the 999 call had been made at 11.53pm.

'How did you get into the park?'

'We hopped the railings. They're low enough.'

The man looked pale.

'I know it's closed and we're not supposed to, but it's a local shortcut.'

'Of course,' Lazarus said. 'What happened next?'

The man swallowed hard and rubbed his face.

'We were walking along the path,' he said.

'Then I needed a piss.'

Debbie slapped his arm.

'Sorry,' the man said.

'I had a call of nature. I saw bushes and went to go behind them.'

Then the life emptied from the man's eyes.

'I went behind the bushes and was just about to, you know…suddenly I saw what I thought was a bundle of rags on the ground. I looked closer and…Jesus Christ.'

He broke away and retched again.

'Sorry,' he croaked when he came back. 'I looked over and saw it was a woman. She was on her back. She looked dead. I'll be honest, I near shat myself. I didn't know what to do. It scared the fucking daylights out of me.'

He shook his head.

'I called Debbie. She looked after her while I called 999. Then the cops and paramedics arrived.'

Debbie nodded.

'That's what happened,' she said quickly.

Lazarus looked away and scanned the park, even though there was no chance the attacker was still around. Apart from the activity at the scene, the area was quiet and pitch black.

'Did you see anyone? Anyone running away? Or even hanging around?' he asked them.

They looked at each other and shook their heads.

'No, nobody,' the man said.

'I was too busy contacting you guys.'

'Nobody at all,' the woman said.

'What about when you walked on the road towards the park?'

They shook their heads again.

'Nobody,' the man repeated. 'It was a quiet night. Not much traffic. One or two cars.'

Lazarus looked to McEvoy.

'This is my colleague Harry. He needs to take a statement from you.'

McEvoy smiled at them.

'We'll go to the station and do it there.'

'Ah, now here,' the man protested.

'What the fuck do we have to go to the station for? We've told you everything.'

Lazarus smiled, but his eyes fixed on the man.

'A woman has been seriously assaulted. I'm sure you'd like to help us catch whoever did this. It could be someone you know the next time.'

The man folded his arms, but said nothing.

'It won't take long,' McEvoy said. 'We just need to get a written statement from you both and some samples for elimination.'

The man's eyes widened.

'Whoa. Hold your horses, big man. Elimination from what?'

The woman hit him in the arm again. He shut up.

'Just listen to the man, Adam. Christ's sake. He's doing his job.'

'We're going to need your DNA,' Lazarus said. 'You will have left some traces, what we call contaminated the scene. This is to eliminate you from any forensic samples we find. And we'll need to have a look at your footwear, too. All the paramedics and gardai who were at the scene will be doing the same. It's purely procedural. We can get a written order from the Commissioner for the sample if you insist, but I'm sure you'll want to cooperate.'

'Bollix to that,' the man said. He shoved his hands into the pockets of his trousers. But Lazarus knew they would comply, despite the hissy fit. He thanked them and walked away. He called McEvoy over.

'Don't forget the footwear. I'm going to meet Winter at the Mater.'

He left McEvoy and was about to get into a waiting marked car when he saw two figures with their backs to him a few metres away. They were engrossed in conversation and didn't see him, but Lazarus tensed when he realised who they were.

Sullivan from *The Globe* stood on the right while his partner Gallagher was on the left. Lazarus cursed as he wondered how they knew about the attack so quickly. He checked his watch. It was 1.45am. They looked as if they had been there a while. Lazarus hadn't seen them when he entered the crime scene, but he wasn't looking for them.

Gallagher wore winter gear. He had a heavy brown jacket with integral fleece zipped up as far as it could go. He wore fingerless gloves, a black woollen hat, runners and black combats.

Sullivan was less prepared. He had the same combats and runners on as at the hotel and wore a black North Face jacket, but had forgotten his gloves and hat. He hopped from foot to foot to keep warm. They were looking towards the northern corner of the park, where a Garda search team was working. Gallagher was videoing them on his smartphone.

'You did well to get the tip so quickly, Conor,' he told Sullivan.

'This footage will look great. Nobody else has a sniff of it.'

'I'll get onto the morning desk,' Sullivan said.

'They start at 5.30am. They'll put it up for 6.30am. It's a great story, should drive plenty of traffic. And we need to get it out before the cops issue a release. They do morning statements at about 8am. I'll break it on Twitter just before we run it online. It will fly.'

'It's a good scoop,' Gallagher said. 'What do we know?'

Sullivan blew out his cheeks.

'The tip just had the bare bones. It said a young woman was attacked as she walked through Griffith Park before midnight. Said she was in a bad way.'

They went silent for a moment as Gallagher shot more video. Lazarus saw a slight smile appear on his face. He wondered why.

The next sentence told him.

'She was found near the bushes and trees?' he asked.

'Yeah.'

'Who's investigating it?'

Gallagher timed it perfectly.

He waited until Sullivan opened his mouth to answer and then cut him off.

'Is it Special Branch?'

Sullivan laughed.

'You're sick,' he said.

Gallagher chortled.

'Are they going to root out the attacker?'

'Christ Almighty.'

'This story is beginning to grow on me…'

'Fuck me, Tony.'

Gallagher laughed again.

Lazarus couldn't help himself.

'You fuckers think this is funny?' he said.

They both jumped at his voice. Sullivan's eyes widened when he recognised Lazarus.

Lazarus expected him to be embarrassed and apologise. But Sullivan chose attack.

'This is a private conversation,' he said, his eyes meeting Lazarus's.

'Don't try that shit with me,' Lazarus spat back.

Sullivan was about to say something else when there was a sudden cry. It was a woman's voice, indistinct but loud. Lazarus realised it was coming from the search team at the edge of the park. The cop had shouted the single word *find*. Lazarus looked into the park and saw McEvoy and two uniforms running towards the voice.

Sullivan gave Lazarus a hard stare then he and Gallagher scurried along the footpath that ran outside the railings. Gallagher now had the SLR camera up and was fixing the settings as he ran.

Lazarus watched them in silence.

12

Lazarus stared at the deserted streets as the Hyundai sped through the city. The only sound was the occasional squawk from the Garda radio. The vehicle pulled up at the entrance to the Mater Hospital emergency department just before 2am. Lazarus got out. The car moved off and headed back to the crime scene at Griffith Park.

Lazarus badged the hospital worker at reception. She nodded and told him to take the lift to level three. Lazarus grimaced. He knew that was where the intensive care unit was located.

Winter met him at the door of the unit. She looked drawn. She was wearing white runners and navy jeans. She had a white blouse under a fleece. She wasn't wearing her Garda raid jacket to protect the victim's privacy. Her mouth was tight and her eyes had a tiredness about them. The bruise on her face from Maloney's punch had turned purple. Winter had almost hidden it with make-up, though.

'How is she doing?' Lazarus said.

She shook her head.

'Not good. They don't know if she will make it.'

They entered the unit. Winter led Lazarus to the second room on the right. It had a heavy pine door with a window of reinforced glass. He looked inside and saw a white iron hospital bed. A young woman lay on it. A nurse in blue scrubs stood over the bed. She looked up and noticed Lazarus and Winter. She let them in.

The nurse was petite and wore oversized blue glasses. She had a sharp nose and a freckled face, with arched eyebrows. Her fair hair was cut short in a bob.

Lazarus walked to the bed. He looked down at the woman. They had dressed her in a white gown. A blood-stained bandage covered her forehead, but her auburn hair above it was free. It splayed on the mattress. It formed a halo around her. Lazarus thought back to earlier in the night and Jenna in the same position in their bed.

The woman was young, early to mid twenties. Although she was in a shapeless gown, Lazarus could see she was of medium height and slight.

It was evident from her face just how ferocious an attack she had suffered. Her nose was misshapen and covered by a dressing. Both her eyes were black and were puffed up. They were nothing more than closed slits. Her upper lip was swollen. There was a large bruise already turning dark purple on her left cheek. Lazarus could also see several cuts, including a deep gash on her chin.

She had thin arms. There was no muscle mass. Lazarus imagined her trying to fight off the monster. He knew she would have no chance. But something told him she would have tried.

A monitor on a stand beside the bed recorded her pulse and heart rate. He heard a slow beep from it every few seconds. He also saw a ventilator. A thick tube ran from it up to the woman's mouth.

'What are her injuries?' he asked.

The nurse looked at the patient. Lazarus noticed the sadness in her eyes.

'Fractured nose. Two black eyes. Burst upper lip. Three cracked ribs on the right side. Bruising to her forehead. Bruising to her left cheek. Bruising to both thighs. Cuts and scrapes on both knees. Large bruise on the back of her head. Looks like she was kicked on the ground. Before we cleaned her up you could see a footprint on her face. He stamped on her.'

'Fucking hell,' Lazarus murmured.

'They're all the superficial injuries, I suppose,' the nurse said. 'What has really done for her is the strangulation. It's very bad. But I'll let the doctor explain that.'

Lazarus noticed the woman's hands. They were bare. He could see bruising and cuts on several of her fingers and he saw three nails on her right hand were missing. He became concerned that they weren't bagged for DNA, especially underneath her fingernails if she did struggle.

'Have her hands been swabbed?' he asked.

'Everything you need has been done,' a woman's clipped voice said behind him. He turned around and saw she wore the green scrubs of a doctor. She was in her early fifties and thin. She had grey hair that she wore in a long ponytail. Her hair was pulled tight off her face and it accentuated her forehead and thin nose. Her cheeks were so hollow she looked emaciated. There were dark rings around her eyes.

'Detective Sergeant John Lazarus meet Dr Mary Ainsworth, the Forensic Clinical Examiner,' Winter said.

Lazarus shook her hand.

'Can you tell me her name?' the doctor said, looking at the woman.

'I don't know who she is. And we need to know her medical history.'

She placed a gentle hand on the woman's left forearm. She kept it there for a long moment.

'We're working on that at the moment,' Lazarus said.

The doctor had pale blue eyes. They were unblinking.

'How is she?' he asked.

'As bad as can be expected. She's lucky to be alive. He could have killed her. I think he wanted to. She is in a coma.'

'A coma?'

'Yes, Sergeant, an induced coma. She was strangled, beaten and left for dead. She may have a significant brain injury.'

She pointed to the woman's neck. There were thick and livid wealds on it.

'See the red marks? They're from the strangulation. It wasn't manual, looks like some sort of ligature was used. A rope, or a tie, maybe a thin belt. She would have gone unconscious within ten seconds. I think he kept going until he thought she was dead.'

She nodded to the ventilator.

'That is breathing for her. The next 24 hours are crucial.'

Lazarus stayed silent.

'Anyway, full rape kit is done,' Dr Ainsworth said.

She nodded to a cardboard box filled with evidence bags on a counter.

'The necessary swabs have been taken and are ready for analysis. All the clothes she was wearing have been individually bagged and sealed. Her whole body has been examined. The other sergeant will take care of that.'

Lazarus realised Flannery was in the corner of the small room. He remembered the techie had left Griffith Park before him. As well as securing the area around the attack for any clues, Ben was also the officer who had to photograph the victim's injuries. And he was in charge of bringing the victim's clothing and other evidence from the hospital to the Forensics Science Ireland laboratories in west Dublin.

Lazarus saw a camera hanging from his neck.

'I think I'm done here. I'm going to head back to the scene. Oh, I got the footprint on her face before it was cleaned off.'

He picked up the cardboard box with the evidence bags, walked towards the door, then stopped and turned to Lazarus. His eyes were red. His face was drawn and pale.

'Get the bastard, Lazarus.'

He remembered Ben had a daughter around the same age as the victim.

'I will, Ben. That's a promise.'

Lazarus turned back to Ainsworth.

'Can you confirm she was raped, doctor?'

'Yes. It was extremely violent.'

'Okay.'

'And there was no semen found. It looks like he used a condom. The tests will confirm that. The forensic scientists can detect trace evidence from the lubricants.'

Lazarus knew the use of a condom meant the attacker was forensically aware. It also showed this was unlikely to be a spur of the moment attack.

Premeditation could mean the victim knew her attacker, Lazarus thought.

'We have given her emergency contraception,' Ainsworth said. 'She's also been given a tetanus jab and the usual medication.'

Rape victims were given a cocktail of drugs during their initial treatment to prevent sexually transmitted infections. Lazarus knew she would have to take the pills for weeks to come to ensure no infections. If she pulled through.

Ainsworth looked to the ground.

Then she brought her angry eyes up to Lazarus.

'There's something else.'

Lazarus braced himself. He wondered how bad what she was about to tell him must be if it horrified a doctor used to dealing with rape victims.

'He left something in her,' she said.

The doctor's gaze was unwavering.

'Money,' she said after a moment.

Lazarus inhaled sharply.

'He placed a two euro coin deep in her throat. I found it during the examination.'

Lazarus felt the room darken.

Ainsworth went over to a steel tray, picked up a clear plastic bag. She held it up. The coin was inside.

'I've never seen anything like it,' Ainsworth said.

The only sounds in the room were the robotic inhaling and exhaling of the ventilator and the regular beep of the heart rate monitor.

Then Lazarus heard his phone buzz. He lifted it out of his pocket and saw it was McEvoy. He excused himself and went out into the corridor.

'Harry,' he whispered.

'I have her, Lazarus.' McEvoy said.

His voice was tinny. Lazarus could hear the wind in the background.

'The uniforms were doing a search of the park,' McEvoy said. 'They found some sort of rope or cord dumped on the path. It could be what he used to strangle her. It's been bagged already.'

Lazarus felt a tingle of excitement. He remembered the officer's shout as he was leaving the park.

'They also found a bag into the undergrowth, just off the path,' McEvoy said.

'There was a purse visible in the opening and I took it out. It has a DCU student card and other stuff. We have an address. Uniforms are doing the knock now.'

Dublin City University had a campus for student teachers on the Drumcondra Road, about a kilometre from the park. The houses in the streets around the park were popular with students from there.

'Give me the name,' Lazarus said.

McEvoy told him.

Lazarus wrote it in his notebook.

Then he had an idea.

'You say she had a student card?'

'Yeah.'

'Does it have her photograph on it?'

'Yeah.'

'Take a picture and WhatsApp me it. Turn off your flash, try to do it under a streetlight.'

'Roger that. Gimme two minutes.'

'You have one,' Lazarus said, then disconnected the call.

He waited in the corridor. Then he saw the red notification on his screen.

He looked at the photograph, nodded to himself.

He walked back into the room.

He went to Ainsworth.

'This is her,' he said.

Winter walked over. They looked at the screen together and saw the photograph.

It was of a young woman with thick auburn hair and soft pale skin. She had a button nose. Lazarus could see the life sparkling in her bright blue eyes. She had a wide smile. It showed off two rows of perfect teeth. He saw a dimple on each cheek and her lips had a subtle red lipstick. Her eyebrows were plucked and tapered. The photograph was a close-up of another close-up, but Lazarus could see the top of a pink sweatshirt at the bottom of the shot.

'The poor girl,' Ainsworth said.

'What's her name?'

Lazarus didn't need to consult his Garda notebook.

Her name was already seared on his mind.

He knew it would be forever.

With the rest of them.

'Delaney,' he said.

'Anne Winefred Delaney.'

13

Lazarus and Winter were done at the hospital by 3.20am. As they left Anne Delaney's room, Lazarus looked back to her lifeless body. He wondered if she would ever waken.

They walked out of the hospital in silence and only started talking when they sat into Winter's car. It was a five-year-old Volkswagen Passat, laser blue with cream leather seats. It smelled new. Lazarus saw a dashcam under the rear-view mirror; it came to life as soon as Winter started the engine. Lazarus looked around the interior. It was spotless.

They were heading to a house on a small street near Griffith Park. Delaney was living in digs on a road off Botanic Avenue, to the south of the park. It was a 15-minute walk from the attack scene. Uniforms had already called to her accommodation and had broken the news to her housemates. They told gardai Anne was from Sligo, on the west coast, and had gone to her best friend's house at about 8.45pm the previous evening. The friend lived in a residential area north of the park. It made sense for Delaney to go through the park as a shortcut. It would have knocked ten minutes off her walk. The friend had already been woken. McEvoy was with her, waiting for them.

Dublin was quiet as Winter drove.

Lazarus turned to her.

'This coin thing…'

Winter's face tightened.

'I've never heard of anything like that,' she said.

'Me neither. What would the experts say? Experts like you.'

Winter blushed. She had just completed a master's degree in criminology and had specialised in the study of sex offenders. She had done the course over two years, and paid for it out of her own pocket. It was one of the reasons why she joined Lazarus's unit.

Lazarus saw her thinking.

'Power,' she said finally.

'Rape is always about power. A man wants control over a woman. What better way to dominate a woman by leaving money in her? Owning her. Then there's the whole thing about labelling her a prostitute'.

'Don't tell Anderson, or even the Super,' Lazarus said.

'Don't put it in any reports. Keep it tight. The only people who are to know about it are me, you, Harry and Flannery. Just the team.'

Lazarus looked out the window.

'The world doesn't need to know he did that to her.'

They arrived at the friend's house ten minutes later. Winter parked close by. They closed their doors softly before walking up the small path. It was a large 1930s semi-detached house. It was bordered by a hedge and a wrought iron gate.

The exterior was grey pebble dash. Lazarus saw an extension on the side, built to cram in another tenant. The front door was dark green with leaded glass windows and a brass knocker. Lazarus noticed an alarm box on the front. No security cameras.

The front door opened as they reached it. It was McEvoy. He moved aside to let them in. Lazarus came into a wide hallway, laminated wood on the floors, salmon-coloured paint on the walls. No posters or art or framed photographs. A white door on their left, closed tight.

'She's in there with Duffy,' McEvoy whispered.

'Orla Diffney. She works in Facebook in town. Aged 23. Has known the injured party for five years. They lived together in university then stayed in contact when she started working and Anne Delaney went to teacher training college.'

Lazarus opened the door and entered the room. Winter was behind him.

Duffy, the uniform, was sitting on a red sofa beside a young woman. Diffney, who was sobbing into a handkerchief, looked younger than 23. She had a small frame, with a thin face. Her dirty blonde hair was long and unbrushed. She sat hunched forward on the sofa. The hair covered much of her face, only her sharp nose and forehead were visible. She wore pink flannel pyjamas and slippers.

She looked up when she heard them enter the room. Lazarus saw her face. Her blue eyes came alive. She jumped to her feet.

'Is she dead?'

She was frantic.

'Please don't tell me she's dead.'

84

Duffy got her back on the sofa. Lazarus and Winter introduced themselves, told her they had just been with Anne and she was alive, but ill. There were two armchairs, the same colour red as the sofa, and they took one each. Winter took out her notebook and pen. Lazarus would be asking the questions. He told the young woman to start at the beginning.

Orla took a long sip of water from a glass, blew her nose on the handkerchief and looked at Lazarus. Her eyes were ringed red.

She took a deep breath, then steadied herself.

'Annie rents over on the other side of the park,' she began, nodding in the direction of Griffith Park.

'Her family lives in Sligo and she was back there for the weekend. We have this thing every Sunday. Her train gets into Dublin just before 8pm. She gets a taxi to her house, dumps her stuff and is in mine by 9pm. We watch Netflix together and have some wine. It's a ritual we have.'

'Is that what happened last night?' Lazarus asked.

She nodded.

'I was out so I went to her place and met her there, then we walked back here together.'

'Why not stay at hers?'

'Mine is quieter on a Sunday. The other girls work in the evening at weekends, so we have the front room to ourselves. We can watch what we want.'

'How did you get here from there?'

'Through the park. It was closed, but we jumped the railings.'

'Everyone does, like. It's no big deal, like,' she said quickly.

Lazarus gave her a soft smile.

'We heard it's popular, it's no problem.

'So, you got here about 9pm?'

'Yeah. We came into this room and watched Netflix.'

'What did you watch?'

'Mindhunter. Annie loves her crime shows. She's seen them all.'

She shook her head.

'Oh my God! Oh My God!'

She started crying again. She used the handkerchief to wipe the tears away.

Then she composed herself.

'I can't believe this has happened. Like, what the fuck? We can't even walk home now. Christ.'

'What time did she leave?' Lazarus asked.

Orla looked down to the carpet and stayed quiet.

She twisted the handkerchief tight.

'This is all my fault. She wanted to leave at around 10.45pm. But there was a bit left on the episode we were watching. I kept at her to stay until the end.'

She closed her eyes.

'She did.'

She put her hands to her face and started crying.

The tears came so hard that when she started talking again, it was as if she was gasping for breath.

'She left at 11. If she had left when she wanted to go, she'd be home safe and sound now. He would have picked someone else.'

'We don't know that, Ms Diffney,' Lazarus said.

'Stranger attacks are rare.'

Orla looked straight at Lazarus.

'You mean someone she knew did this?'

Lazarus held his hands up.

'It's too early to say. We can't rule anything out.'

Orla folded her arms, slumped back in the seat.

'I knew it. That absolute weirdo. I told her he was dangerous. The bastard.'

Lazarus tried to stay calm, but adrenaline started to course through him.

'Who are you talking about?' he asked.

Orla sighed.

'She used to go out with this complete arsehole. She dumped him a few weeks ago. He wouldn't accept it.'

Lazarus's heart jolted.

'He had been hassling her,' Diffney said.

'Kept ringing her and messaging her. He wanted to get back with her.'

She blew her nose again. Then looked back at Lazarus.

'He messaged earlier asking to meet up. She showed me the message. The creep did all that kissy-kissy shit at the end of it.'

She shuddered.

'I made her block him on Facebook and Insta, and Snapchat too. She blocked his number on her phone as well.'

'When?' Lazarus asked.

'When she was with me earlier. Not that it matters. The asshole knows where she lives. She'd seen him hanging around.'

She turned to Duffy.

'That type of stalker who just happens to bump into you, know what I mean? He studies in Trinity in town but somehow chanced upon her as she was heading to college in Drumcondra.'

She grimaced.

'Fucking weirdo.'

'When did he bump into her' Lazarus asked.

'He was doing it all the time. Never left her alone. He was knocking around her house last Friday, I think.'

Winter glanced at Lazarus. They exchanged a long look. Lazarus nodded at her, then turned back to Diffney.

'I need to know everything about him.'

14

Anderson was late.

He entered the room after 8.10am. The conference was due to start at 8am. He didn't apologise.

The room was spacious: white walls and a light blue carpet. A long conference table dominated it. Fallon sat at the head of it. Lazarus to her left, Winter beside him. McEvoy faced them, beside Flannery. Anderson pulled a chair in beside Fallon.

Lazarus saw a false smile on Fallon's face. Anderson's contacts in Garda HQ meant she had to treat him with respect, even if she thought he was a prick.

Lazarus didn't have to, though.

'I rang you four times in the night, Inspector,' he said.

Anderson blushed. His eyes burned into Lazarus. He held the inspector's stare.

Anderson looked away.

'My phone died. I only got the messages when I powered it up.'

Lazarus had managed to get home for 30 minutes in the middle of the night to take a quick shower and get his Giulia. It was around 5.30am. Winter and McEvoy had done the same.

Anderson had been oblivious to it all. They finally got him at 7am.

'Forget about it,' Fallon smiled.

She gave Lazarus a filthy look.

'Move on, Detective Sergeant.'

Lazarus was about to speak when Anderson butted in.

'Just one thing,' he said.

The detective inspector had an iPad on the table.

'I presume we have seen *The Globe*.'

Lazarus felt his heart sink. He hadn't seen the story, but Winter had briefed him earlier. Sullivan had broken the attack as he said he would. His article had the bare details of the incident, but that was enough.

It said a woman was fighting for her life after she was attacked. There were anodyne quotes from a source talking about how violent the attack was and there were fears the woman could die. There were no clues about the victim's identity, where she lived, or whether she was a student or had a job. It didn't even have an age for her.

But it did have several photographs. One was of the officer at the outer cordon. Another was a close-up of the forensics tent at the scene. The third was of the search team around Anne Delaney's bag at the edge of the park.

'It's the first story anyone who logs on sees,' Anderson said.

'It's already had thousands of hits. Something needs to be done about Sullivan's tout in this station. First the Maloney arrest, and now this.'

He looked straight at Lazarus.

'The story is bullshit,' Lazarus snapped.

'He's just making stuff up. Sullivan claims the victim was found semi naked. She was fully clothed.'

Just then, Lazarus saw Harry McEvoy blush and fidget in his seat.

'Finding whatever gobshite took a few quid from Sullivan to leak him stories is not our top priority,' Fallon interrupted.

'I want all our energies put into finding this attacker.'

Anderson said nothing.

Lazarus signalled to Flannery, who pressed down on a remote control. A large TV on a wall came to life. The screen was filled with a photograph of Delaney in hospital.

It had been taken an hour ago. Lazarus saw no change in her condition. She was still unconscious, still in the same white gown. Her eyes were taped closed, the ventilator tube still in her mouth. Her face still bloody and bruised. The bandage around her forehead had more blood.

'The victim is Anne Delaney,' Lazarus said.

'She is 22 and from a small village in County Sligo. She is studying to be a teacher at the St. Patrick's Campus of Dublin City University in Drumcondra. She was found just before midnight by a couple taking a shortcut through Griffith Park. The man had a call of nature and found her in an overgrown area off the main path. We've taken their DNA samples for elimination, but they have a strong alibi. She is in an induced coma. They are planning to carry out a CAT scan in the next few hours to determine if she has brain damage. The injuries were caused by ligature strangulation. She may not survive.'

Flannery pressed the button on the remote again and Delaney's student ID card appeared.

Lazarus felt a sudden sadness when he looked at her smile and her hope-filled eyes.

'Her injuries include a fractured skull, possible bleeding to the brain, ligature marks around the neck, a broken nose and other damage to her face, arms and hands,' Lazarus said.

Flannery pressed the remote control again.

This time a map of Griffith Park and the surrounding area appeared on the screen.

He took control of the briefing.

'The victim lives here.'

A house flashed red on the bottom of the screen.

'It is to the south west of the park.'

Flannery clicked the remote again. A straight line appeared. It ran from the attack site to her address. The line stretched through the park, over Botanic Avenue and into a built-up area. The measurement came up on the screen. Just under 400 metres.

'She was five minutes from home,' Fallon said sadly.

Flannery nodded.

'Yes, ma'am. We carried out an initial search of the park last night and found her handbag dumped in the grass.'

A bag appeared on the screen. It was dark green with brown piping around the open pocket flap. It lay on wet grass and its broken strap extended out to the right, like a tail. There was a wide pocket on its front. Mud and debris were visible on it.

'It's a canvas cross body bag,' Flannery explained.

'The wearer puts the strap over her neck and it hangs diagonally from the shoulder. It is on its way to Forensics as we speak. We searched the immediate area of the attack for fluids, such as blood and semen, with ultraviolet light last night. We are going back now that it is daylight to do a more detailed search.'

The next photo was of a small bungee cord. It was olive green, with a black hook at the ends.

'We also recovered this near the bag,' Flannery said.

'We believe that was the ligature. It is from a pack of four sold by one of the large-scale camping outlets. It's 30 centimetres long. It's used by walkers, mountaineers, campers and the like. It's elastic and very strong. Thousands of them have been sold in Ireland.'

The map reappeared. The area where the two items were discovered pulsed red at the top of the screen, near the north edge of the park. The area was close to the Ferguson Road park entrance, where Orla Diffney lived.

'They were recovered in this grassy area,' Flannery said.

'The bag was 105 metres from where the victim was found and the cord another 1.25 metres further north. I suspect he dumped the bag and cord as he ran. That would put him on a trajectory towards the northern gate of the park.'

The park entrance glowed red. It was about 30 metres from the bag and cord.

'He carries out the attack, then heads north, throwing the items away,' Anderson said. 'Then he legs it out of the park by jumping over the railings close to that entrance.'

'That's what it looks like to me, Inspector,' Flannery said.

'The street at the entrance is called Walsh Road. There are several routes he can take from there.'

'Have the victim's family been notified?' Fallon asked.

'Yes,' Lazarus said.

'The nearest station is Sligo town. We contacted them as soon as we confirmed her address. The knock was done just before 7am. The parents are on their way to Dublin.'

Fallon shivered.

'Glad I didn't have to do that one,' she said.

Cops hated doing such knocks. It was never easy calling to a door to break the worst of news to whoever opened it. Lazarus didn't do them now he was a detective sergeant, but he had done more than his fair share when he was in uniform. He still remembered his first one.

It was December 23, 2005. Lazarus was on the night shift. It was quiet. The Christmas parties had finished. Dubliners were in that phony war period between getting pissed with work colleagues and spending the big day with their families.

He and his then partner, a woman called Roisin Feehan who retired a few years later, got the call at 1.59am. They were out in a squad car. All the dispatcher told them was there had been an incident on a road near the airport. It was outside their patch, but they happened to be on an inquiry five minutes away. They raced to the scene. They were the first to arrive.

Feehan was driving. She rounded a bend and the headlights captured an image from hell.

Lazarus saw a woman hanging upside down in a tree. Blood was gushing from her neck. She was naked. Her arms hung down by her head.

A car was on its side about 20 feet away. Its front end crumpled up against another tree, its left front wheel spinning in the dark. Lazarus ran to the vehicle. He found a woman and a man inside. The man was in the driver's seat. Although he was wearing a seat-belt, he was quite dead. The back of his head had caved in. His face was a bloody pulp. The woman was conscious but trapped in the back seat. Her eyes were wide and unblinking, her mouth open in shock.

The forensic collision investigators later concluded the woman in the tree was not wearing her seat belt and was thrown around the cab of the car when the pissed-up driver lost control and slammed into the tree. She hit the back of the driver's head before being thrown through the window and ending up in the branches.

She was 18. Her name was Monica Reilly.

She wanted to be an architect.

Her parents lived in a small village 30 minutes north of Dublin. Lazarus and Feehan arrived at their home at 7.15am. It was a detached bungalow with a yellow door. He always thought of the girl when he saw the colour.

Slowly, each opened their door and got out of the car. Lazarus led the way. He had a sick feeling in his stomach. He opened the gate leading to a gravel driveway. The crunch of the small stones echoed around them. It made the walk feel longer than it was. Their footsteps had alerted a dog, who was barking inside. As they were approaching the door, a security light came on.

The door opened.

A petite woman in her mid fifties, with a parting on the left of her long brown and grey hair, appeared in the doorway. She was wearing a navy blue business suit and a cherry pink blouse and black flats.

She screamed when she saw them.

Her hands went up to cover her mouth. Her eyes bulged.

'Is it Monica?'

Lazarus swallowed hard.

He heard the trembling in his voice.

'Are you the mother of Monica Reilly?'

'Yes', the woman wailed.

'What has happened to my girl? Please tell me she's okay. Please.'

'Can we talk about this inside please, Mrs Reilly?'

'Is she dead?'

'Please can we come inside…?'

And then the woman collapsed on the tiled floor of the pristine hallway.

A question from Fallon snapped Lazarus out of the memory.

'What was the girl doing out at that time of night?'

'She was at her friend's house. It is on a street off Ferguson Road,' he said.

They looked up at the map.

Lazarus could see Ferguson Road north of the park.

'The friend is called Orla Diffney,' he said.

'She offered to walk her home, but Anne said she would be okay. Orla watched her from the gate. She lost sight of her when she turned left and walked towards the park.'

'She didn't notice anyone following Anne?' Fallon asked.

'No. She said the street was deserted.'

Fallon looked down at the initial report Winter had written up.

Lazarus had a copy and noted she had left out the two euro coin.

'Most rapes are carried out by people who know the victim,' Fallon said.

'The level of violence here would suggest a deep anger or hatred, which might support the theory she was targeted by someone she knew. What is the story with this ex-boyfriend?

'Jamie Darcy is his name,' Lazarus said.

'He is studying for a PhD at Trinity College. Some ology. Very intelligent man. And very weird.'

'So what has he done for this Diffney girl to nominate him?' Fallon said.

Rachel Winter coughed and checked her notebook.

'They started going out with each other about seven months ago, ma'am,' she said

'He is five years older than Anne. They were together up until the end of the summer term but went their separate ways over the holidays.'

'I can see where this is going,' Fallon said.

Winter nodded.

'Ms Diffney says Darcy stayed in Dublin to do some research, while Anne went to California. She worked in a restaurant for a few months, met an Irish boy over there.'

'Who is he?' Fallon asked, her eyes narrowing.

'He's from County Kerry and is studying in England,' Winter said.

'I have already checked him out. He is a student at the University of Manchester. Geography. Ms Diffney believes it was a brief fling and Anne said there was nothing to it. She said Anne told her they were just fuck buddies.'

Winter's face turned red.

'Pardon my language.'

Anderson snorted.

'What does that even mean, detective?'

Winter blushed even more.

'It means they just hook up for sex. No strings attached. It's very common. At the end of the night, if you don't have anyone to go home with, you text your buddy and, well, you can work out the rest.'

'Wish they had that in my day,' Fallon said.

'I believe he was in England last night, based on his social media activity,' Winter said. 'He was tagged in photographs on his Facebook timeline at the students' union bar at 8.37pm. He was tweeting and the tweets were geolocated to the same bar over an hour later at 9.42pm.'

She looked down at her notes again.

'But, to be sure, I checked the flights from Manchester to Dublin. The last one is at 10pm. It lands at 11pm. By the time the jet taxis to the gate, everyone gets off and you go through security and passport control, you're talking at least 11.30pm. Then you have to get to the park from the airport, know where Anne is, wait for her and then attack. Then escape.

'And we know the victim left Ms Diffney's house at 11pm. The park was a few minutes away. She was probably attacked before 11.10pm, anyway.'

Fallon nodded.

'Ask the Manchester police to go and visit him, find out what he did later in the night. Just a formality, I'd say. Also, get Crime and Security in the Depot to check if his passport was used last night.'

'Yes, ma'am.'

'Now,' Fallon said, 'tell me more about this bucko she used to go out with.'

Winter took a long sip of coffee.

'She hooked up with him when she got back to Dublin from America at the end of August. But then, at the start of this month, she broke it off.'

'And?' Fallon said.

'And he didn't take it well,' Winter said.

'He started messaging Anne abuse about two weeks ago. He couldn't get over that she had dumped him. At first, they were quite pleading – he wanted her back and asked her to reconsider ending the relationship. But then he turns nasty. Anne showed some of them to Ms Diffney.'

'What did they say?' Fallon asked.

'He called her a bitch and a tramp. He accused her of leading him on and messing him around.'

'Please tell me she kept the messages,' Fallon said.

Winter shook her head.

'They're long gone. They were mostly snaps, anyway.'

Fallon wore a blank expression.

'Snapchat messages,' Winter explained.

'It's an app on your phone. You can send messages to an individual person, or you can put up a video story all your friends can see. The lads in the station all have it. It's great craic on a night out. The messages automatically delete after they are read. Unless you go out of your way to save them. But nobody does that. And they aren't saved on any server, so when they're gone, they're gone. He also sent some old fashioned text messages and he called her a lot of names. She deleted them, but at least the service providers will be able to give us records of the times he sent them.'

'What's his background?'

'He's from Cork,' Winter said.

'The family are involved in finance and own a few shops and investment properties down there. They're well known. His father William is on the city council.'

Everyone groaned.

'That's all we need. A politician's son as a suspect,' Anderson said.

Lazarus saw Fallon fidget in her seat.

She was on the downslope to retirement and didn't want any controversy in the remainder of her service.

'I'm reluctant to name him a person of interest so soon,' she said.

Then she turned to Flannery.

'When will the forensics be back?'

'We already have the samples taken from the victim at the hospital, if there is any DNA found on her we should have it back by tomorrow,' he said.

'And we also have all her clothing for any contact evidence. That should be back in a couple of days. I am going back to the scene for a more detailed search, so any items I seize there will be sent over later this afternoon.'

'I want to wait for what forensics we get before putting the squeeze on Darcy,' Fallon said.

'He could just be a horny young man who wants the ride. Let's see if there is any DNA we can compare with men on the database first, especially those on the register.'

The Garda had a growing DNA database. The force also had a sex offenders' register, and everyone on that had to provide a DNA sample for the database. Supposedly.

'Let's rule out the usual suspects before we go after an ex-boyfriend,' Fallon said.

'We'll have another conference later. Get to work everyone.'

The room started to clear.

'Inspector Anderson and Sergeant Lazarus, stay back,' Fallon said.

Flannery, McEvoy and Winter left the room.

Lazarus called to McEvoy as they were leaving.

'Harry, wait for me outside.'

McEvoy nodded.

Fallon waited until the door was closed.

She glanced at Anderson, then turned to Lazarus.

'Who do you think should run this?'

Lazarus said nothing.

He had been waiting for this.

Anderson cleared his throat.

'The Superintendent and I spoke on the phone on my way in,' he said.

'This is a major investigation and we need to establish who will be the SIO. It would be me, but I am busy with the supers' competition, so am not available.'

The Senior Investigating Officer was the detective in charge of the inquiry. For a case like this, it would be a detective inspector, but Lazarus knew Anderson was going for promotion. That meant investigating came second.

'We have a choice, John,' Fallon said.

'We either make you the SIO, or we bring in the national unit.'

Lazarus stood up, waved his hands at her.

'You can't do that!'

'Sit the fuck down, Sergeant!'

Fallon was on her feet and pointed an angry finger at Lazarus.

'I'll remind you I am your fucking boss! Sit.'

Lazarus obeyed her.

Fallon glared at him.

'Fucking D/Sergeants. You're all the same. Think you're running the show.'

Then she composed herself.

'We know you have passed the SIO courses with flying colours. But this is heavy shit, John. The girl could die. The media will be all over this.'

'I fear you are not ready,' Anderson said with a tight smile.

Lazarus fought the urge to hit him.

'I am ready,' Lazarus said.

'This is my case. And I will solve it. We don't need MIS.'

The Major Investigations Squad, based in an unassuming office block in the city centre, was an elite Garda national unit. It had its own sex crimes team, who were regarded as the cream of the entire police force. But Lazarus knew them sending one of their people to run this investigation would be a kick in the balls for him.

'The MIS is the best course of action,' Anderson said.

Then, after a beat: 'Just to help the sergeant.'

A smirk appeared on his face.

'I don't need their help,' Lazarus snapped.

The room fell quiet for a long time as Fallon considered things.

Anderson stared at Lazarus. Lazarus glowered back.

Fallon was thinking.

'Okay,' She said after a long moment.

'John, you're the SIO. You deserve a chance. But I want you to go and meet the MIS and see what help they can give you.'

She paused and looked into Lazarus's eyes.

'Detective Sergeant Frankie Cochrane is their lead on random sex attacks. Call on her expertise.'

Lazarus closed his eyes, cursed his luck.

Of course it had to be Cochrane, the detective who was in charge of his sister's case.

'I know her,' he said.

'I know you do,' Fallon snapped.

'Sort it. Now, what about the Maloney case?'

Even though the Delaney probe was Lazarus's priority, he still had to give all the other files their proper attention. And that included Maloney. He had been in custody since the arrest the previous evening.

'There is a delay,' Lazarus said.

'He was due to appear in court this morning, but he complained of being unwell in the cell last night.'

'Not because of the injuries he received in that incident?' Fallon asked. Her face creased in concern.

'No, he got nothing more than a few slaps in the struggle,' Lazarus lied.

A vivid memory came to him of Maloney cowering on the ground while he kicked and punched him. He quite liked it.

'They think he took some pills just before we brought him his room service. It only started to affect him a few hours later. He's been ruled medically unfit for court. He will be either up this evening or tomorrow.'

'Good. That gives you time to go to the Caseys and fill them on the child abuse material charges,' Fallon said.

Lazarus grimaced.

'Take young Winter with you,' Fallon said.

'McEvoy is to stay here and run the incident room.'

Lazarus got up to leave. He was just at the door when Fallon called him.

'This is your one chance,' she said with an icy stare.

'There will be pressure on this one, Sergeant. The media are all over it already. We need a quick result. I'll give you a week. If you don't have it solved by then and the animal in custody, I will be asking MIS to take over.

'A week, Sergeant. Not a minute more.'

Lazarus nodded and walked to the door. She called his name just before he opened it.

'Do not fuck this up.'

Lazarus left the room without answering.

He closed the door and saw McEvoy loitering in the hallway. He looked nervous.

Lazarus approached him.

'All right, spit it out,' he said.

McEvoy fidgeted with his tie.

'Spit what out, Lazarus? I don't know what you're on about.'

Lazarus glowered at him.

'There's something you're holding back. Tell me before I beat it out of you.'

McEvoy let out a long sigh.

'Okay, okay. I didn't want to say anything in there. The Sweeney couple who found Anne Delaney. They gave me a statement when you were at the hospital. Remember?'

Lazarus nodded. There was something evasive about the man Adam. Lazarus had a bad feeling about him.

Lazarus frowned.

'Tell me,' he said.

'I brought them to the station when you and Winter were at the hospital. They were jabbering away and repeated the version of events they told us at the scene, that they found her on her back and fully clothed. I took the full statement.'

He looked at the floor.

'But they came back at about 7am, when you were doing paperwork.'

He looked up at Lazarus.

'I meant to tell you before conference,' he said quickly.

'I just didn't get a chance.'

'What?' Lazarus growled.

McEvoy blanched.

'They had second thoughts, wanted to tell the truth. Turns out her bottoms were around her ankles when the man found her. The woman dressed her when he was calling it in. She said she wanted to give her some dignity.'

Lazarus closed his eyes.

'Fuck.'

Their stupidity had set back the rape investigation right from the start. If the first gardai to arrive at the park knew she was undressed they would have realised it was a sex attack. Lazarus's unit would have been called in immediately. It was almost an hour before he was alerted.

But it also meant Sullivan's story was right.

'Who did you tell about this?' Lazarus asked McEvoy.

'Just a couple of the lads in the station.'

'Fuck's sake,' Lazarus spat.

He thought back to the hotel and Sullivan being there for the arrest of Maloney. McEvoy was there, too.

'Harry, I need you to be honest. It's between me and you. It won't go any further. Are you Sullivan's tout?'

McEvoy's eyes flickered.

'John, I swear to you, I'm not. On my mother's grave. It wasn't me. I don't know the man. I give you my word.'

Lazarus went silent.

'You better be telling the truth, Harry,' Lazarus said.

'Because if you're not, we're both dead.'

15

Winter had been promoted to the front passenger seat now that it was just the two of them.

'Are we near?' she asked.

Lazarus shook his head.

'We're taking the scenic route.'

He took a hand from the wheel and waved towards the streets outside.

'I thought I'd show you the delights of Dublin, give you a tour of your new patch.'

The Caseys lived in a tight cul-de-sac of terraced homes in the shadow of Croke Park stadium. Lazarus's team investigated domestic violence, sexual offences, abuse and neglect cases for a wide area of the capital, covering both sides of the River Liffey.

This was where old and new Dublin sat side by side, with working class communities, like where the Caseys lived, and the shiny developments in the docklands, where Lazarus was driving through now.

He steered the Toyota Camry around the business area just on the south-side of the river, which was packed with modern apartment complexes and office blocks, coffee shops and trendy bars. Well-dressed young men and women strode along the pristine pavements, hope and excitement in their eyes. It was 9.40am.

Lazarus pointed to a gated apartment block.

'There's a man in there who earns €180,000 a year in a tech company. We arrested him three months ago for raping and assaulting an escort. We're awaiting a decision on charges.'

'Much evidence?' Winter asked.

Lazarus drove out of the financial district and back into old Dublin.

'CCTV, forensics, phone data and his DNA,' Lazarus said.

'I look forward to knocking on his door soon. He had one of the most expensive lawyers in the country with him when we interviewed him. Said nothing the whole time.'

They drove around the area. After a few minutes Lazarus pointed out a house on a side street.

'We took three kids from their parents in there last month. They're both users. He robs and she is on the game. Neighbours called us because they heard the children crying for hours.'

'What age?' Winter asked.

'Four, two and ten months.'

She nodded.

'The parents were strung out in the living room when we broke the door down,' Lazarus said.

'The kids were locked in a room upstairs. The two youngest hadn't been changed for days.'

He grimaced.

'The smell was horrendous. They're safe now with foster parents.'

Winter sighed.

'I am that bad company?' Lazarus joked.

'You ever wonder what it's like to have a normal life?' Winter asked.

'No kicking down hotel room doors. No sitting with a rape victim in a hospital all night. No rescuing a child from her brother. Imagine what it's like not to have to do... this.'

She gestured to the inside of the car, as if it was a physical manifestation of the job.

'That sounds like a good night out to me,' Lazarus joked again.

He suspected something was eating at Winter, but didn't want to know.

Then he remembered he was a team leader and had a duty of care. Or something.

'What's up?'

Winter's mouth was tight, her eyes downcast.

'I fucked up in the hotel last night, Lazarus. You know it, you're just too nice to bawl me out of it. Maybe I'm not cut out for this.'

Lazarus stayed silent.

'I was so stupid,' Winter said, more to herself than Lazarus.

'I should have been more careful going over to the wardrobe.'

'It has happened to the best of us,' Lazarus said.

It had never happened to him.

He was lying to make her feel better.

'No,' Winter said.

'You told me to be careful. I thought it was just a normal arrest.'

She went quiet for a moment.

'Can I ask you something?' Winter said.

Lazarus gave her a side eye.

'I'm a married man.'

Winter laughed.

'When you came towards me and Maloney, were you frightened?'

He tightened his hands on the wheel. He didn't like where this was going.

'Damn right I was. He had a firearm in your mouth. I thought your life was in immediate danger.'

Winter stared at him. He realised his mistake.

'I mean, I *initially* thought it was a real firearm. But I was committed by the time I realised it was fake, you know?'

Winter wasn't listening. She was lost in her own thoughts.

'No,' she said slowly.

'I don't think so. I was watching you. There was something in your expression. I saw no fear. It almost looked like you were...enjoying it...'

Lazarus shifted in the seat.

Winter was right. Enjoyed wasn't the right word, but he had, in that moment of exhilarating terror in the hotel room, felt somehow at ease. He knew he was the right person in the right place at the right time. He came alive in a crisis. Some cops are no good in that moment. They go to pieces. Can't think. Can't act.

Lazarus was different. He revelled in danger, felt a deep calmness when everyone else was panicking. He had a sensation of things slowing down for him when he was in the middle of a shitshow.

He had time to think.

Time to act.

He believed he was born for it.

Lazarus had spent five years in the Army before he became a cop. He put the moment with Maloney down to military training.

Close with the enemy.

Don't be passive.

Do something.

Take them on.

Fight.

'We're here,' Lazarus said suddenly.

The timing was perfect.

They entered a narrow cul-de-sac.

The houses on the street were red bricked and on top of each other. The windows were small, but double glazed.

Lazarus parked and cut off the engine. They got out of the car.

The grey footpath was wide and spotless. They walked in silence until he opened the small metal gate at the Casey house.

They walked up the short path. Brown tiles on the ground. Two hanging baskets, bare because the plants could not withstand the approaching Irish winter, hung from either side of the blue front door. It was made of solid wood, with no glass. It was once painted bright blue, but the patina had long ago faded. The surface was dull now. There was a small circular peephole, a brass knocker and a doorbell.

Lazarus pressed the bell. After a few seconds, heavy footsteps clumped in the hallway. Then there was silence. The door remained closed. They were being examined through the peephole, he knew. A moment later, a deadbolt slid back and the door opened.

Mick Casey, Sarah's father, stood in front of them.

'You got the bastard,' he said.

His voice was gravelly from four decades of tobacco. He wore brown boots, a pair of black jeans and a sleeveless white T-shirt. It accentuated his biceps. His head was shaved and he had a flat nose, a reminder of the hours he spent in the ring. He had hazel eyes and a hard face. He looked older than 55. A bushy grey moustache and goatee beard made up for his lack of head hair.

'I think we better come in, Mr Casey,' Lazarus said.

Casey moved aside. The cops walked in.

'In on your right,' Casey said.

Lazarus and Winter followed his instructions and walked into a small living room. There was a large plasma attached to the wall. Two brown leather sofas on a polished wooden floor.

Casey followed them in. He stood by a bookcase crammed with books nestled between the fireplace and one of the sofas.

'Mr Casey,' Lazarus began.

'Call me Mick.'

'Mick, this is Detective Garda Rachel Winter. She is new to my team.' She and Casey shook hands.

Lazarus sat down in one of the sofas, followed by Winter.

'Is Sarah in?' Lazarus asked.

Casey was just about to answer when they heard footsteps on the stairs.

'There's your answer,' he said.

'We've decided to keep her off school for a few days.'

Two people stood in the doorway.

One was Sarah Casey. She was 17, but looked younger. She was thin, about five foot three. She wore a black sweatshirt, red cotton tracksuit bottoms, pale pink crocs. Her face was narrow and she had blue eyes. She had a small nose and tight mouth. Lazarus didn't think he had ever seen her smile. Her skin was waxy from lack of sleep. There was a sadness about her that Lazarus recognised from other victims. She nodded a greeting.

Her older brother Rob stood behind her. Lazarus tensed up when he saw him. He always did that when he was near dangerous criminals. Rob was 24, well-built and athletic. He stood just under six foot, had tight brown hair and hazel eyes, like his da. He had a wide nose and a strong jawline.

'All right, Mr Lazarus,' Rob said.

'Took you long enough to get that prick. If I had my way, this would have been sorted a long time ago.'

He stared at Lazarus with cold eyes.

'Behave, son, Mr Lazarus is a guest in our house,' Mick snapped.

Rob chewed his lip.

Lazarus knew Rob was heavily involved in gangland in the inner city. He was on the Garda radar for drugs, bank robberies and burglaries. He was a suspect for several shootings, including the murder of a dealer ten months earlier. He had been arrested over it, but there was not enough evidence. He had once been part of Danny O'Hara's crew, but left after Maloney's abuse of Sarah came out.

On the surface, the tensions over Sarah and Maloney led to the split, but the drugs unit had briefed Lazarus that Rob was ambitious in his own right. He was now the leader of a 20-strong gang that brought its own coke supplies in from the continent. It had been butting heads with O'Hara's outfit for the last year. There had been beatings and fist fights as they faced off over lucrative middle class areas where there was plenty of demand for cocaine. But the guns had not come out. Yet.

The Casey family kept up a façade of civility towards Lazarus and the rest of his team, but there was intelligence there had been a major row over how to deal with Maloney. Rob, his younger brother Josh and Mick wanted to kill him. Sarah and her mother Joanne had wanted to go to the cops. They got their way. But his later escape had devastated the family. Rob went on a rampage and attacked a younger brother of Maloney, putting him in hospital for a month. Lazarus visited Mick Casey the next day. He looked him in the eye and promised him he would find Maloney and jail him.

Now, 18 long months later, Lazarus had kept his promise. And it looked to him that Rob Casey had been banking on them failing. He had a scowl on his face. He had his hands deep in the pockets of grey tracksuit bottoms. A black polo shirt and expensive trainers completed the gangster look.

Lazarus smiled at Sarah.

'How are you doing?'

'I'm okay,' she said. Her voice was weak.

'How's school?'

'It's okay.'

She chewed at her bottom lip and pushed strands of loose hair behind her ear.

'I have my exams this year. I'm studying hard.'

'That's good,' Lazarus said.

'Have you thought any more about what you want to do?'

'I'd like to be a primary school teacher,' Sarah said. 'I want to get into St. Patrick's, but I need to get good points.'

Lazarus smiled, but felt a pang of sadness when he heard the name of the college. It was the same one Delaney was attending.

He wondered if Anne would ever make it back.

'I'm sure you'll do well. I know the teachers are very happy with you,' he said.

Lazarus had been liaising with the staff in Anne's school for the last two years. She was academically gifted, but Maloney's abuse and the ensuing Garda investigation had taken its toll. She had once been a straight A student, she was now a B, sometimes a C.

'We're all very proud of her,' Mick said.

'She'll be the first Casey to go to college.'

He smiled at his daughter, gave her a wink.

Lazarus felt sick over what he was about to do.

He swallowed hard. He didn't want to tell Mick in front of Sarah. And definitely not in front of Rob.

He turned to Mick.

'Can we go out to the kitchen for a quick chat? Garda Winter can stay here with Sarah and Rob.'

Mick examined Lazarus, trying to read his face.

'Sound,' he said.

They walked outside together.

Casey gestured towards the white panelled door at the end of the narrow hall. They came into a small kitchen cum dining room. It was painted soft blue. A round table, dark brown and big enough for four chairs, sat at the end of the room. Grey patterned lino on the floor. All the appliances were new. A black 50-inch TV was screwed onto the wall at the end of the room. The kitchen smelled of fresh pine. Everything was clean. Everything was in its place.

Mick pulled out one of the chairs from underneath the table. He offered it to Lazarus. Then he took one for himself. The two men sat down.

'When is Maloney up in court?' Casey asked.

'It was supposed to be this morning, but he had to get medical treatment in the station last night. He fell ill. It will be tomorrow. But it's fine, he won't be going anywhere.'

'What happened him?'

'He had taken drugs before we got to him. They didn't agree with him later in the night.'

'Ah shite. I was hoping you gave him a few slaps.'

Lazarus thought back to the hotel room. He saw Maloney on the ground, that evil smile on his face as he called Sarah a slut.

Then he saw himself beating down on the bastard.

He placed his hand on Casey's forearm. He said nothing for a long moment. He tightened the grip. He saw Casey wince and realised the grip was too tight. But he didn't care. He was back in the hotel room, doing what needed to be done.

'I did,' Lazarus said.

'I kicked the shit out of him. I did it for what he did to Sarah. And when he was on the ground and I was kicking and punching him, he told me he was sorry. He told me to apologise to you and the family. And to Sarah.'

Lazarus looked at Casey and he knew he had just done the right thing. A few white lies always helped victims and their families. Casey didn't need to know what Maloney had really said. Or that part, perhaps most, of Lazarus's attack on him was because of the vision of Gabriella that flashed into his head. Nobody needed to know that.

'Good man,' Casey said.

He reached forward and clasped Lazarus's hand. He held it hard. 'Fair play.'

Then he released his grip and sat back in the seat.

'What are the charges?' he asked.

'He has 23 charges of sexually assaulting Sarah,' Lazarus said. Casey showed no emotion. His face was still. He knew about the rapes, had been kept informed of the Director of Public Prosecutions' orders.

'He's also being given new charges,' Lazarus said.

'One of assaulting Garda Winter, another of possession of a firearm with intent to endanger life, another of resisting arrest.'

'Good,' Casey said.

'I read that lad Sullivan's piece in *The Globe*. It mentioned child porn charges, too. Was that animal looking at videos of other kids being abused on the internet? I've heard about these people.'

Lazarus felt a knot in his stomach.

This was it.

'Mick, there's something I have to tell you.'

Casey's eyes darkened. He stood up and walked to the kitchen sink, turned back to face Lazarus.

His fists were balled.

Lazarus knew he knew.

'Go on,' Casey said.

Lazarus took a deep breath.

He thought back to telling Mrs Reilly her precious daughter was dead, upside down in a tree. There was no easy way tell her then, there was no easy way to tell Casey now.

'After Maloney fled the country, we found a flat where he had been staying,' Lazarus said.

'We recovered a laptop. We sent it off for examination and the analysis came back a few weeks ago.'

Lazarus stood up. He walked over to Casey. He gripped his arms, looked him in the eyes.

'They found videos of Sarah on it. I am truly sorry. He filmed the abuse.'

A heavy silence filled the room.

It lasted just an instant.

Then Lazarus heard a guttural roar burst from Casey. He screwed his eyes shut and threw his head back. He waved his arms in the air.

'Don't tell me he did that!'

All control was gone.

'He's fucken dead. I'll kill him myself. I'm telling you now I'll kill that cunt with my own bare hands.'

Casey struggled to get a proper breath as he shouted.

Then he stopped, began to cry. He sank to his knees and punched the lino.

'Sarah, my poor Sarah! That fucken animal!'

Lazarus bent down and tried to comfort him.

'Please, Mick,' he said.

He went to speak again but he was distracted by the roar of an engine on the street. Lazarus knew it was a motorbike. He turned his head to the noise.

'What's that?' he asked, alert.

He stood up, began walking to the front door. Casey followed.

Then Lazarus heard a screech of tyres.

And he knew what was coming.

'Get down!'

He pushed Casey to the floor, then jumped on top of him.

They hit the ground just as Lazarus heard the first shot. There was another loud bang almost immediately. Then another. Then another. It was like someone banging a hammer on a door.

Lazarus felt bullets zipping over his head. He unholstered his Sig. He brought the pistol up in his right hand and half-crouched half-ran towards the front door. He reached it in seconds. But by the time he got to it the shooting had stopped. Lazarus thought maybe 12 rounds had been fired, but he had lost count.

His heart was pumping.

His gun was armed and he was ready to fire.

He listened for any sign of the attackers coming into the house.

But there was nothing.

And he knew he had to go outside and face them.

He stood up, took deep breath and threw open the door.

16

Lazarus crouched as he ran out of the house.

He held the Sig-Sauer out in front in a two-handed grip.

He swung it from side to side and tried to spot the shooter. Then he heard an engine on his left.

He turned the pistol towards the noise. He saw a motorbike about ten metres away. The passenger held a pistol. He wore dark clothing and a white full-face helmet. The visor was up and Lazarus could see half the face – and all the eyes. They were dark and beady.

The bike started to move off. But the passenger raised the weapon and pointed it right at Lazarus. Then in an instant Lazarus heard the crack of a shot being fired and a bullet striking the wall beside him.

Lazarus ducked out of instinct, but then his training took over. He stood to his full height. He raised his Sig and aimed at the shooter. He was still pointing the gun at Lazarus. Lazarus levelled the sights on him. He aimed for the gunman's chest and knew he couldn't miss from this range.

One shot, one kill.

He let out a breath and pressed down on the trigger.

And then he saw the old woman.

He roared at her.

'Get out of the fucking way!'

She stood on the footpath just behind the bike. And right in his line of fire.

Her mouth fell open in shock as she stared at Lazarus and the black gun pointing at her. She was thin and small, barely five foot, but still in the way of his bullet. She wore a green woollen overcoat, a grey skirt, heavy beige tights and a pink headscarf knotted under her neck. She held a bulging plastic bag in each hand. She was in her seventies.

Lazarus knew he couldn't fire. He shuffled two steps to the left, trying to make a clean angle for the shot.

It was too late. The delay had been less than a second, but that was all the biker needed. He wound the throttle and the bike sped off. It weaved from side to side as it flashed along the street. Lazarus knew the moment had gone. The gunman had turned away. There was no longer any threat. He had no legal reason to shoot. He watched, powerless, as the bike disappeared around the corner.

'*Porca Miseria!*' he shouted.

Then he pressed long and hard on the red SOS button on the Tetra radio on his chest. It sent an emergency distress message out to the entire city.

He felt his stomach lurch as he suddenly remembered Winter and the Caseys were in the house. He swept his pistol around the street to make sure there was no threat. The old woman dropped a bag and brought her hand up to her mouth when she saw the gun moving.

He held the palm of his free hand out to calm her.

'It's okay, you're fine. Armed gardai. Relax.'

Then he was running.

He sprinted back to the house, his pistol still up. He heard the faint wail of approaching sirens.

He saw bullet holes in the front door. They were like rivets, small and tight. Three were in the door, one was in the frame, another was in the brickwork between the door and the living room window. That was the one that had been meant for him.

He looked at the window of the front room and froze.

The window had at least six holes, each surrounded by a tight spider's web of cracks.

Sarah and Rob and Winter were still inside.

He barrelled through the front door.

He was frantically calculating the height of the holes and trying to guess their trajectory, wondering if anyone was hit.

Mick Casey stood at the end of the hallway. Alive.

'You okay, Mick?'

Casey nodded. He looked to the living room door. Lazarus saw him dart for it. He held out a firm hand.

'Leave this to me!'

He walked forward and banged on the door, fearing the worst, hoping for the best.

'Rachel, it's Lazarus. I'm coming in.'

Lazarus holstered his pistol, waited a beat.

He had no idea how Winter would react on the other side of the door. She could be trigger happy. She could be panicking. She could be dead.

He took a deep breath, then pushed the door open.

Lazarus peered inside. Rob Casey was on the floor on the right, using a sofa for cover. He was in a foetal position, with his hands over his head.

Lazarus moved into the room. Looked left. Sarah Casey was spread-eagled on the floor, face down. It looked like she had been rugby tackled. Winter lay on top of her. One arm held Sarah down. The other was extended, gun in her hand, her finger on the trigger.

And it was pointed right at Lazarus.

He raised his hands.

Winter relaxed when she realised it was him.

She took her finger off the trigger, lowered the pistol.

'They're gone,' he said.

Winter nodded. She released her iron grip on Sarah before getting to her feet in one easy move. Lazarus noticed how agile and fit she was. And how calm. There was a controlled energy on her face, no sign of panic, or fear.

The sirens were close now. There were several cars and Lazarus could hear their sirens overlapping.

The room was in chaos. Sarah was shrieking. Rob was roaring and cursing. Splinters of glass from the windows glistened on the floor. A fine white dust filled the room from the bullet holes in the wall. Lazarus saw the bullets had gone through the front window and hit the back wall at about nine feet, just beneath the white coving. He counted seven.

'Nobody injured in here,' Winter said.

She hauled Sarah to her feet.

The girl's eyes were pinballing around her sockets. Her face was red.

Rob got to his feet just as Mick burst in.

He ran towards his daughter and grabbed her. He was sobbing and enveloped her in a bear hug. She disappeared into his arms and he held her tight.

Just then, Lazarus heard heavy footsteps on the path outside.

'Armed gardai coming in!'

McEvoy kicked the open door and it slammed into the wall.

He ran in, his pistol in both hands. Five uniformed officers wearing hi-vis bullet proof vests, batons out, piled in after him.

Lazarus put his hands out to show there was no threat.

He looked around the room. Rob Casey was still shouting at the top of his voice and was pacing around. Mick turned to Lazarus.

His face was contorted in rage.

'That bastard O'Hara will pay for this,' he said.

'I'm fucken telling you, Lazarus. He started it. We'll finish it.'

★

The attack on the Casey family home took up the rest of the day for most of the station. The Delaney case went on the backburner.

Gardai from all over the capital streamed to the street after Lazarus pressed the alarm on his radio. More than 20 cars were sent to the house. Some cordoned off the street and began the investigation. Others sped around the area looking for the hit team. When the bike sped away, Lazarus saw it turn right, heading back towards the city. Now, detectives scoured CCTV footage to see where it went from there. But it could have been anywhere in the city centre within five minutes.

A needle in a concrete haystack.

By 3pm, the cordon around the house had been lifted. Forensics had finished their examination. Mick Casey had bought glass and replaced the shattered window. Lazarus and Winter stayed with the family. The house was filled with the smell of fresh putty and paint. The damage to the front door had already been filled in. Mick was starting the undercoat. One of Mick's sisters came over and offered to put him and the family up.

He told her to fuck off.

'These bastards won't make me move,' he said as he dipped the paint-brush into a tin of paint.

'We're staying.'

There were two more unwelcome visitors when Lazarus and Winter were preparing to leave.

'There's a car coming,' Winter said.

Lazarus looked up and went for his holster.

But then he recognised the vehicle and his heart sank.

'Ah, Jesus. Not these two again.'

The black Touareg drove slowly along the street. Lazarus saw Conor Sullivan in the passenger seat. Gallagher was driving. Sullivan eyed Lazarus as they passed the house. Lazarus stared hard back at him.

'Who's that?' Mick Casey asked, brush in hand. Thick white paint dripped from its bristles.

'They're journalists. Conor Sullivan from *The Globe* and his sidekick.'

'The one who wrote that story about you arresting Maloney?'

'Yeah.'

They watched the Touareg reach the end of the cul-de-sac, perform a tight three-point turn and drive back towards them. It came to a halt a few feet before the house.

Both men got out.

'Our advice is not to talk to the media,' Lazarus said.

Casey's nostrils flared.

'With respect Mr Lazarus, get fucked. I decide who I talk to. Nobody else.'

He looked at the approaching pair.

'I read his stuff. I like him.'

Lazarus shrugged his shoulders.

He signalled to Winter it was time to go. They said a quick goodbye to Casey and walked down the path. They reached the gate the same time as Sullivan and Gallagher. The journalists stopped to let the cops walk out. Lazarus and Sullivan ignored each other. Sullivan motioned for Gallagher to stay at the gate while he approached Mick.

'Hello, Sergeant,' Gallagher smiled.

'You and Conor are still not friends, I see.'

'He better not mess up this case,' Lazarus said.

He was worried about the Caseys being named.

Gallagher gripped a camera hanging on a strap from his right shoulder. He let go of it and held out both hands in a motion of surrender.

'I'll make sure he doesn't, Sergeant.'

Lazarus looked back to the house. Sullivan shook hands with Mick. He said a few quiet words of introduction, but then Lazarus heard Mick's raised voice.

'I know who you are and why you're here. Get your notebook out, son. I'll give you a fucken story all right. We're not afraid of these cunts.'

Sullivan reached into his coat pocket and took out the notebook. As he was doing so, he glanced over at Lazarus and gave him a subtle smile.

'What happened, Mr Casey?' Sullivan asked, his eyes still on Lazarus.

'That fucker Maloney shot the gaff up,' Casey spat.

'It was a miracle none of us was killed. The bastard is trying to intimidate us. But, and you can quote me on this, he can GO FUCK HIMSELF.'

He said the words slowly.

'We're not afraid of him or his mates.'

Lazarus saw Sullivan writing.

'They've been at us for over a year. They've done everything to get us to drop the charges,' Casey said.

'Like what?' Sullivan asked.

Casey stuck out a hand and unfurled a finger with each incident.

'They robbed my car and burned it out. They threw paint at the house. Broke a few windows. Scrawled graffiti about my daughter on walls. And they even got other girls in her school at bully her.'

'Jesus,' Sullivan said, excitement in his eyes.

'And did you ever think of dropping the charges?' Sullivan asked.

'Not a fucken chance,' Casey shouted, looking over at Lazarus and shaking his head.

'Maloney is going down for what he did to my little girl. And we'll be there to watch.'

Lazarus tried not to react.

As soon as the abuse allegations came to light, Mick Casey and his two boys had been out for revenge. They had wanted to sort things out themselves and keep the police out of the picture. It was the insistence of Sarah and her mother Joanne that had seen the family go to the gardai.

And now Mick was coming across as holier than thou to a reporter.

Lazarus had to walk away. He couldn't listen.

He motioned to Winter and they headed to the Camry. As he sat into the car, Lazarus looked back to the house and saw Casey still talking, and Sullivan still writing.

17

Lazarus drove home through the darkness.

The neon clock on the dashboard of the Giulia said 7.59pm. He and Winter had spent the last four hours with the team investigating the shooting, reliving every second.

He was halfway home when he got a call from Fallon. She and Anderson were on a citywide management seminar away from the station. They wanted to know everything.

'I'm glad you're okay, Lazarus,' Fallon said.

'The paperwork if you got killed would have been horrendous.'

Lazarus laughed.

'What's the latest?' Fallon asked.

Her voice was tinny and remote. She had him on loudspeaker so Anderson could listen. Lazarus imagined her leaning forward in a chair, arms folded and staring at the phone, while Anderson sat next to her, taking notes.

'Ben Flannery found 12 bullet holes in the house. He recovered matching shell casings on the road outside. They're nine-millimetre. He reckons it was a Glock pistol.'

'Okay,' Fallon said.

'There might be prints or DNA on the casings,' Lazarus said. 'And maybe the same gun was used in another shooting.'

He heard a loud snort from Anderson.

'I doubt that very much. O'Hara is too smart for that. It will be new and clean.'

Lazarus noticed the confidence and certainty in Anderson's voice.

'We'll let the Scenes of Crime Officer worry about that, shall we?' Fallon said.

'What about the bike?'

Lazarus looked over his right shoulder before pressing down on the accelerator. The car surged forward and he moved into the outside lane.

'There is any number of roads it could have taken,' he said.

'They're checking CCTV to get a route and there is a KLO out for the bike, but I didn't get a reg.'

Lazarus only got a glimpse of the bike. He had been focused on the gun pointing at him. It was racing green with a white flash on the engine cowling. It was powerful, maybe 500cc. The team had circulated the description. There was a Keep a Look Out notification all over the city for the bike.

'It's long gone, I'd say,' Anderson said.

'What are DDU hearing?' Fallon asked.

The District Detective Unit already had a good handle on the shooting and confirmed O'Hara was behind it.

'The word is it was a warning to Mick and his family to drop the Maloney charges,' Lazarus said.

'They don't think they were trying to actually kill any of the family.'

He frowned.

'That didn't stop them shooting at me.

'Anyway, nobody has been nominated yet. Could have been any one of O'Hara's gang.'

'What about the Caseys, will they drop the charges? Fallon asked.

'They're not budging,' Lazarus said.

'Good,' Fallon said.

'I don't want them intimidated out of giving evidence.

'This is an important case. We have to show the people of Dublin nobody is above the law, not even O'Hara. I'm deploying more armed patrols to the area and cars are passing the Caseys' house every 15 minutes.'

'We're not the only ones looking after them,' Lazarus said.

'One of the patrols saw some of Rob Casey's friends in cars at the street a few minutes ago.'

'Jesus Christ,' Fallon sighed.

'A gang war is all we need. Make sure you and your team have your ballistic vests on when you go anywhere near that house.'

Lazarus remembered something.

'One other thing, ma'am,' he said.

'Sullivan from *The Globe* called to the house as we were leaving. Mick spoke to him. He is sending O'Hara a message in the paper tomorrow.'

'For God's sake,' Anderson said.

'A story is the last thing we need. Why did you let him speak to Casey?'

Lazarus looked at the phone, gave Anderson the finger and a silently mouthed insult.

Vaffanculo.

Fuck you.

He grinned, alone in the car.

Childishness was good sometimes.

'I asked him not to talk to Sullivan, Inspector, but he made up his own mind,' he said.

'It's not a big deal,' Fallon said, irritated.

'Papers don't refuse ink. Sullivan will move on to something else tomorrow. Let him at it. Today was a bad day. But it could have been much worse. I'm glad you weren't injured, John. Or worse.'

She paused.

'Now, back to work. Tomorrow, you're back on the Griffith Park case. What's your plan?'

'I have Maloney in court first,' Lazarus said. 'The doc says he's fine now. As soon as that is done, I'm meeting Ben Flannery over forensics. Then I'm going to brief Detective Sergeant Cochrane.'

He waited a moment.

'As you directed, ma'am.'

He let the last sentence hang in the air. He was still annoyed the MIS detective had been parachuted in.

Fallon knew he was angry.

'Frankie Cochrane is an expert in this field. Use her,' she said stiffly.

The line went dead.

Twenty minutes later, Lazarus reversed the Giulia into the driveway of his home. He killed the engine and stepped out of the car. The moon gleamed in a cloudless sky. The bitter north wind brought a cold that tugged at Lazarus. He hurried inside.

He walked into the living room. It was a large, wide room, with a low ceiling painted brilliant white. It had a decorative plaster rose in the centre with a stylish lampshade hanging from it. The walls were what Jenna called Wild Sage colour. He called it green. A large mirror hung over the oak fireplace. A patterned rug on the wooden floors.

Jenna was sitting at the end of a red sofa. One hand held a glass of wine, the fingers on the other were massaging her forehead. She stood wearily. Lazarus walked over to her and they embraced.

He kissed her forehead.

'*Buona sera carina,*' he said.

He held her tight.

'How's things?'

When Jenna answered, she sounded drained.

'Give me your gun. I'll do time for them. I'll nobble the jury and make sure they're all stay at home mothers like me. I'll walk. They'll never convict me.'

Lazarus rubbed her back. He smiled.

'Me giving you my gun is what got us in this mess in the first place.'

He moved his hands down to her ass.

'Although, my gun is suddenly locked and loaded.'

Jenna threw her head back and laughed.

She had dirty fair hair that reached her shoulders. She wore a lime green jumper, navy jeans with black ankle boots. She was tall and slender, with blue eyes and pale skin. Although half Italian herself, she looked Irish. She was 37, two years younger than Lazarus. But she looked younger. Lazarus couldn't help admiring her form.

She caressed Lazarus's face and kissed him long on the lips.

'Feed me. I'm starving.'

They walked together into the kitchen. Lazarus opened the fridge. He saw pancetta on the bottom shelf. His eyes moved to the rack where the cheeses were kept. He saw a block of Pecorino and another of Parmesan.

He turned to Jenna. 'Carbonara?'

Her eyes lit up.

'Oh yes. Yes. Fucking yes.'

Lazarus did most of the cooking at home. He was good at it. And he enjoyed it.

'How was work?' Jenna asked as Lazarus took the ingredients from the fridge and laid them on the island.

'It was fine,' he said.

'That bad?'

He laughed.

No-one knew Lazarus like Jenna.

'Same old same old,' he said.

'I don't do happy. You know that.'

He went back to the fridge and took out two bottles of Moretti. He opened them and gave one to Jenna.

He took a long swallow of the Italian beer. Then he smacked his lips and let out a long sigh.

He wiped his mouth with the back of his hand.

Jenna suddenly tensed.

She put her face in her hands.

'Jesus Christ. Not again.'

The dining room door burst open.

Their twins Giovanni Junior and Pietro stood on the threshold, eyes downcast.

'What is it now?' Jenna demanded.

Giovanni Junior hid behind Pietro.

'I'm frightened,' Pietro said.

'I have a sore tummy,' Giovanni Junior added.

'Oh really?' Jenna said.

The boys were aged six and were identical: a mop of dirty brown hair, brown eyes, sallow skin that came from Lazarus. They were thin and had long limbs, Lazarus could tell they would reach six foot. They wore Spiderman pyjamas, rich blue and bright red. Jenna was taking a break from her career as a solicitor to look after them.

'There's nothing to be afraid,' she said.

'Mamma and Papa are here and the landing light is on.'

She looked at the wall clock.

'Look at the time, boys. You have to get up for school in the morning. Back to bed. *Avanti.*'

Pietro's lower lip started to quiver. Giovanni Junior howled.

Lazarus walked towards the boys, formed a gun with his fingers and pointed at them.

'Polizia! Mani in alto!'

Their eyes lit up.

They put their hands in the air, just as Lazarus had ordered. They had their own real-life game of cops and robbers with their father. And they loved it.

'Face the wall!'

Giovanni Junior and Pietro giggled as they turned to the wall.

Lazarus winked at his wife.

'Detective Garda Jenna, please take these prisoners back to their cells.'

The boys giggled again.

Jenna smiled and softly grabbed each one of them by the collar. She marched them upstairs.

Lazarus took another swig of Moretti and began preparing the pasta.

Fifteen minutes later, he was sprinkling fresh parmesan over two bowls of *Spaghetti alla Carbonara* when Jenna came back into the kitchen. She savoured the aroma of cooked bacon, garlic and parmesan.

Steam rose from the bowls.

She waved it towards her face.

'Fantastic.'

Lazarus brought the bowls over to the dining table, before going back to the fridge. He took out a bottle of Pinot Noir and poured two large glasses.

They ate in comfortable silence for a few moments.

'How was work, really?' she asked him, finally.

'It was fine.'

Lazarus kept his eyes on the pasta.

'Nothing happen?' she asked.

'Nothing that stands out.'

Lazarus took a long sip from the glass of cold red wine.

His internal alarm began to ping.

Jenna tried again.

'The news said a house was shot up in Dublin and gardai were there at the time.'

'Yeah?'

'Yes, *John.*'

Lazarus knew he was in trouble.

'I didn't hear the news all day. I was busy.'

Lazarus twirled some eggy cheese and spaghetti around his fork.

Jenna's voice was hard.

'Were you there?'

'Where?'

'At the house.'

Lazarus paused a beat.

'Yes.'

'Jesus Christ. Were you the officer they shot at?'

Lazarus reached over to Jenna and grasped her hand.

'It wasn't that bad.'

Jenna freed herself from his grip then put her hands over her face. Lazarus heard sobbing.

'Please, *carina.* It was just a warning to the people inside,' he said.

'They weren't trying to kill anyone.'

Lazarus thought of that fucker Sullivan. He had broken the shooting online. Again. The rest of the media had picked it up from him.

'The media have blown it out of all proportion,' he said.

He quickly realised his mistake.

Jenna slammed her hands onto the table.

'Some scumbag shoots at you and you say it wasn't that bad?'

'He didn't shoot at me,' Lazarus lied.

He saw himself pointing his Sig at the gunman and pressing the trigger, getting ready to end the bastard. Maybe it was best for them both that the woman appeared in his sights.

Jenna shook her head.

'I can't believe this. Some asshole shoots up a house you're in and you come and make the dinner as normal without even telling me?'

'It was nothing, really.'

'Nothing?' Jenna shouted.

'The kids are asleep,' Lazarus said.

'Don't give me that shit!'

He held his hands up.

'Sorry, *carina.*'

'Tell me what happened,' she said.

He told her a version of what happened.

'I was back in the kitchen talking to the father and some fella came along on a motorbike and fired a few shots at the front window. That's all. They were just warning shots. Honestly. It's all been hyped up.'

Jenna gave him a sad look, shook her head.

'The boys need their father.'

'They have their father right here.'

'What if those bullets had hit you today? Where would they be now?'

'They didn't hit me.'

'They could have.'

'They didn't.'

Jenna sat back in her chair and folded her arms.

She craned her head back and examined the ceiling.

'Have you not done your time?'

'Here we go,' Lazarus sighed.

Jenna ignored him.

'You've been a guard for 16 years, you've almost 15 years done on the streets. Is it not time to move on?'

'Move up, you mean?'

'Yes, John, move up. You're nearly 40 and'

'Thanks.'

'You're too old for this… cops and robbers stuff.'

'It's not stuff, Jenna. I'm making a difference. I'm helping people who need to be helped.'

'You're putting yourself in the firing line. The children need you around. I do, too.'

Lazarus didn't answer.

'I am sick of worrying about you. Every day you go out that door, I say a prayer you come back home alive and not in a wooden box.'

'Jesus, *carina*, steady on.'

Jenna stood up, walked to the island.

'I don't want you to die.'

'Funnily enough, neither do I.'

'Well then, do something about it. Get a transfer into an easier job.'

'We've been through this. I did not join up to sit behind a desk. You know what I do. I catch bad people and protect good people.'

'And you're very good at it. But if you are being honest, you'll admit you're trying to protect the one girl you can't.'

Lazarus tensed.

'What are you on about?'

'You know what I'm saying. Gabriella is gone. There is nothing you can do to bring her back.'

Lazarus felt a stab of anger.

'Don't bring her into this.'

His voice was even.

Jenna walked towards the table, sat down and put her hand in his.

'*Caro*, listen to me. You have to let her go.'

Lazarus closed his eyes.

'I can't.'

Then: 'Somebody has to fight for her.'

Jenna stroked the back of his hand.

'It wasn't your fault.'

Lazarus's voice quivered.

'I should have been there for her.'

'We've been through this a million times. You were working. What could you do?'

They sat in silence for a few moments.

'What about trying for inspector again?' she asked.

Lazarus shook his head.

'I like being a polis man. The higher up I go, the less police work you do. When you're an inspector, it's all politics and forms and committees and reports and stats on PULSE.'

Jenna pulled back from him.

'I hate that word. I hate it. *Polis*. It's so common. What does it even mean?'

'It's what I am. A polis man. An investigator. I'm not some fuckwit in a suit who sits in an office and kisses the commissioner's arse.'

Jenna grimaced.

'Charming.'

'Do you want me to be happy in my job? Do you want me to spend my days doing up rosters in an office?'

'I want you to be safe!'

She remembered the kids were upstairs and lowered her voice again.

'I want you to be able to sleep at night without waking up screaming. I want you to be able to take real time off without all your colleagues ringing you. I want you behind a desk if it means you don't have to look at videos of some poor child being raped or beaten or tortured.'

She stood and walked to the sink. She threw the remnants of her wine into it. She washed the glass, slammed it on the draining board.

'I'm going to bed.'

She walked out.

Lazarus heard her trudge up the stairs.

He sat alone in the kitchen for a long time. Thinking. He lost all track of time.

Then, finally, he got up and went back to the fridge. He needed another drink.

He took out two bottles of Moretti.

They were ice cold and he could see condensation on them. Lazarus went back to the dining table. He sat down and thought about his little sister and how in death she overshadowed his whole life.

Lazarus shook his head as he downed half a bottle of cold Moretti in one swallow.

He turned on the internet radio, got RAI 2. Eros Ramazzotti was on, singing about a beautiful song being enough to change the world, to make things better. Lazarus knew it was nowhere near enough.

Idiota, he told himself yet again as he listened to the music.

He lapsed into Italian under stress. It must be a comfort blanket.

Italian was the first language he had learned, picking it up from his parents. Most of the family's friends were Italian immigrants, or kids of immigrants, and they all spoke the language to each other. He only mastered English when he started primary school. And even as he hit adolescence and moved towards adulthood, Italian was his everyday language.

He preferred it to English, although he was mother tongue fluent in both. English was more utilitarian, whereas Italian came from his heart. He felt as if he was singing when the language came out of his mouth.

He finished the first bottle of Moretti and looked at his watch. 10.40pm. He had been up for 22 hours. The call about Delaney seemed a lifetime ago, now.

Sono stancomorto, he thought. *I'm dead tired.* But not too tired for another beer. He cracked open the second Moretti. The bottles were only 330ml, he told himself. It was gone in three mouthfuls.

He stood up and brought the bottles to the utility room.

Then he went back to the kitchen. He rinsed the dinner bowls and put them in the dishwasher.

He walked to the stairs and took them one at a time, not wanting to wake the kids.

The bedroom door was ajar. He pushed it open and walked inside.

He approached the bed.

He saw Jenna was lying on her side, her back to him.

He knew she was awake.

He undressed and got into the bed.

'Jenna.'

He got no response.

'Jenna, *carina* …'

He heard a loud sigh.

'What, John?'

She was still angry.

'The Super ordered me to have some loving. I always follow orders.'

She laughed turned towards him.

'You're a weirdo,' she said.

She opened the duvet.

Lazarus smiled and moved over to her.

18

Tuesday

Lazarus stood when Judge Scully entered the courtroom just after 10am.

'Good morning,' the judge said.

He sat into the raised bench facing the court. The cops and lawyers answered him. The accused stayed silent. The Criminal Courts of Justice complex was near Phoenix Park in central Dublin.

Court number three was on the ground floor of the circular building. It was large, with a high ceiling. An oak harp above the judge stared down at the court.

The court was full. Regulars sat beside businessmen who had taken one line of coke too many at the weekend and were now paying the price. They looked terrified. The habitual clients were less stressed. Most wore casual gear. Some of them put their hands down the front of their tracksuits and cupped their balls.

Lazarus sat down beside McEvoy and eyed Judge Howard Scully. He was a former defence solicitor. He had a reputation for going hard on gardai. He was small, drowned by a black judicial robe. He wore a pair of oversized glasses and the thick lenses magnified his eyes. He hadn't shaved and his grey stubble drained the life from his bony face. He was 61, looked older. He was bald, except for a few tufts of hair above his ears.

'Jesus, Lazarus,' McEvoy whispered.

'Look at the head on yer man. He's in bits. He must have been on the piss. Imagine going out on the beer with him? I'd say he'd be shiteing on about human rights all night.'

'I've done that,' Lazarus said.

'Jenna knows him. He's good company.'

Lazarus nodded towards the bench.

'He's only a pain when he's sitting up there. But maybe that's a good thing. Maybe he keeps us cops honest.'

The court clerk nodded to Lazarus.

'The Director of Public Prosecutions and Sean Maloney,' she said to the body of the court.

Lazarus stood up.

The clerk announced the case was in camera and ordered everyone except gardai and journalists out. Maloney was in the security-glass panelled dock at the left of the court. A prison officer unlocked his handcuffs.

Maloney, still bruised from the hotel, ignored the officer.

The public left the court, except for three men at the back. Lazarus saw them and his stomach tightened.

The Caseys.

Lazarus bent down to McEvoy and whispered in his ear. McEvoy nodded, got up and left the court.

Lazarus eyed the men with suspicion as he walked to the stand.

Mick Casey was in the middle. His eyes bored into Maloney. He held a copy of *The Globe*. Lazarus had seen it earlier. Sullivan's story was front page. The banner headline read

WE'RE NOT AFRAID

Underneath was a photograph of the Casey house, the bullet holes visible. The damage had been cleaned up before Sullivan got there. Lazarus realised the Caseys gave the photograph to him. In the bottom right corner of the image, an editor had placed a close-up of the bullet holes in the window. The paper had not named the Casey family, nor had they said where they lived. But they had named Maloney and linked him to O'Hara.

Rob Casey was on Mick's left. The intelligence files said he was known for extreme violence and had access to firearms. On Mick's right, Lazarus saw Josh, Rob's younger brother. He was 19, but already had the build of a fully-developed adult. There was plenty of intelligence about Josh Casey, too. It linked him to assaults, robberies and car theft. He was small, with a boxer's physique: thin, tight muscles, lean. He had short ginger hair. His freckled face belied a hardness that too many people had underestimated to their own cost. His mouth was small and tight, his cheeks hollow and he had a flat nose. Lazarus saw a faded scar under his left eye. His blue eyes were cold. He had a black spider's web tattoo on his neck.

The Caseys were allowed to stay because they were family. Lazarus looked at the press box. It had two occupants. Sullivan and Gallagher. *Of course they're here.*

Gallagher gave Lazarus a wink. Sullivan looked up, saw Lazarus and reddened.

Lazarus got to the stand and picked up the New Testament. He raised it in his right hand and recited the oath.

'Judge,' he said, 'on Sunday at 8pm, I arrested Sean Maloney at the Prestige Dublin Airport Hotel. He was then conveyed to Broadstone Garda Station at 9.05pm, where he was charged at 9.55pm.'

He read out all charges. There were 34, with 23 for abusing Sarah Casey; eight for making videos of her; three for the incident in the hotel.

When Lazarus was done reciting them, he asked for Maloney to be remanded in custody. Scully looked to Maloney's solicitor, a man called Oisin George McMahon.

'Will there be any bail application, Mr McMahon?'

McMahon stood up.

"There will, Judge,' the solicitor said.

'I am objecting to bail,' Lazarus said.

'Maloney is a clear flight risk, and I believe the victim and other witnesses are in danger from him and his associates. Maloney also has access to firearms. He had one when I arrested him on Sunday and he threatened to shoot my-'

'That's bollix! I had no fucken piece. The cops planted it!' Maloney shouted.

He pressed an angry face against the security glass. The warders pulled him back.

Scully looked at him, the way someone examines their shoe after trodding in dog shit.

'Control your client,' he said to the solicitor.

McMahon lumbered over to Maloney. He whispered at him through the glass.

'The victim and her mother are in fear of him,' Lazarus said.

'I have confidential information a gun attack on the family home yesterday was carried out by associates of the accused.'

'Mr McMahon?' the judge said.

McMahon was in his fifties, tall and overweight. He wore a cheap black suit that was one size too small. He had brown hair everyone knew was dyed. He wore it greased back.

'Sergeant... uh ... Lazarus,' he said.

Lazarus had sparred with him for years.

McMahon always pretended not to know his name.

'When did you arrest my client?'

'Sunday evening.'

Lazarus kept his answers short.

Give the bastard no rope.

'Has he been in custody since?'

'Yes.'

'Had he access to a phone?'

'No.'

'Any visitors?'

'No.'

McMahon turned to the judge.

'My client clearly had no involvement in the shooting.'

Back to Lazarus.

'Has my client ever been charged with a sexual offence, Sergeant?'

'No.'

'Has he ever failed to turn up for trial?'

'No.'

'Any warrants?'

'Just the one we arrested him over on Sunday, for the charges for which he is now before the court.'

McMahon turned back to Scully.

'These are serious charges, Judge. But my client has a constitutional right to bail. He has no history of sexual offences and has never missed a court date. The trial is at least a year away. If he is refused bail, he will spend a considerable amount of time on remand. He is willing to abide by the most stringent of conditions. And he is happy to provide a substantial bail bond.'

'Would strict conditions satisfy you, Sergeant Lazarus?' Scully asked.

'No, Judge. I fear for the safety of the victim and her family.'

The court went quiet as Scully pondered the application. The courtroom door opened and Lazarus saw McEvoy come back inside. He had rounded up a posse of uniforms. Lazarus had asked him to get back up when he realised the Caseys were present for the hearing.

He had a bad feeling as soon as he saw them.

McEvoy nodded to Lazarus on the stand as he and the uniforms took up positions at the back of the court.

Just then Judge Scully cleared his throat. He had made a decision.

'In view of the seriousness of the charges and the sergeant's fears for the complainant, I am refusing the application.'

'Fuck's sake!' Maloney shouted.

Scully ignored him.

'Remand to next Thursday.'

Lazarus left the stand and passed Maloney as he walked back to his seat.

'Cocksucker!' Maloney shouted.

Lazarus heard a roar from the back of the court.

'Shut the fuck up, you paedo bastard!'

The Caseys jumped to their feet.

'You'll get it up the hole inside, you rat!' Rob Casey shouted.

Mick and Rob ran to the dock, roaring as they moved.

'You're a dead man!'

McEvoy and the uniforms moved towards them. Lazarus did, too.

McEvoy got to Mick Casey and began struggling with him. Mick was a strong man. He pushed McEvoy backwards with such force he fell on his arse. Two of the bigger uniforms dragged Mick away. Two other uniforms went for Rob Casey. He swerved past them and got close enough to kick at the security glass. Lazarus grabbed him. He saw one quick-thinking uniform hurry to the bench and bustle the judge to the exit as the fighting continued.

'I'm gonna fucken kill you!' Rob screamed at Maloney.

'Calm down, Rob,' Lazarus shouted.

Saliva shot from Rob's mouth. He tried to get at the glass. Another uniform came to help Lazarus.

And then Lazarus realised Josh Casey had not become involved. He looked away from Rob towards where his younger brother had been standing.

He had disappeared.

Lazarus swept the room.

He saw movement to his right. Josh sprinted to the dock. He reached it in an instant and put his hands on the top of the frame. He brought a knee up and smoothly vaulted over the partition.

Then he was on Maloney, raining blow after blow on him. Maloney tried to protect himself, but it was no good: the punches kept coming. A warden put himself between Maloney and Casey. He got a few smacks as his colleague tried to pull Maloney away.

Someone pressed the panic button and its loud wail filled the court. Within seconds, half a dozen cops burst in. They ran towards the fight. Two got inside the dock and sprang towards Josh Casey.

Then it ended, just as suddenly as it had begun.

Mick and Rob stopped struggling with the cops outside, Josh finished his barrage of punches inside.

He smiled, stepped away from his victim, raised his hands in the air.

Five minutes later, calm had been restored. A battered and bloody Maloney was bustled away, the Caseys were arrested. Mick nodded at Lazarus and McEvoy as he was taken past in cuffs.

'Had to be done, Mr Lazarus. Family is family.'

'This is just the start, Harry,' Lazarus told McEvoy as he watched the Caseys being led away.

'I feel a war coming on.'

They walked out of the court. Lazarus heard a voice calling him. He ignored it.

'Sergeant Lazarus?' The voice repeated, louder this time.

Lazarus turned to face Sullivan.

'What?'

Sullivan raised his hands in the air.

'Don't shoot.'

Sullivan wore a T-shirt and jeans. He had the black North Face jacket on from the hotel.

Sullivan was trying to use humour to break the thick ice between them. Lazarus decided not to play the game.

'I said, what?'

Sullivan flushed.

'Look, I'm sorry about the row at the hotel. Shit happens, man. We're all tense in these situations.'

'You were a pain in the arse,' Lazarus said.

'That's my job. I'm a reporter.'

He waved his hand around the hall.

'And I'm the only hack who cares enough about this girl to bother coming here.'

He stepped forward.

'This girl matters to me. I'm going to make sure my readers know what she went through. Even if I'm not allowed to name Maloney, people will know it's him.'

Lazarus thought back to the press bench. He was right, no other media had turned up. Maybe she did matter to Sullivan.

He relented.

'Okay. What are you looking for?' Lazarus said.

Sullivan saw an opening. He dived in.

'Maybe we can have a chat about this, for after the trial?'

Lazarus saw his own opening. He dived in, too.

'Maybe. I'll help you if you help me.'

Sullivan's eyes narrowed.

'What do you mean?'

'Who told you we were at the hotel for Maloney?'

Sullivan recoiled, waved a hand like a karate chop.

'No, no, no, no. No. That won't be happening. No.'

'Fine,' Lazarus said. 'You'll get nothing from me.'

Lazarus turned his back on Sullivan just as he felt his phone vibrating in his pocket.

19

Lazarus checked the screen and saw Winter's name.

'Talk to me,' Lazarus said as he connected the call.

He was walking with McEvoy to the Camry.

He covered the phone with his free hand to shield it from the wind.

God he missed Italy.

'We're starting door to door now. I have three uniforms with me,' Winter said.

'Good. What area are you canvasing?'

'We haven't started yet.'

'Let me think,' Lazarus said.

The park where Anne Delaney was attacked was surrounded by hundreds of houses and half a dozen roads. Resources were tight. They did not have the bodies to canvas the whole area at once. It would take Winter and the uniforms days to get to every potential witness.

Lazarus thought back to the map Flannery put on the screen in yesterday's conference. Ferguson Road and the area where Delaney's friend Orla Diffney lived were to the north. That was where Delaney's bag and the bungee cord were found in the park. To the east was Drumcondra Road. That was the route the Sweeneys had come from after leaving the chipper.

'Where are you now?' Lazarus asked Winter.

'At the scene. We're parked up on the Botanic Avenue entrance.'

The Botanic Avenue side was where Lazarus had been driven to on the night of the attack. It was also where he had seen that shit Sullivan with Gallagher. He knew it was a busy road, with many houses facing the park.

'You may as well start there,' he told Winter. 'Maybe one of the houses facing the park has CCTV.'

He hung up just as he got to the Camry. McEvoy drove. The shortest route back to Broadstone was along the North Circular Road. But Lazarus had a plan.

'Drive in through town, Harry,' he said.

'I want to check the Casey house.'

Fallon had ordered all armed detective units to mount passing patrols around the house. Although Mick and his two sons were in custody, they would be released soon. Lazarus knew there would be no prosecution. The family home still needed protection. Lazarus planned to visit the house, log it on the system and get back to finding Delaney's attacker.

They drove in silence along the quays that border the Liffey. They crawled past the Guinness brewery. Then they came to the Four Courts, where all the city's civil courts were housed. It used to host criminal trials before the Criminal Courts of Justice complex they had just left was opened a decade ago. Lazarus had fond memories of the old building.

Then they came to the Ha'penny Bridge that spanned the Liffey.

'You know why it's called that?' McEvoy said.

'I have a feeling you're going to tell me,' Lazarus said.

'There used to be a toll of half a penny to cross it. It was built in the early 1800s.'

Lazarus was poker-faced.

'Did you get to the official opening?' he said.

McEvoy pretended to go for his gun.

Soon they were on O'Connell Bridge. Lazarus saw the GPO and the Spire on his left.

They drove through the north inner city and ten minutes later they turned into the Caseys' street. Lazarus put his hand on the grip of his pistol, tapped his body armour. They went past the house to the end of the cul-de-sac, then did a U-turn and drove out.

There was nobody suspicious around. As they approached the house on the way out, Lazarus saw Joanne, Sarah's mother, at the door. She saw them coming, went in and closed the door behind her.

'Oops,' McEvoy said.

They headed back to the station. They took the North Circular Road again. It brought them past Croke Park. The Gaelic games stadium towered over the other buildings in the area.

Lazarus was marvelling at it when he heard McEvoy shout.

'Fuck me!'

He pointed a stubby finger outside.

Lazarus followed it and tensed when he saw Danny O'Hara.

He was with two younger men. O'Hara was in his late thirties and wore his long black hair in a ponytail. He had a drooping, Mexican-style moustache. He was of medium height and thin. He wore a dark brown waxed coat. It reached below his knees and had a large flap on the shoulders. Lazarus had seen him in the coat before and knew he wore it to make himself look bulkier than he was. He wore heavy black biker boots with silver buckles and zips. Quite the look.

'Do the bastard,' Lazarus said.

McEvoy gunned the Camry.

It surged forward and closed the space between them and O'Hara in an instant.

Lazarus jumped out of the car, started sprinting.

'Get back up, Harry,' he shouted over his shoulder.

He brought his Sig out and pointed it at O'Hara and the others as he ran. 'Armed gardai!' he shouted.

The two younger men moved to bolt, but O'Hara stopped them.

'Take it easy. Relax the kacks,' O'Hara said.

O'Hara smiled and put his hands up. He turned to the wall.

He knew the drill. Lazarus moved his pistol to the men with him.

The man nearest him was in his late twenties and was around six foot and well built. He wore a green parka, blue tapered tracksuit bottoms and black runners. His fair hair was short. He had a tight beard and tanned skin. His eyes were dead.

The second man was younger, smaller and slight. Lazarus thought he was a teenager. He came up to the first man's shoulder. He had spiked greasy blond hair that caressed his collar. He wore a green fleece and, even though it was late October, navy shorts and red runners. His face was dotted with pimples and he sported a wispy moustache.

'Up against the wall,' Lazarus said.

The two men slowly did as they were told. They spread their legs and put their hands high up on the brickwork.

Lazarus tried to keep an eye on all three of them but he could not stop staring at the teenager. He looked even more slender from behind. His arms were thin. The sleeves fell towards his shoulders, exposing milky white skin.

Lazarus saw a large watch on his left wrist. It had a silver link strap that glinted in the light. Lazarus knew expensive watches were status symbols for up and coming criminals. He looked more closely at the watch face and recognised the logo. He figured it was worth at least €9,000. The kid didn't look a day over 16.

Lazarus wondered what the future held for him. Nothing good, he thought.

A coffin or a cell.

McEvoy had joined Lazarus and patted all three down. Lazarus covered him. McEvoy nodded at Lazarus; they were clean.

'Put your hands down and turn around. Backs to the wall,' Lazarus said.

O'Hara smiled again.

'Mr Lazarus. How's things?'

Lazarus ignored him and went to the other two. He put his pistol away and had a notebook and pen in his hands now. He approached the older man first.

'Name?'

'Tommy Spence,' the man said.

Lazarus knew him. He was a criminal from the north-west of the city. He was close to O'Hara. Lazarus had arrested him for drugs before.

Lazarus moved across and came face to face with the teenager with the watch. He looked into his eyes. There was no fear in them.

'What's your name?' Lazarus said.

'You asking me out?'

Lazarus moved forward.

'I won't ask again.'

The teenager rolled his eyes to show he gave exactly zero fucks.

'Luke Armstrong.'

'Address?'

'181 Fuck You Avenue.'

The teen started laughing. Lazarus balled his fist and went to hit him. Armstrong saw his chance. He started shouting at passers-by.

'Help!'

Lazarus grabbed him and shoved him back against the wall.

Then he heard a voice behind him.

'What did they do?' a young man shouted.

He had his phone out and was filming.

McEvoy and Lazarus ignored him. Being videoed by passers-by was a daily occurrence. They concentrated on holding the suspects against the wall until back-up came.

The cameraman found more courage and moved closer. He was about five foot six, with baggy jeans covering sparrow legs. He had an oversized combat jacket that drowned his torso. He had a thin beard and long dark hair.

'Holy shit…it's Jesus Christ,' McEvoy whispered.

'I hope he doesn't have the 12 Apostles with him or we're fucked.'

'What have they done? Why are you harassing them?' Jesus shouted again.

'I'm recording this, you know.'

Lazarus heard more shouting behind him.

But of the welcome kind.

'Move back. Move away now.'

It was Sinead Duffy.

She and her partner had just arrived in their marked Hyundai. Her partner came to Lazarus and McEvoy, she chose Jesus.

She moved around in front of him, shielding his view of Lazarus and McEvoy

'Get back now!'

She gave him half a second. When he didn't comply, she pushed him hard in the chest.

Jesus stumbled backwards, shock on his face. He dropped the phone.

'Leave this area now,' Duffy shouted.

She pushed him again. He reached for his phone, then scurried away.

Lazarus turned back to the three men. O'Hara was eyeing him coldly.

'I hear you had a nasty incident yesterday, Mr Lazarus.'

He had a rough, Dublin accent and his voice was thick. He looked Lazarus up and down.

His eyes paused on Lazarus's black overcoat.

'I see you didn't rip your nice Italian jacket.'

Lazarus caught his breath and looked into O'Hara's eyes. They were the eyes of the gunman who tried to kill him at the Caseys' house.

O'Hara locked his gaze on Lazarus.

And there and then O'Hara knew that Lazarus knew.

His smile died. He swallowed hard.

'That little bitch better be worth it Mr Lazarus,' he said.

'There is going to be hell to pay over this, you know.'

'The only person paying anything will be Maloney,' Lazarus said. 'Your buddy is fucked.'

Lazarus smiled at O'Hara.

'And that means you probably are, too. He's going to prison for a long time. And you know how bad he is in enclosed spaces. He'll do anything to get out early. That includes inform on you. He'll fuck you to save himself.'

O'Hara snarled.

'You're a hard man with that piece on your hip, Lazarus. But you're not the only one with guns.'

Then he paused

'We'll do this again one day. Me and you. Man to man.'

Lazarus pushed O'Hara back into the wall.

'I look forward to that. Piece of shit like you who protects a child rapist. It will be my pleasure.'

O'Hara's face hardened.

'She led him on.'

'She was a kid,' Lazarus said.

'She's a fucken tramp.'

Lazarus's phone rang.

He gave O'Hara a hard look and walked away to answer it.

'Yes,' he snapped.

'Lazarus, it's Winter.'

Her voice was urgent.

'I have something. You need to come up.'

Lazarus walked back to McEvoy and the uniforms, who still had the men against the wall. He called McEvoy aside.

'Anything on them?'

'Nothing, Lazarus. Clean as a whistle. Not even any blow.'

'Let them go. I need to get up to Griffith Park.'

Lazarus moved back to O'Hara and the other two.

'Get out of here,' he said.

Then he put his mouth up to O'Hara's ear and whispered something only for him.

'You got lucky yesterday, O'Hara. Point a gun at me again and I will end you.'

O'Hara laughed.

'I don't know what you're talking about.'

He nodded to his cronies.

'I hope you're not threatening me. I have witnesses.'

'I don't do threats. Just promises,' Lazarus said.

20

Lazarus jumped into the driving seat of the Camry when McEvoy got out at the station.

His partner walked through the door and headed to the incident room. Collating all the reports and statements and analysis was his task in the inquiry. Lazarus was the main investigator, chasing leads, interviewing witnesses, gathering the evidence. But every major investigation needs a Bookman, someone to put together a file for the Director of Public Prosecutions. McEvoy was a rare breed: a detective who loved paperwork. He was a natural choice to run the inquiry from the station, but that meant Lazarus was down a detective. He was using the inexperienced Winter more than he wanted.

He drove to the end of the road, then turned left onto Mountjoy Street. Within minutes he was on Dorset Street heading north. The city looked miserable. He turned the heat on full.

It took him 15 minutes to get to Botanic Avenue and Griffith Park. He slowed down as he scanned the area for Winter. He spotted her on the other side of the road. He pulled into a space.

Forensics had finished with the park. It had returned to normal. A young couple walking their toddler child towards the park's play area. A woman in her late thirties jogging on the path around the park. Pedestrians coming and going, oblivious to or uncaring about Delaney's fate.

Winter stood at a detached bungalow on a rise facing the park. It was red-brick, baskets hanging on either side of a black front door. Clean. Well-maintained. Solid. He examined the facade, saw no CCTV.

He got out of the car, crossed the road and walked towards it. Winter was in the doorway. She wore a heavy hoodie under her Garda jacket and body armour. As Lazarus approached, a woman came out and spoke to her. She was in her late seventies, with a stout frame and thick strawberry blonde hair. She wore a blue skirt and a pink cardigan. She folded her arms over her large bosom.

'Detective Garda Winter,' Lazarus said in a formal tone when he got to her.

'Detective Sergeant Lazarus,' she replied.

'This is Helen O'Shea.'

Lazarus shook her hand.

She had sparkling eyes and a broad smile. Her face was lined, but gentle.

'Nice to meet you,' she said.

Her hand was warm.

'Come in, I'll put the kettle on. I have some nice biscuits,' she said.

Lazarus smiled, spread out his arms.

'You had me at hello, *Signora*.'

O'Shea laughed.

They walked into the house. The heat was on. Many pensioners were tight for money. They often had to choose food or heating. Most of them chose to eat. Lazarus was glad this woman could do both.

She led them into the house.

Winter turned to Lazarus as they walked behind the woman.

'She doesn't talk like any pensioner I know,' she whispered.

Lazarus raised his eyebrows.

'I'll only be a minute,' O'Shea said. 'Make yourselves comfortable while I sort the tea.'

They entered a small living room on the right the woman pointed to as she walked into the kitchen.

There was a sofa and two armchairs, all with a soft blue pastel design. A coffee table with a glass top and black steel legs sat on a thick cream rug. A closed laptop on it. The floor was covered with a brown deep pile carpet, the walls had yellow and white patterned wallpaper. A TV on a black stand in the corner. Lazarus saw a large framed portrait photograph on a wall. The woman was in the centre with a man her rough age and three smiling adult men, all in their thirties. There were also separate framed photographs of each of the young men in graduation gowns.

Lazarus and Winter sat into the sofa as O'Shea came in carrying a tray with three cups, a sugar bowl, a small jug of milk and a plate of chocolate biscuits. She saw Lazarus looking at the photographs and smiled.

'That's my family,' she said.

'My husband Jim died a few years ago. Cancer is a cunt.'

Lazarus's eyes widened.

A foul-mouthed pensioner. *This will be fun.*

'Sorry to hear that,' he said.

The woman sat into an armchair.

'Do you see them much?' Lazarus asked.

'One is in Sydney, one in London. The youngest works for a multinational down in Cork. He gets up when he can. But he is busy as fuck. You know yourself.'

Lazarus tried not to laugh.

'Do you get many other visitors?' he asked her.

The woman looked away.

'I used to, but it has been a bit quiet in recent months. People are bastards, they always let you down.'

Lazarus nodded. She was growing on him.

'It's the same with my family. I don't get to see my father with work. It's hard.'

'Your mother is dead?'

Lazarus grimaced.

'Yes. She died a few years ago.'

'Fucking hell. I'm sorry,' the woman said.

'Make sure you visit your daddy. I know what it's like to be alone.'

'I will,' Lazarus lied.

He hadn't spoken to his father in more than four years. They had butted heads forever. But there was a major falling out when he was just 17. It had been expected he would join the family restaurant business. He knew from a young age that was not for him. When he announced he had decided to join the Army straight from school, his father reacted furiously. They didn't speak for weeks. Lazarus joined up the day after his 18th birthday in July 1998. The father came around after several months and was there when he passed out of basic training.

Lazarus spent five years in the Army. He loved it, reaching the rank of sergeant and serving overseas with the United Nations in Lebanon. One day he was chatting with another sergeant in his infantry unit. His five-year contract was coming to an end and Lazarus was tempted to stay on. His commander had recommended him for an officer's course, but when his buddy told Lazarus the Garda was recruiting, his mind was made up.

They applied together. They were both accepted and joined the same day in 2003. His friend was sent to Galway and was still there today, where he was a detective.

Life was going well for Lazarus in the cops until the night his sister was murdered. Things were never the same since. He was in a drugs unit and was being earmarked for great things there, but Gabriella's death put everything on hold. After a year of zombie-like paralysis, he went for promotion and became a uniformed sergeant. Steady hours allowed him to spend more time with his father and mother as they grieved.

His parents were devastated by Gabriella's murder, but Lazarus began to think they were coming to terms with it. And then on October 30, 2014, two years to the day since Gabriella's murder, his mother Maria said goodbye to Lazarus's father Giacomo and left their home in Dundrum, south Dublin.

She said she was going to the church to light a candle. His father became worried when she failed to return four hours later. He rang Lazarus, who was on a day off. He knew immediately something was wrong. He could still remember the lurch in his stomach as he raced across the city, trying to think where she could be.

And then he knew.

He diverted to Bohernabreena Cemetery, where Gabriella was buried. He parked up and searched for his mother. There was no sign of her at the grave, but he did see fresh flowers at the foot of the headstone.

Then he saw a note.

Lazarus recognised his mother's handwriting. He froze. Then he read it and was gripped by an icy fear.

Mia bella ragazza. Fra poco saremmo assieme per sempre. Io e tu.

★

"My beautiful girl. Soon we will be together forever. Me and you."

Lazarus ran around the cemetery, frantically searching.

He found her after ten minutes.

He saw her white Fiat 500 parked in an isolated area. The engine was off and the windows steamed up. He sprinted to it and grabbed at the driver's door. It was locked.

He ran to a grave and picked up the first thing he saw, a small heart-shaped marble tribute to a dead child. He smashed the window with it. He reached inside and opened the door. Her mother fell out onto the ground. Her skin was pallid. Her eyes were glassy.

He knew at once she was dead. A post-mortem confirmed cause of death as an overdose of sleeping tablets she had been using since Gabriella's murder.

Lazarus found an envelope addressed to his father on the front seat. He assumed it was a suicide note, but his father never told him what it said.

He never asked.

In December 2014, almost two months after the suicide, his father sold up and went back to Italy. Lazarus hadn't spoken to him since. They had a row the night before. The father said things to him that could never be taken back.

Lazarus felt Winter nudging him.

It brought him back to the room, back to the charmingly foul-mouthed pensioner.

'You have some information for us, Mrs O'Shea?' he asked.

The woman smoothed her skirt and nodded at Winter.

'The detective here came to my house earlier about that terrible attack on the poor woman in the park. It's fucking shocking. I can't believe it happened. I walk there most days and I have never had any shit at all.'

'I'm sure it was a one off,' Lazarus said.

Helen O'Shea gave Lazarus a sceptical look.

'Did you see anything on the night?' Lazarus said.

'What? Me? Oh. No. I was explaining to the garda I was in bed before 11pm. I had a bollix of a headache.'

'Okay,' Lazarus said.

He raised an eyebrow to Winter.

'The lady has a video doorbell,' she said.

'It captures all movement. It got something interesting.'

Lazarus perked up.

'Show me,' he said.

O'Shea opened the laptop on the coffee table.

'My son in Australia got me it the last time he was home,' she said.

'It's the dog's bollix, as you young people say.'

Lazarus cursed himself for not seeing the video doorbell when he arrived.

The pensioner clicked the mouse and a video came on the screen. It was a live view from her front door. The camera had a wide field of vision. Lazarus saw the Broadstone Toyota Camry he had parked on the road, a bus and cars passing by. A large section of the park was visible, too. The video was so clear he could see the brown and yellow leaves rustling in the wind.

'It's HD, you know,' the pensioner said.

'It has excellent night vision. It's monochrome, but the quality is top notch.'

Lazarus saw a twinkle in her eyes.

'Just because I'm in my seventies doesn't mean I don't know my shit. I like technology.'

Lazarus smiled. She was cool.

She looked at the screen.

'Any movement causes the camera to record a video that is saved to the cloud. The cloud stores it for 30 days, but I pay a few quid extra every month and my clips are retained for six months. You can also go on to live view and watch the world go by. I do that sometimes. It's fucking great. You'd swear you were watching a movie.'

She fiddled with the mouse.

'The lady detective told me you were interested in any activity between 10pm and 12.30am on the night of the attack. There is quite a lot. But here is a list of recordings.'

Lazarus thought about the timescale. The Sweeney couple who found Delaney made the emergency call just before midnight. He looked at the list of video clips and saw they were ordered by time. He saw one for 12.05am. 'Can we see that one?'

The woman pressed the button and a black and white video appeared. Lazarus could see the reflection of flashing lights and, just at the edge of the screen, he made out the front half of a marked squad car. He knew gardai were on scene at 12.04am, so he could tell the timing on the video was accurate.

They went back to the list. He saw three thumbnails from 11.59pm, 11.56pm and 11.52pm. He asked to see the one from 11.52pm. Grainy footage showed a man and woman jumping over the railings to get into the park. He knew it was the Sweeneys. The railings were low and presented no problem for them. They called 999 at 11.53pm.

'Can we see the clip right before that?' Lazarus said.

The next video was from 11.50pm. It was a car going past the house. There were several more, all of them of either cars, busses or lorries driving past.

'Can we go to the one we saw earlier? The one from around 11.20pm,' Winter asked the woman.

'Sure,' she said.

She moved the mouse to another video and pressed play.

There was a moment's pause as the clip loaded and began to play. Lazarus looked at the time and saw it was from 11.21pm. At first, all he could see was grey gloom. The street was quiet.

But then, from deep in the park, a blur of movement caught his eye. The image was indistinct at first, but as it moved out of the bushes and into the open it became stronger.

Lazarus realised it was a man sprinting towards the railings.

His mouth fell open.

He stood up.

'*Cristo*,' he said.

'Fucking right,' Mrs O'Shea said.

21

Winter took a hurried statement from the pensioner. It confirmed she consented for the clips to be used in the investigation.

Lazarus thanked her, then they bustled out of the house. They sprinted through a gap in the traffic to the car. Lazarus's mind was racing, adrenalin coursing through his veins as he sped back to the station. Winter gripped a silver USB stick with all her might, like a punter with a winning lottery ticket.

'It has to be him,' she said.

'It is absa-fucking-loutely him,' Lazarus said.

'It can't be anyone else.'

Winter looked at the USB.

'What a devious bastard.'

The attacker had dumped the cord he used to strangle Delaney and her handbag at the northern exit of Griffith Park, but the O'Shea video showed him leaving by the southern exit.

'It was too obvious,' Lazarus said.

'He planned this attack. It made no sense for him to dump key evidence in plain sight like that. Unless it was a decoy.'

They were back at Broadstone within minutes. They ran to the incident room. It was small and was crammed with four desks, grey lino on the floor and off-white paint on the walls. It was a place of work, there was no time for aesthetics. No paintings on the walls, just one large screen TV. Each desk had a landline and a computer.

The room looked onto the back of the station and had one window, hidden by venetian blinds. McEvoy was at a desk. He had his head down and was going through paperwork when Lazarus rushed in, Winter in his wake.

'The Super and Inspector are on their way down,' McEvoy told them.

'And Ben Flannery is coming, too. Just as you asked.'

Lazarus had called the emergency meeting as he drove back to base.

Fallon was the first to arrive.

'Hello, detectives,' she said.

Anderson came next. He ignored Lazarus and took a seat.

'What's going on?' he asked.

'This better be important. I had to cut short a call to the assistant commissioner. He wants news on the leak inquiry.'

Lazarus exchanged a look with Fallon just as Flannery walked in. Fallon raised her eyes to heaven.

'Of course it's important,' Lazarus snapped.

'What about the leak inquiry?' Anderson persisted.

'The A/C wants to know.'

'It's on my list, Inspector. Sullivan was in court for Maloney today. I asked him for his source and he refused. I'll go to his office and make a formal request.'

Anderson snorted and turned to Fallon.

'Can we do the station party's phones? Somebody in here tipped Sullivan off.'

Fallon folded her arms. Checking the phone logs of everyone in Broadstone station for contact between them and Sullivan was a big decision. But if the assistant commissioner for Dublin was asking about the inquiry, that meant Garda HQ was taking an interest.

'That is not something I'll do lightly,' Fallon said.

'Our people have a right to privacy that can only be overridden in serious cases. I don't know if a story in a rag meets the threshold. I'll have to consider that. Anyway, right now I'm more concerned about what Detective Sergeant Lazarus has for us.'

Anderson flushed.

'Off you go, Sergeant,' Fallon said.

'Detective Garda Winter called to a house on Botanic Avenue,' Lazarus said.

'The resident is a Helen O'Shea. It's across the road from the park and has an excellent view of it. She has a video doorbell.'

Lazarus took the USB stick off Winter and put it in a slot on the computer at McEvoy's desk.

It took a few seconds for the stick to transfer its data. A dialogue box opened and a video clip appeared on screen. He pressed another button and the TV on the wall came alive. It mirrored the computer.

'The camera takes a one-minute video every time it detects movement,' Lazarus said.

145

'Mrs O'Shea has about 60 clips from between 10pm and midnight when the first units arrive on scene. Ben can go to the house later and download them all, but we have one here.'

Fallon nodded.

Anderson remained impassive.

'It's the one we need,' Lazarus said.

He clicked play.

The desktop whirred and the video appeared on the TV.

'Watch the railings in the centre of the screen,' Lazarus said.

Everyone leaned forward after a few seconds as a figure ran from the bushes in the park towards the railings.

'That's the attacker. He is fleeing the scene,' Lazarus said.

Fallon put a hand to her mouth.

'Jesus.'

Anderson studied the screen, no emotion on his face.

The camera had infrared, and the man appeared in an enhanced black and white. The clothing he wore looked black, but Lazarus knew that was because of the camera. They could have been brown, or blue, or grey, or even dark green.

The man wore a beanie hat and a scarf. They were pulled together, exposing his eyes and nose. He had a running jacket zipped up to under his chin. He carried a bag on his back, like a rucksack.

Lazarus judged him to be between five foot ten and six foot, of medium build. He wore dark bottoms, maybe a tracksuit, as well as dark runners. Mr Average. No distinguishing physical attributes.

It could be anyone, Lazarus thought. That would present a problem if they identified a suspect and put the footage to him.

He paused the video as the man reached for the railings, his hands a strange tint.

'I think he is wearing surgical gloves,' Lazarus said.

'Which means he's forensically aware,' Fallon said.

'Not much chance of DNA or fingerprints.'

Lazarus pressed play again. The room went quiet.

The attacker glanced around. He put his hands on the top of two steel spindles, hauled his feet up and jumped over the railings. He landed on a small patch of grass.

'He's agile anyway,' McEvoy said.

'I can't imagine someone in his fifties getting over railings like that.'

The park was about 40 metres away from the O'Shea house, but the camera was so good it captured him clearly. Once the man landed on the grass, he straightened up, took another quick look around, and sprinted away.

He moved from right to left on the screen.

'The direction he takes along Botanic Avenue is away from the city centre and out to the suburbs,' Lazarus said.

He paused.

'Now, watch this.'

There was a collective intake of breath as the room saw what happened next.

The attacker stopped halfway across the screen, and looked around again.

Then he threw his head back, clenched his fists and waved them triumphantly in the air.

'What the fuck?' Fallon shouted.

The macabre show lasted just a second before the attacker ran off.

The superintendent jabbed an accusing finger at the screen.

'Was that bastard celebrating?'

'Yes,' Lazarus said.

The team watched the clip in silence four more times.

'Fuck me,' Fallon said.

'It's him. And I can't believe he celebrated like that. The animal.'

She turned to Winter.

'Great work, Detective. Fantastic.'

Winter blushed.

'Yes,' Anderson grumbled.

Fallon stood up. She straightened her blue Garda tie and smoothed down her white uniform shirt.

'This is a good start,' she said.

'Now go and find the fucker.'

She left the room. Anderson followed.

Lazarus waited until they closed the door and then turned to the team.

'We need to focus on how he got away,' he said.

'Rachel, knock on more doors on Botanic Avenue, bring more uniforms. Somebody else must have seen something.'

Flannery interrupted.

'Don't be expecting too much up there,' he said.

He tapped the keyboard of his computer. The map of the park and surrounding areas appeared on the TV screen. The spot where the cord and bag had been dropped was at the top left, while the location where Anne Delaney was found was highlighted just off the centre of the park.

The section of railing that the attacker jumped over was at the bottom. Flannery clicked his mouse and the road parallel to the railings pulsed red. It ran along the bottom of the screen.

'That's Botanic Avenue, where this O'Shea woman lives,' Flannery said.

'It is a nightmare. He could have gone anywhere from there.'

Flannery tapped the keyboard and the map zoomed out to show more of the wider area.

Lazarus looked at the expanded map. He saw the blue line of the River Tolka meandering through the park. At the top of the screen, lay Walsh Road and a ribbon of streets around it. At the right edge of the screen, he saw Drumcondra Road, the main thoroughfare into the city from the airport. He also saw Fagan's pub, where the Sweeney couple who found Delaney had been beforehand.

The bottom of the screen showed the red stretch of Botanic Avenue and a warren of streets behind it. The left of the screen showed more of the avenue, more streets, and a main road running north to south.

'Look at the number of streets off the avenue,' Flannery said.

'There is a huge residential area on the left of the road, with 30 streets less than five minutes away by foot.'

He hit another key and the main road heading south to north that Lazarus had noticed seconds earlier pulsed blue.

'That is St. Mobhi Road, it intersects Botanic Avenue,' Flannery said.

'If our man had wheels parked nearby, he has two options when he gets to it. He can turn left, and he is in the city centre in five minutes. Or he can turn right and keep going on until he reaches the M50. The whole country opens up then.'

The M50 motorway ringed Dublin. Most of its exits led to other motorways that branched out of the capital, heading north, south and west.

Lazarus frowned.

'He could be on the M50 within ten minutes.'

Flannery nodded.

'Yeah. Could have gone anywhere, And I think it's a miracle we got this doorbell footage. I have a database of all CCTV on the avenue and that device wasn't on it. Anyway, do you want the bad news or the good news?'

'Give me the bad news first,' Lazarus said.

'GDPR has fucked us.'

The EU-wide General Data Protection Regulations had come into force in Ireland in May 2018, just 17 months earlier, but already they were hampering Garda investigations.

'People are terrified of being sued,' Flannery said.

'Most CCTV cameras have been reoriented. They used to point outwards on to the street and we would get great footage. But now they have all been repositioned so they only film the property they are on. I've seen systems where public areas have been digitally blacked out. Our man could have taken off his clothing and carried a poster with his name on it past the cameras on the road and all we'd see is a black box. I don't think there'll be more CCTV of him in that area.'

He reached for a blue manila folder on his desk.

'That is the bad news. And this,' he said holding up to the folder, 'is the good news.'

Lazarus sat forward.

'What is it?'

Flannery smiled.

Lazarus knew he liked eyes on him.

'The results of some tests are back,' Flannery said.

'We have good solid footprints from the mud and also from one on her face. We analysed them. They are from a Nike runner.'

'What model?' Lazarus asked.

'That will take a few days. It's a complicated programme. But we also have fibres from his clothing that transferred on to the victim. If you lift a suspect and find his clothes and shoes then we should be able to tie him to her.'

Lazarus felt deflated. He was hoping for more from forensics.

But then he saw a smile on Flannery's face.

'The attacker was quite smart and forensically aware. But not *that* smart,' Flannery said.

Lazarus sat up in his chair.

'Ben, if you don't tell me now, I will fucking shoot you right here.'

'Okay, okay,' Flannery protested, his hands up.

'You'll remember that the Forensic Clinical Examiner swabbed Anne Delaney in the hospital when she was brought in. The tests showed there was no semen recovered and analysis showed trace evidence from the lubricants of a condom.'

'The FCE told us about the condom on the night,' Lazarus said. 'What is your point?'

'My point is, my good man, what do condoms come in?'

Lazarus jumped to his feet.

'Wrappers!'

Flannery smiled, took a small evidence bag from the folder, held it up. It contained a small piece of silver foil. Lazarus squinted to get a proper look. It was ragged, and the diameter of a small coin.

Flannery read his mind.

'It's not the whole thing. But enough.'

'*Cristo*,' Lazarus said.

'*Cristo*,' he said again.

'Here's what I think happened,' Flannery said.

'He drags the girl into the undergrowth, maybe comes up behind her as she is walking on the path. Overpowers her, assaults her. He uses one hand to hold the poor girl down. Maybe she was struggling, who knows?'

'She did fight him,' Lazarus said, remembering the broken fingernails on Anne's hand when he saw her in the hospital.

'Well, there was no foreign DNA found under her fingernails, so she didn't get a chance to scratch him,' Flannery said.

'Maybe she tried to grab a branch of a tree as he dragged to the undergrowth and that's how she lost them.

'Anyway, at the height of it, our man – forensically aware as he is – realises he needs a condom to…well, you know. He takes it of his pocket. But it's in its wrapper. He needs to get it out. He can't use two hands to open it, one is holding the girl. So he grips it with his teeth and uses them and his free hand together to pull the wrapper apart. He pockets the wrapper and the condom.'

Flannery grinned.

'A bit of the wrapper comes off in his mouth when he's opening it. He spits it out and either doesn't realise he has done it in the moment or forgets to look for it after he…afterwards.

'Luckily for us, it was a decent size. And *really* luckily for us, it landed on her leggings and stuck to them.'

A memory flashed into Lazarus's mind of Dr Ainsworth motioning to the cardboard box filled with evidence bags back at the hospital, shortly after the attack.

'I found it yesterday when I was examining her clothes. I bagged it and sent it to the lab. The results came back an hour ago. His saliva is all over it. They raised his DNA profile from the saliva.'

Flannery looked at Lazarus.

'We have him, John. The profile we raised is being run through the national DNA database now.

'And we'll know if we have a hit tomorrow.'

22

The anonymous-looking office block on William Street near St. Stephen's Green was like any other complex in central Dublin. It was red-brick, six-storey. Its large windows stared down on the busy street below.

But Lazarus looked at the building with a cop's eyes. CCTV cameras at strategic points. A security hut for a garda sentry. Two long antennae on the roof. More than a dozen unmarked Garda cars outside.

This was no ordinary office block.

This was the MIS HQ.

Lazarus walked over.

He badged the garda at the entrance and went inside.

The Garda Major Investigations Squad dealt with serious offences like rape and murder.

Lazarus walked into the MIS office just after 2.30pm. Detective Inspector Patrick O'Leary was waiting for him. They shook hands.

O'Leary was tall, heavy set and wore a hang-dog expression, aggravated by curly black hair and bushy eyebrows. He wore a creased brown polyester suit. His grey paisley tie was loose, the top button of his white shirt undone.

They walked in silence until they reached a blue door. A sign on it said SCAU.

O'Leary knocked. There was a long silence, then it crashed open. Cochrane appeared in the doorway.

She was in her early forties, had a tired and lined face, with bags under her eyes. Her mouth was tight and wrinkled, like many smokers. She was stick thin and about five foot seven. Her grey hair was in a severe ponytail.

She saw Lazarus and her dark face darkened a bit more.

'Oh for fuck's sake!'

'Nice to see you, too,' Lazarus said.

'You're really getting on my tits now, Lazarus.'

Cochrane had a strong northern accent. Her *now* came out as *nigh*.

'What the fuck do you want?' she said.

Lazarus brought his hands up, bunched the thumb and fingers of each together and wagged them in her face. It was a classic Italian get fucked gesture. He used it a lot.

'I want you to answer my calls, that's what I want.'

Cochrane's eyes darkened.

'I don't have time to listen to your shite.'

Lazarus flared.

'My sister is not shite!'

Cochrane ignored his protest. She was going postal.

'What are you playing at, Lazarus? You're fucken stalking me.'

He jutted out his chin.

'I have rights.'

'Shove your rights up your fucken hole.'

'You're a real lady.'

Cochrane motioned to the door.

'See this sign?'

'I'm not blind,' Lazarus snapped.

'It stands for the Sexual Crime Analysis Unit.'

'I know what it stands for.'

'You have about 80 sex offenders in your division. There are almost 1,500 around the country. I have responsibility for every fucken one of them nationwide. I also have a fuckload of unsolved sex killings on my desk. I'm sorry to say that includes your sister. I wish it didn't. But it does.'

Lazarus looked down at the carpet. It was blue, with a fine black pattern.

'Jesus Christ, you're taking the piss with all the texts and calls. We have no suspects. We have no news,' Cochrane said.

She went quiet.

'I do not need you contacting me every other day.'

Lazarus looked up, fire in his eyes.

'I want to know what is happening to Gabriella's case. She was my little sister,' he said.

'You contacting me every fart's end is not helping. Is that what you want? How am I supposed to find her killer if you harass me all the time?'

O'Leary stepped in.

'Enough.'

He ran a shovel-sized hand through his hair.

His voice was tired.

'I don't know what's going on with you two. And I don't care. The Assistant Commissioner has directed you to work together on the Griffith Park case. And that's what you'll do. HQ is watching this. They are worried about the media coverage. That little shit Sullivan in *The Globe* has been on it. They want a result.'

He pointed at the open door.

'Get in that office and solve it. Now.'

He walked away.

Cochrane glared at Lazarus. Lazarus glared back.

Cochrane broke first.

'I suppose I have no choice on this. You may as well come in.'

She retreated into the office. He followed.

Cochrane wore a white shirt, a navy trouser suit and flat shoes. There was a large holster on her left hip. She carried a Walther P99 9mm pistol, popular with the national units.

Local detectives like Lazarus used the Sig-Sauer P226.

Lazarus walked into the office, closed the door behind him.

'Fucking hell,' Lazarus said.

He sat in a chair, put his hands to his face.

He closed his eyes and took deep breaths. The vision of Gabriella dead and brutalised in the ditch came to him again.

He suddenly felt sick.

He opened his eyes after a long moment.

Cochrane hadn't moved.

But her face had softened.

'You all right?' she asked.

Lazarus nodded.

'I'm sorry,' he said.

'It's her anniversary soon. My mother's, too – you know what happened to her?'

'It's in the file.'

'It just gets to me around this time every year,' Lazarus said.

He relaxed his shoulder.

'I'm sorry for the texts. But you should have contacted me rather than my Super if you had a problem.'

Cochrane bit her bottom lip.

She sat into the chair behind her desk.

'Can we start again? Maybe we're both being gobshites?'

He knew she was right.

'Fine,' he said. 'But try to speak English. My Nordie is not what it should be.'

'Dead on big lad,' Cochrane said with a smile.

'Sure I'll teach you. You'll be fluent before you know it.'

Lazarus smiled then checked out the office. It was small with just enough space for two desks. He looked at Cochrane's. He saw a pile of files at one corner. He shuddered to think what was inside. An empty coffee cup, a vaping pen, an A4 diary. A notebook. Scraps of paper, too. Then he saw a row of neat black crosses on the side her computer. He counted eight. They were like decals on a model airplane.

'What's the story with them?'

Cochrane stared at the crosses impassively.

'Each one is a man who killed himself before we could charge him. Most of them were for abusing kids. Every time one of them tops himself, I put a cross on the computer. Then I go home and have a fuck off glass of wine. And I think of the taxpayers' money that has been saved.'

Jesus, Lazarus thought. *That's cold.*

He saw a whiteboard on the wall behind Cochrane. It was covered with photographs. One was a newspaper cutting of Cochrane leading a man in handcuffs into court. He looked familiar. He was fat and bald, with a bulbous nose and thin lips. Dark eyes. He was small and wore a white boiler suit. Late forties.

Cochrane saw him looking.

'Eamon Whelan,' she said.

'Best day of my illustrious career.'

Lazarus remembered him. He was a van driver who went on a murder spree across Ireland five years ago. He sexually assaulted and killed boys all over Ireland.

'It took us a year and six murders to catch the fucker,' Cochrane said. Her eyes burrowed into the photograph.

'He murdered them in the van.'

Her voice went quiet.

'He videoed what he did to them next. We got him after a member of the public saw him bundling a child into the van and got a partial index number. Thank fuck for that woman. She saved a ten-year-old. And God only knows how many more there would have been if not for her.'

She stared at his photograph.

'They've told me he'll never get out. I pray to God that's true.'

Lazarus looked at the other photos. There were 13, all women and children. Three of them were kids. One was an old woman. The rest were young, late teens to mid thirties. All were females, except one young boy.

'That's my murder board,' Cochrane said.

'I collate every homicide of a woman or a child, whether there was a sexual motive or not.'

'Are they all from this year?' Lazarus asked.

Cochrane nodded.

'There are usually around 15 a year. We're in October and we have 13. We could hit 20. I've been involved in a few of them.'

Cochrane pointed at the first photograph. A woman in her early twenties. She had sandy fair hair down to her shoulders, a thin face and large blue eyes. She sat on a carpet and her back rested against a grey sofa. She held a glass of white wine and smiled to the camera.

'New Year's morning,' Cochrane said.

'Her fella stabbed her. Said she was flirting at a party. It happened three hours after he took that photograph.'

The pensioner was next. She sat in an armchair that dwarfed her tiny frame. She had a soft face under a mop of thick white hair. Her cheeks were sunken and she wore a gold chain with a large crucifix over a blue jumper.

'Beaten to death by her son,' Cochrane said.

'She was 81. He had mental health issues. He should have been in a facility, but there was no bed.'

The next photograph was of a girl.

'A seven-year-old,' Cochrane said.

Lazarus noticed a tremor in her voice.

'Her father had been in a custody row with his ex. He broke into the house one evening, beat the shite out of the mother and took the child. He strangled her in his car, then stabbed himself. He tied the knife to the steering wheel with heavy duty tape and slammed his chest into the blade. He took an hour to die. I wish it was longer.'

She went through every victim. It took her 15 minutes. Just over a minute for each life.

Stabbed, shot, kicked, beaten, strangled. Ten women, two girls, one toddler boy. Lazarus was struck by how many of the stories were similar. Most were killed in their own home by a partner or husband or ex or son or father.

All except one.

Cochrane pointed to the most recent photo.

'Alison Tracey,' Cochrane said. 'Twenty nine. She was a solicitor. She went on a Tinder date. The date raped her. Strangled her. Did a runner. We got him at Dublin Port as he was boarding a ferry to France.'

Lazarus stayed silent for a moment.

'Is that the only sex murder this year?'

'Aye,' Cochrane said. 'Stranger sex attacks are rare. Stranger sex killings even more so.'

'How's your victim?' Cochrane asked.

'She's still in ICU,' Lazarus said. 'Too soon to say.'

'Any forensics?'

'We got his DNA.'

'Good,' Cochrane said.

'If he's on the register, we'll have him soon enough. Any suspects?'

'Her friend has nominated the ex-boyfriend called Darcy,' he said. 'We have CCTV of the attacker taking a route that brings him near his house. He had been stalking her. We don't have enough to arrest him yet. The Super won't sanction it. We're looking into his background and we're going to his place to ask him to make a voluntary statement.'

He thought of Delaney's battered body and face.

'Could the violence in our case suggest it was personal?' he asked.

Cochrane shook her head.

'Everyone who comes to us thinks I'll magic a profile out of my arse and serve the attacker up on a plate. That's bollix. Good police work gets results, nothing else. I'm not the answer here. You are.'

Cochrane sat in her chair.

'I had a murder about ten years ago when I was in west Dublin,' she said.

'Castleknock. Nasty case. A man stabbed in his home. I mean *really* stabbed.'

She moved her fist back and forward, mimicking a knife.

'The post-mortem found 58 wounds on his body. In his torso, hands, arms, head, face, throat, even in one eye. Everywhere. He was like a colander, God love him. The bosses brought in a profiler. She said the violence suggested a personal motive. We spent months checking all his family, friends, neighbours and workmates.'

'Turned out it was a stranger?' Lazarus asked.

'A burglary,' Cochrane said.

'The deceased came home sick from work and found him in the bedroom. Yer man took out a knife and killed him. We got him after he told a mate, who came forward when a reward was offered. He confessed straight away.'

'Did he say why he used so much violence?' Lazarus asked.

Cochrane grimaced.

'He said once he decided to kill him, he had to make sure he died. Literally overkill. Don't assume the violence in your case shows a grudge. He may just be an evil fucker. It could be anyone. But we do have the sex offenders' register for a reason, so we can start there.'

People convicted of a sexual offence in Ireland went on the register. They had to give gardai their address and other details. Lazarus's unit looked after the register for his division. There were 82 men on it. That was high, but the patch included hostels for released prisoners. Cochrane's unit had access to statistics for the whole country.

'How big is the national register?' Lazarus asked.

Cochrane sat forward and tapped the keyboard.

'As of last night, 1,465. Eleven women, the rest men.'

'Holy shit,' Lazarus said.

Cochrane tapped more keys.

'We can cut the numbers,' she said.

'Of the 1,454 men on the list, 734 are in Dublin and the surrounding areas. It is possible the attacker came from the country, but unlikely. It's probable he's from Dublin or Wicklow, Kildare, Meath and Louth.'

The counties she mentioned surrounded Dublin or were within an hour's drive.

'It's all about percentages,' Cochrane said.

'We can assume whoever did this had to be fit. I don't think one of the old priests would be in any condition to attack a young, fit woman. I'll go for the age range 20 to 45.'

She hit a few buttons and then nodded.

'That brings us down to 382.'

'Still high,' Lazarus said.

'Yes, but we can reduce it again,' Cochrane said.

'Every sex offender has his own thing. We call it paraphilia. One is into boys, another 15-year-old girls. Another might have raped a woman at a party. A paedophile is unlikely to go after a woman. A date rapist probably won't target a stranger on the street. There are maybe 3,000 reported rapes and serious sexual assaults every year. But how many do you think are stranger attacks like yours?'

Lazarus had around 60 rapes a year, just over one a week. He could only think of a few where there was no connection between the attacker and victim.

'It's around ten,' Cochrane said.

'For the whole country. The number of stranger rapists is quite small. So, with the help of ViClas, I have compiled a target list.'

Lazarus had heard of ViClas. It was the Violent Crime Linkage Analysis Scheme, a computer package bought from America.

'It analyses all violent attacks,' Cochrane said.

'I fed in the initial details from your attack.'

She looked down at a file on her desk.

'ViClas looked at the M/O and nominated 38 suspects. Eight are in prison, two are dead. Others are too old. Some live too far away.'

Lazarus waited for the magic number.

'I cut that down to 15,' she said.

'That sounds much better,' Lazarus said. 'It gives us a fighting chance.'

Cochrane stuck a finger up to stop him.

'But there is one who stands out. I really think he's a good fit for this.'

Lazarus felt his heart skip a beat.

Cochrane glared at her computer.

'A fucker called Martin Glennon.'

23

'Why Martin Glennon?' Lazarus asked Cochrane.

She was in the driving seat of a red Ford Mondeo.

Cochrane grabbed the gearstick, slammed it into reverse.

'Because he is a monster.'

She sped out of the space, righted the car and drove down the road.

'And he always fucken will be.'

Cochrane had printed out Martin Glennon's profile from PULSE, the Garda computer system. Lazarus studied it as she turned left at St. Stephen's Green. It said Glennon was 35. Right in Cochrane's age range.

He stared at his mugshot. He looked older. Lazarus thought 45. His brown greasy hair was swept back, accentuating a large forehead.

His face was hard and thin, exposing his cheekbones.

His brown eyes were dead, dark and sunken. They reminded Lazarus of two pebbles in the snow.

Cochrane sucked hard on a vaping pen, lowered the window and breathed steam into the cold air. She shifted down a gear, undertook a car without looking. A screech of tyres and the blare of a horn behind them.

Lazarus closed his eyes, gripped the overhead safety handle.

'I should book you,' he said.

'Make sure you've picked out your favourite coffin first, big lad,' Cochrane said.

Her hands were tight on the wheel. She wore a man's large Rolex on her wrist.

Cochrane saw him looking at it.

'I caught the fucker who murdered a nine-year-old down the country a few years ago,' she said.

'His parents gave me this when he was locked up. The father bought it for his boy the week he was born. It was to be his 21st birthday present. I wear to it remember him.'

Lazarus was struck by how matter of factly she spoke about murders, even kids.

He realised this was her normal.

'What's Glennon's story?' Lazarus said.

'I see he has a few convictions for rape.'

Cochrane took another long drag of the vaping pen.

'Martin Glennon is as dysfunc'

'Fuck's sake!' she shouted.

A pensioner had stepped in front of the Mondeo. She froze as she saw the car bearing down on her. Cochrane slammed on the brakes. She managed to stop just inches from her.

The old lady wore a grey rain jacket and a clear plastic hood tied around her neck. Cochrane jumped out of the car. She did it with such aggression that Lazarus thought she was going to launch into the pensioner. But she gently took her by the arm, stopped traffic with her other hand and escorted her to the pavement.

She got back to the car, took a deep breath.

'Glennon is Mr Dysfunctional,' she said as she sat back in her seat.

'Mother was an addict who died of an overdose. Christ knows who the father was. Glennon got involved in crime at the age of 12. Shoplifting, street fights, acting as a runner for drugs gangs. Then when he was 16, he started burgling houses. He was already an addict by then.'

She clamped the vaping pen between her teeth.

'He was a creeper, breaking into houses and taking the keys to take the car outside. He made good money, but injected most of it. Then, one night, he discovered he liked raping women.'

A car in front dallied.

Cochrane pressed down hard on the horn.

'Fucken move, you bollix!'

Lazarus turned side on to face her.

'He carried out his first attack when he was 20,' she said.

They were stopped at lights.

'He did a place on the southside. He thought it was empty, and went upstairs looking for jewellery. He came into a bedroom, and found a woman in bed.

'She sat up, turned the light on.'

Cochrane grimaced.

'The victim said he stood on the threshold for a few seconds. Looking at her. And then he moved into the room, closed the door behind him.'

The car moved off from the lights.

'He spent two hours with her. Tied her up, choked her, threatened to kill her. Raped her three times. He told us later he never felt more alive than when he had a woman like that. At his mercy. He got a thrill from dominating a woman. He liked having power over them.'

Lazarus remembered Winter telling him the same thing as they drove to Orla Diffney's house.

'Burglary became secondary,' Cochrane said.

'There were so many women living alone it was easy for him. He spent the mornings driving around the suburbs, looking for the right house. He picked properties that had one car in the driveway. He came back in the evening, parked up and watched until the occupant returned. If it was a man, or a couple, he moved on. If it was a woman by herself, he returned at night. He staked out each house for days, establishing the woman's routine and confirming she lived alone. And then, when he was ready, he made his move. The victims said he wore a ski mask, dressed in black and used a rope on them.'

'How many?' Lazarus said.

'Eight,' Cochrane said.

'It was superb detective work that got him in the end.'

Lazarus glanced through the front window. The sun was hidden by dark clouds.

'I wasn't in the MIS at the time,' Cochrane said.

'O'Leary got him,' she said.

'You're shitting me,' Lazarus said.

He could not believe O'Leary had ever investigated anything.

He remembered back to meeting O'Leary. There was nothing on his face. No excitement. No energy. No anger. Nothing.

Cochrane was at the bitter stage. But O'Leary was far past that. He looked as if he didn't care, that he was numbed by everything he had seen. And Lazarus realised he was on the same train as them.

His stomach tightened.

'I know what you're thinking,' Cochrane said.

'But O'Leary was a top investigator once. Anyway, he looked at the cases and suspected the attacker was a housebreaker,' she said.

'He spent days trawling CCTV, logging every car in the area of each attack. Looking for a repeat car, looking for a pattern. One night, he was examining CCTV from a bank a few hundred yards from one attack. The footage was from a week before the rape. He saw a light blue Nissan Micra heading towards the property. It came back five minutes later. The colour triggered something in him. He checked his database of logged cars and realised similar vehicles had been spotted near other attacks. When he looked more closely, he saw a metallic light blue Nissan Micra was in the areas between 7am and 9.30am on the days of three more rapes. Then he checked the evenings of the attacks and saw a similar car on CCTV again. He knew it was him. Now all he had to do was identify the owner of the Micra.'

They were passing the Guinness Brewery in central Dublin. The black gates under the sandstone brick arch were open. A car emerged. Cochrane flashed and let the driver out.

'Back then, the CCTV quality was poor,' she said, then stopped herself.

'But you know that anyway because of Gabriella's case. I'm sorry.'

There was CCTV in Gabriella's case, but Cochrane was right. It wasn't good enough to pick out number plates.

'Most of the recordings were crap,' Cochrane said.

'They had been overwritten so often that O'Leary had to discard them. The cameras never caught a clear shot of the suspect's face. He always wore a baseball cap. But, after a fucken eternity of trawling, he did find enough clips of the Micra to put together a partial index plate. It started 95 D 13, but O'Leary couldn't get the last three digits.'

Lazarus raised an eyebrow.

'Impressive.'

'Best investigator I ever worked with,' Cochrane said.

'The job has fucked him.'

She looked out the window.

'This job fucks us all in the end.'

She went quiet and Lazarus wondered what cases she was thinking about.

'He checked on the system and found there were 120 Micras with a Dublin registration from the year 1995,' she said after a long moment.

'Of them, 17 were the same colour as the suspect's car. He checked with a dealer, it was colour code BPO, or metallic light blue.'

'Of the 17 cars of that colour on the system, only six had the sequence 13 after the D. So that shortened his odds. But, to be sure, he did a search for any colour, mindful of the possibility the car could have been resprayed at some stage. That wider search brought the number back up to 11. He drew up a list of the registered owners and prepared to visit each one of them.'

Cochrane smiled.

'He checked each car on PULSE first, just to see if there was anything on them,' she said.

'He was on his fifth name when he got a hit. The car was registered to a Molly Glennon. She had once gone bail for her grandson Martin. O'Leary also saw Glennon had been linked on PULSE to the car on four occasions. He clicked on his name and the system led him to Glennon's own PULSE entry.

'As soon as he saw his convictions for burglary O'Leary knew it was game over. He led the arrest operation against him the following morning. His DNA linked him to all eight attacks. He pleaded guilty and got 15 years. With remission and time served, he walked free in late 2017.'

'He's out a while,' Lazarus said.

'He refused treatment inside,' Cochrane said.

'He got clean on the outside and now claims he has found God.'

She snorted.

'He has in his hole. The devil is in him.'

She pulled into a parking space without indicating and hit the brakes.

Lazarus put his hand on the dashboard to protect himself.

'We're here,' she said.

'Let me show you a monster.'

24

Lazarus hung back as Cochrane pressed the buzzer.

The distance gave him a better angle on the large Georgian house. It was a redbrick, four storeys high, with a basement. He counted 12 windows, one for each button on the intercom. The glass was dirty. One window had a long crack. Another had been smashed and repaired by cardboard. The window frames were green. Some were rotting.

Cochrane came back to him.

The overgrown garden teemed with weeds and litter. A discarded cigarette packet. A bottle of cheap German beer. A pizza box. Two black refuse bags.

'I like what he's done to the place,' Lazarus said.

Cochrane laughed.

She looked up at a window. She shook her head, went back to the door and pressed the intercom again. She held her finger down on the button.

Cochrane let go of it, stepped back.

'There are 12 of the fuckers here,' she said.

'It's a halfway house for released prisoners. Two ordinary criminals, the rest are sex offenders. Four priests, an accountant, a mechanic, a doctor, a bus driver, a scout leader – surprise, surprise – and Glennon.'

Lazarus heard feet on stairs in the house.

Cochrane flipped open the lid of a small bottle and squeezed a clear liquid onto her palm. She gave him the container and then massaged the gel into her hands.

'Sanitiser. You never know what you can catch from these dirty fuckers,' she said.

The door eased open. Martin Glennon stood in front of them.

'Garda Síochána,' Cochrane said. Her northern twang turned the soft CH in Síochána into a hard K.

She flashed her ID.

Glennon looked at the ground.

'I know who you are, Sergeant.'

'We need a word.'

Glennon shrugged.

'Okay.'

He turned and walked up the stairs.

As they followed him, Cochrane took out a small tin of Vaseline. She dipped her index finger into the jelly and smeared it under her nostrils. She offered the tin to Lazarus. He declined.

Glennon turned left at the landing and pushed a heavy white door.

He gestured for them to enter.

Lazarus crossed the threshold and recoiled. A rancid smell hit him in the back of his throat. It was a combination of smoke, shit, garlic and rotten food. He almost retched. He regretted not taking the Vaseline from Cochrane.

'Fuck me, what died in here, Martin? Cochrane gasped.

'Sorry, Miss Cochrane.'

Glennon walked over and opened a large window. Welcome cold air rushed in.

The flat was once a bedroom, now repurposed as a bedsit. It had a kitchenette at one end, a bed at the other and living space in between.

The kitchenette had a microwave and dirty hob. Two pots simmered on it. There was a small fridge. Its handle was broken. The floor was dark orange lino, littered with holes. There was a tattered grey sofa in the living area, an armchair of the same colour and a television. The walls were yellow, with rising damp in the corners. At the back of the room there was an open door to a small toilet and shower, where the worst of the smell came from.

Lazarus examined Glennon. He had changed since the prison mugshot. His hair was grey. He had it short. No grease. He was clean shaven, his eyes laser blue. He had a strong chin. His nose was out of shape. He was around five foot ten, with a wiry frame. He wore a faded off-white T-shirt, black jeans and blue runners. Lazarus examined the runners. They weren't Nike.

Glennon stood by the window, clasping a cigarette.

Lazarus saw an old-fashioned mobile phone on the table. It was a dumbphone, one that only made calls or texts. No internet. Three cups and a bowl caked with cereal competed with the phone and a Bible for space on the table.

There were two posters on the walls. One was of Christ on the cross. Another was of the Virgin Mary in a white dress and headscarf and a blue shawl. She was in the clouds, looking down on the world with her hands spread.

Glennon walked to the coffee table. He took another cigarette from a packet and lit it with the smouldering butt he was holding. He took a long drag, then exhaled.

Cochrane stood a few feet from him. She kept both hands in her trouser pockets. Lazarus remembered reading an article about body language. It was supposed to be a tell of confidence, especially for women talking to men. He hoped she was doing it on purpose.

'How are you spending your time, Martin?' Cochrane asked.

Glennon walked back to the half-open window. He stared through the glass, his back to them.

He took another drag.

'I go to mass every morning. Then I have a few bets, a few pints. I go for a walk in the evening. Not much else to do.'

'Where do you go for your walks?' Cochrane asked.

'Around.'

'Around where?'

'Anywhere I can to get out of this place. The walls can close in on you.'

She turned to Lazarus.

'This is Detective Sergeant Lazarus from Broadstone station.'

Glennon looked to Lazarus and nodded.

'Where were you on Sunday night?' Cochrane asked him.

'Why?'

Cochrane's voice hardened.

'Answer the fucken question.'

Glennon turned back to the window.

'What am I supposed to have done?'

Cochrane took her hands out of her trousers.

'Listen to me. We are investigating a serious sexual assault. We need to know where you were on Sunday night.'

Glennon walked back to the coffee table and stubbed the cigarette out in the overflowing ashtray. Lazarus saw Cochrane's fists balled.

'I have done my time, Miss Cochrane,' Glennon said.

'I am not a rapist. I *was* a rapist. I was off my head on drugs when I did what I did. My sins are in the past. I pray for the women I hurt. I pray they can forgive me.'

Cochrane seemed to be considering his answer.

Then she sprang towards him. Her fists were balled, her face was just inches from his.

'Don't give me your Jesus freak bollixology, you cunt. You were born a monster and you'll die a monster. And if you don't tell me where you were on Sunday night, you'll die sooner than you fucken think.'

Glennon's eyes bulged. He raised his hands in surrender.

'Jesus!' he croaked.

'Where were you?' Cochrane shouted.

'I was here! Please!'

'Who were you with?'

'Nobody!'

'When did you get home?'

Glennon tried to swallow.

'I was in a pub until nine, then I came home. I was in bed by 11, I swear on the Bible!'

Cochrane stepped back.

'Right,' she said.

'That wasn't so hard, Martin. Good boy.'

'There was no need for that,' Glennon said.

He massaged his temple.

'I know I have to suffer for my sins. I regret them every day, but I have found the Lord Jesus Christ. He has forgiven me.'

Cochrane laughed at him. Glennon looked at the floor. Then his forehead creased. A frown came on his face.

He turned to Lazarus, puzzlement in his eyes.

'Lazarus? That's your name, Sir?'

'What of it?' Lazarus said.

'Lazarus…Lazarus… Did you ever arrest me, when I… when I was a sinner?'

'No,' Lazarus said.

Glennon furrowed his brow.

'There's something…I…that name…Do you know the Bible story of Lazarus?' he asked.

'Everyone does,' Lazarus said evenly.

He had researched the family name. Although he was Italian through and through, the name was originally Jewish. His people had come from the Middle East to Italy centuries earlier.

'It's about the power of the Lord Jesus Christ,' Glennon said.

'He can bring people back from the dead. If he can do that, he can save sinners.'

He patted his chest.

'He saved me. He forgave me. Jesus can do anything.'

He smiled.

'I am Lazarus. I am back from the dead. Now I'm alive. Thanks be to God.'

Glennon's eyes bore into Lazarus. He began to feel uncomfortable. He stared back, refusing to blink. He had been taught on day one on the streets never to show them any weakness.

'Stop talking shite, Glennon,' Cochrane interrupted.

'Your case workers and the do-gooder pinko liberal charity muppets who suck your smelly little mickey every day may fall for your shite, but I don't. And we're the ones who matter. We are watching you, waiting for you to take one bad step.'

She pointed at him.

'And when you do, I will be there. If you have lied to me and we link this to you, you are a dead man.'

She nodded to Lazarus.

'We're done.'

She walked to the door. Lazarus followed.

Glennon called after them as Lazarus was closing the door.

'I am Lazarus. Back from the dead.'

They walked down the stairs in silence, a silence that continued until they sat into the car.

Lazarus waited until Cochrane started the engine.

'What was that about back there?' he asked.

Cochrane concentrated on reversing. She gunned the accelerator. The car flew backwards. Then she hit the brakes, changed into first gear, hit the accelerator again and the Mondeo sped off with a screech of tyres.

Cochrane kept her eyes on the road, said nothing for a long moment. The car sped along the road.

'The last two women he raped, Glennon made them thank him,' she said, finally.

'They had to say, "thank you for fucking me". In their own house. In their own bed. He slapped them on the face. Not hard, more like how you might slap a child on the arm. Then he spat in their faces. He choked them so tightly they thought they were going to die. He did that because he wanted control over those women.'

169

She looked at Lazarus.

'I am going to make sure he never has any power over any woman again.'

She pressed down on the accelerator again.

The car leapt forward with a growl.

Her eyes were blazing.

'And especially not me.'

25

Cochrane dropped Lazarus on O'Connell Bridge in the city centre 20 minutes later. She drove off, almost before he had time to get out. It was 4.15pm and she was in a rush to beat the traffic.

'Nutcase!' he shouted after the Mondeo.

The driver's window rolled down. Cochrane gave him the finger.

Lazarus cursed again and began the walk to his next appointment. It was for 4.35pm, at Sir John Rogerson's Quay, on the south bank of the Liffey. It was already dark and he battled through a wall of commuters heading home.

The Liffey was high. The current was fast. The water was black. It looked cold. He had gone into it three times when he was in uniform. The rest of the unit always volunteered him because he had done lifesaving in the Army. He still remembered the breath leaving him at the shock of the freezing water.

He had a good record. Only one of the three died. He often wondered if the other two got the help they needed, or if some other garda later pulled them out of the same water.

He kept a steady pace and soon passed Butt Bridge. Liberty Hall appeared on the opposite bank, then the Custom House. He was close to his destination when he rang Winter.

'Head over to me now,' he said.

'This won't take long.'

He was on his way to interview Sullivan. Lazarus knew what the reporter was going to say. But Anderson was like a dog with a bone. The sooner he got a no comment from Sullivan, the sooner he could concentrate on finding Delaney's attacker.

He got to *The Globe* five minutes early. He had rung Sullivan while he was with Cochrane to agree a time.

The newspaper was based in a modern office building overlooking the quay, across from the Dublin Convention Centre, with its iconic glass front bathed in electric blue light.

An Irish Naval Service ship was tied up beside the *Globe* office on Sir John Rogerson's Quay. It was battleship grey with the letters P31 on its side. It was the LÉ Eithne. He had been on it when it visited Beirut while he was serving there with the United Nations in 2001. He and some pals were given two nights' leave from their camp in southern Lebanon and spent it drinking in Beirut with the sailors.

He walked up steps at the entrance to the building, a five-storey modern block with mirrored windows. A bank of flat-screen TVs on a wall in the foyer played Sky News, RTÉ, BBC and CNN.

He walked to reception. A man in his sixties sat behind the low desk. He wore a white shirt and a black jumper with the logo of a security company.

Lazarus smiled.

'This how you pass the time now?'

Alan Daly laughed, stood up and came around to embrace Lazarus. Daly used to be a beat cop and spent a year mentoring a young Lazarus. He had retired three years ago.

'The last I heard you were sunning yourself in Marbella,' Lazarus said.

Daly had short white hair and a salt and pepper goatee. He was about five foot ten. Lazarus remembered him as being taller. He wondered if he was shrinking with age. He looked in good shape, though.

'I got bored,' Daly said.

'There is only so much Sangria you can have. I came back a few months ago. The missus is delighted. She didn't want to go to Spain in the first place. She missed the family. I do this three days a week. Keeps me out of the house.'

Lazarus told him he was there to meet Sullivan.

Daly raised his eyes to heaven as he lifted the phone, dialled a number and spoke into the handset.

'He's hard work, that fella,' Daly said when the phone was back in its cradle.

'Really?'

'Yeah. Something about him, lad. Something not quite.' He stopped when a door opened behind him and Sullivan appeared. He had brushed his hair, but had a light five o'clock shadow. He wore a blue denim shirt over a white T-shirt, black cargo pants and grey hiking boots.

'Sergeant Lazarus,' he said swiping an access card at a turnstile. He stuck out his hand. Lazarus shook it and held eye contact. The firmness of Sullivan's handshake surprised him. Sullivan brought him through the turnstile to the door, which opened to a small landing. They took a lift to the third floor, then walked in silence through a corridor until they came to another door.

Sullivan pressed a card against a reader. It beeped and the door opened.

'This is where the magic happens,' he smiled.

Lazarus didn't answer.

They entered an open-plan office. Mirrored-glass windows showed the city in front of them. The newsroom was to the left. White desks were grouped together. Each desk had an iMac on it and most had young people typing on keyboards. The walls were a garish red and were covered with framed front and back pages of *The Globe*.

Sullivan walked him into a glass-fronted room.

'It's the editor's office,' he explained.

There was a large desk at the back, and a high-backed leather chair behind it. A teak table and four chairs were in front of the desk.

One chair was occupied by a distinguished looking man. He was around six foot two and thin. He wore a grey wool three-piece suit. The shirt underneath was navy blue with a white collar. He wore gold cufflinks and a bright red tie. He had short fair hair that was greying at the temples, a solid face, bushy eyebrows and thick spectacles.

'Nick Bell, our legal advisor,' Sullivan said.

'We've met,' Lazarus said.

Bell stood and they shook hands.

'Indeed we have, Sergeant,' Bell said.

'Hope you're well.'

Bell's voice was rich and plummy. He was in his late forties and was one of Dublin's best-known criminal defence solicitors. He was from Dublin 4, the richest part of the capital. He was old money. He joked his family were so rich their butler was born with a silver spoon in his mouth.

'How's your good lady?' he asked.

Jenna used to work for him.

'She's fine. How could she not be? I'm a catch.'

Bell laughed.

Lazarus peeled off his overcoat. They all sat down.

Lazarus took a manila folder from a brown leather briefcase.

'My news editor will be here in a second,' Sullivan said.

'We can't start without her.'

At that, the office door opened. Lazarus expected to see a woman. But it was Gallagher.

He winked at Lazarus.

'When you take him out, will you cuff him with his hands in front. It will make a better photo, Sergeant.'

Lazarus smiled, despite himself.

He couldn't help liking Gallagher. Lazarus thought he was the polar opposite of that little shit Sullivan.

'I just popped my head in to say hello,' Gallagher said. 'I can't stay. I have another job.'

He looked pointedly at Sullivan.

'With a real reporter.'

Sullivan laughed.

'It's a pity,' Gallagher said.

'I would have like to have stayed. Personally, I'll give Sullivan 30 seconds before he is on the floor crying.'

Sullivan feigned outrage.

'With enemies like you, who needs friends?' he joked.

'See you around, Sergeant,' Gallagher said.

He smiled and walked out. As he was leaving, a small woman stormed in.

She was around 40 and heavy. She hid her shape under a baggy green jumper and loose blue jeans. Her face was round and she wore the expression of an always busy executive. She had straight chestnut hair which she wore in a fringe. She was small, maybe five foot four.

She had her head turned to the door as she walked, talking back to a younger man just outside.

'There is no fucking way I am putting Jason Rees-Mogg on the front page. It's not happening,' she said.

'Jacob,' the man said.

'What?'

'Jacob Rees-Mogg. Not Jason.'

She dismissed him with a wave of her hand.

'I don't give a shiny shite what his name is. Neither he nor Brexit will sell a single paper for us. Unless and until the Brits invade us again, it will never be a splash. Find something else. Now.'

She slammed the door in his face.

'What a day,' she sighed. 'I'm knackered.'

'Madame News Editor,' Bell said with a bow.

She threw her head back and laughed.

'You posh boys crack me up,' she said.

Then she saw Lazarus.

Her eyes widened.

She looked him up and down.

She smiled, extended her hand.

'*Hola guapo*,' she said. 'Ciara Farrell. Head of News.'

Lazarus felt his face flush, but he stood and shook her hand.

'Detective Sergeant John Lazarus,' he said.

Farrell smiled again.

'You can't be a cop. Cops are ugly big bastards from down the country.'

She winked.

'You're definitely not from the country.'

She held his hand for a long moment.

'What's a girl gotta do to get you to arrest her?' she said.

'I'll confess to anything.'

Lazarus withdrew his hand.

'That's a lovely suit,' Farrell said, giving him another appreciative look.

'What is it? Italian?'

'Yes,' Lazarus said.

The suit was a light brown two-piece. Pure wool. He wore it with brogues and a light blue shirt. No tie, top two buttons on the shirt open, exposing his bare olive skin.

'What does it look like on the floor?'

Bell laughed then immediately put a fist to his mouth to stifle it.

A silence descended on the room. Lazarus decided to let it play out. Farrell kept her appraising eyes on him, but she broke after a few seconds.

She walked to the free seat.

'Okay,' she said.

'Let's get this over with. What shit have you got us into now, Sullivan?'

Sullivan laughed, but was embarrassed.

Lazarus coughed to clear his throat, then turned to Sullivan.

'Mr Sullivan.'

'Call me Conor,' Sullivan said. 'Can I get you coffee?'

'No thanks.'

'Tea?'

'No.'

Sullivan looked to Bell and rolled his eyes.

175

Lazarus opened the manila folder.

'Mr Sullivan, I have been sent here over stories in *The Globe* newspaper in relation to two separate Garda inquiries into…'

'No comment,' Sullivan said.

Lazarus looked up.

'I haven't asked anything yet.'

Sullivan kept his eyes on the table.

'No comment.'

Lazarus stared at him for a few seconds, then turned back to the questions he had already prepared.

'These stories quote sources, claiming to have information on the arrest of Sean Maloney, and about a serious sexual assault in Griffith Park.'

'No comment.'

'Where did you get your information?'

'No comment.'

'Did a serving garda give you information?'

'No comment.'

'Did you pay a serving garda for any information for your stories?'

'No comment.'

'How did you know Sean Maloney was being arrested?'

'No comment.'

'You were there before we arrived.'

'No comment.'

'Did you tip off Sean Maloney that we were there? Someone did…'

'No comment.'

'Is Maloney paying you for information?'

'No comment.'

'Your information about the Griffith Park attack must have come from a garda, only a handful of members had those details.'

'No comment.'

'You were there less than an hour after it was reported. How did you know so quickly?'

'No comment.'

'How did you know she had been strangled?'

'No comment.'

'You have included information that could prove not only damaging to the Garda investigation, but may also prejudice any trial.'

'No comment.'

Sullivan folded his arms, stared at the table.

'How did you know the victim in Griffith Park was found half-naked? That was kept very tight. Did you even consider the victim before you included that in your article?'

Bell butted in.

'Sergeant, my client has told you he does not wish to comment. If you keep asking questions, I fear we are facing a situation where such questioning will be seen as oppressive.'

'I have been directed to put these questions to Mr Sullivan,' Lazarus said.

'Journalists have a right to protect their sources,' Bell said. 'That's what Mr Sullivan is doing. He is not willing to answer any questions. He has made that clear.'

Lazarus knew the meeting was over. There was no point him asking any more questions. It had gone exactly as he thought it would.

Sullivan smirked at him. Lazarus eyeballed him back.

The confrontation lasted 30 seconds. Neither man flinched.

But Bell did.

'I think that concludes matters, Sergeant?'

Lazarus looked down at the folder, took a sheet from it.

'I need you to sign this memo,' he told Sullivan.

'It says I asked you questions and you refused to comment.'

Lazarus had prepared it earlier. He knew what Sullivan was going to say.

'My client won't be signing anything,' Bell said.

Lazarus shrugged his shoulders. He placed the paperwork back in the folder, closed it over and put it back in his briefcase.

He looked hard at Sullivan.

'Do you not think you're damaging the Griffith Park inquiry? You're letting the attacker know what we know? Could you not step back from this? We have to find this guy. Your article was close to the bone.'

It smarted with Lazarus that Sullivan knew about Delaney's state of dress before he did.

'No comment,' Sullivan said.

'The interview is over,' Lazarus said.

'No comment.'

Lazarus shook his head.

'We're done.'

'No comment.'

'*Porca Miseria*,' Lazarus muttered.

His angry self was his Italian self.

He stood up.

'I have to see you out, Detective Sergeant,' Sullivan said.

'I'm not a child,' Lazarus snapped.

'It's health and safety.' Sullivan said.

They walked out together. Lazarus huffed the whole way.

When they were a few metres from the exit, Sullivan tried his line, a line Lazarus new was coming.

'Sorry about that,' he said. 'I have to protect my sources.'

Lazarus didn't reply.

They were at the security desk now.

'You know now I'm not going to spill on my informants,' Sullivan said. 'I'd rather go to jail. Maybe we could go for a coffee some time?'

He stopped and looked in Lazarus's eyes.

'I guarantee I'll protect you.'

Lazarus snorted, walked to the exit.

He turned back to Sullivan.

'No comment,' he said.

And then he stepped out into the busy Dublin evening.

26

Winter was outside in the Camry. They had a few hours until their next job and went for food in a bar close to Trinity College.

It was busy, but they got a table in a corner. The ceiling was low and the décor was old world Irish. Lazarus was on duty, but really wanted a beer, so he picked a Moretti Zero.

Winter ordered Irish Stew, with a thick dollop of mashed potato on top. Lazarus went for the burger and chips.

Lazarus filled her in on Sullivan's interview as they ate. She laughed when he told her of the reporter's effort to recruit him.

'He was ballsy enough to try,' Lazarus said.

Winter turned the conversation to Darcy, Anne Delaney's ex.

'He's a bad boy,' she said, as she speared a chunk of lamb.

'I did a search of social media. He's on Twitter, Snapchat, Instagram and Facebook. He makes a lot of jokes about women. Fancies himself, too. Has loads of selfies, you know those ones where you're taking a photo in the mirror so you can show off your body.'

She chewed the meat.

'He has been posting about how he is having no luck with women. He has posted drunk a few times, even mentioned Anne. He calls her a bitch. Accused her of leading him on.'

The burger was halfway to Lazarus's mouth.

'Does he fit the profile?' he asked.

Winter nodded.

'Definitely. He is in good shape, is the right size and is 28. He has a few photographs of him in sports gear. Playing football, running, that sort of thing.'

Lazarus's eyes tightened.

'Can you see the runners he has on?'

'Yes,' Winter said.

'They are dark Nike.'

'Just like the runners in the video,' Lazarus said.

'That doesn't mean much, though, by itself,' Winter said.

'Half the country has Nike runners.'

Lazarus nodded.

'Yeah, but he also fits the physique of the attacker. And he was hassling Anne before the attack. I'm going to talk to Fallon about him,' he said.

They finished their meal and went back to the station. Lazarus wrote a report on his meeting with Sullivan and emailed it to Fallon. He would talk to her face to face about Darcy. Winter did more checking on him. She printed out the abusive posts about women, including Anne.

Both tasks took them up to 9pm, and Lazarus decided it was the right time for their last job. They left Broadstone in the Camry. Lazarus drove around for more than an hour, visiting several parts of the city without success.

It was not until 10.20pm that they got lucky.

Lazarus had reached Mespil Road, south of the city centre, and was feeling glum over his failure to find any working women. Most of them plied their trade online, but there were still some who walked the streets. He just couldn't find them.

Suddenly as they turned a corner, Winter shouted.

'Lazarus, there!'

She pointed to a woman who had emerged into the light of a streetlamp. Lazarus drove past her, then pulled in.

'I'll do the talking,' Winter said as they got out.

'You sure?' Lazarus was conscious Winter was still new.

She nodded.

'I need to get to know them.'

Lazarus recognised the woman as he approached her. She was called Jackie Lynch. She was stick thin. Her face was heavily wrinkled and her nose was flat from a beating by a punter or a pimp. Her long white hair was tied back and had a nicotine-stained fringe. She wore large silver hoop earrings, a brown jumper and a blue denim micro skirt. Her legs were blue from the cold.

She was 25, her face and body were that of someone twice her age.

'Busy tonight?' Winter asked.

'Wasn't too bad until you came along. They'll vanish now.'

'This is important. Where are the others?' Winter asked.

Lynch folded her arms. Lazarus saw scars on both forearms. He saw more scarring on her throat. Lynch had started injecting heroin into her system there.

Jackie turned around and let out a shout. There was no response at first. But then Lazarus noticed movement. One by one, women emerged from the shadows. One looked so small Lazarus thought she was a child. She had auburn curly hair, was flat chested and wore the clothes of a teenager; white plimsolls, runners, a sweatshirt. Another wore a red crop top and black leggings that stopped halfway down her calves. Then there was another woman; mid forties, with large breasts that sagged down low under a red jumper. She had long pink hair and wore black tracksuit bottoms.

'Make it snappy,' Jackie said. 'We're losing money every minute.'

Winter waited until they had formed a semi-circle around her. None of them looked happy to see them.

'We are investigating a serious assault over in Drumcondra,' she said. 'You may have seen it on the news.'

Griffith Park was around four miles away on the other side of the river. Many of the women facing her were from the north inner city and would know it.

'I read about that in the paper,' the woman with the pink hair said.

'You'll investigate a rape on some girl up from the country, but you won't when it fucken happens to us. These fuckers batter us all the time and you do fuck all about it.'

Winter spread her arms.

'I've investigated attacks on workers and I have got the men who did it jailed. Anything happens, come to me and I'll go after them.'

Winter addressed them all.

'We need to find the man who did it. Before he does it to one of you, or me, or any other woman.'

The girls just stared at her.

She tried again. 'We suspect he may have been with some girls on the street. We are wondering if there have been any punters in recent weeks who have used violence.'

'They all use violence! Every fucken night!'

It was the woman who looked like a teenager. Her arms were folded over her tiny chest and she was shivering. None of them was wearing coats. They needed to show themselves off to the buyers.

Lazarus recognised her now. Her name was Lucy Fowler. She was from a flats complex in the city centre. She was 22, but already had old eyes and an old face. She was an addict. She ended up on the streets when she was 15 and soon started selling the only thing she had to score the drugs.

'If anyone is violent towards you, report it to us and we will go after them,' Winter said.

'You have the same rights as anyone else.'

Fowler shook her head and tapped her foot angrily.

'Just keep an eye out for anyone out of the ordinary,' Winter said. 'Any punters who are violent. They might even be regulars. We're here 24/7. You all know where we are. Come to us if you want to talk. It will be in confidence, I assure you all of that.'

There was no reaction.

'Let's go, Rachel,' Lazarus said after a moment.

He walked towards their car.

The crowd dispersed to their spots. As Lazarus got to the Camry, he looked back at them. Lucy Fowler was staring at him and Winter. The distance between them made her look even more childlike.

The detectives sat into their car.

Instead of going straight back to the station, they decided on a detour. Lazarus wanted to check up on the Casey family. He drove through town. It was quiet.

They reached the Caseys' just after 11.15pm. Winter put her hand on her pistol and scoured the street as Lazarus dropped down into second and drove along the road.

'Clear,' she said and relaxed.

Lazarus nodded, drove to the end of the cul-de-sac and performed a U-turn.

As they came back past the Casey house, Lazarus saw Joanne, Sarah's mother, emerge into the doorway. She was framed by the light in the hall.

'Talk about making yourself an easy target,' Winter said.

Lazarus stopped the car. They walked to the house.

'Hello Joanne,' Winter said. 'Just checking in.'

It was the second time Winter had met her. The first was when Joanne hurried home from work after the family home was shot up.

Lazarus saw worry etched on her face.

She ushered Lazarus and Winter into the living room. Lazarus looked up at the back wall. It was pristine. No damage visible. They all sat down.

'Is Sarah in?' he asked.

'She's in bed,' Joanne said.

'Has been studying all night. She wants to do well in her exams.'

'How is she?' Winter asked.

'She's been in brutal form for the last week. I don't know what to do with her, Ms Winter.'

Joanne was in her mid fifties. She wore a pink jumper, stonewashed jeans, black ankle boots. The jeans accentuated her thin legs. She had a tired face, with long auburn hair that reached her shoulders.

'Is Mick about?' Lazarus asked.

Joanne shook her head.

'He's down at the pub,' she said.

She looked down at the floor.

'It's hard for him. He dotes on Sarah. He has hopes for her future. She's very bright. He can't cope with what has happened to her. She didn't deserve it.'

'I know this is hard for you,' Lazarus said. 'But you are doing a wonderful job.'

Joanne shook her head.

'You don't know the half of it.'

She took a scrunched-up tissue from the sleeve of her jumper and blew her nose.

'I walked into her room last night. It was a few hours after the, you know…'

She couldn't bring herself to acknowledge her house had been attacked.

'Sarah was self-harming. She had a razor blade and was cutting her arms.'

She started crying.

They sat still for a long time, Joanne's sobbing the only sound in the room.

'I'm sorry,' she said finally.

She blew her nose again, got up and walked to the window.

'She has started disappearing in the evenings, too. She goes out for these walks in the dark. By herself. She just vanishes for a few hours. We ask where she has been and she just says she was out.'

She folded her arms, looked at the cops with sadness and anger in her eyes.

'We made a mistake going to youse,' she said.

'Mick was right. I realise that now. We should have dealt with this in our own way. It's a fucken disaster.'

She waved a hand around the room.

'This wouldn't have happened if we did. People wouldn't be fucken laughing at us in the street. That bastard Maloney would have had his comeuppance years ago for what he did to Sarah. And she would have been able to get on with her life. This case is killing her.'

She shook her head.

'I thought I was doing the right thing bringing her to the station that day, I really did. I thought I was teaching Sarah that there was a different way. That people like us could trust the system to get justice. But fuck was I wrong. There'll be no justice for Sarah in this now. No matter what happens in court. O'Hara and his bastards have made her name muck around here. Little bastards call her a slut when she's walking to school. One fella filmed himself asking her for a ride and put it up on Snapchat. It went around the place like wildfire. Rob heard about it and beat the bollix out of him. I'm glad he did. There's only one language these bastards understand.'

She stared at Lazarus.

'We trusted you people. But enough is enough. We're not taking any more shite. From anybody.'

And Lazarus suddenly had a feeling that a bad situation was going to get even worse.

27

Wednesday

Lazarus tensed when he heard the first shout.

He tightened his grip on the steering wheel. His eyes darted to the rear-view mirror.

'*Ragazzi!*'

There was a moment's silence, then Giovanni Junior began to cry. His cheeks were red. Lazarus looked over at Pietro, who like his brother, sat on a booster seat in the back of the Giulia.

'What's going on?' he shouted.

'It's his fault,' the boys shouted, each pointing a finger at the other.

'He hit me,' Giovanni Junior wailed.

'He said I was smelly,' Pietro shouted

'You are smelly!'

'*Basta!*' Lazarus shouted. *Enough.*

The boys went quiet, but glared at each other. Lazarus shook his head and looked at the clock. Just before 9am. He needed to be quick. Jenna was meeting friends – escaping the nut house, she called it – and Lazarus was dropping the boys to his brother Massimo. School was off today. Half-term.

He pulled up to Massimo's apartment complex five minutes later. Massimo lived in Ballsbridge, south of the Liffey. The restaurant business he inherited from their father was doing well. The apartment was in a gated complex, with CCTV cameras and an electronic access system. Lazarus knew the code and punched it into the keypad. The heavy iron gates glided open and he drove into a courtyard. It was surrounded by four apartment blocks. Massimo had two allocated parking spaces, one for him, the other for visitors. It was usually occupied. He was a popular man. Lazarus drove into the free space. It was beside Massimo's car, a black 18 reg BMW. Lazarus admired it as he got the kids out of the Giulia.

The boys scampered to the entrance door of one of the blocks. Lazarus heard a buzz and the door opened as the boys reached it. They ran inside. Lazarus waved at the video camera above the door. Massimo was watching.

They got into a lift with a deep-pile carpet and floor to ceiling mirrors. The boys fought to press the button. Giovanni Junior won. They were wearing the same clothes, something their mother insisted on. It drove Lazarus crazy, but Jenna thought it was cute. Blue runners, brown cords, a dark blue T-shirt and a white long-sleeved vest underneath.

The lift opened on the top floor and the boys scampered out. Massimo was waiting for them. They ran to him and he grabbed them in a bear-hug. They hugged his thighs and giggled as he tickled them.

'How's my two favourite boys?' he shouted.

Lazarus got to the door and Massimo let go of the boys, ushered them inside. Then he embraced Lazarus. They kissed each other on both cheeks.

'*Fratellino, ciao,*' Massimo said.

Massimo always called Lazarus little brother, even though he towered over him by four inches. He supposed he would always be the kid brother.

'How's Ireland's best-looking cop?' Massimo asked as they separated.

'I'll ask him when I find him,' Lazarus said. 'But anyone would be hand-some beside you.'

Massimo was far from good-looking. He stood five foot nine. He was heavyset, with broad shoulders and thick legs. He had black curly hair. He had a fat face and a stubby nose, a wide mouth and brown sparkling eyes. He hadn't shaved. He wore a black dressing gown, open at the front, exposing blue and white striped boxer shorts and a grey T-shirt. The T-shirt fought a losing battle to hide his belly.

'Cover yourself up, man,' Lazarus said. 'It's too early in the morning for that.'

Massimo threw his head back and laughed.

'The ladies love it. Gives them something to hold on to.'

Massimo had always been a hit with women; Lazarus less so. Even though he was taller and thinner and more appealing on the eye, Lazarus never quite possessed Massimo's charm. Women fell for his humour and chat up lines, regardless of his physique. At 43, he was still single. Still chasing women. Still succeeding. Lazarus suspected his conquests in recent years owed more to his wallet than his patter. He was a millionaire. He had added four restaurants to the three his father left him. The chain was called *Il Vecchio Mulino*, the old mill. He was planning franchises all over the country.

They walked into the apartment. It was massive. The lounge had a marble floor covered by an expensive Venetian rug. Two three-seater black leather sofas and a Lazy Boy recliner filled the room.

'No special visitors last night?' Lazarus asked.

Massimo grinned.

'Been and gone, *fratellino*, been and gone. I didn't want her here when you arrived. You would only get depressed.'

Then, conscious of the kids nearby, he mouthed the word *hot* and winked at Lazarus.

Lazarus ignored him. He was happy with his lot. The idea of clubbing and chasing skirt every night no longer appealed to him.

'So what's the plan for today?' Lazarus said.

Massimo yawned, stretched.

'I'm planning to take my two fantastic nephews bowling.'

He turned to the boys,

'What do you think, *ragazzi*?'

Giovanni Junior and Pietro cheered and put their arms in the air.

'That's a yes, then,' Massimo laughed. 'We'll go for breakfast in town and then head to the bowling alley.'

'Cool,' Lazarus said. 'Gotta scoot. Jenna will pick them up around 4pm. *Va bene?*'

'*Va bene,*' Massimo smiled. Okay.

Lazarus high-fived the boys, told them to behave and walked to the door.

'Hey, Giovanni, one second,' Massimo said.

'What?' Lazarus said, warily.

Massimo only called him Giovanni when he was being serious.

'*Papa,*' Massimo said.

Lazarus felt his heart sink.

'What about him? Is he ill?' Lazarus said.

'No, he's fine. But you know…maybe you could try again? He's your father…'

'He hasn't spoken to me in years,' Lazarus said. 'I've tried and tried again. He has made up his mind. He blames me. There's nothing I can do.'

After the deaths of his wife and only daughter, their father Giacomo had moved back to Italy. He could not bear to be in Ireland where he had lost them. The night before he left, Lazarus asked him, one last time, to stay.

The father exploded in pent-up anger.

'*Colpa tua,*' his father said.

"This is your fault."

Lazarus was stunned.

'Why did you not pick up Gabriella that night? Why did you leave her by herself?' the father asked him.

Lazarus tried, again, to explain he was on a job at the time and could not just leave the station. His father waved his explanation away.

'You could have saved her. You're a cop. You were her brother. You were supposed to protect her. And now your mamma is gone, too.'

Lazarus stormed out and never spoke to his father again. He and Jenna had years earlier bought the family homestead in Schio, north of Venice, so the father purchased a small house in a village called Torrebelvicino, about five miles to the west.

Lazarus spent months trying to contact his father, but he never took his call. Eventually, Lazarus stopped. He still holidayed in Schio and occasionally drove to Torrebelvicino.

But he never knocked at his father's door. He knew there was no point.

Instead, he watched him from a distance as he walked around the village, oblivious to the damaged son observing him.

Masimo slapped Lazarus softly on the face.

'He's your father,' he said again.

'And I'm his son,' Lazarus snapped.

'Come on,' Massimo protested.

'No,' Lazarus said. 'I've tried. I'm tired of trying.'

He looked down at the ground.

'It wasn't my fault.'

Massimo cupped Lazarus's face in his hands.

'I know, Giovanni. I know. But, please, try again. For me. Life is short.'

Lazarus gripped Massimo's hands and took them from his face.

'Basta.' Enough.

Then, with tears in his eyes, he turned and left the apartment.

28

Cochrane stood beside Lazarus and stared through a window into the room.

Lazarus gripped his Juventus cup and could smell the aroma of the Americano inside. Cochrane, who had landed in Broadstone 20 minutes earlier, gripped her vape pen. Its mouthpiece was gnarled with bite marks.

They were in the intensive care unit of the Mater Hospital just after 10.45am. Anne Delaney was on the other side of the glass. Nothing had changed since Lazarus saw her on Monday, two hours after she was found.

She was on her back, in a white hospital gown. Her arms were by her side, outside the bedsheet. She was connected to a bank of monitors. The ventilator was breathing for her. The bruises on her face and arms had gone from red to purple. The bandage around her forehead had been changed.

'Is this poor wee girl fucked?' Cochrane said.

'She looks fucked to me.'

'They think maybe brain damage,' Lazarus said.

'They're doing another scan today.'

Cochrane bit down on the vape pen.

'Are the parents going to have to make a decision?'

'Perhaps,' Lazarus said.

The victim's parents had mounted a bedside vigil since Monday morning. Lazarus had waited until they left to get breakfast before he brought Cochrane over today. He preferred to leave family to the liaison officer. His job was not to comfort the parents, it was to catch the victim's attacker.

The doctors had briefed Lazarus and Cochrane. Delaney had suffered a fractured skull. But the worst damage was caused by the strangulation. He had tried to kill her, and she was lucky to have survived. He kept going until he thought she was dead. Although she was alive, the lack of oxygen to the brain may have caused damage. Doctors were trying to establish if

189

there was enough brain activity for her to breath by herself. If there wasn't, the parents would have to take the decision to turn off life support.

'Tough choice,' Cochrane said.

'We've seen enough,' Lazarus said. 'Let's get back to the station. We're useless here.'

They walked out of ICU and took a lift to the ground floor. It was busy. A middle-aged man sobbed in a corner. A woman held him.

'You were supposed to meet me at ten,' Lazarus said.

Cochrane flushed.

'Something came up,' she said.

'Anything I need to know about?'

'No, no, no.'

Cochrane looked away.

Lazarus glared at her.

'If you're doing something on this case, I want to know.'

Cochrane held her hands up.

'I wasn't. I promise.'

They walked outside in silence.

They crossed the road and walked back towards Broadstone. Lazarus had wanted Cochrane to see Delaney, but they needed to get back to the incident room. Flannery had promised an update on the DNA profile.

Lazarus filled Cochrane in on the events of last night at the Casey house as they walked. She grimaced when he told her Sarah had started cutting herself and walking alone at night.

'I remember dealing with a girl around the same age a few years ago,' she said.

'She was about 18, I think she'd be about 25 now.'

A long-distance look appeared on her face.

'She was raped by her eldest brother from the age of seven until she was 12. Then the middle brother decided he wanted a go. Her mother was dead, and she later confided in her father. He raped her too'

'Christ,' Lazarus said.

'She finally told a friend, who came to us,' Cochrane said.

'We got her out and all three of them were locked up. Ten years for the old man, eight for each of the boys. She was put in care, but started to wander off at night. Uniforms would find her and bring her back to the foster home. We thought she was unhappy there.'

They were on Western Way now, a few metres from the station entrance. Cochrane stopped suddenly. She looked at Lazarus.

'It turned out she just liked walking the streets at night. I asked her why. She told me she had already been through everything and what was the worst that could happen? Be dragged down an alleyway and raped? Her own family did that to her. She went out walking to show she was afraid of no man.'

They walked through the entrance into Broadstone station's public office. It was a small room, with benches around the side. It was painted white and had two noticeboards on the walls, with witness appeals over unsolved murders and missing persons' cases. There were also posters for the Samaritans, Alcoholics' Anonymous and a homeless shelter.

Lazarus went to a door beside the counter. He keyed the code in a pad beside it. The lock clicked. He opened the door, held it for Cochrane, and they walked upstairs to the incident room.

McEvoy and Winter were at their desks. There was no sign of Flannery. Lazarus was about to call the scenes of crime officer on his mobile when McEvoy interrupted him.

'You need to see something, Lazarus,' he said.

He tapped on the keyboard of his computer. The flat screen TV on the wall lit up.

'I don't like the sound of this,' Lazarus said.

'Fucking right, *amigo*.'

McEvoy hit another key and the screen filled with CCTV footage.

It was from an inner city Dublin pub. The camera was behind the counter, looking out onto the bar. The bar was mock 1940s, with a wooden counter and old-fashioned beer pumps.

It was almost empty. High tables and chairs dotted the room. The walls had been pared back to their original brickwork and were covered in framed posters. One was of the Dublin GAA squad, another was of the Irish football team. Lazarus also saw one for U2's original Joshua Tree tour in the 1980s and another print of central Dublin from the air.

Danny O'Hara sat on a highchair at a table on the left. He faced the camera and had his arms folded over his chest. Two men were with him. Spence and Armstrong, the kid with the expensive watch.

O'Hara and Spence were drinking Guinness, Armstrong had chosen some long-necked beer. Lazarus checked the clock on the screen. It said 11.23pm. That was around the same time he and Winter were at the Casey house.

He remembered Joanne telling him Mick was at the pub. And then he knew what was coming.

191

He saw movement on the screen. Five men, masked and carrying base-ball bats, burst into the pub. They barrelled past a few punters and ran towards O'Hara and his men.

O'Hara reacted first.

He jumped down and threw his glass at the attackers.

It slammed into one of them. The man hit the deck. O'Hara grabbed more glasses and threw them at two more men who were just feet from him. Both missed. Spence and Armstrong jumped from their chairs and turned to face the gang, just as the attackers lit on them. Four landed quick blows of the baseball bats on their heads. Then, when Spence and Armstrong faltered from the initial hit, they slowed down and used longer swings. They brought the bats up over their shoulders in a two-handed grip and slammed the wood hard down on them, again and again and again. The onslaught continued as Spence and Armstrong lay defenceless on the ground.

'Jesus,' Lazarus said.

Just then, one of the attackers peeled off and turned towards O'Hara.

Lazarus recognised him, even with a mask. His physique gave it away.

'Mick Casey,' he said.

'Watch this,' McEvoy said.

Mick took a pistol from his coat. He gripped the weapon in both hands. He was just over a metre from O'Hara. He couldn't miss.

He brought the gun up, aimed it his nemesis.

Lazarus saw him pull the trigger.

And nothing happened.

'It jammed,' McEvoy said.

'How lucky was that bastard?'

O'Hara saw his chance. He swung a desperate punch. Mick ducked and the haymaker flew over his head. O'Hara didn't hang around. He turned and ran.

Mick tried to free the blockage in the pistol.

But he realised the chance was gone and signalled to the others. They rushed out, leaving Spence and Armstrong unconscious on the floor.

'Lucky boy,' McEvoy said.

He ended the video.

'The owner called 999 and a car got to the scene in three minutes, but they were gone. The incident lasts 46 seconds. No messing.'

'How badly injured are the other two?' Lazarus asked.

McEvoy sat back and clasped his hands behind his head.

'They're grand. They took a bit of a battering, but walked to the ambulances. Scrotes like them have thick skulls. If that had been me or you, we'd be fucked.'

'I am guessing O'Hara declined to cooperate.' Lazarus aid to said.

'Yup,' McEvoy said.

'Told the uniforms to fuck off. Refused to make a complaint. One of the lads heard him tell the owner to say fuck all and he'd pay for the damage. I'd say he'll do his own clean up in a few days. If I was Mick Casey, I'd emigrate. He had one chance and he missed. The dickhead.'

'This is all we need,' Lazarus groaned.

He heard movement behind him. He looked around and saw Flannery. He held a file and Lazarus knew it was what he had been waiting for.

'I may as well come to the point,' Flannery said.

'The DNA doesn't match anyone on the Irish database.'

'Ah shite,' Cochrane said.

Lazarus felt the atmosphere turn heavy. He closed his eyes and rubbed his face.

'It's not the end of the world,' he said.

'A match on the database would have been great, but we'll just have to keep going.'

The national DNA database had been up and running for three years. The last Lazarus heard, it contained samples from more than 15,000 people.

He turned to Cochrane.

'Does this mean we can rule out every convicted sex offender?'

Cochrane flushed.

Lazarus frowned.

'What are you not telling us?'

She bit the mouthpiece of her vaping pen.

'The database is run by a unit in Garda HQ,' she said.

'They collate all the samples and upload them onto the system. But there have been a few teething problems and some samples have gone missing.'

Lazarus's eyes narrowed.

'Some?'

Cochrane's shoulders sagged.

'About 1,500.'

'Jesus Christ,' McEvoy shouted.

Cochrane held her hands up.

'You know management. They set up the unit without the proper resources or training. It's shite.'

'Job's fucked,' McEvoy grumbled.

'What does it mean for us?' Lazarus asked.

'Do we have to find every one of the 1,500?'

Cochrane shook her head.

'No. Remember I told you yesterday the number of offenders who would do something like this is very small? The good news is the vast bulk of them are already on the database.'

She opened her case and took out a sheaf of papers.

'I have worked on the list of 15 I mentioned to you before,' she said. 'All but three of the men I picked are on the DNA database.'

Lazarus thought back to yesterday.

'What about Martin Glennon?'

Cochrane grimaced.

'He's in the clear. Unfortunately.'

'Where are the other three?'

'No idea,' Cochrane said.

'They are in the wind. They failed to sign on the register and went to ground. My bet is they have left the country.'

'How many of the 1,500 will we have to trace?' Lazarus asked.

Cochrane bit her lip.

'Most of them are abusers who targeted people they know. Grandfathers, fathers, uncles, cousins, that sort of thing. I'll draw up a list of those who match the age profile and have any convictions for violence. You're talking about 20. We'll have to go through them all, find them and get their DNA. I can also talk to Interpol and see if they can help us track down the missing three.'

She sucked on her vaping pen.

'I thought it was one of the 15 on my list. There aren't too many men known for this type of attack. I think our pal is one of two things. He is either someone who has carried out previous attacks and hasn't been caught.'

'Or?' Lazarus asked.

'Or she knew him,' Cochrane said.

'Jamie Darcy,' Winter said.

Lazarus knew Fallon would have to allow the team to go after Delaney's ex now.

Flannery coughed.

'Is there something you're not telling us, Ben?' Lazarus asked.

Flannery was a typical techie. Slightly odd, more at home dealing with computers and machines than with people.

Flannery smiled.

'You didn't let me finish,' he said.

He stepped over to his desk.

'We have access to other European countries' DNA databases. I sent out a request yesterday evening. We just got a hit.'

Lazarus felt his mouth go dry.

'Where? When?'

'Holland,' Flannery said.

He looked at his notes.

'On January 29, 2016, a woman was raped in Scheveningen, in The Hague, which is the capital. She was attacked as she walked through a park. She was grabbed from behind and dragged into the undergrowth. He held her by the neck in a chokehold as he was pulling her along with his other hand over his mouth. He got her into the wooded area and raped her, then strangled her and left her for dead.'

'Did he use a ligature?' Cochrane asked.

'No. He used his bare hands. Beat her about the head and face, too. The victim has no recollection of that, so the team over there think it was while she was unconscious. All she remembers is he was dressed in dark clothing and had a scarf over his face. He didn't speak the whole time.'

'How did they get his DNA?' Lazarus asked.

'He didn't use a condom.'

'Did they ever get him?' Lazarus asked.

Flannery shook his head.

'No. The Dutch ran the DNA through the system, but there was no match. They have tens of thousands of people on theirs. He has never been caught.'

Lazarus looked at Cochrane.

'What do you think?'

'I wouldn't be surprised if he has struck in other countries that Ben has not heard from yet,' she said.

'Some countries are faster than others,' Flannery conceded.

'Could he be foreign?' Lazarus asked.

'I'd bet my next pay cheque he's Irish,' Cochrane said.

'He used a condom in the Dublin attack, but not in Holland. That tells me he was more careful here than there. And that would indicate he's local. I've been to Scheveningen. It's a tourist area. Griffith Park is not. Our man had local knowledge. He didn't speak during the Dutch attack. I think he didn't want her to know he was foreign.'

She turned to Lazarus.

'We have a serial rapist on our hands. And the fucker is Irish.'

29

Winter scanned the house numbers as Lazarus drove along the quiet street.

'There,' she said, pointing at a red door.

Lazarus pulled into a space. They got out of the Camry and walked to the house, a 1940s semi-detached, red-brick, with a small front garden.

'We're early,' Lazarus said.

'It's 2pm,' Winter said.

'Exactly. He's probably still in bed.'

'Not all students were like you,' Winter said. 'Some of us did full days in college.'

'The fools,' Lazarus said.

'What did you study?' Winter asked.

'French and Italian. I did it part-time after I joined the Army. Scraped a two-one. No doubt you got a first,' Lazarus said.

Winter blushed. They were walking together towards the house.

'I did okay.'

'I'd say you studied law,' Lazarus guessed.

'No.'

'Women's Studies?'

'Fuck the fuck off.'

'Sociology?'

'Jesus, no. I did Journalism.'

'Journalism? I should get you to do my reports,' Lazarus said.

'I've read them. You need all the help you can get,' Winter said.

'Why did you not become a journalist? It has to be better than this,' Lazarus said.

Winter's eyes darkened.

'I had a best friend in college,' she said.

'Her father was a Protestant clergyman.'

Lazarus did not like where this was going.

'One night when he was alone with her, he raped her.'

They reached the house, started walking up the path.

'Just out of the blue,' Winter said. 'She was 17.'

'She confided to me in college a few years later. I went to her local station with her. I held her hand through the whole process. The garda who was dealing with it was brilliant. And I knew that's what I wanted to do. Finished my degree and joined. Best decision I ever made.'

'What did he get?' Lazarus asked.

'Ten years.'

'Good sentence.'

'She's living a life sentence,' Winter said.

They reached the door. Winter pressed the bell. She activated the recorder on her phone. Cops had started recording interactions with civvies for their own protection.

A man in his late twenties opened the door. He was about five foot ten, slim, with broad shoulders and a flat stomach. He wore his thick black hair to his collar. His face was long and unshaven. He had brown eyes and a pale complexion.

'All right?' he said with an easy confidence.

He had a mid-Atlantic accent.

'Jamie Darcy?' Lazarus said.

Darcy smiled at Winter.

'That's me. What's up?'

Lazarus badged him.

His smile vanished.

'Is this about Anne Delaney?'

'Can we come inside?' Winter said.

Darcy hesitated, then stood aside and let them in.

'The living room is through there,' he said, gesturing to the left. They were in a narrow hallway. There was a door to the right, which Lazarus guessed was a parlour turned into a bedroom. At the end of the hallway was another door, half open. He saw white kitchen units, an island and a wooden floor.

They went into the living room. It was sparsely furnished. Magnolia walls. A large mirror over a black fireplace. Sanded floorboards. A large flat-screen TV in the bay window. Lazarus noticed a DVD player, satellite receiver and Xbox console. A coffee table, a worn red sofa, two armchairs of the same colour.

Darcy took one of the armchairs. They sat on the sofa. He leaned forward and placed his elbows on his thighs. He clasped his hands together.

'Is this about Anne Delaney?' Darcy repeated.

'I saw it on the news. We know it's her.'

'Who's we?' Lazarus asked.

Darcy looked at Winter.

'All our friends. Students. Everyone is talking about it.'

He shook his head.

'Poor Anne.'

Lazarus looked to Winter and nodded.

'We need to caution you, Mr Darcy,' she said.

'Whaaaaaat?' Darcy said.

'Is this a fucking joke?'

'We have a few questions for you,' Lazarus said.

'You're not a suspect, but as a matter of routine we do have to caution anyone we talk to as part of the investigation.

Darcy's eyes widened. He went pale.

'Am I in in trouble here?'

'No, Mr Darcy, it's just routine. Honestly,' Lazarus said.

'We want to talk to you about your relationship with Ms Delaney. We're trying to build up as comprehensive picture of her life as we can. Your name came up. I'm sure you'd like to help us.'

'Jesus H,' Darcy said, panic in his voice.

'We're going to caution you, okay?' Winter said.

'We can ask our questions here, or if you prefer you can come with us to the station,' Lazarus said.

Lazarus winced. He sounded like a cop in a bad movie.

Darcy slumped back in the armchair.

'Go on, then. I've got nothing to hide.'

Winter read the caution.

'What's your date of birth?' Lazarus asked when she was done.

Darcy told them. He was 29 next month.

'Where are you from?'

'Cork.'

'Where in Cork?'

Darcy named a posh suburb.

'You don't have a Cork accent,' Lazarus said.

'You don't have an Irish name,' Darcy answered.

Lazarus blushed.

'I came up to Dublin when I was 18. You lose touch with home,' Darcy said.

'How do you know Anne Delaney?' Lazarus asked.

Darcy scratched his stubble.

'We dated for a while. Nothing serious. We broke up a few months ago.'

'How did it end?'

'I'm busy with my studies and have to go away next year. I don't have time for anything serious, so I thought it was best to, you know...anyways, we're both young. Plenty of time for serious shit later. She was fine about it. For a while.'

'She's much younger than you,' Lazarus said.

Darcy held his hands up.

'We're both adults. I was 27, she was 22. Nothing wrong with that. We were having fun.'

'How was your relationship with her afterwards?' Lazarus asked.

Darcy crossed his legs. He ran a hand through his thick hair.

'Look, man, we broke up. These things are never easy, especially when we have mutuals. We had a few rows, but I was hoping we could still be friends.'

'What sort of rows?'

'Just rows.'

'About what?'

'The break-up, I suppose.'

'Face to face?'

'She rang me a few times. Sent me a few messages. She wanted to try again. I said no. She didn't take it too well.'

'Did you ever message her?'

'Just to answer hers.'

Lazarus stood up and walked to the fireplace.

He glanced at the mirror, saw his own hard face.

He turned to Darcy.

'How did you message her?'

'Snapchat.'

'Those messages auto delete.'

Darcy said nothing.

'How was your relationship with Ms Delaney recently?'

Darcy fidgeted in the chair.

'There is no relationship, dude. It's over. I ended it. She couldn't accept that and sent me a few fucked up messages.'

'Like what?'

'Like, clingy. A bunny boiler, you know?'

Winter had been taking notes, but stopped. She exchanged a look with Lazarus.

'Did you send Ms Delaney any messages you might regret?' Lazarus asked.

'No,' Darcy snapped.

'We believe you did. We have been told you had been giving her a hard time, so much so that she blocked you.'

Darcy's face reddened.

'Is that bitch Orla Diffney causing shit again?'

Lazarus had his legs apart and his hands at his side.

Ready.

'Calm down, Mr Darcy,' he said quietly.

Darcy put a hand to his forehead.

'I fucking knew it was her. She has it in for me. She never liked me. She sent a letter of complaint to my professor. Tried to get me kicked out of my programme.'

Then, under his breath: 'Fucking bitch.'

'Where were you on Sunday evening?' Lazarus asked.

Darcy looked up.

'Do I need a lawyer, man?'

'Where were you between 10pm and midnight. It was only four nights ago.'

Blood had drained from Darcy's face. He was staring at the ground.

'I didn't attack Anne,' he murmured.

'Where were you?'

Darcy sighed again.

'I play five-a-side at DCU every Sunday from 5pm to 6pm,' he said.

Dublin City University had a complex on Collins Avenue, about two miles north of Griffith Park.

'What time did you leave?' Lazarus said.

'About 6.30. I went to the uni library. Left there at about nine, went for a few with the lads.'

'What pub?'

Darcy named it.

It was popular with students.

Lazarus glanced at Winter. She nodded subtly, wrote the name of the pub in her notebook. They might need to check its CCTV.

'What did you do after that?' Lazarus said.

'I came home. I had a meeting with my tutor the next morning, so I needed to prepare.'

Lazarus knew the route from the pub to the house, south of Botanic Avenue, took Darcy past Griffith Park.

'What time did you get home?'

'About 10.30pm'

'Who was with you?'

'Nobody.'

'How did you get home?'

'I walked.'

'Which way?'

'St. Mobhi Road.'

Lazarus pictured the map Flannery had shown them of the attack area. He knew St. Mobhi Road skirted the park.

'Did you walk home past Griffith Park?' he asked.

'It's on the way. Well, I mean, the top of it is on St. Mobhi Road. I had to.'

'Any other tenants here when you got home?'

'I don't know. I went straight to my room. I didn't see anyone.'

No alibi.

Lazarus examined him. He was wearing a black Free Palestine T-shirt, baggy pink shorts, flip flops.

'What runners do you have?' Lazarus said.

'Runners?' Darcy asked, puzzled.

'Let me ask the questions,' Lazarus said.

Darcy blushed.

'Eh, Nike.'

'What colour are they?'

'Why is that relevant?'

'If you don't mind, Mr Darcy, we just need to know.'

'They're black. Air Max. I bought them a few months ago.'

'Can we see them?' Lazarus said.

Darcy's eyes widened.

'Seriously man, am I in trouble here? Do I need a solicitor? I know my rights.'

He swallowed hard.

'You don't need a solicitor because you are not under arrest,' Lazarus said.

'You're a witness. You're helping us out. Can we please see your runners? If you don't want to let us see them, I'm sure we can make this more official. We could get a warrant...'

Darcy stood up.

'Fuck sake, man. I didn't attack Anne!'

'Relax, young fella,' Lazarus growled.

'Show us the runners.'

Darcy looked agitated as he considered his options.

Then he relaxed, as if he had come to a decision.

He smiled.

'Okay. That's no problem. They're upstairs in my room. I'll go and get them. Is that allowed?'

'It's your house,' Lazarus said.

He walked to the door, left it open as he walked out.

Lazarus turned to Winter.

'What do you think?' he whispered.

'Something dodgy about him. He looks nervous,' Winter said.

'And he's lying about the texts and his relationship with Anne. Now I have his DOB, I'll check him out on the system when we get back to the station. He might have previous.'

Lazarus rubbed his chin.

'He has no alibi for the time of the attack.'

'He places himself close to the park on the night as well,' Winter said.

'I'm beginning to have a feeling about him,' Lazarus said. 'He did lie about the messages to Anne. And he clearly hates Orla Diffney.'

Lazarus decided he would seize Darcy's runners if they were dirty and resembled the attacker's. It had been raining on the night of the attack and the rapist had left muddy footprints at the scene. Almost as good as fingerprints. That might just be enough to persuade Fallon to bring Darcy in for questioning and a DNA test.

Lazarus was mulling over the possibilities when he heard a violent thud upstairs.

He looked at Winter. He saw realisation in her eyes. He knew, too.

He started running. Winter sprang to her feet and followed. They were in the hall when Lazarus had an idea.

'The kitchen. Quick!' he shouted.

Winter veered off and ran to the half-open kitchen door. Lazarus took the stairs two at a time. His heart was in his mouth. He got to the landing in seconds.

He saw four identical doors, all white. He had to make a quick decision. He chose one on his right.

He opened it.

He scanned the room.

Nothing.

He ran back to the landing.

'Jamie! Where are you?' he shouted.

No answer.

He ran to another door.

He tried the handle.

It was locked.

Lazarus took a step back, then lunged forward and landed a kick just under the handle.

The lock was no match for him.

The frame splintered and the door burst open.

Lazarus raced inside.

He looked to his left and saw a desk, a MacBook Pro open on it. He looked right and saw a double bed with a patterned duvet. A white chair was on its side in front of the bed.

Then Lazarus saw feet dangling in the air.

He looked up and saw the rest of Jamie Darcy.

He was naked from the waist up and was hanging from a noose. It was tight around his neck and was looped over an oak roof beam. The noose was black and Lazarus knew Darcy made it from his T-shirt.

'Jamie!' he shouted.

He heard a gurgling noise.

Darcy thrashed and kicked his feet. His hands grabbed at the home-made noose as he fought for his life. His tongue was stuck out grotesquely and his face was purple.

Lazarus knew he had seconds left.

He ran to him, past the chair Darcy had used to reach the beam. He grabbed Darcy's swinging legs and brought them together. Then he pushed him up towards the ceiling to take the weight off his neck.

Winter appeared in the doorway, a large knife in her hand.

Her eyes were calm as she took in the scene. She ran forward, righted the chair and stood on it. She brought the knife up and started cutting the T-shirt. She cried out as she missed and cut her hand. Lazarus saw blood gushing from the wound, but still she persisted.

Lazarus was struggling with Darcy's dead weight now.

He felt himself falter.

But then he heard a cry from Winter as she cut through the T-shirt.

Darcy fell, brought Lazarus with him.

They crashed on to the carpet. Lazarus came face to face with him. Darcy's black tongue snaked out from his gaping mouth.

'Call 999,' he shouted to Winter.

He rolled Darcy on to his back and brought his mouth down hard on the student's. He pinched his nose and started pumping his own air into Darcy's lungs.

'Stay with us, Jamie, stay with us!' he shouted.

He gave him more mouth to mouth.

Winter stood up, breathing hard, and took out her phone.

Blood was pumping from her cut hand. She used the other to tap the screen.

There was second's delay as the 999 operator answered

'Ambulance!' she shouted as Lazarus did more mouth to mouth.

30

Thursday

Fallon rested her elbows on the desk and read Lazarus's report.

He sat across from her, Winter beside him. He gave her a wink of reassurance. It didn't work. She was a bag of nerves.

It was 9.30am, almost 20 hours after they knocked on Darcy's door. Lazarus still found it hard to fathom what had happened. His report explained the bald facts, but it could never convey the terror he felt as he battled to save him.

Fallon closed the report and looked up.

'How is the young buck now?'

'He'll survive,' Lazarus said. 'He has a bad injury to the neck, but no permanent damage. His parents are with him. They're admitting him to hospital. He has had ongoing mental health issues for the last few years, has been in hospital before.'

Fallon shrugged her shoulders.

Mental health was something cops were dealing with more and more. It affected every area of policing.

She looked back down at the report.

'Now,' Fallon said. 'Is he still a person of interest?'

'No,' Lazarus said.

'Another tenant was in the kitchen and saw him coming in at 10.40pm, before the attack. The door was open and he could see out to the hallway. He was cooking and stayed at the same spot until just before midnight. He would have seen him going out. He didn't. Darcy didn't notice him when he came in because he was looking at his phone and had his Beats on.'

'What about the runners?' she asked.

'I looked when it had all calmed down,' Lazarus said. 'The markings are totally different from the cast. These were circles. The cast was lines.'

'I don't think we need to ask him for DNA now, do you?' Fallon asked.

'No,' Lazarus said.

'If he is in the clear, his actions are even more peculiar,' Fallon said.

'Wonder why he did it?'

'It definitely wasn't anything to do with us,' Winter said quickly.

Fallon held her hands up.

'I'm not saying it was. Just… it's a bit strange how he reacted.'

'We did everything by the book,' Lazarus said.

'He panicked. Maybe he thought he was in trouble over his messages to Anne Delaney. Who knows?'

Just then, there was a knock on the door.

'In you come,' Fallon shouted.

Duffy walked in.

'Sorry to interrupt,' she said.

'A female has come to the public office and says she has information about Griffith Park. She wants to speak to Detective Sergeant Lazarus. I've put her in interview room two.'

Lazarus felt his pulse quicken.

A press release had been sent out earlier asking for the public's help. And Sullivan's stories, although infuriating, put the attack firmly on page one. Maybe someone had read them and decided to come forward.

'Go see what she has,' Fallon said.

Lazarus and Winter got up and left the office.

Lazarus felt adrenalin rush through him as he went down the stairs.

He opened the door of room two. It was small and sparsely furnished. The walls were painted a sober cream, the carpet was grey. A heavy brown desk sat against one wall. It had four chairs, two pairs facing each other. A red panic button was fitted to the wall and a large recording device sat on the edge of the desk.

Lazarus's eyes widened when he saw Lucy Fowler, one of the sex workers from Arbour Hill two nights earlier. She was hunched over the table, smoking a cigarette. She casually flicked the ash into a tinfoil ashtray.

'Hello Lucy,' Lazarus said.

He paused on the threshold with Winter, then they walked in and he closed the door. Lucy stared at him with pale green eyes that had already seen too much. Lazarus saw no light in them, no spark of youth, no hint of happiness. He was momentarily gripped with an unbearable sadness when he looked into those desperate eyes.

He cleared his throat and sat down with Winter opposite Lucy. He remembered thinking how she resembled a teenager when she came out of the shadows at Arbour Hill. He thought she looked even younger in the artificial light of the interview room. Her curly auburn hair was dirty and unkempt. Her skin was unhealthily pale, apart from a red blotch from the cold on each thin cheek.

Lazarus got up, went to the door and called Duffy back from the public office. He asked her to get Lucy a cup of sweet tea and whatever chocolate there was in the vending machine. He handed her five euro in coins and returned to his seat.

As he sat down, Lazarus noticed a cut over Lucy's left eyebrow. He also saw a scab on her chin. He wondered if they were from a punter or her pimp. Or maybe a dealer she owed money to. He knew she'd never tell.

Back at Arbour Hill, she had no overcoat on because she was selling herself, but today she wore an oversized blue padded jacket. There was a rip on the left elbow and the padding oozed from it like pus. The zip was broken and she held the jacket closed around her thin frame with a bony hand. The hand that held the cigarette was filthy and there was grime under her fingernails. The jacket was open from her bust up. She wore a dirt-stained red T-shirt. She was so thin her collarbone stood out against her grey skin.

Lazarus smiled at her.

'How's things?'

Lucy looked down at the table and took another drag on her smoke.

'All right, Mr Lazarus.'

'You want to talk about the attack on the woman in Griffith Park? Our colleague suggested you might have some information.'

Lucy was just about to say something when there was a knock on the door. Duffy walked in. She was carrying a cup of tea and two Snickers bars.

'That'll warm you up,' Lazarus smiled.

Duffy handed Lucy the chocolate and tea.

She opened the first Snickers and wolfed it down. Lazarus wondered when she had last eaten a proper meal.

'Yeah, it's fucken Baltic out there,' Lucy said with her mouth full.

The two cops shared a quick glance. Lazarus raised his eyebrows.

Winter took the hint.

She turned to Lucy.

'You were up at Arbour Hill the other day when John and I spoke to a few of the girls.'

'Yeah, I remember,' Lucy said.

She took a long drink of the hot tea and put the cup down on the table.

'I was thinking about what you said. You know, about other women being in danger. Then I read an article in the paper about the attack. I spent all day yesterday building up the courage to come in.'

She paused. Her mouth trembled.

'I didn't think you'd believe me.'

Winter sat forward.

'We'll never turn away anyone who wants to help.'

Lucy didn't answer. The room fell into silence.

'Take your time, Lucy,' Winter said.

'There's no problem. We're here to listen. We're not here to judge you.'

Lucy took a deep breath.

Then her eyes narrowed as she thought of something.

'Here, if I help youse and this fucker gets locked up, is there anything in it for me? The paper said there was some reward.'

Lazarus had been prepared for this.

A local anti-crime charity was offering a cash reward for information that helped bring Delaney's attacker to justice. It didn't say how much was on offer, it never did. But Lazarus knew from experience it could be as much as €10,000.

A life changing amount for someone like Lucy. Or enough to kill her.

'That's a long way down the road,' Winter said.

There were terms and conditions for all rewards and Lazarus wondered if the charity would be happy giving cash to a drug addicted sex worker. But that was not his problem. He nudged Winter under the table.

'Why don't you tell us what's on your mind and we'll take it from there?' she said.

Fowler nodded, then took a long drag of her cigarette. She exhaled and the smoke spread over the desk towards Lazarus and Winter. Lazarus stifled a cough.

She took another sip of the tea.

'There's this punter who has been with me a few times,' she said after a long moment.

'He pays me more for the ride, know what I mean? Most of them just want a blow job or for me to wank them off.'

She blushed, looked away.

'Sorry.'

Winter smiled a soft smile.

'We're all adults here, Lucy. John and I are people of the world.'

Lucy nodded.

'Ok. He pays me two hundred euro to go the whole way. He picks me up on the street and takes me somewhere quiet in his car. He ri..., we do it in the back of his car.'

'Okay,' Winter said. 'Do you know what kind of car it is?'

Lucy shook her head.

'It's a fuck-off black one. That's all I know. It's nice inside. Big, too.'

'Is it an estate? Or a jeep?' Winter asked.

'No,' Lucy said. 'It's an ordinary car, like a taxi, something like that.'

'Just a normal car,' Winter said.

'Yeah,' Lucy said.

'So what about him? Why have you come about him?' Winter said.

Lucy looked down at the ashtray.

'He has never done anything to me, in fairness,' she said finally.

'He's grand. Just a bit kinky, you know?'

'Kinky in what way?' Winter said.

'He likes it rough.'

'Does he hit you?'

'Jesus no. That's the mad thing. He doesn't hurt me at all. He just pretends to strangle me.'

Lazarus perked up.

'Strangle you?' Winter said.

'Yeah,' Fowler said.

'He, like, puts his hands around my throat. He says it makes him cum better.'

'Does he say anything when it's happening?'

Lucy grimaced. Her sad eyes became just a bit sadder.

'He shouts out that I'm a slut.'

Then she looked up quickly to defend her tormentor.

'He says he's sorry afterwards and says he doesn't mean it. I get that shit a lot, know what I mean?'

She looked down at the table.

Her voice became feeble.

'A lot of men call me a slut.'

'What else does he say?' Winter asked.

Lucy clasped the cup.

'That's the thing. I always thought he was joking...'

'About what?'

Winter and Lazarus sat forward in unison.

'He has told me a few times that he fantasises about killing a woman,' Lucy said.

'He asked me to play a game with him once. He wanted to pretend rape me. You know, he'd grab me from behind, I would have to fight and scream, he'd drag me into the bushes. All that shit. He said we could do it at night in a park.'

She flicked ash into the ashtray again.

'I told him to fuck off.'

Her eyes danced between Winter and Lazarus.

'The fucken weirdo went too far. I'm not into that shit.'

'How many times have you been with him?' Winter asked.

Lucy took a long drag, sat back in the chair and blew the smoke towards the ceiling. She held the cigarette away from her face as she trawled her memory bank.

'He's been a punter of mine for about a year,' she said.

'The third Sunday of the month, regular as clockwork. He must get paid or something. He always flashes the cash.'

The attack on Delaney happened on a Sunday and it was the third of the month.

'Can you remember the last time he visited you?' Winter asked her.

'He didn't come to me last Sunday. That was the first time he hasn't since he started coming to me. It was last month.'

Lazarus's pulse quickened.

'How does he contact you?' Winter asked.

'Eh, by phone,' Lucy said, giving Winter a look that said she believed the detective had just asked the most stupid question in history. Ever, like.

'He rings me all the time. Fucken hounds me. No wonder he does what he does. But they're all like that, aren't they? I mean, that's their job, hounding people.'

Lazarus frowned, looked at Winter.

'What do you mean by hounding? What does he do?' Winter asked.

Lucy picked up the second Snickers, unwrapped it and started eating it. She waited until she swallowed the mouthful of chocolate.

'He's one of those reporters, or whatever the fuck they're called. That's what they do, isn't it? They hassle people all the time. Like stalk them.'

Winter sat forward in her seat.

'He's a journalist?'

Lucy clicked her fingers.

'That's it. A journalist.'

'Do you know his name?' Winter asked.

Lucy gave her another look.

'Of course I fucken do. Sure he's famous. His photo is always in the paper.'

'What is it?' Winter asked.

Lazarus held his breath. Waited.

Lucy stared Winter in the eye.

'Sullivan,' she said after a beat.

'Conor Sullivan.'

31

Three hours later, when they were done with her and she had told the story over and over, Lazarus escorted Lucy Fowler out of the interview room.

They headed down the narrow corridor into the public waiting area, neither talking. They walked out of the station. It was lunchtime and the street was busy. Lazarus looked to the grey sky.

'Looks like rain,' he said.

'I can get an officer to drop you home.'

Lucy shook her head and laughed.

'I'm all right, Mr Lazarus. Can you imagine what my mates would do if I arrived up in the back of a cop car? They'd fucken batter me.'

Lazarus thought he knew the real reason for her refusal.

Lucy took a packet of smokes from her bag and lit up.

She exhaled long and slow.

'What time do you start?' Lazarus asked.

'About nine. I'll go out for a while, meet a few people, score some…'

She went quiet.

'Relax, Lucy,' Lazarus said.

'I'm not interested if you're using, only what you told us in there.'

He nodded back to the interview room.

'Not many girls would come to us. They would either not trust the police or stay quiet and keep taking the money from him.'

Lucy took a long drag of the cigarette.

'I knew as soon as you mentioned it to us the other night it was yer man Sullivan. I just knew it. But I was too afraid to say anything in front of the other girls. I'm fucked if they think I am ratting to the cops.'

She gave him a glance of apology.

'No offence, like.'

Lazarus smiled.

'None taken.'

Lucy shivered and wrapped the jacket with the broken zip and the foam oozing from the cut in the sleeve tight around her body.

'Fuck knows I've messed up often enough, Mr Lazarus. I thought it was time to do the right thing for once. Maybe help some other girl. Maybe save her.'

'You did do the right thing, Lucy,' Lazarus said.

'Will he know it was me?'

Lazarus knew he could not bullshit her.

'Yes. We'll have to put what you said to him if and when we arrest him. You may be called as a witness, but that will be months away. If it's him.'

'Does that mean my name will be in the papers?'

'We'll do everything we can to protect you. But that will be a decision for the judge. He might give you anonymity.'

'I hope so. He scares me.'

'He won't harm you. I'll make sure of that, Lucy.'

Lucy smiled a sad smile.

'Sound,' she said.

'Will you protect me from the other punters as well?'

Lazarus pursed his lips, said nothing. He knew there was nothing he could say. She'd probably be raped tonight by some bastard. And then be back working an hour later.

'Sorry,' he said, finally.

'I know,' Lucy said.

'Story of my life.'

She finished her smoke, threw the butt onto the pavement.

'I better go,' she said.

'Take care, Lucy,' Lazarus said.

'And thanks. You've been very helpful.'

She walked out onto the street. She stopped after a few seconds, looked back at Lazarus.

'Just make sure you nail the bastard,' she said.

'I'll do my best,' Lazarus said. 'We all will.'

Lucy nodded and walked away. She headed along the street, towards the city centre. Her head was down and she walked slowly, as if she was carrying a heavy weight.

And Lazarus thought she had been all her life.

Lazarus watched her until she disappeared from sight. Then he turned and went back into the station.

McEvoy, Cochrane and Winter were waiting for him in the incident room.

'Fuck me pink and call me Porky, I was not expecting that,' Cochrane said.

'Plot twist,' Winter said.

'This is heavy,' McEvoy said.

Lazarus saw worry on his face.

'We need to be careful, *amigo*,' McEvoy said. 'This fella Sullivan is a celebrity. And I have no doubt he has friends in the Depot. Let's measure twice and cut once here.'

Lazarus glared at him.

'He can be friends with the Commissioner, the Pope and the President for all I care, Harry. He's been nominated as suspect. So we're going to look at him.'

He walked over to an enlarged still of the attacker from the CCTV footage. It was of him celebrating, with his hands in the air. It was taped to a corkboard on the wall. He tapped it with a pen.

'The physique is a good match, for starters,' he said.

'Same build, same rough height.'

McEvoy had added an enlarged photo of Sullivan to the board. It was his by-line photograph taken from *The Globe* website. He stared dolefully right into the camera. Lucy had identified him from it.

Lazarus felt a jolt of excitement as he remembered something.

'Sullivan and his buddy Gallagher were at the scene that night,' he said.

'They were the only media I saw.'

'I saw them when I arrived at about 12.40am,' McEvoy said.

'The call only came in around midnight.'

'Wait a second,' Lazarus said. 'Sullivan's rag broke this. They had it up online before the press office even released the details.'

He looked to Winter.

'Rachel, pull up his story from that morning.'

Winter swivelled in her chair and typed on her computer.

'I have it,' she said after a few seconds.

'It says, *"Gardai are hunting a fiend who raped and strangled a young woman as she walked home late last night. The woman, who is in her 20s, was subjected to a shocking attack in the grounds of Griffith Park in central Dublin.*

"Sources have confirmed the woman was raped, beaten, and strangled in the shocking attack. She was found unconscious in bushes at around midnight.

"Globe *sources have also revealed she was found semi-naked and is now crit-ically ill in the city's Mater Hospital. A major investigation has been launched by detectives.'*

'Stop!' Lazarus shouted.

Something had hit him. Something massive.

'What time was that story published?' he said.

'Let me check,' Winter said.

'They usually put the time of publication under the headline.'

She scrolled back to the top of the story, put a finger up to the screen to make sure she read it properly.

'It says it was published at 6.45am,' she said.

Lazarus closed his eyes.

'*Porca Miseria,*' he said slowly.

'What is it, John?' Cochrane asked. Her eyes were wide.

Lazarus shook his head, and when he spoke, it was more to himself than his team.

'It was right in front of us the whole time,' he said.

'You're not making sense, big lad,' Cochrane said.

Lazarus didn't hear her. He was too busy kicking himself.

He turned to McEvoy.

'Harry, this is important. What exact time did the Sweeneys come back and tell you they dressed her?'

McEvoy blew out his lips.

He took his Garda notebook from a pocket of his suit jacket.

'Let me see,' he said as he flicked through the pages.

'Ah, here we are!' he shouted.

'They came to the public office at 6.57am. I started taking the state-ment from them in one of the interview rooms at 7.04am.'

'Jesus Christ,' Cochrane said.

'That's nearly 20 minutes after Sullivan's yarn went online.'

'Sullivan knew something we didn't,' Lazarus said.

'No garda or paramedic saw her half-dressed. So he can't have got that information from the emergency services. And it's unlikely the Sweeneys told him.'

Lazarus shook his head.

'We didn't know about it. But the attacker did.'

He looked at his colleagues.

'And so did Sullivan.'

'I don't know,' Cochrane said.

She turned to Lazarus.

'There is still an outside chance that somebody told Sullivan. Maybe the Sweeneys blabbed to a friend. Maybe they have a friend that they spoke to for advice in the early hours before coming to us. These reporter types, they have sources everywhere. Someone could have told him.'

Cochrane folded her arms.

'It's not enough, John.'

'We have Fowler, too,' Lazarus said.

Cochrane raised her eyes to heaven.

'Does she have much form?' she asked.

'Loads,' Winter said.

She pulled Lucy's rap sheet profile up on the computer.

'She has 54 previous convictions,' she said.

Lazarus groaned.

'How serious?' he asked.

Winter blew out her cheeks as she scanned Lucy's record on the Garda computer system.

'Theft, shoplifting, dealing, robbing, soliciting when it was an offence, the works. She has done prison five times, the longest stretch six months. She's been in trouble from around the age of 12. Her stepfather was sexually abusing her and she kept on running away from home. She made a complaint and he got seven years. She was taken into care and sent to a foster home. The man of the house raped her as well. She ran away and ended up on the streets. She got hooked on gear and started selling herself and robbing to feed her habit.'

'What a life,' Lazarus said. He thought of her trudging away from the station, weighed down by that life.

'She'll be a shocking witness, John,' Cochrane said.

Lazarus knew she was right. Lucy's credibility would be shot to pieces on the witness stand.

'We need more, something to corroborate her story,' he said.

'We can start by doing their phones,' Cochrane said.

'She said he was in contact with her. There'll be a record of that.'

Lazarus said nothing. It had become dark outside. He knew he was about to take a leap into another type of darkness. Probing a high-profile journalist like Sullivan would catapult the investigation into another stratosphere, one that would involve Garda HQ, and most likely the Commissioner himself.

He had 14 years to go before he could retire with 30 under his belt and a full pension in his pocket. He knew if he took one misstep with Sullivan, his career was finished.

'Accessing a reporter's phone records is way above my pay grade,' he said, after a long moment.

'That is political. This is one for Fallon.'

The more savvy detectives in the city would take one look at Lucy's statement and throw it in the bin. They would see madness in listening to a sex worker. Even the idea of submitting a file to prosecutors with a key element being a statement from a heroin addict who robs to feed her habit would horrify them.

But he wasn't like them.

Delaney mattered to him.

So did Lucy Fowler.

And if a well-connected journalist was in the frame, then so be it.

'Start digging around,' he told the team.

'See if you can back up her story. I'm off to see the brass.'

He walked out of the incident room and made his way upstairs to Fallon's office. He knocked and opened the door. Fallon was behind her large desk, doing paperwork. She looked up and smiled when she saw him.

'Hello, young buck,' she said.

He smiled back, but then his face hardened when he saw Anderson sitting on the sofa, a sheaf of papers in his hand.

He stared at Lazarus.

'What did the woman have to say?' Fallon said.

Lazarus told them what she said and what he wanted Fallon to do.

There was a moment's silence.

Then Anderson threw the paperwork onto the sofa.

He jumped to his feet.

'Is this a joke?' he shouted.

'You want to investigate one of the country's most respected crime journalists over the rape and attempted murder of a woman on the word of a brasser? Have you lost your mind?'

'Wind your neck in Inspector!' Fallon shouted.

'We do not call them brassers. This is not the eighties. They are sex workers and deserve to be believed as much as the next person.

'She is a citizen like anyone else.'

Anderson blanched and sat down.

Lazarus enjoyed that. He turned back to Fallon.

217

'The witness has implicated a man for the attack. We know that man has details about the incident that have been confidential. Details only a few of us know. I thought there was a leak from the investigation, but how can a garda have leaked something we didn't know? The story was up online before the Sweeneys came back to us and said they dressed her.

'Nobody in this station knew.'

He took a step towards Fallon.

'What if Sullivan knew about her being left half-naked because he was there?'

Anderson snorted, folded his arms in protest.

'He's a journalist, for Christ's sake,' he said.

'He has touts all over the place. We know one of your team is leaking to him. Jesus, I can't believe you want to look at him for this. It's crazy. Ridiculous. Doing his phones on the word of a prostitute is a joke. The civil liberties crowd will go nuts if we access his phones. Not to mention the politicians. This has to be a joke.'

Lazarus felt the dam give way.

'The joke is that you, as a detective inspector, can't see why this man should be looked at. You're just worried about the political ramifications of going after him. I don't care about that. I go where the evidence takes me. There is evidence making him a person of interest. And checking his phone records will help me eliminate or implicate Sullivan. This is basic stuff.'

Anderson jumped to his feet. Again.

'Watch your mouth, Lazarus.'

His face was red with anger.

Fallon slammed her palm down on the desk.

'Sit the fuck down you two. Jesus, it's like dealing with spoilt kids.'

She brushed a hand through her hair.

'Okay, here's what is going to happen,' she said finally.

'There is no way I will authorise accessing his phone records.'

Lazarus folded his arms.

Fallon gave him a filthy look and jabbed an angry finger at him.

'At. The. Fucking. Moment. Get your team together. Check him out. See if you can find anything to convince me. Then we'll talk.'

Anderson was still on his feet.

'Superintendent, I will be placing on record my opposition to this course of action. I'll be telling the Assistant Commissioner I regard this as a waste of time.'

'You do that,' Fallon snapped.

'I do not care. He's a person of interest. That's my decision. Now get out the pair of you.'

Anderson stormed out. He slammed the door after him.

Lazarus was walking to the door when Fallon called him.

'You better be right, John. If this goes pear-shaped, it will be your beautiful Italian arse in the bacon slicer. Not that gobshite Anderson's. And definitely not mine.'

Lazarus nodded and walked out of the office.

He was ready to lead the investigation into Sullivan.

And he knew exactly where to start.

32

Lazarus used his own Giulia. He thought even an unmarked Garda car would stand out. He parked the Giulia on a side street. He took out his iPhone and sent a WhatsApp.

All clear?

The tick went blue almost immediately. The response came within seconds.

Roger that, John. He left 10 minutes ago. Gone for the night

Lazarus paid for parking on the app and locked the car. Three minutes later, he was on Sir John Rogerson's Quay and was walking into *The Globe* building. Daly waited for him at the entrance.

Lazarus saw the excitement in his eyes.

Daly looked around and spoke in a conspiratorial voice.

'Follow me,' he said.

'He's definitely gone?' Lazarus asked as they came to a door just past reception.

It was brown and windowless with a heavy-duty lock. It had a black and white sign that said SECURITY.

'Yes,' Daly murmured.

'I asked the little bollix myself.'

Daly typed a code into a security pad at the door. He gripped the handle, pulled the door open and ushered Lazarus inside.

'Welcome to the nerve centre,' Daly said, his voice back to normal.

'We can talk freely. No one will hear us. Now, I think I should be able to help you.'

Lazarus had called Daly and asked him to check the CCTV for Sunday evening for any footage of Sullivan. If he was in the newsroom at the time of the attack, then the investigation would be dead before it had even begun.

The room was stuffy and dark. Three desks had been pushed together in the middle and four computers sat on them. On the wall to the left, Lazarus saw a large whiteboard with numbers on it in green ink. He saw the number for nearby Pearse Street Garda Station. It was circled in red. Another board to the right had three columns of writing. One was a list of names. Lazarus saw Sullivan's on it and assumed it was a list of employees. The two other columns detailed the cars they drove and their registration plates. It said Sullivan drove a 2016, black BMW 3 series, Dublin registration.

His pulse quickened. Another piece in the jigsaw. He remembered Lucy saying Sullivan drove a black car when he used her. He took out his phone and sent McEvoy a text message with the details, so he could check the car on PULSE.

He put the phone back in his pocket and examined the rest of the room. The wall in front of him was dominated by a bank of television screens. Each one had a different scene from the CCTV system.

'I never liked that Sullivan fella, you know,' Daly said.

'He's an arrogant prick. What's he supposed to have done?'

Lazarus held his hands out.

'You know I can't get into that.'

'It's the rape, isn't it?'

Lazarus's didn't answer.

Daly smiled.

'John, I was a cop for 33 years. I still have friends in the job. I know you are investigating the attack in Griffith Park. It's all over the paper.'

'Alan...' Lazarus said.

Daly ignored him.

'And now you've asked me for anything to do with that shit Sullivan on Sunday evening.'

Lazarus sighed.

'Can we keep this to ourselves? It's early days.'

'I won't breathe a word to anyone. I promise.'

Daly sat into a black office chair in front of one of the computers and tapped the keyboard. After a few seconds, Sullivan's face appeared.

Daly examined the screen, frowned.

'Oh, now that is interesting.'

'What does it say?' Lazarus asked.

He took a notebook and pen from the pocket of his overcoat.

'This is Sullivan's employee page. It has everything. Photo, employee number, next of kin, address, telephone number, car registration. The works.'

Lazarus nodded.

'You can't get in or out without swiping your card through a reader,' Daly said.

'*The Globe* ID card has a magnetic swipe, so it doubles up as a fob for access. Each time your card is used, it is recorded on the system, to the second. Sullivan parks in the underground. The card works on that entrance, too.'

He clicked the mouse. A table of dates and times came up. The columns alternated blue and red.

'Blue is for in, red is for out,' Daly explained.

'This is Sullivan's activity all day Sunday.'

Lazarus looked more closely at the data.

'Sullivan entered the car park at 11.39am,' Daly said. 'He swiped his card on a reader at a door from the car park to the lift at 11.41am. At 11.42am, he entered the newsroom.

Lazarus wrote the times down.

'He stays there all day,' Daly said, 'doesn't go out for lunch, but they have a canteen.'

He scrolled down further.

'He left the carpark at 6.43pm.'

'That fits,' Lazarus said. He must have been heading out to the Prestige Airport Hotel for the arrest of Sean Maloney.

Then he thought of something.

'I had a row with him at a scene later that evening, but he was in a different vehicle. It was an SUV registered to Tony Gallagher. You know him? Is he on the system?'

'He works out in the field, he's never in here,' Daly said.

'Sound lad, actually. They're like chalk and cheese. They must have met up somewhere and Sullivan got into Tony's SUV. I think it's a Volkswagen. They do that a lot, one drives and the other takes photographs. They tell me in the old days, you were either a journalist or a photographer, but it's a brave new world now. There are no photographers anymore. Just reporters who take photos sometimes. It's all about cost-cutting, really. One lad does two jobs. The only reason Tony and Sullivan work together is that they are both experts in crime and the bosses think it is safer for them to work as a pair rather than alone on jobs.' Daly turned back to the computer.

He pointed to an entry.

'He came back later.'

'What time?' Lazarus asked.

The hairs on the back of his neck began to tingle.

'He entered the car park at 11.47pm. He leaves again at 12.29am,' Daly said.

Lazarus did the maths. Sullivan arrived at his office more than 45 minutes after Delaney left Orla Diffney's house around 11pm, and 26 minutes after the attacker was caught on the camera at Helen O'Shea's house at 11.21pm. Twenty six minutes to get to Sir John Rogerson's Quay slap bang in the city centre from Griffith Park.

It was maybe four miles.

The roads would have been deserted. Even sticking to 40 kilometres per hour, he could easily have completed the journey in 20 minutes.

Lazarus's heart began to beat faster.

'Are his movements recorded on CCTV?' he asked. 'I might need to prove it is him using his swipe card.'

'There are cameras all over,' Daly said.

'Every time his pass is used, the system records a 30-second video and saves it. Same for when a vehicle uses the car park. But it will take a while to download the files. We have time for a coffee.'

Daly started downloading the files and then got up from his chair. He walked towards a door at the corner of the room. It led to a small kitchen with beige walls and white appliances and a Formica table and chairs. There was a silver urn beside the sink that served boiling water.

'We only have instant,' Daly smirked, 'none of your fancy Italian stuff.'

Lazarus laughed. He was a coffee snob. He had his own supply of ground coffee at the station and a glass cafetière at his desk.

'It'll do,' he said.

He took the coffee and sat down at the table. Daly produced Chocolate Hobnobs from a drawer. They each took a biscuit. They ate in a comfortable silence.

'You glad to be out?' Lazarus asked.

Daly smiled.

'This is where I'm supposed to say retiring was the best thing I ever did.'

He put his cup down on the table.

'I miss it every single day. I come in here and do my shift a few days a week. The lads are grand, but I am just an old man behind a desk. I'm invisible to the staff. But when I was in the job I mattered, I had status.'

He placed a blemished hand on Lazarus's forearm.

'Stay in as long as you can, Lazarus. Suck out every last minute of the job. You'll understand when you're out.'

'Come on,' he said after a long moment. 'It should be done by now.'
Then he paused.

'Whatever I give you is on the QT. You'll have to come back with a warrant if it goes official.'

Lazarus nodded.

They walked back to the desk. Daly looked at the computer.

'Here we are,' he said. CCTV footage filled the screen. It was from a camera at the car park entrance. A black car came into view and the driver's window slid down. Sullivan reached out and put his card to the reader. The heavy gate trundled open and Sullivan drove in. The 24-hour timestamp said 23:47.25. Daly pressed another icon and more video came up, this time of Sullivan entering the office building from the basement. Lazarus checked his clothing. He had on the same black North Face jacket that he remembered him having at the scene and dark blue combats. He remembered the O'Shea video. Dark clothing on the attacker. Could be black.

When he was a rookie cop chasing shoplifters, he was told to check the shoes. They always change clothing to try to escape detection as they went from one shop to the other. But never the footwear.

He looked at Sullivan's footwear and saw they were black, with the familiar white swoosh.

Nike.

He was just about to ask Daly if he could download the videos onto a USB stick when he heard his iPhone beep. He checked the message. It was from Winter.

> *Harry is with me. We have some news.*
> *Can we meet up back at the station ASAP?*

Lazarus put the phone away and gave the USB to Daly. The files were large and it took five minutes for them to transfer. The time crawled for Lazarus. He wanted to get back to Broadstone to hear Winter and McEvoy's findings, and tell them his.

He finally took the USB, said goodbye and made for the exit. Within seconds he was on the footpath and was running back to his Giulia.

He had a sense of things speeding up now, of everything falling – no, collapsing – into place.

Collapsing into place around Conor Sullivan.

33

Lazarus felt the electric atmosphere inside the incident room as soon as he entered. It was the buzz that came from rapid progress in an investigation.

Winter was at her computer. McEvoy was shuffling some paperwork. They looked up when he barrelled in. Cochrane stood at the window, arms folded, looking back into the room.

'Sullivan was at his office late on Sunday night,' he said.

'He's caught on CCTV arriving at 11.47pm. He could have made it from Griffith Park to the city centre after the attack. Plenty of time to get back to work. They also have him leaving the building at 12.30am, which fits with Harry seeing him around 12.40am.'

'I have something, too,' McEvoy said.

He hit a button on his computer and the flat screen TV came to light. It was a map of Griffith Park. McEvoy zoomed out and more of Dublin appeared. He pointed out some landmarks. The park was to the left of the map, Botanic Avenue, and Helen O'Shea's house, glowed red south of the park. Lazarus shuddered when he saw the pulsing over Darcy's digs a few streets away.

Drumcondra Road, the thoroughfare from the city north to the airport, ran through the centre of the map. To the right, Lazarus saw Dublin Bay. Between that and Drumcondra Road, sat the large oval of Croke Park GAA stadium.

McEvoy looked over at Lazarus.

'I checked Sullivan's car. He has had it for about 18 months. It's an early 2016 BMW 3 series.'

He read out the reg.

'It's been collated at a few scenes, but that's to be expected.'

Uniformed gardai always took details of cars at scenes, in case the criminals came back. But that meant reporters who covered them also had their cars noted.

'I checked with the Castle for ANPR,' McEvoy said.

'And this is where it gets interesting.'

Lazarus felt another tingle of excitement. Dublin Castle was home to the Garda Traffic Corps. The unit patrolled the city in cars equipped with Automatic Number Plate Recognition cameras. They captured registration plates of vehicles and flagged up any that had no insurance or tax, or that had been linked to crimes.

'They had a car in the city centre on Sunday night,' McEvoy said.

'It was on the southside between 9.30pm and 10.45pm. But then it moved north of the river and pulled in on Drumcondra Road Lower at 11pm.'

McEvoy clicked the mouse and the location of the ANPR car pulsed blue on the map. It was outside the Bank of Ireland, just past Clonliffe Avenue, the road that led to Croke Park. It was a few hundred metres before Drumcondra Road became Dorset Street in the heart of the city centre.

'It started recording cars at 11.06pm and stayed there until 11.53pm,' McEvoy said.

'It caught Sullivan's car heading towards the city centre at 11.34pm.'

'*Porca Miseria*,' Lazarus said.

An image came on the screen. It showed the front of a black BMW, the registration visible. It was Sullivan's. The image showed the windscreen of the car. The driver was obscured by the darkness. That didn't matter. Lazarus had CCTV from Daly of Sullivan driving it a few minutes later. What did matter was that the ANPR located his car on a road close to the rape scene shortly after the attack.

'I had a hunch I knew what route he took,' McEvoy said.

'I know a pub owner further up on Drumcondra Road, just about here.'

McEvoy hit another button and an icon flashed green on the map. It was north-east of Griffith Park, on a stretch of busy road that had several pubs and restaurants.

'He checked his CCTV,' McEvoy said.

'We know the attacker left the scene at 11.21pm and Sullivan's car was caught on ANPR at 11.34pm. That's a 13-minute window. Piece of piss for these digital systems. He downloaded it and emailed me it. I found this.'

McEvoy clicked his mouse again.

The TV screen flashed black, then footage from another CCTV system came up. It showed a stretch of Drumcondra Road. The footage was clear, thanks to the quality of the digital camera, but also to the street lighting. The timestamp said 23:31.28.

A group of six young people walked on the footpath. Lazarus looked past them to the road and saw a bus heading north.

Then he noticed movement. It was a car driving right to left, north to south. It was black.

'That is a 3 series BMW,' McEvoy said.

'Just like Sullivan's.'

The footage was of a car heading towards the city from the north. That meant Sullivan, if it was him, had to have gone out and then back on himself.

McEvoy read Lazarus's mind.

He walked over to the screen.

'I think I know what he did.'

He pointed a stubby finger at the park.

'We know he came out over the railings here,' he said.

He traced his finger along Botanic Avenue, heading west, past Helen O'Shea's house, following the route the attacker was seen to take on the video.

'The avenue comes out on to St. Mobhi Road, which heads north.'

He pointed to the road.

'Just say he had his Beemer parked here and drove along it to here,' he said, bringing his finger to a right turn further up St. Mobhi Road.

'That's Home Farm Road. It's 400 metres from the junction of Botanic Avenue and St. Mobhi Road. It would take him less than a minute.'

Then he traced his finger to the right, along the extent of Home Farm Road.

'That is 900 metres,' McEvoy said.

That road ended in a T-junction. McEvoy brought his finger to the right at the junction, and Lazarus knew he was moving along Drumcondra Road, past the pub that gave him the CCTV. He continued over a blue line that was the Tolka River. That river also ran through Griffith Park. It was close.

McEvoy's finger kept moving. It was in the city centre now and soon approached the Royal Canal.

And then he jabbed the finger at the screen again.

'This is where the ANPR car was. It's in a direct line from the pub with the CCTV.

'It's about three minutes later. It fits, Lazarus. I checked Google Maps. The time for a car journey up St. Mobhi Road, across Home Farm Road, down Drumcondra Road then across the city centre to *The Globe* on

St. John Rogerson's Quay is 20 minutes. Sullivan arrived at *The Globe* at 11.47pm and the attacker left the park at 11.21pm. That's 26 minutes.'

Lazarus went quiet.

As Senior Investigating Officer, it was his decision to arrest Sullivan. The warning of Fallon bounced around his head. If he got this wrong, it would be the end of his career. He was about to tell McEvoy he needed time to think when he heard Winter cough.

Her eyes were wide with excitement, like she was straining at the bit. Then he remembered her text where she said both she and McEvoy had uncovered information.

'I have been checking Sullivan out,' Winter said.

'The first place I looked was PULSE.'

The Garda computer system included details of incidents and arrests and even intelligence on individuals. He was not surprised Sullivan had his own entry on the system. Lazarus went over to Winter and started reading.

The entry gave Sullivan's date of birth as July 17, 1983, which made him 36. There were two addresses for him. One was *The Globe* Newspaper. The other was in Harold's Cross, a suburb four miles south of the city centre. Three years earlier in 2016 gardai had mounted armed patrols around his house following a death threat.

Lazarus looked at another entry for the address and his heart skipped a beat.

'*On June 18, 2017, members called to the above address,*' the report's narrative began. '*The occupier, Conor Martin Sullivan (17/07/1983) was arrested on suspicion of committing an offence under section 10 of the Non-Fatal Offences Against the Person Act (1997).*'

'Stalking,' Winter said.

Lazarus read more.

'*The complainant alleged Mr Sullivan had been harassing her by phone and in person for six weeks. Mr Sullivan denied the allegations in interview. He was later released after six hours' detention pending the preparation of a file to the Director of Public Prosecutions.*'

Cochrane and McEvoy stood beside Lazarus. They read the report together. Lazarus rubbed his chin as he considered his next step. He felt the surge of adrenalin that comes when you know you are opening a door into a major new phase of an investigation.

'He claimed he was trying to talk to the woman for reasons of legitimate journalism,' Winter said.

'The complainant was a witness in a murder trial. Sullivan wanted her story. The team sent a file to the DPP who concluded there was not enough evidence to sustain a conviction. No charges.'

She clicked off PULSE and went into the internet browser.

'And then I started doing my own digging and found this on the *Irish Times* website.'

Lazarus could see Winter had clicked on a court report.

'Two months ago, Sullivan and his newspaper lost a High Court defamation case,' Winter said.

'A woman claimed Sullivan defamed her. A jury awarded her €95,000 in damages, plus costs. The report says Sullivan became agitated and shouted at the woman outside the court after the verdict. He had to be pulled away by colleagues.'

'A fucken incel,' Cochrane said.

Winter nodded.

'I have a few friends from college who are in journalism.'

She stopped, realised. Looked to Lazarus.

'I tell them nothing.'

Lazarus waved away her protest.

'One of them knows Sullivan. She told me he broke up with his girl-friend five weeks ago. She ended it.'

Cochrane snorted.

'He loses a high-profile court case to a woman, then his missus dumps him,' she said.

'This is classic.'

'There's more,' Winter grimaced.

'Much more.'

She clicked the mouse and another web page opened.

Facebook.

Winter didn't take her eyes off the computer.

'This is his page,' she said.

She clicked on one of the photographs.

'Look at this.'

Sullivan was in a group outside a large, concrete building. Tony Gallagher was with two other journalists at the side. They were at the entrance. It was obscured by security glass. Behind the glass, Lazarus saw large silver lettering that made his eyes widen in shock.

EUROPOL

'Is that where I think it is?' he asked.

'The Netherlands,' Winter said.

'More specifically, The Hague. He was there on a press junket. You can see some well-known journalists with him.'

She moved the mouse to the right, where Sullivan had written a post.

'*Over in Europol with other crime reporters to see the future of European policing – should be interesting.*'

Winter pointed the cursor at the date.

Lazarus's mouth fell open.

'January 28, 2016,' he said.

'The day before the woman was attacked in Scheveningen. Christ.'

Winter nodded.

'It's a mile from the park where she was attacked.'

'Jesus H,' McEvoy said.

'Holy shit,' Cochrane said.

Lazarus felt his heart pounding fast, so fast he thought it was going to burst out of his ribcage. All the information McEvoy and Winter had given him in the last 20 minutes swam around his mind. Cars. CCTV evidence. Sullivan's swipe card. A social media photograph of a group of reporters enjoying themselves on a junket in Holland. An angry man shouting at a woman outside a court.

And it all pointed to one, unavoidable fact.

He left the room, knew what he had to do.

He sprinted up to Fallon's office, his pulse pounding in his ears.

He took a deep breath to calm himself, then knocked.

'This better be good,' Fallon said.

Anderson was on the sofa as usual.

Lazarus spent ten minutes filling them in on the evidence he and his team had gathered against Sullivan.

When he finished, Fallon looked down at the notes she had been taking in her official Garda journal.

It was a hard-backed A4 book.

She was thinking.

Anderson wasn't.

'This is bullshit,' he said.

'You have nothing concrete on him. A waste of time. We're toast if this comes out. We're targeting a journalist.'

He put his head in his hands.

Lazarus ignored him. He didn't count.

Fallon had the final decision.

She looked up from her notes.

'There is a lot of circumstantial evidence here,' she said.

'But no real evidence,' Anderson interrupted.

Fallon stared at the detective inspector.

'Circumstantial evidence carries as much weight as conventional evidence, Inspector. You should know that.'

Anderson looked away.

Fallon turned to Lazarus, raised her eyes to heaven.

'What's your plan?'

'I want to arrest him to put our evidence to him but also to take his DNA. If it's a match to the Griffith Park sample, we have him.'

Fallon went silent. Drummed her fingers on the journal.

Then her eyes hardened.

They moved to Anderson, settled on Lazarus.

'Tell your team to go home and get some kip,' she said.

'Tomorrow is going to be a long day. I'll request his phone records now.'

She smiled a tight smile.

'Take him.'

34

Friday

Lazarus seethed as he sat in the Camry passenger seat. He threw an angry glance in the rear-view mirror to the cause of his fury.

It was a grey Hyundai i40 unmarked Garda car. Rachel Winter was behind the wheel.

And Anderson sat in the passenger seat.

'*Bastardo*,' Lazarus said through gritted teeth.

'I still don't understand why Ankles came with us,' McEvoy said.

Lazarus shook his head.

The two cars were parked up across from *The Globe* office. It was just after 9.20am.

'He told Fallon we needed a supervisor to manage the arrest because Sullivan is so high profile,' Lazarus said.

'That's bullshit. It's always about him. We're just pawns in his game. He's trying to make himself look important for the interview panel for superintendent.'

'Fucking gobshite,' McEvoy said.

'And what the fuck are we doing twiddling our thumbs on the street?' McEvoy jabbed a finger at the entrance to *The Globe*.

'We should be in there dragging the little bollix out by the hair.'

Lazarus grimaced.

'Anderson vetoed it this morning,' he said.

'I told him and Fallon we were going into the office. The blood drained from his face. He disappeared for a few minutes, came back and said he had spoken to Garda HQ. They were worried about the optics of us going into a newsroom and arresting one of them. So he insisted we wait outside and move against him in the street. I was furious. We could be here all day waiting for Sullivan to come out. I nearly floored Anderson when he told me.'

McEvoy raised an eyebrow.

'Again?' he said.

Lazarus smiled at the jibe, then smiled even more at the memory of slapping Anderson in the pub that night.

He checked the mirror.

Anderson was talking excitedly to Winter. She looked bored.

'He probably wants t–'

'John!'

McEvoy placed a hand on Lazarus's arm.

'There he is.'

Sullivan came down the steps of *The Globe* building. He wore his usual black jacket, dark jeans. It was a cold morning, but he was bareheaded and his coat was unbuttoned, exposing a denim shirt.

'Double denim,' McEvoy said. 'Outrageous.'

Sullivan looked around as he walked, didn't see the danger.

He reached into his trouser pocket and withdrew a phone, started tapping on the screen. Sullivan turned right into a side street.

Lazarus reached for his Tetra radio.

'Go, go, go,' he shouted.

McEvoy sped out of the parking space. The Camry's tyres screeched as McEvoy turned into the side street. He sped down the street then came to a hard stop just feet past Sullivan. The reporter had heard the screech of the tyres and had looked up at the noise.

Now he was frozen in shock, his hand clutching the mobile phone, his mouth agape, his eyes wide.

Lazarus got out of the car and ran.

McEvoy was nearer and reached Sullivan first.

He rugby tackled him, knocked him to the ground.

Lazarus heard McEvoy shouting.

'Don't move! Armed gardai! Stay still!'

Winter had driven the Hyundai furiously and stopped beside the Camry. She left the engine running, the door open. She sprinted towards McEvoy and Sullivan. She held a radio up to her mouth, talked into it rapidly as she ran.

Lazarus heard an explosion of sirens. The plan had been for Winter to call for uniformed back-up as soon as they moved in on their target. They were seconds away.

Winter ran over and pressed her knees onto Sullivan's back. Sullivan was trying to struggle, but McEvoy had him on the ground.

'Stop struggling!' Winter shouted. She pushed Sullivan's face into the pavement.

Sullivan tried to shout, but his voice was muffled. Lazarus ignored the struggle. He was too busy looking for the phone that Sullivan had been holding when they moved in on him.

And then he saw it.

The phone was perched on the edge of the kerbstone, about two metres from where Sullivan was pinned to the ground. The force of McEvoy's tackle had made it fly from his grip.

Lazarus took a purple glove from his pocket and used it to lift the phone. With his other hand, he fished out a small evidence bag from a pocket and placed the phone inside. Then he turned to Sullivan, just as McEvoy and Winter were hauling him to his feet.

They pushed him against a wall.

McEvoy kicked his legs open. He patted Sullivan down while Winter brought his arms around behind his back and cuffed him.

They turned him around.

He saw Lazarus and his eyes bulged.

'This is an outrage. What sort of police force arrests journalists in the street? This isn't North Korea.'

'Calm down, Conor,' Lazarus said.

He was centimetres from Sullivan. He placed his hand on the reporter's arm.

'Conor Sullivan. I am arresting you on suspicion of rape and attempted murder. You are not obliged to say anything unless you wish to do so, but anything you say will be taken down in writing and may be given in evidence. Do you understand?'

The colour drained from Sullivan's face.

'What the actual.'

'Do you understand, Conor?' Lazarus repeated.

Sullivan's eyes pinballed in their sockets.

Suddenly, Lazarus heard another voice.

'Mr Sullivan, do you understand the caution?' Anderson asked.

Sullivan saw him and exploded.

'Is this all your doing, Anderson? What the fuck are you at? You can get fucked!'

Anderson jutted out his chin, stared at Sullivan.

'The decision has been made to arrest you for two serious offences, Mr Sullivan. I advise you to think very carefully about what you say.'

He paused, stared hard at Sullivan.

'Very carefully.'

Sullivan blinked, swallowed hard.

'No comment.'

'Do you understand the caution, Conor?' Lazarus asked.

'No comment.'

Lazarus grabbed Sullivan's arm, pulled him towards the Camry. McEvoy had the back door already open. Lazarus placed his hand on Sullivan's head and pushed him down into the back seat. He then ran around and jumped into the seat beside him.

McEvoy gunned the engine and sped off.

Sir John Rogerson's Quay, home to *The Globe*, soon became City Quay. Then the Camry turned left onto Lombard Street. The architecture changed from plush offices to council houses and flats.

There was a shorter route to the station, but Lazarus had a strategy, one that included getting under Sullivan's skin.

And for that he needed time.

'The last time I was asking you questions, you were acting the comedian in your office,' he said.

'You even had the cheek to try to recruit me. Let's see how cocky you are in the interview room.'

Sullivan stared out the window.

'Where were you going when we lifted you, Sullivan? Calling one of your touts?'

No answer.

They were on Pearse Street now, past Trinity College where Delaney's former boyfriend Darcy was studying before Lazarus and Winter knocked on his door and ruined his life.

Traffic was heavy, even though, at 9.35am, rush hour had long passed. It took them seven minutes to travel the 400 metres to Tara Street, past a hotel and fire station. They crawled along Tara Street, coming to the *Irish Times* building.

Lazarus nodded to the newspaper building.

'You'll never get to work in there now. The journalists, proper ones, will be writing about you soon enough. You'll be front page news.'

Sullivan stayed silent. But his breathing was out of control.

McEvoy turned left, then came to O'Connell Bridge.

Lazarus held up the evidence bag containing the phone he found on the street.

'We have your burner phone now, Sullivan,' Lazarus said as they reached the bridge.

'I can't wait to see what the techies get from that. We'll have your touts. They'll be sacked.'

Sullivan ignored him. The car was on O'Connell Street and moving past the General Post Office.

'Let me see,' Lazarus said.

He pressed a button on the phone through the evidence bag and it came alive.

'That is so sloppy You don't have it PIN protected. Rookie mistake.'

Sullivan kept looking out the window.

'You're staying silent now, but you'll fold. They always do. I am going to really enjoy breaking you.'

For the first time, Sullivan reacted.

He leaned into Lazarus.

Their faces were close.

Sullivan spoke.

'Jesus, man, what did you have for your breakfast? Your breath is rank.'

Lazarus smiled.

'You'd want to get used to smells where you are going,' he said.

'Other prisoners like pissing in sex offenders' meals. They throw shit at them when they're walking in the wing.'

He and Sullivan stared into each other's eyes.

Sullivan blinked.

He returned to the window. It took McEvoy a few minutes to get to Broadstone, where he sped into the car park at the back of the station.

Lazarus's heart sank. He saw a dozen-strong crowd of plain clothes and uniformed officers.

News of the arrest had leaked.

Winter and Anderson had taken a shorter route back to the station after the arrest and were at the front of the crowd.

McEvoy was the first out of the car. He opened the rear passenger door. He reached in and grabbed Sullivan's arm.

Lazarus caught up with them as they reached the back door to the station. He keyed in the access code and together with McEvoy walked Sullivan to the public office. Ian Bradley, the sergeant in charge for the station, stared at them. Bradley was in his late fifties and stocky, around five foot nine. He had wavy hair that was once black but was now grey. His eyebrows were still black, as was his thick moustache. His mouth sat in a permanent scowl. He was running down the clock on indoor duties until next year when he could take the half sheet and walk off into the sunset with his pension and a nice tax-free gratuity.

Lazarus had briefed him earlier about the arrest. He had a custody record ready on a desk. He sighed and reached for it before turning to Sullivan.

'What is your full name and address?'

Sullivan told him.

'Occupation?'

'Guess.'

Bradley turned to Lazarus.

'Time of arrest?'

'9.29am.'

'Location?'

'Sir John Rogerson's Quay, Dublin 2.'

Bradley wrote that down, then he glanced at the wall clock and noted in the record that Sullivan arrived at the station at 10.07am.

'You have been arrested on suspicion of the rape and attempted murder of a female at Griffith Park in the city of Dublin on the night of Sunday October 20,' Bradley said.

'I am authorising your detention under Section Four of the Criminal Justice Act. Do you understand?'

Sullivan nodded.

'You are entitled to consult a solicitor while you are detained. Do you have one in mind?'

'Nick Bell,' Sullivan said. The lawyer he had used in the newspaper office confrontation.

'You can be held for an initial six hours,' Bradley said.

'There is the scope for you to be detained for up to 24 hours, but that…'

'I know the procedure,' Sullivan interrupted.

Bradley nodded.

'I have to tell you, nevertheless. Your detention may be extended by a senior officer. We will let you know if that happens.'

Bradley brought Sullivan into another room where he was searched, photographed and had a saliva swab taken from inside his mouth. A uniformed officer also took his possessions, including his phone and wallet.

He took his shoes, socks and belt.

'We need your phone PIN,' Lazarus said.

'Fuck off,' Sullivan said.

Lazarus had been expecting that.

He knew Sullivan would guard the privacy of his main phone, especially after Lazarus saw the burner handset was unlocked. Keeping the PIN meant Lazarus's team could not access it.

'That's fine,' Lazarus said.

'We'll send your phone off to the experts in Israel who have programmes to break the code. It costs a fortune, but you're worth it.'

Sullivan grimaced.

'This way,' Bradley said. He took hold of Sullivan's arm.

He walked him down a tight corridor, heavy grey cell doors on either side of it. Bradley got to the last one on the left, opened it.

He held out a hand to show Sullivan the inside of the cell.

'In you go, Mr Sullivan. You'll be in here for a while until the detectives are ready to interview you.'

Sullivan said nothing. He walked into the cell, looked around.

It was small with a built-in bed and a thin blue mattress. The walls were grey and hard. He perched on the bed, stared straight ahead.

The heavy steel door clanked shut.

Lazarus looked in through the peephole.

Sullivan rested his head against the wall and closed his eyes.

35

Sullivan sat at a table in a small interview room. Bell was beside him. The solicitor wore a navy suit, white shirt and bright pink tie.

They were engrossed in conversation, but Lazarus could not hear it. The sound had been turned off so Sullivan could consult his lawyer in private. Sullivan nodded after a few moments. The men separated and sat back in their chairs. Then the room's brown door opened. Winter and Cochrane walked in and took chairs facing the men.

McEvoy did Jazz Hands.

'It's show time,' he said in an exaggerated American accent.

He sat beside Lazarus in a viewing room. They had come in after a conference with Winter and Cochrane.

McEvoy reached into the breast pocket of his brown suit jacket and took out two bars of chocolate.

Lazarus tutted.

'Why did you buy me that shit? You know I don't eat junk food.'

McEvoy blushed.

'They're both for me.'

He reached into another pocket and fished out a muesli bar.

'Here's your rabbit food.'

Suddenly Lazarus heard a buzzing noise as Winter activated the microphones in the interview room.

Bell straightened his tie. He looked over to Sullivan and winked. Cochrane sat opposite Sullivan, Winter faced Bell.

'Mr Sullivan,' Cochrane said.

'I am Detective Sergeant Frankie Cochrane from the Major Investigations Squad.'

'I know who you are,' Sullivan said.

He folded his arms.

'This is a load of crap. I did not rape anyone. I did not attack anyone. You're doing this just to get at my contacts. It's a witch hunt.'

Bell placed his hand on Sullivan's arm.

'Remember the plan,' he murmured.

Cochrane ignored the outburst.

'This is my colleague Detective Garda Rachel Winter from Broadstone Garda Station. You have been informed why you have been arrested and detained today.'

Sullivan cleared his throat.

'I won't be answering any questions. If I do, I could inadvertently identify a source. I have to protect them.'

'That's a new one on me, now,' Cochrane said.

'What?'

'I've interviewed hundreds of suspects, but I've never heard them use protecting their touts as a reason for not answering questions.'

'Have you interviewed many journalists before, Sergeant?' Bell interrupted.

Cochrane didn't answer.

'How are you feeling, Mr Sullivan? Do you need anything?' she said.

'I need you to let me go.'

Bell pulled him back.

He whispered in his ear.

He jerked a thumb towards the door.

Sullivan's shoulders slumped.

'He must be trying to calm him down,' McEvoy said.

Lazarus sipped the coffee.

'No, he's telling him to answer Frankie's questions so they can get out of here,' he said.

As if on cue, Sullivan nodded and looked at the detectives.

'I apologise. This is a tense situation for me. I will answer whatever questions I can without betraying my sources.'

'Thank you. I have no interest in your sources. Has it been explained to you why you are here?' Cochrane said.

'I didn't rape anyone.'

'We'll get to that. Can I call you Conor?'

'Call me what you want. I didn't fucking rape anyone.'

Cochrane opened a file on the table.

'I know you're upset, Conor. But maybe try to moderate your language.'

Sullivan reddened. He sighed and brushed a hand though his hair.

'Let's just have a chat for a while, I like to know as much as possible about the person I am interviewing,' Cochrane said.

'It helps me get a better picture of them. You might say something that puts you out of the frame. Bear with me, all right?'

Sullivan didn't answer.

'I see you are 36,' Cochrane said.

'Yes.'

'You look younger.'

'It's the stress-free lifestyle I lead.'

'I can imagine your job is stressful.'

'It has its moments.'

'I remember a few of your stories in the paper. How long have you worked there?'

'Thirteen years.'

'How long have you been a journalist?'

'Fourteen years.'

'Did you study journalism?'

'I did a degree in it at Dublin City University.'

Sullivan looked down at the table.

'When was that?'

'I graduated 15 years ago.'

'But you've been a reporter for 14 years?'

'I travelled for a year and then came back to Dublin.'

'Where did you travel?'

'All over. Europe. Asia. America.'

'You live in Harold's Cross now, but are you from Dublin?'

'Yes.'

'What part?'

'Crumlin.'

'The G. Is that why you became a crime reporter?'

Crumlin was a working-class area of south Dublin, known in the Garda as G District, or just the G. It had suffered from gangland criminality in recent years.

Sullivan snorted.

'Crumlin is full of good people. It gets a bad press.'

He realised his mistake as soon as the words came out of his mouth.

'That's your colleagues' fault, not mine,' Cochrane said.

Winter was the note-taker, even though the session was being recorded. She scribbled on an A4 pad as the two talked.

'Have you always worked in *The Globe*?' Cochrane asked.

'I freelanced for a year in different papers. Then I was poached by *The Globe*.'

'Why did they poach you?'

'I won an award.'

'For what?'

Sullivan's eyes darkened.

'I was walking near Trinity College and I saw a homeless woman outside a shop. She had a black eye and a cut lip. Everyone else walked past her, but I stopped. I asked her if she would like a coffee. I brought her to a nearby café. She started crying when I laid the drink and a sausage sandwich on the table for her. Her name was Carol and she was living in a tent in Phoenix Park.'

For a moment, Sullivan was out of the room and back in the cafe.

'She was an addict and had been left pregnant after a rape. She couldn't afford the boat fare to Britain for an abortion. She didn't know what to do. A few nights earlier, her rapist had come looking for her. He raped her again and set fire to her tent. I persuaded her to do a story. I freelanced it to *The Irish Times*. Politicians read it and got involved. The council gave her a nice flat and I got an award.'

Cochrane whistled.

'That's a pretty big deal.'

Sullivan stared at Cochrane.

'She died in the flat two months later of an overdose. The baby inside her died, too.'

Lazarus saw Winter had stopped writing notes.

'This prick is good,' Lazarus said.

'He knows how to tell a story. Winter has fallen for it.'

'She's just the note taker, Lazarus,' McEvoy said. 'Cochrane won't.'

They turned back to the screen.

'Were you always a crime reporter?' Cochrane asked him.

'Yes.'

'Do you like it? My job can be stressful. I'm sure yours must be.'

'It's very challenging and rewarding.'

'What is your typical day? Do you work late shifts or are you in early?'

'My paper goes to bed at 1am, so I am on call until then. Anything happens crime-wise and I cover it. That could be at midnight or 10am – it's all the same to me.'

'Goes to bed? What does that mean?'

'It means when the paper is finished and ready for printing. We call it going to bed. Then there is online, so it's 24 hours.'

'Do you go in the office every day?'

'Sometimes. Especially on weekend shifts when it's quiet."

'Have you ever had threats?'

'It goes with the beat.'

'What is security like in your office?'

'There is a guard at the front desk 24/7.'

'Can anyone just walk in?'

'No, of course not. There is an access system. We all have cards to get in and I have a parking space in the basement.'

'So, you have your own fob that records your entry and exit every day?'

'Yes.'

'That's mad,' Cochrane smiled.

'That sounds like a modern-day clock on, clock off system. The bosses are always watching, aren't they? You can never slope off early. We don't have them. At least that lets me get out of dodge early on a Friday. I just tell my super I'm going to meet a tout.'

'As long as they get a good story from me every day, they don't care where I am,' Sullivan said.

'You meet touts a lot?'

'No comment.'

Cochrane held her hands up.

'Relax, Conor. Just making conversation. This isn't about who's talking to you in the job. Tell me, are you married?'

'Divorced.'

'How long were you married?'

'Is this relevant?'

'I'm only asking questions, Conor. Just trying to build up a picture.'

'We were married for seven years. We separated four years ago. The divorce came through a few months ago.'

'Were you unfaithful?'

'Pardon me?'

'Did you cheat on her?'

'No, I did not. She did. She had an affair. I found out. That was the end of that.'

Cochrane folded her arms and sat back in the chair.

'You must have been angry.'

'I'm over it. It was a long time ago. I have moved on.'

'Okay. Are you with anyone now?'

'No.'

'No girlfriend?'

'I was going out with a girl there for a while, but we broke up.'

'When was that?'

'About a month, maybe five weeks ago.'

Lazarus felt his pulse quicken. Cochrane acted casual, but Lazarus suspected she was as excited by the answer as he was. Sullivan had been cuckolded in his marriage. He had now broken up with another woman shortly before Delaney was attacked and around the same time his divorce came through.

'What happened?' Cochrane asked, and Lazarus could tell she was interested behind her casual mask.

'It was nothing.'

'Must have been something.'

Sullivan let out a long breath.

'She wasn't happy with my working hours. Decided to end it.'

'That must have been hard,' Cochrane said.

'I've had worse.'

'Does work get in the way of your private life?'

'I bet it does to yours, too,' Sullivan said.

'How do you get to work?' Cochrane asked.

'I drive,' Sullivan said. 'I never know when I will be heading off down the country for a murder or some other story. I need my car.'

'You came up on the system as having a black BMW.'

Cochrane looked down at her notes and read out the registration number.

'Is that still your car?'

'What has my car got to do with anything?'

'Just ticking some more boxes. Is the BMW a work vehicle?'

'No. It's mine.'

'Does anyone else drive it? Do you lend it to anyone?'

'Just me.'

'Tell me,' Cochrane said, 'your mobile phone number, what is it?'

He recited it.

'And is that your phone, or does anyone have access to it?' Cochrane asked.

'Mine alone.'

Then he smirked.

He turned to Bell.

'I see what they are doing here.'

'I'm just asking some initial questions, Conor,' Cochrane said.

'What level are you?' Sullivan said.

'Level?' Cochrane asked. 'What do you mean?'

'Ah come on. You're forgetting my job.'

Cochrane stayed silent.

'Are you a level three?'

Bell looked puzzled.

'What's this?'

'There are four levels of interviewer in the cops,' Sullivan told him.

'Levels three and four are the best. Detectives are usually level three. That involves sitting in an interview room and asking the questions.'

Sullivan nodded towards the CCTV camera.

It looked to Lazarus as if he was staring right at him.

'Level four usually sits outside and manages the interview strategy. That gobshite Lazarus is sitting in a room with the fat one watching this now.'

'The bollix,' McEvoy said.

He sucked in his belly.

'Isn't that right, Sergeant?' Sullivan asked Cochrane. 'All part of the plan?'

'What plan would that be, now, Conor?' Cochrane said.

'Every question you're asking me is deliberate,' Sullivan said.

'You're trying to get stuff out of me. You have where I live. You know my car details. You know my work address. You know if I'm with anyone. You know my mobile phone number. You want me to admit no one else has access to my car or my phone.

'You're just playing games. This is an enjoyable chat. But maybe ask me what you want to ask me, then we can all get home.'

He sat back in his chair, folded his arms and stared at the ceiling.

'I must agree with my client,' Bell said.

'I object strongly to this time wasting and I will be letting Superintendent Fallon know of my anger at what you are doing here. You're clearly up to something.'

He leaned forward.

'I suggest you stop it. Now. Because if you don't I will have no hesitation in calling a press conference in front of this station to say my client is in an interview room here and you are not putting any evidence or allegations to him.'

36

Lazarus stared at Bell through the screen.

'Asshole,' he said.

McEvoy nodded.

'You're not wrong. Arrogant snobby bollix.'

He opened the second chocolate bar.

'They're on to us,' he said through a full mouth.

'No point putting it off now. He complains to Fallon and we'll be in no end of shit. Let's just do it.'

Lazarus said nothing.

The interview plan had been worked out earlier. They were starting off with the rapport phase. The idea was to draw Sullivan out by asking seemingly trivial questions unconnected to his arrest. But every word out of Cochrane's mouth had been planned to lead up to the challenge phase – where the evidence and allegations would be put to him.

Now Sullivan and his lawyer were fucking with that plan.

Lazarus felt his shoulders slump in resignation.

'You're right,' he said.

'Go in and get Cochrane and Winter out.'

McEvoy walked out, just as Lazarus received a message on his phone. It was from Flannery. He was leading the search operation at Sullivan's house. He read the message.

> Search nearly done, Lazarus. We seized a few items of clothing similar to
> our man's in the video. We'll be sending them off for comparison with the
> fibres on the victim's clothing. But feel free to show him them first.
> Nike running shoes, too. Should be back in station in 20 mins.

It was more than Lazarus had been hoping for.

He was composing a reply when the door opened. McEvoy walked in, with Cochrane and Winter.

Cochrane's face betrayed her anger.

'He's a wee shite,' she said.

She gripped a cup of tea.

'You know what he's at, don't you?' she said.

'He figures Bell acting the prick will make us release him earlier than we have planned and before the DNA comes back. Then he can fuck off.'

Lazarus grimaced.

The team at Forensics Science Ireland was busy with other DNA samples. Lazarus had been told it could be up to 36 hours before Sullivan's sample was compared to the attacker's DNA. Lazarus had pleaded with the team to bump Sullivan up the list, but they made no promises.

The longest they could hold Sullivan was 24 hours. The initial period of detention was six hours. Fallon could authorise another six, but would then have to ask the chief superintendent for the final 12. The chief would only do that if there were legitimate reasons to continue the detention. Lazarus had structured the interview plan so there would not be time to put everything to Sullivan in 12 hours.

But Sullivan and Bell both knew policing and the rules of detention.

Lazarus knew they hoped their complaints would bully the team into releasing Sullivan after just 12 hours' detention – before the DNA came back. If that happened, Sullivan could leave the station a free man.

Cochrane took a long sip of her tea, then let out an angry sigh.

'We let him out without charge and that fucker will just disappear,' she said.

This was Lazarus's big fear.

Gardai had no power to stop a suspect leaving the country before they were charged. Lazarus imagined Sullivan rushing home, getting his passport and going straight to the airport.

Away from Ireland. Away from justice.

Lazarus knew there and then what he had to do.

'We need to break him,' he said to the room.

'We have to get him to confess today. We can't wait for the DNA, it could be days. I don't want this animal walking the streets.'

Lazarus turned to Winter.

'I'm going in with Sergeant Cochrane in the next session,' he said.

'The techies have Sullivan's car, head over to the garage and supervise the search. They find anything of interest, come back with it at once.'

'Roger,' Winter said.

★

An hour later, at 2.30pm, Lazarus and Cochrane entered the interview room. Sullivan had been given a meal break, and another consultation with Bell.

Lazarus carried a brown evidence bag.

He sat opposite Bell.

Sullivan shot him a foul look.

'Is this because I stood up to you at the hotel when you arrested Maloney?' he asked.

Sullivan sat back in the chair.

'It's pathetic, that's what it is.'

Lazarus said nothing. But his eyes met Sullivan's. The two men stared at each other. Lazarus thought for a second that Sullivan was going to reach across the table and attack him.

Part of him wished he did.

'We understand you are interested in the outdoors,' Cochrane said.

'What's wrong with that?'

'Do you go camping?'

'Yes.'

He stared pointedly at Lazarus.

'It's a great antidote to the horrible people I see in my job. I go up the mountains by myself.'

'Do you stay over?' Cochrane asked.

'Of course I do. That's what camping is.'

Lazarus reached into the evidence bag at his feet and brought out a small clear plastic bag. He placed it on the desk in front of Sullivan.

'Know what that is, Conor?' Cochrane asked.

Sullivan looked at it.

'It's a bungee cord.'

'Yes. It was recovered close to the scene of the attack.'

'And?'

Lazarus kept his eyes on Sullivan as he slid another small bag over to Cochrane.

'We searched your house and car this morning,' Cochrane said.

'We found these.'

Cochrane held up the evidence bag.

It contained three bungee cords.

'They were found in the search of your car. Detective Garda Winter brought them over in the last 20 minutes. They are the same as the cord found at the scene. We checked. They come in sets of four. There were three in your car. Where is the fourth one?'

Sullivan chewed the inside of his cheek. Sweat formed on his brow.

'I must have lost it camping, or on a job or something. It happens.'

'The cord found at the scene is still being analysed. I think we'll find your DNA on it.'

Sullivan shook his head.

'Not a chance.'

Lazarus put the bags away.

Cochrane looked down at a folder on the table. She took out an A4 photograph.

It was a still from the CCTV footage Winter had taken from O'Shea's house on Botanic Avenue.

It showed the attacker in full frame, his arms raised in celebration.

Sullivan looked at it, and Lazarus saw a reaction on his face.

'This image shows the attacker leaving the scene,' Cochrane said.

Sullivan's eyes were glued to the photograph.

'We had it analysed by our experts in C and S in the Depot. You know who they are, don't you?'

Sullivan's attention was fixed on the photograph. His eyes moved slowly as he examined it.

'Crime and Security,' he said distractedly.

'Very good. They have computer programmes that can enhance CCTV,' Cochrane said.

'Their analysis is the man in the photo is slim – we can all see that – and between five foot ten and six foot one. What height are you?'

Sullivan looked up at Cochrane and Lazarus.

'I didn't do this.'

'You've said that already. What height are you?'

'No comment.'

'That's no problem,' Cochrane said and nodded to Lazarus.

He put a larger evidence bag on the table.

'We found this black running jacket at your house today,' Cochrane said.

Sullivan looked at the bag.

'Do you see the resemblance between it and the jacket the attacker is wearing in the video? Same dark colour. Same tight-fitting body. Same hood. Do you see all that? I think it's the same jacket. What do you think?'

'I'm innocent.'

'We have your black North Face jacket as well from today, but we think this is a better fit,' Cochrane said.

'It would have been no problem for you to change out of it into the North Face one at your car. Would it?'

Sullivan said nothing.

'We'll be examining both, Conor,' Cochrane said.

'Grass. Mud. Blood. You'd be surprised what sticks.'

Lazarus put another evidence bag on the desk.

'A pair of black Nike runners. Also seized from your house,' Cochrane said.

'No comment.'

'The attacker stamped on the woman he tried to kill. He left a footprint on her face. They match other footprints recovered in the mud at the scene. You forgot about the mud, didn't you? When you were escaping after you raped Anne Delaney and tried to kill her. You forgot it had rained earlier and it was mucky. You left footprints.'

'I didn't do it,' Sullivan murmured.

He looked at the ground beside the desk.

'The tests show those prints come off a Nike runner. Your runners are Nike, Conor.'

'Common brand,' Sullivan said.

'The prints are off a size nine shoe. What size shoes do you wear?'

'I didn't attack her. I wasn't there.'

'Your shoes will be analysed. We'll know soon enough if they match. But to me the pattern on the soles of these do look *very* similar to the prints from the scene.'

She stared at Sullivan.

'Lots of coincidences, Conor. If you're innocent. You're running out of road.'

'No comment.'

'I put it to you that is you in the photograph.'

'It's not me.'

'I put it to you the jacket in the photograph was the jacket we seized from your house.'

'No.'

'I put it to you the runners will match the prints from the scene and the victim.'

'No.'

'I put it to you that you raped Anne Delaney, left her for dead and celebrated as you ran away.'

'No.'

'Tell us now, Conor. We have forensic tests to come back. I think I know what those tests will show. I think you know as well. You're done for.'

Sullivan glared at her. His nostrils flared.

'I didn't do it. I didn't fucking do it.'

37

Lazarus and Cochrane left the interview room just after 5pm. Sullivan stayed inside to have another consultation with Bell.

He would soon be taken back to the holding cell and given a meal. Custody rules meant Cochrane and Lazarus had to kick their heels for 90 minutes while Sullivan was allowed food and a rest, as well as the legal consultation. Bradley usually sent an officer to a chipper. The sergeant-in-charge had interrupted the questioning of Sullivan four times to inquire if he needed anything. Bradley's job was not to help with the investigation, but to protect Sullivan. Taking the side of a prisoner was something he relished. Sullivan asked for burger and chips and a can of Coke.

In his last visit, Bradley told Sullivan the original six hours' detention period was up. He said Superintendent Fallon had granted a six-hour extension, which would bring his period of detention up to 10.15pm.

McEvoy was waiting for Lazarus and Cochrane in the viewing room.

'Any word on the DNA?' Lazarus asked.

'Nothing.'

'Shit.'

'We'll get it when it's ready,' McEvoy said.

'Anyway, we have something else to worry about.'

McEvoy gestured to the window.

'We have guests.'

Lazarus walked over and looked through the glass.

He threw his hands in the air.

'Porca Miseria.'

A satellite van with RTÉ in large letters on its side was parked up. A gaggle of media huddled together nearby.

McEvoy joined Lazarus.

'It was on the news. The press office rang a while ago to let us know it was out and to expect media. I told them I could already see the fuckers.'

Lazarus looked at the press pack.

They wore heavy coats to guard from the cold. Most had hats and scarves. But one man was bareheaded. He stood apart from the crowd. He wore a brown padded overcoat, dark blue jeans and black boots.

A black camera with a long lens hung around his neck.

Gallagher had his hands in his coat pockets.

Then he raised his eyes to the Garda station. They fell on Lazarus.

The two men stared at each other. Lazarus saw a look on Gallagher's face.

Disappointment.

Lazarus thought he looked disappointed in him.

After a moment, Gallagher shook his head sadly and turned to the other media.

'Ignore them,' Lazarus said, still looking at Gallagher.

'Let's just plan the next session. It will be our last unless I can persuade the Super to ask the Chief for another 12 hours.'

Exactly 85 minutes later, Lazarus walked back into the interview room, Cochrane at his side.

Lazarus was asking the questions this time, so he sat opposite Sullivan.

Strain was written all over Sullivan's face. His eyes were bloodshot. His hair unkempt.

'How are you feeling?' Lazarus asked.

Sullivan snorted and looked over at Bell.

'This guy's a comedian. This is all his fault and he asks how I am?

Lazarus shrugged.

'Okay Conor–'

'Mr Sullivan.'

Lazarus didn't react.

'The attack we are questioning you about happened at around 11pm last Sunday. Where were you at that time?'

'No comment.'

'It's a simple question. You give us a verifiable alibi and you're in the clear.'

'Nothing to say.'

'Are you trying to protect a source?'

'No comment.'

'Would a source want you locked up like this?'

Sullivan said nothing.

Lazarus waited a beat.

'We noticed you and Mr Gallagher at the scene at 12.40am. How did you know about it so quickly?'

'No comment?'

'Who told you about it?'

'No comment.'

'Did you tell yourself? You attacked the woman, then tipped yourself off so you could get an exclusive at the same time?'

'I did not rape anyone.'

'You keep saying that, but you're not offering any alibi evidence to show you weren't there. Talk is cheap. Prove that it wasn't you. Help us out.'

'Sergeant Lazarus,' Bell snapped. 'That's not how it works. My client does not have to prove anything. That is your job.'

Lazarus's olive cheeks burned. He looked down at his notes. He slid a sheet of paper across the desk.

'This is a copy of the story with your name on it that *The Globe* put up online before 7am the morning after the attack.'

Sullivan glanced down at it.

'You have a lot of detail, Mr Sullivan. Far more than any other outlet.'

'Thanks,' Sullivan said.

Lazarus didn't bite.

'See this,' he said, pointing with his pen at a line in the story that had already been underlined.

'It says, "*Globe* sources have also revealed she was found semi-naked and is now critically ill in the city's Mater Hospital.".'

'And?' Sullivan said.

'The victim was fully clothed when gardai got to her,' Lazarus said.

'I read the story at the time and thought you made it up. But it turns out you were right. The couple who found her later admitted to us they had dressed her before we arrived.'

'So?'

'That means you knew something we didn't. How did you know?'

'No comment.'

'You know because you were there.'

'No.'

'The Sweeneys say they never heard of you. We checked their phone records. They didn't call or message anyone for more than ten hours after they found her. They were in shock. Your story was long done by then.'

'No comment.'

'They didn't tell you, and no garda knew. How did you know?'

'No comment.'

'Your story says she was strangled.'

'No comment.'

'By the time you wrote that, five people knew. Me, detective garda Winter and McEvoy, the scenes of crime officer and the doctor who treated her.'

'No comment.'

'Ben Flannery is adamant he told nobody. I trust him. Rachel Winter was busy. She didn't speak to any other garda, so it wasn't her. Harry was with me. And we've checked all the phones. None of us has been in contact with you ever. I certainly wasn't.'

Lazarus sat forward in his chair.

'If we didn't tell you, that leaves the doctor.'

'No comment.'

'Do you think a doctor who specialises in treating victims of rape and sexual assault would do such a thing? There's no evidence she has before. We checked. Why would she do it now?'

Sullivan folded his arms.

'No comment.'

'I am sure she didn't,' Lazarus said.

'She has given us a statement. I am confident she doesn't even know *The Globe* exists. She's more an *Irish Times* sort of person.'

'Nobody's perfect,' Sullivan said.

'If we didn't and the medic didn't,' Lazarus said, 'then the only conclusion I can draw is you knew about the strangulation because you did it.'

'I'm innocent,' Sullivan said.

Lazarus opened the folder again.

'I want to talk to you about a sex worker called Lucy Fowler. Do you know her, Mr Sullivan?'

Sullivan's eyes widened.

'No comment.'

'Lucy knows you. She told us. She made a statement after seeing an appeal in the media.'

Sullivan went pale.

'No comment.'

'She tells us you use her. The third Sunday of the month. Like clockwork. Is that around the time you get paid, Conor?'

'No comment.'

'Lucy says you keep talking about killing a woman. She says it's your fantasy.'

'No comment.'

'Do you fantasise about raping women?'

'Jesus, that's disgusting.'

'I put it to you raped Anne Delaney,' Lazarus said.

'I didn't rape anyone.'

'We checked Lucy's phone records and yours. What's the relationship between you two?'

'No comment.'

Lazarus slid another sheet of paper over towards Sullivan.

'This is an analysis of the phone traffic between you and Ms Fowler over the last year.'

'No comment.'

'You rang her 65 times. You sent her 105 texts. She texted you 27 times and rang you 24 times. What were you talking to her about?'

'No comment.'

'Where were you last Sunday night?'

'No comment.'

Lazarus held up an A4 sheet inside a plastic folder.

'This is the security log from your office from Sunday. We got a warrant for it earlier.'

Sullivan said nothing.

'It shows your access to your office on the day.'

'No comment.'

'It is your card. You have had it since...' Lazarus checked his notes... 'Sunday, May 13, 2012. Nobody else has access to it. It shows you went into the office early on, but then you were out later.'

'No comment.'

'You come in at 11.40am.'

'No comment.'

'You leave at 6.43pm. I saw you at the hotel when we arrested Sean Maloney and we had our little spat in the evening. Do you remember that? I'm sure you do. You threatened me. That was at about 8.30pm.'

Sullivan stared at Lazarus, said nothing.

'You come back to the office at 11.47pm. That's more than three hours between me and you having our row and you getting to the office. Where were you?'

'No comment.'

'Anne was attacked at around 11pm. The attacker left her at 11.21pm. He escaped by running up Botanic Avenue.'

'No comment.'

'Saint Mobhi Road intersects the avenue. If you turn right onto it and go up a few hundred metres you can get on to Home Farm Road. You go the full length of that and before you know it, you're in Drumcondra and are heading back into town.'

'No comment.'

'Two colleagues did that journey last night. They timed it. It took 19 minutes to get from Botanic Avenue to your office via Home Farm Road.'

'No comment.'

'You drive and own a black BMW.'

Lazarus red out the reg.

'And you said no one else had access to it.'

Sullivan swallowed.

'No comment.'

'Do you know what ANPR is?'

'No comment.'

'I think you know ANPR is Automatic Number Plate Recognition. The Traffic Corps uses it.'

'No comment.'

'One of the cars was on duty in north Dublin that evening.'

'No comment.'

'It can read six number plates per second. It picked up the number plate associated with your BMW at the junction of Drumcondra Road and Clonliffe Road at 11.34pm. You were heading into town. Away from the rape scene.'

'No comment.'

'We have other CCTV which shows a car I believe to be yours driving into the city centre from Drumcondra a few minutes earlier. You know the road. It's the one from the airport into the city centre.'

Lazarus saw a flash of recognition in Sullivan.

'That car was yours, Conor. I can see it in your eyes,' he said.

'You were on the Drumcondra Road close to Griffith Park less than 15 minutes after the attack.'

'No comment,' Sullivan said.

'You reached your office car park at 11.47pm. Then you used your card to get into your office at 11.48pm.'

'No comment.'

'Where were you, Conor? Where were you coming from?'

'No comment.'

'Your car is seen coming back from the direction of the attack after it happened.'

'No comment.'

'Tell us where you were.'

'No comment.'

'If you were meeting someone, tell us.'

More sweat appeared on Sullivan's brow.

'I have no comment,' he said.

'Are you sure?' Lazarus said.

'You seem to be trying to convince yourself. Tell us. End this now.'

Sullivan shook his head angrily.

'You're in the shit, Conor,' Lazarus said.

'Tell us if you were meeting someone. Do you realise how precarious your situation is here?'

Sullivan stayed silent for a few seconds.

But Lazarus could see he was thinking.

Considering his next move.

Lazarus pressed on.

'We checked your phone records for the day of the attack on Ms Delaney.'

'No comment.'

'The phone was off between 9pm and 11.48pm. It was dead. No texts sent or received. No calls made, none answered. It was a brick. That would mean nothing to most people.'

Lazarus paused a beat.

'But I'm not most people. A void like that is significant. An absence of evidence can be just as important as an abundance of information.'

'No comment.'

'If your phone had been on at the time, we would have been able to track your movement. It's called cell site analysis. We can map where your phone was by the masts it passed through. Every time there is activity on your phone, it pings off the nearest mobile phone mast. You see where I am going here?'

'No comment.'

'If you were driving from your office to somewhere, the calls and texts you made and received on the way would create a map for us to show your route.'

'No comment.'

'Your phone tells us where you are at all times, as long as there is activity on it.'

'Nothing to say.'

'But when it comes to the evening of the attack there is no activity between 9pm and 11.48pm. No data for us at all. Your phone was off. That tells me you are forensically aware and you turned your handset off because you were worried about being tracked.'

Sullivan bit his lower lip.

'Why were you worried about that, Conor? What were you doing that you did not want to be mapped?'

'No comment.'

'All this evidence builds a picture. And that's what we have to do. We have to give the prosecution the tools to build a picture for the jury. The evidence is pointing to one thing: you were responsible for the rape and attempted murder of Anne Delaney.'

'No.'

Lazarus pressed on.

'This is your chance to do the right thing. You've covered more criminal cases than most. Imagine what the judge will do when he hears you confessed. You will get a chunk of time off your sentence. And I presume you do know the maximum penalty for rape is life?'

'I'm innocent.'

Lazarus had his hands steepled in front of his mouth as if he was in prayer. He stared at Sullivan.

'Your wife cheated on you. Your new girlfriend dumped you. You lost a massive defamation case to a woman. Another woman accused you of stalking her. You attacked Anne Delaney because you want to know what it's like to kill a woman. You hate them, don't you. You're an incel. You think women have ruined your life. This was payback. Wasn't it?'

Sullivan was rocking in his chair.

His eyes were flickering.

He bit his lower lip.

Lazarus had seen this moment countless times in interview rooms.

The moment when a prisoner breaks.

All the evidence they had put to him must have been taking its toll on Sullivan. Taken together, it was a compelling picture, enough to persuade a guilty man he was fucked. A few gentle words from Lazarus could push him towards a confession.

It was always a key moment.

Lazarus's technique was to let the suspect stew in an uncomfortable silence as the demons in his head battled it out.

The Atmosphere in the room was charged.

'Take your chance, Conor. Get it out. The judges take an early plea into account.'

Sullivan said nothing.

Lazarus took a red Garda photograph book from the folder. He opened it, flicked through it until he found the photo he wanted.

He turned the book towards Sullivan.

It was of Delaney in a coma.

'Look closely,' Lazarus said.

'This is what you did to Anne Delaney. Look at her face. Look at the bruises. Look at her nose. Look at her neck.'

'Fucking hell,' Sullivan said.

'You know how this is going to end. There is significant evidence against you and we both know the DNA is going to come back a match.'

Sullivan looked down at the table.

Lazarus saw a crack and tried to make it bigger.

'I'll speak up for you in court. I'll highlight your lack of convictions. I'll say you showed remorse.'

The silence hung in the room.

'Do it, Conor. Think of your family and friends.'

Sullivan's eyes welled up. He looked up from the desk. Lazarus felt a thrill of anticipation course through his body.

He knew it was going to happen.

Any second now.

Sullivan looked up and stared into Lazarus's eyes.

And then: 'No comment.'

38

Lazarus sat in gloomy silence in Fallon's office while she read the memos of the interviews with Sullivan.

He knew what was coming, but that didn't make it any less palatable.

Fallon put the papers down, took off her reading glasses.

'Have you anything left to put to him?'

Lazarus shook his head glumly.

'We're waiting for forensics on his clothing we seized.'

'Don't mind the forensics. There's no way they will be back in time. Look at the bungee cord. They've had that for almost a week and there is still nothing back. It's complicated science.'

She gave him a disapproving look.

'We know this, John. Now, have you anything left to put to him?'

Lazarus grimaced. He looked up at the wall clock. 10pm. The team had just 15 minutes before Sullivan's detention ran out.

They had the chance to get another 12 hours, but that was up to the Chief Superintendent. Fallon had come back from home and was in her civilian clothing. She would be the one making the case to the Chief, Brenda Kavanagh, for the extension.

But first Lazarus had to persuade Fallon.

'Have you anything else?' Fallon repeated.

'No,' Lazarus said.

'Right,' Fallon said, 'what about the DNA?'

'Flannery brought it to the lab early today. I asked them to hurry it. But they're dealing with two murders. We're down the pecking order.'

'So you won't get the DNA tonight, or even tomorrow?'

'It could be a few days,' Lazarus said.

Fallon looked over to Cochrane.

'Thoughts?'

'He's as guilty as sin, Super,' Cochrane said.

'He did it and he knows we know he did it. The clincher for me was when we showed the photos of the damage he did to the girl. He couldn't cope with that. I thought he was going to puke. And he knew it was over when we put all the technical evidence to him. He's toast.'

Fallon looked at Lazarus for a long moment.

Then she scanned the interview notes again.

She shook her head.

'You've run out of road, John,' she said.

'The DNA won't be back and the forensics on his clothing and that cord will take even longer. I'm sorry. There is no basis to extend the prisoner's detention. I'm not going to ask the Chief. She would laugh me out of it. It will have to be a file to the DPP job.

'Let him go.'

Lazarus closed his eyes and sighed a deep sigh.

*

Ten minutes later, Lazarus stood with Bradley as he opened the heavy door in the holding cell.

Lazarus looked inside. Sullivan sat on the bed, his knees up, back to the wall.

'You still here?' Sullivan asked Lazarus.

'The overtime must be good.'

Lazarus ignored him.

'Come with us,' Bradley said.

'What's happening? he asked, suspicious.

'You are being released without charge,' Bradly said.

'There will be a file prepared for the Director of Public Prosecutions. That office will decide if you're to face any charges.'

Sullivan laughed.

'That's you fucked, Lazarus. The DPP will take one look at this and laugh you out of court.'

He knitted his eyebrows as he thought about what he had just said.

'What am I saying? This won't get near any court.'

Lazarus said nothing.

Sullivan got up and followed the cops down the corridor. In less than a minute, they were in the custody room where Sullivan had been processed earlier. McEvoy was waiting for them.

McEvoy gave Sullivan a subtle nod, but Lazarus just stared at him. Bradley went through the paperwork and retrieved Sullivan's property from a locker. He was handed his belt, wallet and house keys.

'Where are my phones? And my car key?' Sullivan protested.

'We have seized your phones. They are being examined by forensics. The same goes for your car,' Lazarus said.

'For fuck's sake,' Sullivan said.

'You can ring whoever you want for a lift or we can order you a taxi,' Bradley said.

'I need a phone,' he said.

'Over there,' Bradley nodded towards a handset on the wall. Sullivan walked over and punched in a number.

He waited a beat then started talking when the other person answered.

'You're up, then? Not past your bedtime?'

Sullivan listened for a moment, then broke in.

'You're outside? Already?' Lazarus realised he was speaking to Gallagher.

Sullivan stared at Lazarus with angry eyes.

'The bastards leaked my arrest. What a surprise. I presume you're not alone?'

Sullivan listened.

'I should have realised they would do that,' he said.

'I'll see you outside in one minute. Just pull the jeep up at the entrance.'

He hung up.

'Thanks for shafting me, Lazarus. They are waiting for me. You did this on purpose. You want me doing the walk of shame, don't you? You want me in all the papers tomorrow.'

Lazarus stared at him.

'I don't talk to journalists, Sullivan.'

Sullivan laughed.

'Don't take me for a fool. This is all part of your strategy.'

Sullivan grabbed at his possessions and signed the receipt before walking through another corridor. Lazarus followed him.

They came into the waiting area.

Duffy stood at the open glass hatch that separated the waiting room from the public office.

She pointed at the door with a pen.

'The exit is that way.'

'I presume there is a welcoming committee for me, Garda?' Sullivan said with a weak smile.

Duffy smiled back, despite herself.

'I'm sure they're all friends of yours.'

'That's what I'm worried about.'

Lazarus could see Sullivan was terrified. His hands were shaking. After a few seconds' hesitation, Sullivan walked towards the open doorway. He took a deep breath, so deep his shoulders hunched up and his chest expanded. And then he stepped outside. Lazarus moved to the doorway to watch.

There was a moment's stillness.

Then the night exploded in a hundred flashes. Lazarus heard the rapid-fire click of lens shutters. Journalists surrounded Sullivan as he walked out of the station towards Gallagher's black Volkswagen Touareg. The smoked windows were so dark Lazarus could not see inside.

Two lights came on as the camera operators turned their attention to Sullivan. The lights were so strong they hurt Lazarus's eyes. The media started devouring Sullivan. He bustled towards the SUV.

Its engine gunned. It was pointing uphill, out of town.

Sullivan put his head down as he fought his way through the baying press pack.

'Did you do it?' Lazarus heard a female voice shout.

'Are you a rapist, Conor?' another woman reporter demanded.

'Are you a danger to women, Conor?'

'Do women have anything to fear from you?'

'Did you admit it, Conor? Did you confess?'

Sullivan said nothing. The cameras were in his face now and a few hacks pushed microphones up close. Sullivan raised his head to look for Gallagher and saw the Touareg was in front of him, the passenger door ajar. He ignored the questions.

'Did you attack her, Conor?' Another voice shouted.

'Surely you want to say something? You would if you were innocent,' Lazarus heard a male reporter shout.

He recognised the voice as that of a well-known TV crime journalist, David O'Brien. He was grey haired, about 50, with a pointy nose, bushy eyebrows and a strong jaw. O'Brien was well built and tall, with muscular arms, one of which was extended like a bar towards Sullivan. He held a microphone with a large muffler on it. O'Brien had pushed through the crowd with his camera woman to get in Sullivan's face. Lazarus saw Sullivan flinch when O'Brien started shouting at him. He sensed there was tension between the two men.

'Is it true you fantasise about rape and murder Sullivan?' O'Brien shouted.

'Fuck off!' Sullivan shouted.

Lazarus saw a smile spread on O'Brien's face.

'Did you pretend to strangle a prostitute?' O'Brien said.

Sullivan's fists clenched and Lazarus thought for a second he was going to attack.

'Were you ever investigated for stalking, Sullivan? Did a woman go to the gardai about you?'

Sullivan reached the door of the Touareg and yanked it open. He dived inside and tried to close it, but O'Brien held it open.

'You were in Holland the night a woman was raped and the DNA from that attacker matched that from the Griffith Park rape, that's a bit of a coincidence, isn't it, Sullivan? How do you explain it?'

Lazarus flinched. The Super had instructed the team not to put the Dutch attack to Sullivan. It happened outside Ireland and had no standing here. But someone had leaked it to O'Brien.

Sullivan brought up his left foot and used it to nudge O'Brien away from the door. He pulled it shut and the engine engaged.

The SUV sped off, with the media scrum running after it, cameras and smartphones in their hands.

39

Saturday

Lazarus woke at 6.30am.

Jenna was still asleep. He tip-toed into the bathroom. His mouth felt furry from four Moretti he drank when he arrived home just after midnight.

He showered and shaved then got dressed and went downstairs. It was still dark. He hated the Irish winter and longed to be back home in Italy in the summer, when the days were long and the sun warmed his bones.

He took a glass to the fridge and filled it with ice-cold water. Then he dropped a vitamin tablet into it. While he waited for it to dissolve, he made himself a coffee. He chose a double espresso. He took it with two sugars and drank from a sturdy white cup with a thick handle and a black rim. There were two words on it in large black capital letters: *Forza Juve. Come on Juventus.*

He sipped the coffee, turned on the radio and started preparing porridge. He was just adding the honey and banana when he heard the jingle for the 7am news. The first item was about Brexit. He couldn't help smiling as he remembered Ciara Farrell getting Jacob Rees-Mogg's name wrong a few days earlier.

Sullivan was next. The newsreader said he had been released without charge and a file would be sent to the Director of Public Prosecutions.

He ate his porridge and finished his espresso, before putting the bowl and cup in the dishwasher. He walked out of the house just as the light was breaking. There were no clouds in the sky and he could smell the early morning sea. He wore a dark blue Italian blazer, a white shirt, no tie, black shoes and brown trousers. He carried his overcoat over his arm and placed it and his briefcase in the passenger seat of the car.

He got to the station at 7.45am. He was the first in the team to arrive. He went to his desk in the incident room and checked for messages. He had been hoping the DNA results would have come back. Nothing.

He fidgeted at his desk, waiting for Flannery to arrive.

He did some administration, then went online, clicked into the *Irish Independent*. Sullivan was the top story. It was dominated by a large photograph of him walking from the station.

He stared at the camera. His face impassive. His lips open. The flash had lit up Sullivan's pale skin. His hair was bushed up at the front, as if he was just out of bed and hadn't had a chance to comb it.

Lazarus examined the rest of the photo. He could see the TV reporter O'Brien brandishing a microphone in Sullivan's face. O'Brien's eyes were bulging, his mouth open. The camerawoman was beside him. Her right eye was closed, her left tight against the viewfinder as she tracked Sullivan. Two reporters were on the other side of Sullivan. Lazarus started reading the story.

A leading crime reporter arrested over a violent rape launched a foul-mouth tirade when he walked out of a Garda station last night – as the detective who interrogated him looked on.

Lazarus went back to the photograph. He looked past Sullivan and saw himself framed in the station doorway.

He was staring at Sullivan.

'You're a celebrity now, I see,' a voice said.

Lazarus turned and saw Cochrane with Flannery in the doorway.

Flannery was in his usual gear of work boots, navy blue cargo pants with side pockets on the thighs and a black polo shirt with a gold Garda crest on his chest.

Cochrane held a print copy of the newspaper in one hand, a large mug in the other.

'They must have been short of news,' Lazarus said.

'You'd need to be careful, Lazarus. The Depot does not like detective sergeants in the spotlight.'

Lazarus shrugged his shoulders.

He turned to Flannery.

'When will they give us the DNA results?'

Flannery screwed his face in thought.

'I'll wait until 11am. That's 24 hours after the sample was taken. If I don't hear from them by then, I'll give them a bell. It's a Saturday, but they are on seven days a week.'

It was 8.35am. Fewer than three hours.

He looked back to Flannery. He was about to tell him to make it 11am on the button when he saw a Manila envelope in his left hand.

'What's that?' he asked.

'It's the XRY report from Sullivan's phone,' Flannery said.

'I did it this morning. Probably while you were still in your scratcher.'

XRY was a piece of software law enforcement used to harvest data from a suspect's phone. All Flannery had to do was connect the phone to his computer, open the software and the programme extracted the data. Every call made and received, same with texts. It could download messages, even those deleted.

Lazarus thought back to yesterday morning in the custody suite and he remembered an angry Sullivan refusing to reveal the PIN of his iPhone. His was the newest model and Lazarus knew the software had not yet been developed to crack its security, despite what he told Sullivan. The experts played a never-ending game of cat and mouse with Apple. They had managed to break into older iPhones, but each new model had to be broken in its own right. It took more than a year for the latest model to be accessible.

'This is from his burner,' Flannery said, reading Lazarus's mind.

Lazarus had forgotten about Sullivan's throwaway phone.

He looked at the envelope and saw it was bulging with sheets.

'It's a goldmine,' Flannery said.

'Plenty for you to read.'

Lazarus grabbed the envelope.

He was just opening it when he heard the heavy thud of feet in the corridor outside.

McEvoy appeared in the doorway, his face flushed.

He wore a brown jacket, blue shirt, blue tie.

And his body armour.

'Shooting at the Casey house,' he panted.

He turned and started running.

Lazarus slapped the envelope down on the desk, grabbed his own vest and ran after him.

They made it to the Camry in the car park in less than a minute. McEvoy jumped into the driver's seat.

He switched on the blue lights and siren and gunned the accelerator. The engine roared. The tyres screeched. The Camry shot out of its parking space.

The sound of the siren was deafening.

'How bad?' Lazarus shouted.

'Control says at least one casualty.'

The car was on Western Way within five seconds. McEvoy kept his eyes on the road, his hands gripping the steering wheel so hard his knuckles were white. He took a hard left, the tyres struggling to stay to the road. McEvoy pressed down hard on the accelerator, forcing every ounce of speed out of the engine. He came to a turn for Wellington Street on the right, took it hard, kept the speed up. He flashed along the small road. It was only 150 metres long. After what felt like an instant for Lazarus, McEvoy jerked the wheel to his left and the Camry screeched on to Dorset Street. He hit 80 kilometres per hour. McEvoy didn't relent until he reached the junction of Dorset Street and the North Circular Road, 400 metres away. Even then, he didn't come to a halt, he slowed down to around 40 kilometres per hour.

'Clear left!' Lazarus shouted, looking to his left and seeing the vehicles on his side had stopped for their lights and siren.

'Clear right!' McEvoy said at the same time.

The car flashed right at the junction onto the North Circular. Lazarus heard more sirens as other cars began responding to the shooting.

The Casey house was one mile away now. Lazarus figured it would take them two minutes to get there. He took out his black Sig-Sauer from its holster. He pulled the slide back and forced a round into the chamber.

Suddenly, an urgent voice filled the car.

It was the Garda radio.

'All units. Look out for a motorbike, rider and passenger. Pillion is armed. Last seen going on Ballybough Road, possibly heading onto the North Circular.'

Lazarus and McEvoy glanced at each other.

'It's coming our way, Harry,' Lazarus said.

'Turn off the siren,' he said.

He lowered his window.

McEvoy pressed a button and the wailing stopped.

He kept his eyes fixed on the road, but reached down and took out his own pistol.

Lazarus stuck his head out and listened.

Then he heard a rumble in the distance, like thunder coming in from the sea.

It became louder with every beat of his heart.

McEvoy slowed down.

The car was almost at a crawl.

They scanned the road in front of them. And still the noise continued to get louder. Coming towards them.

Everything else seemed to fade away.

All Lazarus could hear was the roar of a motorbike.

And he knew.

'It's going to be us Harry. Block the road.'

McEvoy swung the Camry across the road.

They were half-way down the road that led from Dorset Street to Summerhill. It was 50 metres before a sharp bend. The bend meant they could not see down to Summerhill, where the bike was coming from.

But it also meant the bike could not see them.

Lazarus stepped out of the car and tapped his body armour to reassure himself. He kept his gun down by his side, his finger hovering over the trigger guard.

The noise of the approaching motorcycle filled his head.

It had to be close.

And then he saw it.

The bike sped around the corner, weaving from side to side, the biker struggling to control it. It was a powerful machine. It was a rich green, with a flash of white down the side of the front panel.

The same bike that that O'Hara had used when he shot up the Casey house a few days earlier.

The wheels were black and small and wide. The headlight was just above the wheel and it shone with a fierce intensity. The front fairing had a small semi-circle of plexiglass and the rider was crouched over it, his hands wide on the grips of the handlebar. He wore dark clothing and a black helmet. The pillion wore a white helmet and gripped the side handrails.

Lazarus stepped into the middle of the road and raised his Sig.

He pointed it straight at the bike.

The rider saw him and hit the brakes.

Lazarus heard the tyres screech, then the bike wobbled and veered to the left.

The rider tried to right it, but over compensated and the bike toppled onto its side.

They rider and passenger were both thrown from it.

Lazarus watched in slow motion as they slammed into the ground, then somersaulted with their arms and legs flailing.

There was a moment's stillness as the pair came to a shuddering stop.

Lazarus started running, his pistol extended in a two-handed grip. The two figures were about five metres apart and Lazarus knew he could not cover them both.

He picked the passenger because he knew he was the shooter.

He was on his feet already. He was beginning to run, his head moving from side to side as he looked for an escape route.

He searched to his left but saw nothing. Then Lazarus saw him turn to his right and sprint towards a small alley.

'Stop!' Lazarus shouted.

He ran towards the man.

'Stop! Armed gardaí!'

The man glanced back. In an instant Lazarus saw the same eyes as the shooter who had tried to kill him outside the Casey house.

Danny O'Hara.

O'Hara hesitated, then pumped his legs and ran down the passage. Lazarus was fitter and faster and closed on him. He could see a slight limp and realised O'Hara must have received a knock falling off the bike.

'Stop, Danny, stop! Armed gardaí!' Lazarus shouted.

O'Hara kept running.

He reached a left turn about 50 metres into the passage, dived into it.

O'Hara ran on, Lazarus gaining on him, his limp getting more and more pronounced.

Then he faltered.

A heavy iron gate, seven metres high, blocked his escape route. O'Hara saw an alleyway in the row of tight terraced houses on his right. He ran into it, Lazarus chasing him still.

Lazarus was 20 metres from O'Hara.

He heard his shoes clomping on the tarmac, their echo filling the tiny street.

Lazarus saw the path come to a shuddering halt against a high concrete wall about 30 metres away.

He stopped running.

He knew there was nowhere for O'Hara to go.

The path was a dead end.

O'Hara realised it was over and faltered to a stop.

He was five metres from Lazarus.

For a second, he didn't move as he appeared to be considering his options.

Then he turned to face Lazarus, a black pistol in his hand.

Lazarus levelled his Sig at O'Hara's chest.

He moved his finger onto the trigger.

Still O'Hara brought his pistol up.

'Don't do it, Danny,' Lazarus shouted.

He was panting from the foot chase, but he held his gun steady.

'Drop the gun, Danny.'

O'Hara continued to raise the pistol, his fingers tight on the grip, his index finger curling on the trigger.

'Don't do it, Danny. I'll shoot you. I will fucking shoot you.'

O'Hara kept raising the pistol.

Lazarus knew he was approaching the point of no return.

'Armed gardai!' he shouted.

'Drop your weapon!'

One last time.

One last chance for O'Hara.

Lazarus knew another ten centimetres on the arc O'Hara was moving the pistol along and the muzzle would be pointing right at him.

He couldn't let that happen.

Lazarus knew he had to fire.

He started the final squeeze on the trigger, making sure the iron sights were on O'Hara's chest.

A brief memory of his army days flashed in his head.

Hours spent on the range, honing his marksmanship skills.

One shot, one kill.

O'Hara's gun came up level and straight.

It was pointing at Lazarus.

Lazarus pulled the trigger.

The Sig coughed once.

Lazarus saw a red flower explode in O'Hara's chest.

The bullet knocked him backwards.

He collapsed onto the tarmac.

He landed on his back and his helmet hit the ground.

The helmet bounced up and slammed back down with a loud crack.

O'Hara's arms extended as if he was being crucified.

The pistol flew from his right hand and landed on the ground.

Lazarus kept his Sig trained on O'Hara as he ran towards him.

He got down on his knees.

He leant over O'Hara.

He put his own gun away. The threat was gone. He unsnapped the chinstrap and removed the helmet, holding the back of O'Hara's head and lowering it gently to the ground.

He felt dampness on O'Hara's hair and he realised it was sweat.

O'Hara's eyes were glassy.

Lazarus placed two forefingers on O'Hara's neck.

He found a faint pulse.

He lowered his ear down to O'Hara's mouth and heard him take short, sharp breaths.

'Can you hear me, Danny?' he said.

A gurgling noise came from O'Hara's throat.

He looked up at Lazarus.

Lazarus held his gaze.

Then he smiled down at him.

'I always keep my promises, Danny.'

40

Lazarus stared out the window of Fallon's office.

He watched people walk the busy streets and wondered what it was like to be normal.

The movie of him shooting Danny O'Hara played on loop in his head. The bullet hitting him. Exploding his chest. Smoke curling from the muzzle of Lazarus's pistol. O'Hara collapsing. The gun flying from his hand.

He had already been interviewed by GSOC, the outside police oversight body. He knew that was only the first step. They would want to speak to him again and again. They'd taken his Sig, too, for examination. He patted his hip absent-mindedly and felt naked without his pistol. He wondered how long it would be before he got it back. Months, probably.

It was 1.15pm, more than four hours after the shooting. He had come out of an interview room 20 minutes earlier. He had been grilled by GSOC and Internal Affairs separately. Now he was telling Fallon what happened in the alleyway.

O'Hara's heart stopped moments after two Dublin Fire Brigade paramedics had arrived on scene.

Lazarus watched as they tried to save him.

One performed CPR, two hands together, the palms pumping on O'Hara's chest. After a minute, the second paramedic took over. He pumped even harder. Blood spurted from O'Hara's mouth every time the paramedic pushed down.

Then O'Hara convulsed and sucked in a long gurgle of blood and air into his lungs.

They rushed him to the Mater. The hospital was so close, the ambulance got to the alley within three minutes and O'Hara was in accident and emergency seven minutes later.

The doctors had been working on him since.

Lazarus imagined the frenetic activity behind the Mater's glass exterior as they fought to keep him alive.

The sound of Fallon's desk phone ringing dragged Lazarus back into the room.

The superintendent snatched at the handset.

He examined Fallon as she listened in silence to the other person on the call.

She sat behind her large desk.

Anderson stood beside the sofa. Impassive.

'Okay, thank you,' Fallon said into the phone, then hung up.

She held the handset.

She stared down at it for a long moment then looked at Lazarus.

Her face was ashen.

'Danny O'Hara died three minutes ago,' she said.

She got up and walked over to him, placed a gentle hand on his arm.

'They did their best.'

Lazarus didn't answer. He didn't know what to say. He should have been devastated at taking another human's life. But all he felt was a comforting calmness.

'I'm fine,' he said after a moment.

Fallon glanced at Anderson for moral support. He didn't react.

'John, Danny O'Hara is dead. You shot him.'

'I heard you the first time, Super.'

'Well, are you okay? Because...because you just killed a man.'

Lazarus looked her in the eye.

'O'Hara was going to kill me. About to leave Jenna a widow and my boys fatherless. I'm just happy I got him before he got me.'

'Jesus Christ, Lazarus,' Fallon said.

'It was him or me. I'm glad it was him,' Lazarus said.

An awkward silence descended on the room.

Fallon looked shocked at his callousness.

Lazarus didn't care.

'How is Mick Casey?' he asked.

'Fuck Mick Casey,' Fallon snapped.

'I'm worried about you, not him. There'll be one hell of an investigation into this. You can't just say you're fine. For fuck's sake, man.'

She took a deep breath and stroked her hair.

'I'm sorry. You're right, you deserve to know. O'Hara got him outside his house,' she said.

'He fired seven times but missed with four. Mick was walking to his car when he saw the motorbike coming down the road. He turned and ran, but O'Hara went after him. One round hit him in the shoulder. Another hit him in the side and broke one of his ribs. The third one grazed his head. He's a lucky boy. Could have been worse. Could have been holding hands with O'Hara in the morgue.'

Lazarus took a long swallow from a cup of hot tea. He was usually an espresso man, but Fallon had insisted he take the tea with lots of sugar. It was in a blue mug with the iconic NYPD crest. Fallon had brought it on a trip to America.

Fallon had left the tea bag in too long and had not put in enough milk. But the taste was masked by the sugar.

Anderson spoke up.

'This is not what I need right now,' he said, almost to himself.

He shook his head.

'Another major case.'

Lazarus felt a sudden rage.

'You all right, Inspector?'

Anderson flushed.

'Excuse me?' he said.

'John,' Fallon said slowly.

Lazarus put the mug down on the window sill.

'You look a bit peaky, Inspector. You're not worried about me, are you? I'm fine. The prick deserved it.'

'Watch your mouth, Lazarus,' Anderson said.

'Or could it be, Inspector, you're worrying about your own arse?' Lazarus said.

'Excuse me?'

Lazarus moved forward.

'You're worried about the Super's competition. Aren't you?'

'That's enough, Sergeant,' Anderson said.

'You're afraid,' Lazarus said.

'Your beloved father-in-law the fucking Deputy fucking Commissioner can't be on the selection board. Even the Garda has limits. They couldn't allow that. So you might get someone who will evaluate your skills and experience and leadership qualities. And they will ask you how you as D/I have so many unsolved crimes on your patch. And you won't have an answer because you're an incompetent prick.'

'That's enough! Sergeant Lazarus! Stop!' Fallon shouted.

Lazarus ignored her.

'And a racist one at that.'

Fallon stormed around her desk and stood between Lazarus and Anderson.

'Listen to me, Lazarus,' Fallon said.

'I know you've had a shit day. I know you're in shock. But you will not speak to a superior officer like that. Do you understand?'

'He's not superior to me,' Lazarus said.

'Do you understand?' she asked again.

Lazarus was in balls deep. Past the point of no return. And he didn't care. He was about to launch another broadside when there was a heavy knock on the door.

'Not now!' Fallon shouted, her eyes still locked on Lazarus.

'It's urgent, Super,' the voice on the other side insisted.

Fallon's shoulders slumped.

'Jesus Christ.'

She breathed a deep sigh.

'We'll talk about this again, John,' she said.

Then she shouted at the door.

'Come in.'

Flannery walked in, paper in his hand.

He had run up the stairs from the incident room and was out of breath.

He held up the sheet of paper.

'The laboratory has just sent the results of the comparison between Conor Sullivan's sample and the attacker's DNA.'

Lazarus stopped breathing.

'Well?' Fallon asked.

Flannery looked over at Lazarus.

Then looked away.

'It's not a match,' he said.

41

The room started spinning. Lazarus had to grab on to the window sill for support.

He closed his eyes as he tried to regain his balance. He kept his eyes closed for a long moment as he tried to compute Flannery's news.

It was devastating.

They – he – had arrested an innocent man. A man who he knew now would come after Lazarus's blood.

And he knew he had no defence.

He finally opened his eyes and saw Anderson staring coldly at him.

A thin smile appeared on the detective inspector's face.

The anger Lazarus felt moments earlier had vanished.

It had been replaced by fear.

The room fell quiet. It was an uncomfortable silence, like two people on a blind date who run out of things to talk about before the second course.

Lazarus rubbed his chin and tried to stay calm on the outside, on the inside his heart was in his mouth.

'Are they sure?' he asked.

Fallon grabbed the sheet from Flannery.

She scanned it.

'He's not your man, Lazarus. The science does not lie.'

She nodded to Flannery.

'Thanks, Ben.'

Flannery walked out of the office.

Fallon waited until the door was closed then let out a long breath.

'Fuck.'

She slapped the paper onto her desk.

'Fuck,' she said again.

'We're fucked.'

She walked back to her desk, turned to Lazarus.

'This is a disaster, John.'

He saw anger in her eyes.

'You arrested one of Ireland's top journalists. There was a circus outside the station last night because one of your fuckers leaked it. His face is on the front page of the papers and I even heard his name on the radio this morning.'

She sat into her chair, put her hands to her face.

'And now he's fucking innocent. Jesus Christ of Almighty.'

Anderson drew himself up to his full height and smoothed his oily hair.

'Super, I objected to this arrest by Sergeant Lazarus. I warned him this was a foolish strategy. He took the word of a prostitute, for God's sake. Sullivan has friends in the Depot. It's political now. This could end badly. For all of us.'

Fallon looked up.

'How badly?'

She was pure cop. She was not political. But Anderson was. He had spent most of his service in the Depot, Garda Headquarters, where everything was political. Who you had lunch with was political.

Who you promoted was political.

Who you shafted was political.

It was as far away from real policing as possible. Anderson had thrived there as much as he had floundered as an investigator on the streets.

Lazarus saw a new look in Anderson.

A mixture of glee, arrogance, and confidence. He had spent the last 18 months a fish out of water investigating crime.

Now Lazarus and Fallon had moved into his world.

And he was loving it.

He saw Anderson consider Fallon's question.

'He could hold a press conference and accuse us of framing him,' he said finally.

'Jesus,' Fallon said.

'He has a national reputation and brand,' Anderson said.

'He'll say the arrest was a smokescreen to get at his sources. The press will eat that up.'

'Jesus,' Fallon said again.

Fallon glanced over at Lazarus, then lowered her eyes.

Lazarus knew now she was worried for herself. He didn't count any more. She was in self-preservation mode. All the kickings they had taken together on the streets, all the arrests they had made, all the times he had covered for her drinking.

Gone.

'It's a very serious situation, Superintendent,' Anderson said.

That smile again. Lazarus fought an urge to close the distance between them and punch him.

'The publicity will be bad,' Anderson said.

'But there will be worse.'

Fallon's eyes widened in panic.

'Worse? What? What are you talking about?'

Anderson's mock sincerity made Lazarus want to puke.

'He'll sue the force.' Anderson said.

'He'd be a fool not to. He has a strong case. He'll get a fortune.'

Anderson brought his right hand up and stuck out a finger with each point he listed off.

'Wrongful arrest. False imprisonment. Breach of privacy. Defamation.'

'What is this shit?' Lazarus shouted. He held his hands out in protest.

'It was a righteous arrest. There were valid reasons to detain hi-'

Fallon gave Lazarus the hand.

'Enough,' she snapped.

'I've heard enough from you for one day, Detective Sergeant. This is a disaster. Shut your mouth and listen for once. You're the problem here. I need solutions.'

Anderson smirked.

'Defamation,' he repeated.

'The media got to hear he had been arrested. That can only have come from someone in the job.'

He held up his hands in mock surrender.

'I'm not saying he is right, Superintendent. But that doesn't matter. What matters is what he says in the witness stand in the High Court. And boy will he give them a sob story. We're exposed on this.'

He paused for a beat.

'The Commissioner won't be happy.'

Sweat appeared on Fallon's brow.

She chewed her bottom lip.

She always did that when she was frightened. Lazarus was on patrol with her one night when they were surrounded by a pissed-up mob. She chewed her lip as the drunks squared up to them and they waited for back-up. They were back to back, protecting each other, lashing out with their batons as the crowd came onto them.

'We have a major problem,' Fallon said to Anderson.

'How do we fix it, Mark? What can we do to mitigate it?'

And Lazarus knew there and then he was fucked.

Anderson smiled another tight smile.

'It's all about damage limitation,' Anderson said.

'The most important thing is the DNA results don't leave this room. Nobody is to know. The press office has a line that Sullivan was released pending a file to the Director of Public Prosecutions. We need to stick to that. Any media queries and we just say investigations are ongoing. We can say the case is a complex one, that the file is being worked on. We can spin that it will take months. Hopefully things will die down after a few weeks.'

He paused and gazed at Lazarus, who held his stare.

But then Lazarus blinked.

'I have an idea,' Anderson said.

Fallon's eyes lit up, the way a rat does when it is cornered but sees the smallest of gaps to escape through.

'Sergeant Lazarus is not going to like it, but in the circumstances, I don't think we have any choice,' Anderson said.

'Spit it out,' Fallon said.

'Let's shake up the investigation team,' Anderson said.

'I wanted the national unit to run it from the start. I suspected it was beyond Sergeant Lazarus. I have, regretfully, been proved right. Sergeant Cochrane should run it now. Sergeant Lazarus can take a back seat. Anyway, he will be busy dealing with the internal investigation into O'Hara. And GSOC, of course.'

Lazarus was too smart to even think of protesting.

He knew an execution when he saw one.

'We can leak that we have brought in the experts from the MIS after you and I ordered a review,' Anderson said.

'That might take the heat off. Hopefully things will die down after a while. Any legal case Sullivan launches won't come before the courts for at least four years, maybe five. A lot of things can happen in that timeframe. And I would venture it won't go to trial. HQ will settle. Sullivan will get a huge amount of money, but you and I will be long gone from here.'

Lazarus almost felt like clapping.

Anderson was offering Fallon a way out. She had a year to go until she took the half sheet. A retirement on a full pension, a nice cash sum and an unblemished record. Anderson was going up the ladder and in four or five years would be a chief superintendent somewhere. Both would be out of Broadstone before the court case started.

Everyone would be a winner, Lazarus realised.

Except him.

If Fallon gave the plan the go ahead, Lazarus knew his career was over. He would be seen as a failure and would never be trusted with a major investigation again. He realised he would never be promoted. His name would be mud in the job. And mud sticks.

Now it was all up to Fallon.

She could go with Anderson's plan to fuck him and save themselves. Or she could stand by him, the way he had stood by her that night outside the pub when they got their shit kicked in. They stood together and fought together and went to ground together under the barrage of kicks and punches.

He turned to his friend and saw a hard look in Fallon's eyes.

'You're off the case, John,' she said.

'Hand over the reins to Detective Sergeant Frankie Cochrane. Effective immediately. That is an order. You need time to get over what happened with O'Hara anyway.'

Lazarus didn't answer.

He walked to the door, opened it and walked out.

His last act of defiance was to slam the door behind him.

42

Lazarus stormed down the stairs.

He wanted to punch the wall.

All he could see was Anderson smiling his weak as shit smile.

It infuriated him.

The idea Anderson had just driven his career down a dead end was too much for Lazarus.

How could he have been so wrong? How did so much evidence point towards Sullivan? How was he going to tell Jenna he had fucked up everything?

Their life. Their future. Their dreams.

He reached the incident room and opened the door. Cochrane and McEvoy were doing paperwork at their desks. They looked up. Cochrane, who was not used to Lazarus's ways, regarded him with a detached interest. McEvoy, who knew about his temper, tightened his eyes.

'What's the craic, Lazarus?' he asked.

Lazarus shook his head.

He walked to the row of coat hooks on the wall. He ripped his overcoat from it. He counted to ten. Took a long breath. He turned to face them.

News travelled fast within the Garda and the look on their faces told Lazarus they both knew.

'I guess you heard about the DNA coming back?' he said.

'Yeah,' Cochrane said.

'That's bad luck. But it happens. We'll start again. There is a few of the sex offenders who never gave up their DNA sample. We'll go at them. And we'll soon have a list of every phone that was active in the area at the time. That gives us plenty to work on. This isn't over. Not by a long shot. Sullivan was a good suspect. Your theory was sound.'

'That's what I would do,' Lazarus said.

'What are you saying?' Cochrane said, suspicious.

282

Lazarus put on his overcoat.

'I'm off the case. It's all yours, Frankie.'

'Fuck that!' McEvoy said.

He jumped to his feet.

'She can't do that.'

'She can and she did,' Lazarus said.

He walked to the door, then stopped and looked back.

'Watch Anderson,' he told Cochrane.

'He'll fuck you over in a heartbeat. Be careful.'

Cochrane was beside McEvoy.

'Roger that,' she said.

'Shite always slides downwards. I know the job,' she said.

'I'm outta here,' Lazarus said.

He headed to the door.

'Lazarus!' Cochrane shouted.

He turned around.

'You're not a bad shot for a local detective, you know,' she said.

He smiled and walked out.

In a few seconds, he was on the bottom floor and at the public area. It was the same route Sullivan had taken the previous night.

Lazarus was following his footsteps. He almost laughed at the irony.

Then he was outside and the cold air slapped his face. He glanced to the sky. It was heavy with clouds. He buttoned his coat and buried his hands in his pockets to guard against the chill.

He could have driven, but he needed the walk, hoped to clear his head. He failed miserably.

He trudged along Western Way, then on to Mountjoy Street. He took a few rat runs down narrow streets and within ten minutes he came out on to Eccles Street. He crossed at a set of traffic lights. They led to the Accident and Emergency unit of the Mater Hospital. He turned, braced for a confrontation.

McEvoy ran towards him.

'Easy, Harry, you'll give yourself a heart attack.'

McEvoy was red-faced and sweating.

'Fuck Fallon,' McEvoy panted.

'She came down to the incident room after you left and called Cochrane out. I heard them whispering outside. Then Cochrane came back in, took her jacket and fucked off. I figured if she was gone, I may as well join you.'

'You're a good friend,' Lazarus said.

McEvoy pretended to recoil.

'Don't fucking hug me in the street, *amigo*, people will think we're riding each other.'

They walked through the hospital together.

Soon they came to a white door with a small window.

It was identical to the door through which Lazarus had observed Delaney. That night when he saw her unconscious on the bed of the high dependency unit seemed like a lifetime ago now.

The victim's condition had made the team even more determined to catch her attacker. She was hovering between life and death a few floors up, but Lazarus knew there was nothing he could do to save her. What he could do was catch her attacker.

The realisation he had failed was like a hammer blow to his gut.

He had let her down, like the cops had let his sister Gabriella down. He wondered if the victim's family would still be gripped with trauma and anger and disappointment over her attack in seven years, like he was to this day over Gabriella.

He hoped that, unlike him, they would find peace.

And suddenly he hated himself for not finding the tranquillity Jenna and the kids deserved.

He walked into the room.

Mick Casey lay on an iron bed. He wore a white hospital gown with a blue diamond pattern. He was on his back, his head and shoulders propped on pillows.

A tube was connected to his left arm and a pulse oximeter hung from his index finger. His head and forehead were heavily bandaged. Blood was seeping through the bandage just above his left eyebrow. Just like Delaney when he saw her first.

A thin tube ran from behind one ear, under his nose and then to the other ear. Two smaller tubes sprouted from it and disappeared into his nostrils. Oxygen. Lazarus saw bandages on his torso under the gown.

Casey's head was deep in the pillows. His eyes observed Lazarus from an angle.

'All right,' Casey said.

'Hello, Mick,' McEvoy said.

'How you doing, pal?'

'I've had worse days in the ring,' Casey said.

Casey tried to laugh, but the pain took over and he grimaced.

'Where did he hit you?' Lazarus asked.

'One bullet grazed my head. One in the side. Another got me in the shoulder. He missed with the rest. But that's because I saw him coming and ran like fuck. And, anyway, the poxbottle couldn't hit a barn door from 20 feet.'

'What the fuck happened your head?' McEvoy asked. 'That looks worse than a nick.'

Casey laughed. It was a throaty growl.

'I fell as I ran into the house to get away from the prick. Hit my head.'

Then he looked over to Lazarus, went quiet.

'You got him, Mr Lazarus,' he said finally.

Lazarus held Casey's gaze.

'Nothing stays quiet in this town,' Lazarus said.

'Is he dead?'

There was no point lying.

'Yes,' Lazarus said.

Casey nodded, satisfied.

'Good. He got what he deserved. It had been a long time coming.'

Lazarus said nothing.

'Was it Danny O'Hara?' Casey asked.

Lazarus didn't answer.

'It was, wasn't it? He's the prick who nearly killed you at my house.'

'You didn't tell us you knew who did that,' Lazarus said.

'Your statement afterwards said you had no idea which of his gang it was.'

Casey's face flushed red.

'There's lots of things the police aren't told, Mr Lazarus,' he said.

'Lots of things you don't need to know.'

'Like the incident in the pub the other night?' Lazarus said.

'What would that be?' Casey said. His voice was even.

Lazarus snorted. As if Casey had no idea.

'Someone tried to kill O'Hara. He got lucky. The gun jammed.'

'Yeah? That's terrible,' Casey said.

'A man can't even have a pint nowadays. Shocking.'

Lazarus was too tired to challenge his bullshit.

He let it go.

The room went quiet.

'Who was on the bike with O'Hara?' Casey asked, after a long moment.

'I can't get into that,' Lazarus said.

Casey ignored him.

'Young Luke Armstrong from around the corner has been hanging around with that bollix. I bet it's him.'

Casey was right. The teen with the expensive watch was in custody. McEvoy had arrested him seconds after the crash, while Lazarus chased after O'Hara. The cockiness he showed Lazarus when he stopped him with O'Hara a few days earlier had vanished. He was facing a decade behind bars. He was singing like a canary. He was crying for his mother, too.

Just then the door opened. Lazarus turned around and saw Sarah and Rob Casey.

Sarah walked over to her father and kissed his cheek. She had a bottle of water in one hand and a chocolate bar in the other.

'All right, da,' she said.

'This is all they had.'

Lazarus saw her downturned mouth and sad eyes.

And he realised those eyes would always be sad, that mouth would always be downturned.

'That's perfect, love,' Casey said.

'Open the bottle for me, will ya?'

Sarah took the bottle back and unscrewed the lid. She leaned over the edge of the bed and held the bottle up to her father's mouth. He glugged at it. He grunted in satisfaction and Sarah took the bottle away. She placed it on the top of a unit beside the bed and started unwrapping the bar.

'You know what they say about hospital food, Mr Lazarus,' Rob Casey said.

He wore expensive white runners, grey tracksuit bottoms, a shiny black Adidas jacket. It was unzipped and exposed a white T-shirt underneath. He had a dark blue Adidas baseball cap on his head, the peak pulled down over his eyes.

'I hope I never have to find out,' Lazarus said.

Lazarus saw a faint smile. It was almost a smirk. He stared hard at Rob, unease growing inside him.

The door opened again.

It was Sinead Duffy. She greeted Lazarus and McEvoy. She wore a Garda tunic over an open fleece. Under that Lazarus could see her body armour.

'We're putting a garda outside the door here for the duration of your stay,' Lazarus said.

'Garda Duffy will be here for a few hours, then she'll be replaced. You're safe, Mick. They won't come after you here.'

'An unarmed female copper isn't going to stop anyone,' Mick Casey said, then looked apologetically towards Duffy.

'No offence, love.'

Duffy smiled.

'None taken. They'll have to get past me to get at you. And I'm in the biggest gang in Dublin.'

She tapped the radio clipped on the chest of her ballistic vest.

'One press of the emergency button on my radio and my mates will be here before you know it. I think we'll be okay.'

Rob Casey smirked as she walked out of the room to take up security duty outside.

'Fat lot of use you were at our house a few hours ago,' he said.

'O'Hara could have killed him. He just waltzed onto our street and shot him. We tried the cops' way. It didn't work.'

He turned to Lazarus.

'Maloney will need to be careful in prison. People can have accidents.'

Lazarus eyed him.

'There's one law in this town, son. You break it and I'll come after you hard.'

'Yeah?'

Rob moved towards Lazarus.

'Yeah,' Lazarus growled.

They both stared at each other hard.

Neither was backing down. Lazarus knew this would only end one way. He balled his fist, got ready to strike.

And then he heard a soft voice behind him.

'Don't mind him, Mr Lazarus,' Sarah said.

He looked around. She was smiling at him. It was a small, sad smile. But a smile nonetheless.

'Rob is talking bollix,' she said.

'I decide what I'm going to do. Not Rob. I'm not a baby, I'll be 18 soon enough. I had a chat with mam last night. We've decided I'm going ahead with the case. I want that man jailed for what he did to me.'

Her eyes blazed.

'Not beaten. Not stabbed. And not shot. Jailed. And I want to be in court when he is taken away.'

Mick Casey examined the ceiling. Rob Casey glared at Sarah. Sarah stared at Lazarus. Then she walked over to him.

She spread her arms wide and enveloped him in a hug.

She held him for a long moment, then disengaged.

She smiled at him again and nodded.

'I'm going to do it right,' she said.

Lazarus smiled back at her and nodded.

'I know you will, Sarah. Thank you.'

He looked at McEvoy.

'Let's go,' he said.

'Take care, Mick,' Lazarus said as they walked to the door.

'You might not be so lucky next time.'

'There won't be a next time,' Sarah said quickly. She was beside her dad now. She took his hand and squeezed it.

Lazarus shot a glance at Rob Casey. He was breathing hard, throwing him daggers. His eyes were wide with anger. There would definitely be a next time for him, Lazarus thought. Rob Casey was not going away.

Duffy sat outside the door. They said goodbye to her as they left. She winked, gave Lazarus a mock salute.

'I'll look after them,' she said.

And Lazarus knew she meant it.

They emerged from the hospital and found themselves back on Eccles Street.

'Let's get back to the office, old man,' Lazarus said.

'I think I've had enough for one day.'

McEvoy laughed, punched Lazarus playfully on the arm.

They walked leisurely back to the station. It was a little over 500 metres away. They didn't talk. They didn't need to. The silence between them was comfortable. Comforting even.

They had just turned on to Western Way and were 100 metres from the station when Lazarus felt his phone vibrate.

He took it out and saw a WhatsApp from Massimo.

Fratellino! Just heard one of your lot shot some scumbag in town.
Hope all's okay with your team. Gimme a shout later. Maybe we'll go
out for a pint this week? Ciao!

Lazarus put the phone away. He knew he would have to tell Massimo and Jenna. But not now. It was too raw.

He walked along the footpath, lost in his thoughts. He felt as if he were on autopilot, like someone who is on a long car journey and realises they have driven for an hour and can't remember any of it. His head was down and he was walking into a cold wind.

Suddenly, he felt hard contact on his left shoulder. He had bumped into a pedestrian.

'Sorry,' Lazarus said, and put his hands up in surrender.

'Sorry, my fault,' the other person said.

Lazarus nodded absentmindedly, but then stopped.

He recognised the voice.

He looked up.

Martin Glennon faced him.

He was as dishevelled as the last time Lazarus saw him at his flat with Cochrane.

He wore the same blue runners, but they were caked in mud. Lazarus noticed a hole in the right toecap.

He wore a pair of black cotton tracksuit bottoms under a heavy over-coat. It was the sort old men wore. It was dirty brown and reached his knees. He had fastened all the buttons and his hands were deep in its pockets.

His face was heavy with stubble.

Lazarus looked at him for a moment and Glennon stared back, fear in his eyes. Lazarus realised he didn't recognise him and wondered if he was afraid he was about to be attacked by a vigilante.

'Hello Glennon,' Lazarus said.

Then he saw a flash of recognition in Glennon's eyes.

But there was something else.

Lazarus thought he looked embarrassed.

Uncomfortable.

'Mr Lazarus,' Glennon stammered. 'All right?'

'What are you doing here?' Lazarus asked.

Glennon fidgeted.

'Just out for a walk, Mr Lazarus.'

Lazarus knew he was lying.

'Where are you going?'

'Out and about.'

Glennon was blinking hard and his Adam's apple bobbed.

His eyes darted from side to side.

Lazarus sighed a long, tired sigh.

'I don't believe you, Glennon. I know you're up to something,' he said.

'But you know what? I don't give a shit. I'm sick and tired of dealing with you people.'

'Come on Lazarus,' McEvoy said, pulling at his elbow.

Lazarus shrugged off his hand.

'You're not human. You'll never change. You can get all the counselling you want and say all the prayers you want. But you're bad. It's a matter of time before you do something bad again.

'God is on my side,' Glennon said.

'He is keeping me right.'

'Bullshit. God gave up on you a long time ago.'

'Lazarus,' McEvoy said.

Lazarus couldn't stop himself.

'The best thing you can do is go to the Liffey and accidentally fall in. Do us all a favour, yeah?'

'Lazarus!' McEvoy shouted.

He dragged Lazarus away this time.

'Fuck's sake,' he hissed.

'You can't be talking to pricks like that in the street. You never know who's watching.'

He looked around as he bustled Lazarus towards the station entrance.

Lazarus held his hands up.

'I'm okay. It's cool.'

McEvoy gave him a long, hard look, but said nothing. They got to the entrance, McEvoy shadowing Lazarus in case he went back to confront Glennon again.

Lazarus looked down the road and saw Glennon trudging along the footpath, his head bowed.

'I think we need a pint,' McEvoy said.

43

Lazarus held a bottle up to his audience.

He felt himself sway a little too much as he stood in the centre of a back room in a local pub and ranted at more than 30 cops.

'And then the *pezzo di merda* went down,' he shouted.

'And then he fucking stayed down!'

The audience exploded into cheers and applause.

Lazarus calmed them with his hands, like a presidential candidate on the campaign trail.

'And lemme tell you, the only way he'll get up again is when his coffin is put on six other bastards' shoulders.'

The audience, some in uniforms with their ties unclipped and their top shirt button undone, some in plain clothes, started laughing.

Word of the shooting had spread around the city like wildfire. Neither he nor McEvoy had bought a round since they walked into the pub 90 minutes earlier. Off duty gardai from stations across the city queued to congratulate him.

Now, with Dutch courage, Lazarus was regaling them.

'He should have surrendered after the bike crash,' he said.

'The fucker gets up and decides to run – well, limp – away.'

More laughter.

'Mistake number one.'

He extended his thumb.

'He tried to escape down a dead end.

'Mistake number two.'

His index finger came out.

'Then he tried to shoot me.'

His middle finger emerged from his balled fist.

'Mistake numero fucking three!'

More shouts and applause and cheers from the audience, most of whom held up pints to salute him.

'I did try to save him,' Lazarus lied.

He was nowhere near the *in vino veritas* stage.

'I tried to save him because that is what we do as members of An Garda Síochána. No matter how much of a scumbag they are, we go to help them. Because we are guards – guardians of the peace!'

More cheers.

'But I can't lie' he said, after lying.

The audience went quiet.

'I won't shed a tear at his death. He was a bad man. He inflicted misery on addicts all over Dub-'

'He was a waste of oxygen,' McEvoy shouted from the side.

He warmed to his theme.

'He was a tall man for a small man. A gobshite. A fuckdog. A wanker.'

'So you weren't a fan, then?' Lazarus asked.

The audience erupted in cheers.

'He *was* a bad man. And if I didn't kill him, he would have killed me…'

He held the bottle up again.

'So fuck him. *Saluti!*'

He brought the bottle to his lips. He downed the contents in one go as everyone clapped again.

He slammed the bottle onto the table and walked towards the audience who mobbed him in hugs.

By 9pm, he was on his tenth bottle and was beginning to fade. McEvoy, a man who had a prodigious capacity for sinking pints, was out for the night. He was in a corner telling lads his own war story.

Lazarus saw him gesticulating wildly as he told a story he knew would be told for years to come.

Lazarus was tired, though. And the tiredness was making him morose. For the previous ten minutes, he had slumped in a seat in a quiet corner.

He was on his phone when he sensed movement in front of him.

He looked up. Cochrane, a fresh bottle of Moretti in her hand, smiled down at him.

'Here you go, hotshot,' she said.

She was drinking a gin and tonic.

They clinked as she sat down.

'You all right?' she asked when she swallowed some of her drink.

'Couldn't feel allrighter,' Lazarus smiled.

They both laughed.

Cochrane looked around the packed pub.

'Thank God this is private. There'd be war if civvies could see us,' she said.

'The less they know the better,' Lazarus said.

They sat in silence for a few moments.

'No hard feelings about the Delaney case?' Cochrane said.

Lazarus felt his stomach tighten.

'I'd almost forgotten about that,' he said.

'It's not your fault, Frankie. I fucked up. Everything pointed to him. I was convinced it was Sullivan.'

'Me too,' Cochrane said.

'I've examined the file. It was top notch. You didn't put a foot wrong.'

'Except arrest an innocent man,' Lazarus murmured.

'Well, yeah, there is that,' Cochrane laughed.

She sat deeper in her chair.

'I have two things for you, Lazarus.'

She opened her bag, took out a small envelope, handed it to him.

Lazarus opened it and laughed when he saw what was inside.

It was a small black cross. He remembered visiting Cochrane in her own office and seeing the row of them on the frame of her desktop computer: one cross for each dead monster.

'Stick it somewhere in the office,' she said.

'Somewhere you see it a lot, so you can remind yourself how lucky you were today.'

Lazarus smiled, but it quickly turned into a frown.

'Lucky? What do you mean lucky?' he asked her.

'Yeah, lucky,' Cochrane said.

'You were an awful eejit today.'

'Pardon?' Lazarus's eyes widened.

'A fucken eejit,' Cochrane repeated.

'That's the only word for someone who goes down an alley alone to take on a gunman. It was perfect for an ambush. And if he was any quicker, you were a gonner. You'll realise this when all these backslappers have pissed off home and you're by yourself tonight.'

She looked over at the crowd of cops with disgust.

Lazarus went quiet.

He fiddled with the decal, then put it back in the envelope.

'What's the second thing?' he asked.

293

'Advice,' she said.

She gestured towards the crowd.

'See these fuckers? They don't count. Most of them would still go out on the piss if it was you on the slab, not O'Hara.'

'Thanks,' Lazarus said.

'It's the truth. They don't give a shite about you.'

Cochrane stirred the ice in the G and T with her finger.

She looked back at him.

'I can't have children. And it kills me. It's why I work so hard. I've nothing to go home to. My job is my life, because there is nothing else. But you? You have everything. A loving wife. Two kids who I am told think the sun shines out of your arse. What the hell are you doing here? You should be with them.'

Lazarus said nothing.

'You can't see what you have. You're putting everything important to the back of the queue and everything trivial to the front. You are – again – an eejit.'

Lazarus picked at the bottle label.

'I've seen your type in the national units before,' Cochrane said.

'Lads who throw themselves into work and forget about their family. How many times have you lied to your wife about work? How many times have you missed family events to do a job?'

Lazarus couldn't look Cochrane in the eye. He had lost count of the times he had put work before Jenna and the kids, just like last Sunday when he stood up the boys to take Maloney at the hotel.

That seemed like a lifetime ago now.

'Go home to your family,' Cochrane said.

'They nearly lost you today. They are all that matters.'

She drained her glass and stood up.

'See you around, big lad,' Cochrane said.

Then she ambled towards the door.

Lazarus looked over at the crowd. They were talking to each other as they guzzled pints and bottles. Not one of them even glanced over to him to see if he was okay. He was an excuse for a piss-up. Nothing more.

And suddenly Lazarus had had enough.

Enough death.

Enough fake friends.

Enough of Broadstone and its treachery.

He felt overwhelmed with guilt.

He realised Jenna had been right all along. All the rows they had had and she was completely right.

He had thrown himself into work for years.

He thought he was doing the right thing, that he could somehow make up for Gabriella's murder by putting every child abuser, wife beater, rapist and paedophile in central Dublin behind bars.

He had locked a lot of them up.

But Gabriella was still dead, and he still felt crushed by the guilt of her murder.

He thought of the life he had just taken, O'Hara's corpse lying on the cold mortuary slab.

He thought of the Annie Delaney attack, a case he had worked his arse off over for the last week that then collapsed into dust in front of his eyes.

And he thought of Fallon, the woman he believed was his friend, but who had shown him there was no such thing as loyalty in policing.

He looked to Cochrane. She was almost at the door.

And suddenly he knew what he needed to do.

He slammed the Moretti onto the table, jumped from his seat.

'Wait Frankie!' he shouted.

Cochrane looked around.

Lazarus ran towards her, ignoring the sloppy backslaps from the drunk cops who all of a sudden remembered him again.

'Frankie,' he panted when he reached her.

'I need a lift home.'

Cochrane smiled, linked her arm in his and walked him out of the pub.

44

Sunday

They lay in bed, entwined in each other.

Lazarus was on his back. Jenna on her side, facing him. She was caressing his chest. He stroked her hair.

They had been up most of the night.

First talking, then when the words were spent they made love. When they were finished they collapsed, exhausted, into bed.

'I've been a fool,' Lazarus said as he stared at the ceiling.

Jenna shushed him and placed her index finger on his lips.

'We sorted this last night, *caro*. The past is the past. You can't control it. We're going to look to the future now.'

'I've ignored you all,' he said.

'Don't beat yourself up over it,' Jenna said. 'You're human. We move on together and do what we decided last night. Okay?'

He brooded for a few seconds and then: 'Okay.'

After he spent an hour crying and grovelling to her about his treatment of the family, Lazarus had told Jenna last night he was leaving Broadstone. He had decided to hand in a transfer request. He'd go anywhere.

'You sure you're happy to get out?' Jenna asked him for the tenth time.

Lazarus kissed her forehead.

'Yes. Now is the time to go. Start afresh. Another unit somewhere.'

'And not sex crimes?' Jenna said.

'No. I promise. I've had enough of it. I'm not saying I'm going to take a desk job, but I've seen too much.'

Just then, all the victims appeared one by one in his mind in a stream of horror and despair.

He remembered them all.

He was trying to chase them away when the bedroom door opened.

Pietro and Giovanni Junior bustled in.

'We're hungry,' they said.

Lazarus threw his head back into the pillow and laughed.

Jenna was already up, wrapping a green nightgown around her.

'When are you going to do it?' she asked as she walked towards the boys.

'Today,' Lazarus said.

It was his last day before four days off in a row. He was due in at 10am.

'Promise?'

Lazarus smiled.

'I promise.'

'Good,' Jenna said.

'Then we can start again.'

★

Lazarus bumped into McEvoy in the station car park and they headed to the detective office together.

'I'm bollixed,' McEvoy said.

'You look it,' Lazarus said. He felt fresh, despite the tears and lack of sleep. Resolution will do that to a man.

'What time did you finish up?' he asked McEvoy.

McEvoy shrugged his shoulders.

'No idea. Maybe 2am. Fuck knows.'

His eyes were bloodshot and he had cut himself shaving.

Although he was showered and in a new suit, the stench of stale booze seeped from his pores.

'Here, you need one of these,' Lazarus said.

He gave him a mint.

Then, on second thoughts, he handed over the whole packet.

They entered the incident room just after 10am.

Flannery, the only one in, was engrossed in a spreadsheet on his computer.

'Where is everyone?' Lazarus said.

Flannery waved his hand.

'Cochrane is off on some mystery job, she wouldn't tell me what it was. Just got a call and vamoosed. Probably some national stuff. Young Winter has gone for coffee.'

'What are you doing' Lazarus said.

Flannery nodded at the computer.

'C and S got the records of all phones active around the park on the night of the attack. I'm compiling a list of possibles.'

Crime and Security had contacted providers and retrieved data on all phones whose signal bounced off cell sites close to Griffith Park on Sunday night around the time of the attack on Delaney.

'They identified phones active within 500 metres of the park over a two-hour period,' Flannery said.

'Calls and texts. The hope is the attacker had his phone with him and can be traced.'

'How many are on the list?' Lazarus asked.

'About 800,' Flannery said.

'But we can weed out a lot of them. Pensioners, women, children, that sort of thing. We'll be able to cut it down by 60 per cent.'

Lazarus whistled,

'More than 300. Ouch,' Lazarus said.

But then he realised it was no longer his investigation.

'It's Cochrane's problem now,' he said with a shrug.

Flannery checked his watch, got up and headed to the door.

'I'm done. They've cut the overtime. I was only in for an hour.'

Lazarus watched him leave then looked at McEvoy.

No time like the present.

'I'm also done, Harry,' he said.

McEvoy looked at him suspiciously.

'What do you mean done?'

'I'm putting in for a transfer,' Lazarus said.

'Ah come on, Lazarus!' McEvoy shouted.

'I can't stay here any more after the Sullivan thing,' Lazarus said. 'I'm toxic. Best if I move on.'

'We all would have made the same decisions as you,' McEvoy said quickly.

'I know. And thanks. But I'm finished here. Fallon has deserted me. Anderson wants to destroy me. This is his chance. I can't let that happen.'

He sat down at his desk.

'You should avoid me until I leave. I'm bad news. Anderson will go after anyone who is close to me. You got to think of yourself.'

'Fuck him,' McEvoy said.

He walked over to Lazarus.

'That bastard can't touch me. I'm an appointed detective. He can't take that away from me.'

He balled his fist, punched Lazarus's desk to hammer home his point. He was staring at Lazarus and did not see where his hand landed. It slammed down on a manila envelope.

The force of the punch dislodged it and it fell to the floor.

McEvoy strained to bend down. He picked up the envelope, put it back on Lazarus's desk.

Lazarus looked at it, puzzled.

Then he remembered.

'What is it, Lazarus?' McEvoy said.

'It's the analysis of Sullivan's burner phone. Flannery gave me it yesterday morning. I forgot all about it.'

Lazarus picked up the enveloped and examined it.

He considered putting the report in his desk drawer and forgetting about it. He couldn't give a crap who was touting to Sullivan, and he didn't think Anderson cared, now that he was getting Lazarus out of his hair.

But he hated loose ends.

Fallon had given him a job. He had to finish it.

He sighed. He opened the envelope, withdrew the report.

McEvoy frowned.

'You're not still going after Sullivan's tout, John? After everything that has happened? The poor fucker is in the clear. Maybe throw him some slack?'

'I have no intention of getting anyone in the shit,' Lazarus said.

'I have to do a report, though. I'll say I was unable to identify Sullivan's source.'

He patted the report.

'If this tells me who it is, I'll pull them aside and have a quiet word. I'm not going to end anyone's career.'

McEvoy grumbled a protest.

'Relax, old man,' Lazarus said. 'I just want to know. I like finding things out. That's what detectives do. You know?'

He started reading the report.

The introduction said that unlike Sullivan's iPhone, the throwaway handset was not PIN protected and was easily accessed. It was a cheap handset Sullivan had bought in a market. It had been jailbroken and was no longer tied to any service provider. That meant Sullivan could use any SIM card in it.

'That explains why he didn't use a PIN,' Lazarus said as he read. 'He could just throw it away when he was done with it.'

The lower security on the phone meant Flannery could use special software called XRY to examine the contents of the SIM and turn it into a tabulated report.

The introduction said the SIM in Sullivan's handset had been bought in central Dublin on March 2, along with €100 credit. But Sullivan did not use it until September 2.

Flannery wrote that Sullivan's phone had been in contact with one number. The SIM for that was bought in Blanchardstown in west Dublin in January 2018, 21 months ago.

Flannery had created a list of times and dates of top ups activated on both phones. Lazarus noticed Sullivan always used different shops all over the city and waited several months before activating the top ups. The other person had bought top up just a few weeks ago in a shop in town.

McEvoy came around the desk and they read the report together.

He pointed to one of the sentences and laughed.

'Look at the false name Sullivan used to buy the SIM. Brilliant.'

It was the name of the current Assistant Commissioner in Crime and Security, the unit that accesses people's phone records.

'That's a real fuck you if ever I saw one,' McEvoy said.

The phones communicated only by text, the report said. Flannery had tabulated the messages. He labelled the reporter's phone SULLIVAN and the second phone HANDSET 2.

The phone data tables were divided into columns. The first gave the date of the message. The second noted the time. The third said whether the message was from Sullivan or the second handset.

The last column gave the contents of the message.

Lazarus started reading the messages, McEvoy craned to do the same over his boss's shoulder.

The first was from Sullivan on September 2 at 8.01pm.

SULLIVAN: Howya. New number. Anything happening?

The answer came seven minutes later.

HANDSET 2: Cool. Not a thing.

The next message was to Sullivan on September 8 at 7.47pm.

HANDSET 2: Shooting in Ballyer. Paudie McNally.

'Rings a bell,' McEvoy said.

Lazarus didn't recall it. Ballyfermot was on the southside of the city, far from his patch.

McEvoy went to his computer, logged into the PULSE system.

'Here we are,' he said after a few seconds.

'McNally was shot dead on September 8. A gang leader over there. The first 999 call was received at 7.32pm.'

He whistled.

'Sullivan's tout was on the ball.'

Lazarus went back to the manuscript.

SULLIVAN: Sheeet! Not THE Paudie McNally? He brown bread?

HANDSET 2: The very one. Paramedics workin on him. But its lukin bad. Shot six times. One to the head. Rest to the body. Hes knocking on heavens door.

SULLIVAN: Think of the OT!

Lazarus smiled. Sullivan knew cops and their love of overtime.

Twenty seven minutes later, at 8.14 pm, HANDSET 2 messaged Sullivan.

RIP.

'Does PULSE say time of death?' Lazarus asked.

'8.01pm.'

'He knew within minutes,' Lazarus said.

An idea began to formulate in Lazarus's head. He did not like what it was telling him.

The next message came on September 13 at 6.05pm.

It was to Sullivan.

HANDSET 2: Skipper lifted in Cork for abusing his daughters.

SULLIVAN: Jaysus. He suspended?

HANDSET 2: Yeah. Don't know if it will go anywhere.

A Garda sergeant arrested on suspicion of sexually abusing his own kids at the other end of the country.

The unwelcome whispers in Lazarus's head became louder. More insistent.

Another message came in at 9.45pm on September 27.

HANDSET 2: DOCB just got a massive seizure near the airport in last 15 mins. 110ks of coke. Over 8m. Two in.

Lazarus quickly translated the jobspeak.

The Drugs and Organised Crime Bureau had seized 110 kgs of cocaine and had arrested two suspects. He knew from his drugs unit days that a kilo of coke was worth €75,000 on the street. He did the maths. €8.25 million.

He recalled that seizure, didn't need McEvoy to check the system for that. It had made national headlines.

He read the next message. October 3 at 1.03pm.

HANDSET 2: Murder-suicide down in Kilkee. Husband shot his wife and three kids, then himself.

Kilkee was a small village in County Clare on the west coast, right on the Atlantic Ocean. It was three hours south-west of Dublin.

'Fuck,' Lazarus said. The whispers were roaring in his head now.

SULLIVAN: Holy shitballs.

HANDSET 2: Bodies found 30 mins ago. Not out yet.

SULLIVAN: I better get going. Could you help me with names?

HANDSET 2: Roger. The killer is a Henry Warren. I'll get the other names in a while. Drive carefully. Don't speed, cops all over the place. LOL.

Lazarus had an idea.

He warmed up his computer and opened Twitter to search for Sullivan's account.

It was easy to find. He was the only Irish journalist of that name. Lazarus saw the blue tick that showed Sullivan had a verified account. He had 43,000 followers. His profile pic was of him with Gallagher, an arm around each other's shoulder. Each was doing the thumbs up and smiling. They were at a crime scene. Lazarus could see the white and blue Garda tape in the background.

He read Sullivan's bio.

> Conor Sullivan. Crime Correspondent for The Globe in Dublin.
> I write about cops and robbers. Some of them even like me. DMs are open.
> All views mine. The fella in the pic with me is ace hack Tony Gallagher,
> my best friend. He has better contacts than me. ❤ ❤

Lazarus scrolled through Sullivan's mentions. They were filled with abusive tweets following his arrest.

Then he saw a supportive tweet from Gallagher.

It was sent at 9.15am today.

> I'm proud to be your friend. Ignore the trolls. Am worried for you.
> I'll be over later. I know you're innocent.

'You and me both, buddy,' Lazarus said.

And he thought standing up for his friend was just the sort of thing Gallagher would do.

The abuse Sullivan was getting must have been unbearable. There were dozens of tweets. People were calling him a rapist, a monster, even a few tweets accused him of being a paedophile.

Lazarus was tempted to contact Sullivan and tell him he was in the clear, but remembered the order from Anderson to keep it quiet.

He checked Sullivan's timeline. He had tweeted all the incidents HANDSET 2 had tipped him off about, often within minutes. He looked at his tweets for September 8, the date of the Paudie McNally shooting. The message hit the burner at 7.47pm. Sullivan sent out a tweet at 7.58pm.

BREAKING: gardai at scene of a shooting in Ballyfermot, south Dublin. Major drug dealer shot. Just out of prison a week. Paramedics working on him.

Lazarus noted Sullivan waited an hour to break the airport drug seizure. He suspected he did that on purpose to give it time to circulate within the force and protect the source.

He tweeted the Cork abuse investigation the next morning, but Lazarus suspected he held it so it would appear in the paper first. It was his exclusive.

He broke the murder suicide in County Clare at 1.12pm, nine minutes after the message.

BREAKING: gardai investigating tragic incident in Kilkee, Co Clare. Father killed wife and three children, then himself.

Reading that tweet sent an icy shiver down Lazarus's spine.

It confirmed that the voices in his head were right.

He was in dangerous territory.

Territory that no street-smart detective would even think of entering.

McEvoy read his mind.

'You know what this means?'

'Yeah,' Lazarus said.

'There is no way some garda in a Dublin station could have heard about that murder-suicide so quickly. Or the coke bust. And how the fuck would he or she know about a skipper being done down the country?' McEvoy said.

'You're right. That doesn't make sense,' Lazarus said.

'Are you thinking what I'm thinking?' McEvoy said.

'Sullivan's informant is a senior officer,' Lazarus said.

'Yup,' McEvoy said.

'It's someone with fast access to sensitive information from all over Ireland. It can only be top brass in HQ,' Lazarus said.

'I'm told the high ups have their own WhatsApp groups. They are told about incidents within minutes. And it looks like one of them is passing stuff to Sullivan.'

McEvoy suddenly looked worried.

'I don't like this, Lazarus,' he said.

'Let's drop it. Just say it's a chief superintendent or, fuck me, an A/C? That would be a career ender.'

McEvoy was right. It *would* be a career ender.

Not for the Chief or the Assistant Commissioner, but for the stupid Detective Sergeant who unmasked them.

'Even if you find the tout, they'll be protected,' McEvoy said.

'You name anyone in the report and you know what will happen.'

'It will be filed in the bin,' Lazarus said.

McEvoy grimaced.

'And you with it. Drop this, John. Forget about it.'

Lazarus felt his shoulders sag.

'You're right, Harry.'

He knew he had to let it go.

He would just report he could not identify the source.

Done and dusted.

Then he could move on.

Shake Linda Fallon and her station off his expensive Italian shoes.

He picked up the report, went to put it back in the envelope.

And then he froze.

Something caught his eye.

He did a double take.

But he saw it the second time, too.

The words Griffith and Park jumped out from lower down the page of texts.

He felt an icy chill in his neck.

He stared at the message.

HANDSET 2: Terrible one in Broadstone District. Young woman beaten and raped in Griffith Park.

It was sent from HANDSET 2 to Sullivan at 12.25am.

Twenty one minutes after gardai arrived on the scene.

Lazarus didn't dare breathe.

He read the rest of it.

> *She is in a bad way. He beat the bollix out of her and strangled her.*
> *Sick fucker left her half-naked in the dirt. And get this, he put a €2 coin*
> *in her mouth! Sick cunt.*

Lazarus felt his chest tighten so hard he thought he was having a heart attack.

He scanned Sullivan's reply: *Jesus! I'll head up there now. Was in a pub with a lad not too far from there earlier. Mad.*

He re-read the original message from Handset 2.

> *Sick fucker left her half-naked in the dirt. And get this,*
> *he put a €2 coin in her mouth!*

Lazarus stayed quite still and quite quiet for a full minute, thinking.

How did Sullivan's informant know about the money in the victim's throat? The doctor didn't tell Lazarus and Winter until after 2am following her examination.

It was impossible for any cop to know that at 12.25am. But that was the time Sullivan received the message.

It was impossible, Lazarus said to himself again.

Unless.

Unless.

The realisation hit him like a speeding train.

And he knew what he had to do.

He jumped up, shouted at McEvoy.

And he was running to the door.

45

Lazarus heard McEvoy lumbering behind him.

'What are you doing, Lazarus?'

Lazarus shouted to McEvoy over his shoulder as he ran.

'Move your arse.'

He hurried to the Camry.

Lazarus tapped impatiently on the car roof as he waited for McEvoy to unlock it.

'Hurry up, Harry! Come on. Come on!'

'Jesus, Lazarus, calm down,' McEvoy panted as he reached the car.

Lazarus heard the central locking click. He wrenched open the passenger door and sat into the seat.

'Drive!' he shouted.

'Where to, for fuck's sake?' McEvoy said as he sat into the driver's seat and turned on the ignition.

'O'Connell Street. Move. I'll fill you in on the way.'

McEvoy gunned the engine and drove out the gate. The Camry moved out into the Sunday traffic on Western Way. It was nearly 10.40am, the road was quiet. O'Connell Street was right in the centre of the city. It was minutes from the station.

Lazarus stared through the windscreen. He felt that beautiful sensation again. Just like he had when he tiptoed down the hotel corridor a week ago approaching Maloney's room.

That beautiful moment when a hunter knows he has his prey in his sights.

'We're going to find Anne Delaney's attacker,' he said.

'What the fuck? The Super took you off it, Lazarus. You'll get us sacked,' McEvoy shouted.

'That's the least of our worries,' Lazarus shouted back.

And then: 'The attacker is a cop.'

McEvoy's mouth fell open.

'I mean it,' Lazarus spat.

'The man who controlled Handset 2 told Sullivan about the attack on Anne about 20 minutes after units got to the scene.'

The car reached Dorset Street. McEvoy turned right towards the city centre. It was an illegal turn down Frederick Street, but fuck it.

'So?' McEvoy asked as he drove down the narrow road.

'Sullivan has a top source. Big deal. All the senior heads talk. You know that.'

Lazarus shook his head angrily, like an adult scolding a child.

They were passing the Garden of Remembrance now.

'This one's different,' Lazarus said.

'Whoever had that phone knew about the coin shoved down Anne's throat when he texted Sullivan before you and I were even at the scene.'

'Jesus,' McEvoy said.

His face went dark as the jigsaw fell into place in his mind.

'The doctor only told you about the coin at 2am. Nobody else knew.'

He was weaving in and out of traffic.

'Look at all the tips Sullivan received on the phone,' Lazarus said.

'He got them within minutes. They were all high-grade. His informant is a cop. And whoever he is, he raped Anne Delaney. It's the only explanation.'

Lazarus looked at the Dublin streets passing by.

'It must be someone in management,' he said.

'Fuck,' McEvoy said.

'There's no other answer,' Lazarus said.

'The attacker bought credit for the burner phone he contacted Sullivan on at a shop on O'Connell Street a few weeks ago.

'The records show the exact time and date, 6.15pm on Tuesday, October 1.'

McEvoy's eyes widened as he realised Lazarus's endgame.

'The CCTV!' he shouted.

Lazarus nodded.

'We find the man who bought the phone credit that day and we find the rapist.'

Lazarus started scrolling through a mental list of superintendents, chiefs and assistant commissioners in the Dublin region. There were dozens of them. But he knew them all, was certain he would recognise whatever monster was caught on camera at the shop.

He said a silent prayer that the store hadn't destroyed the CTTV from the day. It was three and a half weeks ago. They might have deleted it already.

The car flashed on to O'Connell Street. It sped past the Gresham Hotel. The shop was 200 metres away. Seconds away.

Lazarus felt his stomach tighten as McEvoy pulled up to it. He jumped out and ran to the shop.

A large Asian man with a fluorescent yellow security armband stood at the door. He was six foot three, with broad shoulders, black hair, sallow skin and brown eyes.

Lazarus badged him.

'I need to see your CCTV from October 1.'

The guard put his hands up.

'Easy man, easy,' he said.

Lazarus ignored the protest.

'Do you still have footage from that day?' Lazarus said.

'Yes, man, I think we do.'

'The security office. Now,' Lazarus said.

'Okay, be cool. This way,' the man said.

He walked to the back of the store. It was a narrow shop, brightly lit with three tight isles. They came to a brown door. The security man took a bunch of keys from his pocket. He shuffled it until he got the right key then put it in the lock. The door opened. Lazarus rushed inside.

Automatic lights flashed on above him and he found himself in a narrow staircase.

He ran up the stairs, the security man with him. They reached the landing in seconds. The guard unlocked another door.

It opened into a small security office. Lazarus saw a flat screen monitor on a white desk. A black keyboard sat in front of it. They hurried inside.

The guard sat into a small chair and tapped on the keyboard.

The monitor came alive.

It was divided in four; each quadrant showing a live feed from a HD security camera.

'We actually have six cameras. Two on the entrance, one over the till and three in the shop itself. What one would you like to see?' the guard asked.

'The camera over the till,' Lazarus said without hesitation.

'Start at 6pm.'

An overhead view of the till came up. The camera was behind the counter, high up on the wall. It gave a view of the cash register. Lazarus saw the back of a woman's head behind the counter. She had blonde hair in a bun. She was small and slim and wore a lime green jumper and black skinny jeans. Lazarus could see over her and examine every customer.

He looked at the 24-hour clock timestamp on the screen. 18:01.

'Hurry it up,' he said.

The guard clicked the mouse and the figures in the shop began to walk quickly. They sped towards the till, jerked their payment to the worker and then scrambled away.

The footage got to 18:13 and Lazarus hadn't seen a senior cop he recognised.

But he knew he would. It was just a question of which one.

'Slow it down,' he said.

The guard nodded. The footage came back to normal.

At 18:13.05, a young man approached the till. Lazarus thought he looked like a student. He was tall and thin, unshaven and with brown hair in a tight man bun. There was no sound on the CCTV system. Lazarus saw the student mouth something to the worker behind the till. She nodded, turned from him and went out of shot. She came back a few seconds later with a packet of cigarettes. The man smiled, tapped his bank card on the shop's reader. He waited a second for the purchase to go through. Then took the smokes from the counter and walked away.

A woman came to the till at 18:13.53. She was in her thirties, stocky with pink glasses and flowing hair the same colour. She wore a black PVC raincoat, tied tight by a belt around her waist. She had a magazine in one hand and gave the cashier a €5 note with the other. The worker took the note then handed the woman her change in coins.

The woman mouthed thanks and walked away.

At 18:14.25 Lazarus saw a man approach the counter, a note in his hand.

And everything stopped.

And everything made sense.

Lazarus saw that familiar thick bushy ginger hair.

That familiar goatee with traces of grey in it.

That familiar wiry frame.

Lazarus and McEvoy reacted at the same time.

'Jesus!' McEvoy shouted.

'*Porca Miseria,*' Lazarus exclaimed.

They looked at each other.

McEvoy's eyes were wide.

Lazarus knew his were, too.

They turned back to the screen in unison.

Lazarus looked at the man again, to be sure his eyes weren't deceiving him.

They weren't.

He watched as Sullivan's best friend Tony Gallagher gave the shop worker a €20 note.

She handed him a slip of white paper.

Phone top-up.

Then Gallagher smiled and walked out of camera shot.

46

'You want me to keep going?' the guard asked them.

McEvoy blew out his cheeks.

'Turn it off. We've got what we came for.'

'No problem.'.

The guard took a DVD from a pile beside the screen and pushed it into side of the monitor. The machine started whirring.

Lazarus was oblivious to the noise. He was too busy watching everything crash together in his mind's eye, like those videos of explosions that have been reversed by some internet geek. The clip starts with bright flashes and smoke and debris in the air. It ends with everything fitting into its proper place.

Tony Gallagher, Sullivan's sidekick.

The man who joked about the attack when Lazarus saw them together outside the park. The man who was beside Sullivan in the photograph of the press trip to Europol. The man who Sullivan said on his Twitter page had better Garda contacts than him.

Suddenly Lazarus remembered Gallagher's tweet.

Am worried for you. I'll be over later.

And Lazarus knew Gallagher's endgame.

He turned and sprinted for the door.

'He's going to kill Sullivan!'

Lazarus bounded down the stairs and jumped the last three steps, landing heavy on the carpet.

'Hurry the fuck up, Harry,' he shouted over his shoulder.

He pulled open the door and ran through the shop. He swerved to avoid a woman pushing a buggy. The delay gave a wheezing McEvoy time to catch up.

They reached the car.

McEvoy started the engine, activated the lights and sirens.

The Camry screeched onto the road and sped along O'Connell Street. They came to O'Connell Bridge. The lights were on red.

'Clear left!' Lazarus shouted.

McEvoy sped through the lights onto D'Olier Street. Trinity College loomed on their left. He followed the road onto Dame Street. Most cars pulled in for him, but one family saloon dallied.

McEvoy jerked the steering wheel hard right and crossed into the oncoming traffic. Cars swerved out of his way. He sped on. They flew past Dublin Castle. Traffic calmed and McEvoy veered back onto the proper side of the road.

He turned left on to Patrick Street at Christchurch Cathedral.

'Talk to me Lazarus!' McEvoy shouted over the roar of the engine and the wail of the siren.

'Gallagher set up Sullivan,' Lazarus shouted.

'This whole thing has been about framing him. I know Gallagher is going to kill him. He tweeted earlier he was going to visit Sullivan.'

He looked out the window. The city flew past in a blur.

'And just happen to find him dead.'

The reached Emmett Bridge, sped over the Canal.

They were two minutes from Sullivan's house in Harold's Cross.

'Kill the siren, Harry!'

The wailing stopped.

He kept the blue lights flashing and his foot stayed hard on the accelerator.

The Camry took a right fork in the road at Harold's Cross park and within ten seconds they were at Sullivan's estate.

'Nice and slow,' Lazarus said.

McEvoy drove 100 metres along the roadway, came to a gentle right turn and saw Sullivan's modern house at the end of a row on the left.

Lazarus saw a black SUV in front of it, the bonnet pointing towards them.

Gallagher's Touareg.

'Shit,' McEvoy hissed.

He stopped at the house, a red-brick semi. Both men jumped out, McEvoy left the engine running.

They ran towards Sullivan's house.

There was a large bay window on the left and a white door on the right.

Lazarus saw a narrow path on the right. He pointed to it.

'Take the back,' he said to McEvoy.

Then he got to the front door.

He reached for his holster.

'Shit!'

He remembered his service pistol had been taken from him by the investigators.

He steeled himself, pushed down on the handle.

It was unlocked.

He ran inside, entered a tight hallway.

He saw a door on his left, barged it open.

It was the living room.

He scanned it. Nothing.

He ran back out to the hallway.

He looked right and saw stairs.

He thought it might be happening up there, but then he saw an open door leading to the kitchen at the end of the hallway.

He heard muffled screaming and knew they were in there.

'Armed gardaí! Armed police!' he shouted.

He ran along the narrow hallway.

He burst into the kitchen.

What he saw inside took the breath from him.

In front of him was an oak dining table with white leather chairs. Behind it was a cream wall. Someone had taken a brush to it

I'M SORRY

It said in lurid red paint.

The paint was fresh, was dripping. He looked to his left and saw more paint on another wall.

FORGIVE ME

He looked to his right.

Sullivan was on his stomach on the ground.

His hands were tied behind his back. Heavy masking tape was wrapped tight around his mouth. His feet were bound, too.

Gallagher was kneeling on top of him, one knee in the small of his back, the other on the dark floor tiles. The floor was covered in a plastic sheet. Gallagher was wearing a white forensics suit and blue latex gloves.

He was pulling on a thin rope that was taut around Sullivan's neck. Just like the one he used on Anne Delaney.

313

Sullivan's eyes were bulging, his face a violent red.

Gallagher had a faraway look in his eyes. He was smiling.

He was killing Sullivan.

The heavy duty tape covered Sullivan's mouth, and Lazarus could see him trying to draw breath in through his nose.

Dying breaths.

Lazarus heard McEvoy trying to break a door somewhere to get in.

But he knew there was no time.

He threw himself on Gallagher.

He connected with the side of his body. The force pushed Gallagher off Sullivan.

Lazarus's momentum drove him in a roll over Sullivan. He tumbled onto to the floor past him.

He continued his roll and came up on his knees, trying to get his bearings and find Gallagher.

Gallagher came at him, a blade glinting in his left hand.

Lazarus brought up his right hand and parried the attack. Gallagher swung again, over his head this time.

Lazarus formed an X with his forearms and stopped the knife dead.

The point the blade came to a halt inches from his face. Lazarus closed both hands around Gallagher's wrist and yanked down. The knife flew out of Gallagher's hand. It skidded across the floor.

Gallagher lunged forward. He punched Lazarus on the head with his free hand.

Lazarus reeled from it. He fell backwards onto the floor. Gallagher jumped on top of him. He had his large hands around Lazarus's neck. He started squeezing.

Lazarus tried to break the grip by chopping at the inside of Gallagher's elbows. They didn't budge.

Gallagher stared at him, his eyes wide, his teeth bared, saliva glistening on them.

Lazarus punched Gallagher's ribs. It had no effect.

Dots exploded in Lazarus's vision as the oxygen supply to his brain was cut.

He tried another punch. It landed on Gallagher's chin.

Gallagher didn't falter. He used all his weight to squeeze down on Lazarus's neck.

Lazarus's eyes began to close.

He was losing consciousness.

He felt his strength ebbing away as he struggled for air.

The blackness was circling him.

An image of Jenna and the kids came to him.

They were smiling.

And he knew he wasn't ready to go.

He knew he had to fight.

He knew he had one chance.

He brought up his right knee with all his remaining energy.

It slammed hard into Gallagher's balls.

Right in the sweet spot.

Gallagher howled and faltered.

He instinctively released his grip on Lazarus's throat, reached for his balls.

Lazarus saw a chink of light in the darkness. He made his move.

He launched a right hook.

It hit Gallagher square on the chin.

Lazarus hit him again.

On the nose this time. He heard a crack, saw an explosion of red on Gallagher's face.

Gallagher fell back.

Lazarus slithered out from under him.

He clambered to his feet.

Gallagher was on his knees, in front of him, trying to stand.

Lazarus kicked him hard in the face.

The crack of his boot connecting with bone filled the room.

The blow knocked Gallagher back down.

Lazarus kicked him again.

The kick connected with Gallagher's temple and drove his head back, smashing it into the hard floor.

This time he stayed down.

Lazarus kicked him again.

Hard, on the face. More blood.

Gallagher wasn't moving.

Lazarus knew he was out for the count.

He knew it was over, too.

He put his hands on his knees and gulped air into his lungs just as McEvoy barrelled in through a door, his pistol in his hand.

'Cuff the bastard,' Lazarus gasped.

47

Tuesday

The clawing smell of antiseptic hit the back of his throat as Lazarus walked along the corridor.

It had just been cleaned. A yellow sign in the middle of the hallway said, 'Danger, wet floor'.

Lazarus decided to risk it. He was in the right place if he went on his arse.

He saw the name he was looking for on a door halfway down.

He thought the door was just like all the other hospital doors he had walked through in the last week.

Too many.

He opened the door and walked inside.

Sullivan sat up in bed. The room was painted off-white, with two wooden armchairs at an angle to the bed. A black flat-screen television was on the wall facing Sullivan's bed. Sky News was on low.

Sullivan wore a black T-shirt and was perched up, two pillows supporting his back. A white cabinet sat to the right of the bed and it had a vase with pink flowers on its top. There were three get well soon cards, a bottle of sparkling water and a box of sweets.

'No grapes?' Lazarus joked, but it fell on deaf ears.

Sullivan hadn't realised he was in the room. He was too busy tapping on the keyboard of a MacBook.

After a few moments, Sullivan sensed he had a visitor. He stopped typing and looked up.

He closed the laptop, took earphones out.

'No comment.'

Lazarus smiled and threw a black iPhone onto his bed.

Sullivan's eyes lit up. He lifted the phone, examined it.

'Don't worry,' Lazarus said.

'It's intact. We didn't break the PIN. Your sources are safe.'

Sullivan relaxed.

'How are you?' Lazarus said.

Sullivan rubbed his throat. It was covered in a thick bandage that hid the deep red marks caused by Gallagher's rope 48 hours earlier.

His voice was raspy.

'They say there won't be any lasting damage and I should be back to normal in a week or so. I might need to take time away from the front line, though, I've got a book to write.'

'About this?' Lazarus asked.

Sullivan nodded.

'It will be good to go as soon as the trial is over. I've had two publishers on to me already.'

Lazarus shook his head.

'Might not be a trial,' Lazarus said.

'You think he'll plead?' Sullivan asked.

'He's fucked. His DNA matched. There's more, too.'

Lazarus walked to the window.

Sullivan's room was on a private ward in St. James's Hospital in the south inner city. Lazarus could see the Guinness Brewery in the distance.

He turned back to Sullivan.

'Off the record?'

'Of course.'

'The team found a hard drive hidden in his house. There was a photo of Anne Delaney on it.'

'From Facebook?' Sullivan asked.

'No. He took a photograph of her after the attack. She is on the ground. Unconscious.'

Sullivan gasped.

'Jesus.'

Lazarus looked to the door to make sure it was closed.

'He had photos of four more women.'

'Christ.'

'Italy, Holland, Spain and England.'

Sullivan put his head back into his pillow, looked to the ceiling.

'He attacked a woman near The Hague in January 2016,' Lazarus said.

The reporter's eyes widened.

'I was there with him then for a Europol gig.'

317

Lazarus nodded.

'That was one of the reasons we had you down for Anne Delaney. The DNA from that attack matched our sample.'

'That's why David O'Brien shouted at me as I left the station,' Sullivan said.

'I was wondering what he was on about.'

'We weren't allowed to question you about it as it happened abroad,' Lazarus said.

Sullivan shook his head.

'Six months before that in June 2015 a pensioner was raped in south London and two years earlier in September 2013 a sex worker was attacked in Milan,' Lazarus said.

'The last one was Spain in late 2017. We checked. He was in the cities at the time. When we're done with him here, he'll be extradited to the Netherlands. They have his DNA already. And when they're finished with him, the next country will go after him, too. He will never see the light of day.'

Sullivan was ashen-faced.

'Was this his first attack in Ireland?'

'They're looking.'

Sullivan looked down at his MacBook.

'How is Anne?' he asked.

'She came out of the coma yesterday.'

'Thank God,' Sullivan said.

'She has a long road ahead of her,' Lazarus said. 'But she's alive. And there is no brain damage. The physical injuries will heal, eventually…'

'Can I ask you something?' Sullivan said. His mouth was trembling.

'Did he hurt her to get at me?'

'I don't know, Conor,' Lazarus said.

'He didn't answer any questions in custody. He didn't even acknowledge the interview team. Not that it matters. He's finished. He appeared in court yesterday.'

'I know,' Sullivan said.

'Rape and two counts of attempted murder.'

He rubbed his neck.

'But I can say he did his best to frame you,' Lazarus said.

'He stole the bungee cord from your car and left it where it would be found. Your DNA was on it, of course. Just as he knew it would be. He spent a year feeding you stories on burner phones, building up your trust in him, made it look as if he was a senior cop.'

Sullivan grimaced.

'He had fantastic sources. Always had,' he said.

'He told you about the coin in Anne's throat,' Lazarus said.

'I think he did it so you would report it and become a suspect more quickly. But you never printed it.'

'I thought it crossed a line. Too much,' Sullivan said.

'And then there is young Lucy Fowler,' Lazarus said.

Sullivan shook his head.

'I'm sorry. I can't.'

'She's not being charged,' Lazarus said.

'She's cooperating. That has saved her from being prosecuted for making a false statement. Gallagher paid her three grand to frame you. We know the whole story. Gallagher was one of her clients, not you. She was an informant of yours.'

'No comment,' Sullivan said.

'Gallagher knew you would protect her, no matter what she said about you.'

Sullivan frowned.

'Nothing to say.'

Lazarus ignored him.

'We have Gallagher's bank records. He took out €3,000 in two batches.'

Sullivan shook his head. He wasn't going there.

He changed the subject.

'What's next for you, Lazarus?'

Lazarus shrugged his shoulders.

'I'll be getting a transfer. Maybe I'll go to a national unit after all the publicity about this case,' Lazarus said.

The press had seized on the rescue of Sullivan and charging of Gallagher. It was still top news, two days later. Lazarus was quite famous now.

'What about Maloney's trial?' Sullivan asked.

'I'll come back for it. I have to give evidence. I want to see it through. And I'm going to help fund Sarah through college.'

That was a white lie. Lazarus had persuaded Massimo to fund it. He could afford it.

'I'm sorry for laughing at Gallagher's jokes at the park,' Sullivan said.

'I feel bad about that. But reporters laugh at a lot of things we shouldn't. It's our defence mechanism.'

Lazarus smiled.

'We're the same. If we don't laugh, we cry.'

'And while I'm at it, I'm sorry for acting up at the hotel,' Sullivan said.

'I have no problem with the media,' Lazarus said.

Sullivan smirked.

'The last time you said that you pointed a gun at me.'

Lazarus laughed.

'By the way, we found out who tipped Maloney off about the raid,' he said.

The smile faded from Sullivan's face.

'Please tell me it wasn't Gallagher,' he said.

'No. A hotel worker. Sacked yesterday.'

'At least it wasn't Tony,' Sullivan said.

And he went quiet.

A heavy silence fell on the room.

Sullivan covered his face.

Lazarus saw his shoulders shake.

After a few moments, he regained his composure and lowered his hands.

His eyes were red.

Lazarus sat on the bed.

He looked Sullivan in the eye.

'Why did he pick you, Conor?

Sullivan's lips trembled.

Lazarus saw a look in his eyes that reminded him of that sweet moment when a suspect breaks in the interview. It was a mixture of regret and relief. Regret at what they did. Relief at letting it out.

Sullivan took a deep breath.

'When my wife left me, I was in a bad way,' he said.

'It destroyed me. I went off the deep end. Tony and his partner Claire were there for me. They saved me, babysat me, I suppose. One night, he was away on a job. Claire came to check on me, brought a bottle of wine...' His voice trailed off.

'Ah,' Lazarus said.

Suddenly everything made sense.

'It was only the once,' Sullivan said quickly.

'Jesus did we regret it the next morning. We swore never to mention it. I put it out of my mind after a while. It was a mistake. I put it behind me.'

He closed his eyes.

'I only realised he knew when he was...you know. He came to visit me to check up on me after my arrest. We were talking in the kitchen. I went to put the kettle on. That's all I can remember.

'I think he put me in a chokehold. It was lights out for me. When I came to, I was tied up on the floor. He told me Claire confessed almost immediately. He said he spent years planning how to ruin me. He said the world would think I was a rapist who had killed himself because he could not cope with the guilt.'

'That explains the graffiti on the walls,' Lazarus said.

Sullivan nodded.

'He told me exactly what he was going to do to me. He said he would garrot me, then when I was dead, he'd take my body and hang me by a noose from the banister. I had no defensive injuries. I didn't have a chance to fight him and I was bound when I regained consciousness. It would have looked like a straightforward suicide.'

Lazarus remembered Twitter.

'He had it all teed up,' he said.

'He tweeted he was worried about you, and would have found your body when he called on you to see if you were okay.'

'Yeah,' Sullivan said.

'It was the perfect crime. Almost.'

Sullivan looked at Lazarus.

'You saved me. I don't know how to thank you.'

He put out his right hand.

Lazarus gripped it.

'Just doing my job, ma'am,' he said.

Sullivan laughed.

Lazarus waited a beat.

'I saved you. Another cop had the chance to, but he chose not to.'

Sullivan froze.

'Pardon?'

'You were with a cop when Anne was attacked. All you had to do was tell us in the interview. A perfect alibi.'

Sullivan's face darkened.

'No idea what you're talking about.'

Lazarus got up and walked to the door.

Then, as he touched the handle, he turned back to Sullivan.

'You stayed quiet. If you had said you were with him, he was finished. But you didn't. You protected him. To the point of almost being framed for attacking Anne.'

'I thought about it,' Sullivan said, finally.

'I was tempted when you were hitting me with everything in the interview room. I almost told you.'

Lazarus remembered back to the room, when he believed Sullivan was going to break.

'But I signed an oath to protect sources. That's what I did.'

Lazarus nodded.

'We inhabit different worlds,' he said.

'I probably would have done the same if I was you.'

He smiled again.

'I have to go. Good luck, Conor. See you around,' he said.

'Maybe we will talk in the future.'

Sullivan smiled sadly.

'I would like that, Sergeant.'

Lazarus walked out, closed the door behind him.

He was making his way along the corridor when his phone vibrated. He took the handset out of his pocket. It was a WhatsApp from Winter.

His heart sank as he read it.

> *We just got a call from the prison. Gallagher was found dead in his cell overnight. Hanged himself with bedsheets. Brass are going nuts. He was on suicide watch. Disaster.*

Lazarus slumped against the wall.

He closed his eyes and thought of the people Gallagher had just cheated out of justice. Anne Delaney. The women in Europe. Sullivan. None of the would have their day in court now.

'Coward,' he whispered.

He stood up straight. The door to Sullivan's room was within touching distance. He stretched out his hand to grasp the handle, ready to break the news.

And then he stopped.

Let Sullivan have a few hours' peace before he was given the news.

And let someone else tell him.

Anyway, Lazarus had something much more important to do.

He turned from the door and walked down the corridor.

48

Lazarus knocked on the door and waited.

There was no answer. Anderson always did that. He liked his underlings to wait, rap again when their first knock went unanswered.

Lazarus wasn't going to play that game.

Lazarus counted off the seconds. He was at 27 when his phone buzzed. He took the handset from his pocket and saw a message from Fallon.

My office. Pronto.

He figured he had a few minutes.

That was all he needed.

Just then the door opened.

Anderson had blinked first.

'Come in,' he said.

Lazarus went in. Anderson closed the door. The office was one of the largest in the station, second only to Fallon's. Clean white walls, a grey carpet. A large desk to accommodate Anderson's papers. And his ego.

The walls had large photographs mounted in expensive frames. One was of Anderson in a graduation gown beside the Commissioner. Another was of all the detectives in the station, with Anderson front and centre. His hands rested on his thighs and he wore a self-satisfied smile. As a detective sergeant, Lazarus also had to sit in the front row, but he chose a seat away from Anderson.

Another was a press photograph of Anderson coming out of the Criminal Courts of Justice complex in the city centre. It had been taken from the side. The photographer had framed the shot so all that could be seen was Anderson at the word JUSTICE.

It gave Lazarus an idea. He took a piece of paper from his overcoat pocket.

Anderson walked behind the desk and sat into a black leather chair.

'What can I do for you?' he said.

'I don't want to work with you anymore,' Lazarus said.

'I don't think you want to work with me either.'

Anderson snorted and sat back in the chair, his hands behind his head.

'You break one big case and you think you can demand a transfer? It doesn't work like that, kid. Fallon is retiring soon. I'll be taking over when I get promoted. I'll decide whether you move or not.'

He smirked.

'Don't hold your breath.'

Lazarus threw the paper onto his desk.

'Here's another photograph for your wall.'

Anderson gave it a suspicious glance. He pulled it across the desk.

He looked down at it.

Lazarus saw the blood drain from his face.

The photograph was black and white, but in perfect definition.

Anderson stayed silent for a long moment.

'What do you want?' he said finally.

'It was a text Sullivan sent Gallagher on the burner the night of the attack that gave you away,' Lazarus said.

'He said he had just been out with a fella having a pint before he got the tip about the attack. I know the route he took back to his office, so I worked backwards and realised he was meeting a contact over on the northside. He went past Drumcondra where we got his BMW on CCTV. So, I knew Sullivan had been north of that.'

Anderson said nothing.

'All I had to do was work out where a garda would meet a journalist in that part of the city without being spotted.'

He named a bar near the road that led to the airport.

'Cosy booths where people could talk without being seen or overheard. Perfect for a secret meeting.'

Anderson kept his eyes on the photo.

'I went there this morning and had a look at their CCTV.'

Lazarus reached forward and snapped the sheet out of Anderson's hand. He examined the image for the hundredth time that day.

Anderson and Sullivan were on CCTV walking through the pub.

The timestamp said 11.24pm. Both men were in casual clothing. Both were laughing.

'What do you want?' Anderson repeated.

'I should arrest you for wasting Garda time,' Lazarus said.

'You knew Sullivan was innocent. You sat in all the meetings. You said nothing. You let it all happen. Then you had the balls to be part of the arrest team. I thought you wanted the publicity. I remember you telling him to think very carefully about what he was saying. You came with us to tell Sullivan to shut up. To protect yourself.'

Anderson stared at the desk.

'When the Commissioner saw the Maloney story, he kicked up a stink,' Lazarus said. 'You ordered the internal investigation to be seen to be doing something.'

More silence from Anderson.

'Sullivan left his office to get to the hotel at 6.43pm,' Lazarus said.

'That was ten minutes after Fallon gave the okay for Maloney's arrest. You contacted him straightaway. That's why he was there before we even arrived.'

Anderson said nothing.

'Do you know what the worst thing is, Anderson? You made me distrust my team. I believed it was Harry first, then Rachel Winter. She told me she studied journalism. I thought she was the mole. But it was you.'

Anderson said nothing.

'I could arrest you,' Lazarus said again.

'I won't. You and I both know your pals in HQ would circle the wagons and protect you. But plenty of journalists would love this photograph. They're all miles behind Sullivan on the Gallagher case and are desperate for anything.'

'What do you fucking want, Lazarus?' Anderson asked for the third time.

His voice was louder now, a mix of anger and desperation.

'I want out of here,' Lazarus said, holding his gaze.

'Into a national unit. Maybe Special Branch. Or Organised Crime. I'm taking leave now and I will be back in two weeks' time. I'll let you know where I want to go.'

His eyes glinted.

'And you, you prick, will sort it.'

Anderson gritted his teeth, said nothing.

Lazarus walked to the door, gripped the brushed steel handle.

He opened the door and pulled it back.

But then he thought of something.

He turned back to Anderson.

'That night in the pub when you called me a Wop and I slapped you in the face,' Lazarus said.

'I want you to know I regret it.'

Anderson looked up, hope in his eyes.

Then, after a beat, Lazarus said: 'I regret not hitting you harder.'

He smiled and walked out of the office.

49

Fallon was waiting for Lazarus on the stairs outside her office.
She smiled.

Lazarus saw the regret in her eyes.

He got to the final step and she moved forward to envelop him in a hug.
He embraced her back. He felt his anger fade away.

'I'm sorry, Lazarus,' she said.

'I fucked up. I was terrified the whole Sullivan arrest was going to be a
PR disaster. I just panicked.'

'It's all cool,' Lazarus said.

And it really was.

'HQ loves you. The case is all over the news. You're a celebrity,' Fallon
said.

'Great,' Lazarus said dryly.

He didn't do fame.

He was a polis man.

Nothing more.

Fallon went quiet, bit her bottom lip.

'Something has come up' she said.

Lazarus tensed.

'There are people in here to see you,' she said.

She walked to her office door, opened it and signalled for him to enter.

Lazarus felt a knot in his stomach.

A thousand different scenarios ran through his head, none of them
good.

He swallowed hard and walked inside.

Cochrane stood behind Fallon's desk. She nodded, said nothing.

He looked over to the sofa. His eyes widened when he saw the two
people sitting on it. The first was Donal Flynn. He was the Assistant
Commissioner in charge of major crime investigations.

He was well-built man in his late fifties, with tight grey hair and blue hard eyes. He wore a charcoal suit, blue shirt and an expense black silk tie. He had massive hands, like shovels. He stood and walked to Lazarus, extending one of those huge hands.

'Sergeant Lazarus,' Flynn said.

'Great work on the Griffith Park case. Outstanding. The Commissioner asked me to pass on his personal congratulations.'

His praise did not register with Lazarus. He was too busy staring at the other person on the sofa and wondering why Jenna was in the room.

His wife stood, hurried towards him.

She wore that brown patterned dress he bought her in Milan last summer. He remembered her eyes lighting up when she saw it in the boutique. The bloody thing cost him €500, but it was worth every cent.

She wore black sandals with straps around the ankles, and a white cardigan. Lazarus saw a large gold crucifix hanging from her neck. He could also see a crumpled handkerchief in her fist.

And eyes that were red from tears.

He was suddenly gripped by unbearable fear.

'Is it the boys?' he stammered.

Jenna shook her head.

'No *caro*, don't worry. Everything is fine. Massimo has them.'

Lazarus breathed a sigh of relief. He thought if Jenna and the kids were okay, he could deal with whatever bad news the A/C had been sent to tell him.

Flynn placed a hand on his shoulder. Fallon stood beside Cochrane at the super's desk. Lazarus realised everyone was either smiling or crying.

'Sergeant Lazarus,' Flynn said.

'We have some news for you. Take a seat, please.'

Lazarus was shaking.

Flynn looked to Cochrane.

'This is your case, Sergeant Cochrane, your hard work,' Flynn said. 'Please do the honours.'

She turned to Lazarus, smiled a sad smile.

'Martin Glennon has come forward with information about the murder of Gabriella,' she said.

Lazarus felt the blood drain from his face. His knees went. He collapsed into the sofa.

'He has been talking to me since that day we visited him at his flat. Sorry. I couldn't tell you.'

'He made a statement,' she added.

Lazarus remembered attacking Glennon outside Broadstone on Saturday after he was taken off the Delaney case.

He put his head in his hands.

'Glennon was in prison at the time of Gabriella's murder. It can't have been him,' he said.

'It wasn't,' Cochrane said.

'But he knows who the killer is.'

She moved forward.

'I was sceptical about all this religious shite,' she said.

She flushed.

'Sorry, Commissioner.'

The A/C waved his hand.

'But it looks like he has changed for the better,' Cochrane said.

'I can't believe I'm saying this, but I think he's telling the truth.'

Lazarus was struggling to breathe. His pulse was pounding in his ears.

'Glennon has been clean since he left prison,' Cochrane said.

'But for most of the years he was locked up, he was off his head on heroin. Can't remember most of his time inside. When I introduced you to him in the flat, something came back to him. It was your name. Lazarus.'

Lazarus recalled the encounter. He thought back to the stinking flat, remembered the strange look Glennon gave him.

'There's something...I...that name...Lazarus...Lazarus...'

'He told me the memory came back to him after we left,' Cochrane said.

'He remembered sharing a cell with another prisoner for a few months. Not a sex offender. A man who was in for assault. A bad one, on a woman. Anyway, one night they got drunk on smuggled in booze and the other fella opened up.'

Lazarus put a balled fist to his mouth. It shook.

'He told Glennon he murdered a woman,' Cochrane said.

'Yer man said he saw her stumbling along near St. Stephen's Green one night and decided to take her. He was a van driver and pulled over, got her into his vehicle. Took her up the mountains and, well...'

Jenna squeezed Lazarus's other hand.

'Glennon said he dismissed what yer man was saying, thought it was the usual cell block bollixology-'.

She again looked at the A/C apologetically, he just smiled.

'Anyway,' she said. 'He had completely forgotten about it until we called to him. He said he spent the evening after we left reading the Bible and praying, asking God for advice. He said God told him to do the right thing. Glennon slept on it. He wasn't nervous about telling us, he just wanted to make sure he wasn't imagining things. He said the heroin messed with his mind.

'He woke up on Wednesday morning and he knew that he wasn't imagining it. So he came looking for me. He went to my team. They rang me and I met him before I came in here.'

She smiled.

'I was being truthful,' Cochrane said.

'I was not on anything related to the Delaney case. I just couldn't tell you. I didn't want to build your hopes up.'

Lazarus thought back to that morning. He had brought Cochrane to see the victim in the hospital, but she had been late. He thought she was holding something back about the case. More or less accused her of lying to him.

He suddenly felt very stupid.

'He made the statement to my colleagues in MIS later that day,' Cochrane said.

'He couldn't remember the prisoner's name – he bunked with so many in his time. The team looked at all the prison records and came up with six potentials. He agreed to look at their mugshots, but for some weird reason, I'm the only detective he trusts.'

Lazarus remembered Cochrane giving Glennon a hard time in his flat. He gave her a look. She winked at him.

'So we did it here on Saturday, when you, eh, left the station,' she said.

'You mean when I threw my toys out of the pram and stormed out after the DNA on Sullivan came back?' Lazarus said.

Cochrane laughed.

'Aye, then. Superintendent Fallon called to the incident room and told me he was here.'

Lazarus turned to Fallon.

'You knew, ma'am?'

She nodded, mouthed the word 'sorry'.

Lazarus saw she was fighting back tears.

He smiled at her.

'It's okay, my friend.' he said.

'So he came into one of the interview rooms,' Cochrane said.

'I laid out the six photos and he pointed at one straight away. He said he was 100 per cent.'

Everything stood still for Lazarus. Even his heart stopped beating.

He asked one simple question.

A question that had haunted him for years.

'Who is he?'

Cochrane had notes in her hand. She didn't need them.

'His name is Jeremiah Connelly,' she said.

She went back to Fallon's desk, took an A4 sheet of paper from a file on it.

'I have his mugshot if you want to see him, John.'

Lazarus said nothing, but held out his hand.

She handed him the photo. Lazarus closed his eyes for moment, then he opened them and looked down at the image of the man who had destroyed his sister.

The man was in his mid fifties. He had a receding brown hair, greying at the temples. A high forehead, tight lips, grey stubble on cheeks. His face was round and he had a double chin. Brown eyes that stared right into the camera.

Lazarus examined the mugshot for a long time, trying to see if there was anything that betrayed Connelly's dark secret.

Any mark of Cain.

But there was nothing.

He looked just like any other middle-aged man.

The banality of evil.

'He's 55 now, was 48 at the time. He lives in County Meath,' Cochrane said.

Cochrane named a small village 60 kilometres north-west of central Dublin.

'But he's from my part of the world originally. County Antrim. I'll tell you the relevance of that in a minute. We checked his background. He was a self-employed courier at the time. Remember the original investigation team looked at all the vehicles in the area around the time Gabriella went missing?'

Lazarus nodded.

'They had no reg numbers because of the poor quality CCTV at the time,' Cochrane said.

'But they did have makes and models. They got all registered vehicles on the database and worked their way through them, visiting every registered owner of a vehicle that was the same model as one caught on CCTV. There were thousands of them. But they found every one, eliminated every one of them, too.'

And then Lazarus knew.

'He had a UK-registered van, didn't he?' he said.

'Yes,' she said.

'A white 2003 Ford Transit that he used for his business. He never registered it to Ireland, always had the British plates. It was never on our system. The devious bastard.'

She didn't apologise to A/C Flynn this time.

'The team lifted him yesterday. They found his van as well. He had kept it for parts. It was out the back of his house. It's being analysed as we speak. There's still a chance there might be some forensics that will link it to Gabriella.'

Lazarus tried not to think what that evidence would be.

'But in a way it's irrelevant,' Cochrane said.

She moved closer to Lazarus.

'John. I want you to know that Gabriella, your fantastic and brave and beautiful sister, gave us all the evidence we need. She fought him. She fought for her life. She scratched at him and cut his face. You know there was DNA under her fingernails.'

She paused.

'They took his sample yesterday. The results came through earlier. The chances of the DNA from the scene not being his are 40 billion to one. It's him, John. It's him.'

The room started spinning.

'The Director of Public Prosecutions came through with a direction two hours ago,' Cochrane said.

'He is to be charged with the abduction and murder of Gabriella Maria Lazarus on October 30, 2012. We have the bastard. He's in another station in the city. I'm heading over there to charge him myself.'

A single tear meandered down her cheek.

'And it will be the honour of my life to do it. For Gabriella. And for you.'

And at that, after seven years and thousands of nightmares, John Lazarus broke.

He fell back in the seat and started sobbing, the tears rolling down his cheeks as he cried for his sister.

Jenna held him and let him weep.

*

It was an hour before the meeting broke up.

Lazarus had a million questions. He got some answers.

The killer had convictions for assault, including beating his ex-wife and a former business partner. He was in jail for attacking a woman in a road rage incident when Glennon met him. He put her in hospital for a month. He had never been on the Garda radar for any sex offences. Now Cochrane and her unit were combing through his past, trying to connect him to other missing women.

They were sure Gabriella was not his only victim.

The meeting ended with hugs and backslapping all round.

Even from the Commissioner.

'Connelly is for court in the morning,' Cochrane said as she walked Lazarus and Jenna down the stairs.

'I'll be there. I wouldn't miss it for the world,' Lazarus said.

'That makes two of us,' Cochrane smiled.

Lazarus held Jenna's hand.

They walked into the public office and headed to the exit.

They were outside in an instant, standing on the footpath.

It was a bitter day.

'This country is always freezing,' Lazarus said.

'But it's our country,' Jenna said.

He rubbed her arm through her heavy overcoat. Lazarus glanced up. There were no clouds in the sky.

He stood with Jenna and gave her a slow embrace.

'Do you want to go to the graves? It's their anniversary in three days,' she asked him as her face nestled into his neck.

He shook his head.

'No, *carina*. I think it's time to let them rest.'

He put an arm around Jenna's petite and beautiful shoulders.

'Lets go home,' he said.

They walked together down the street, his arm still around her shoulder, hers around his waist.

The sun was in Lazarus's eyes.

He had to squint.

And he thought the sunlight was wonderful.

THE END

Author's Note

I've been a crime journalist for more than 20 years, a reporter for almost 30.

In that time, I have come into contact with thousands of people; some good, some bad.

Some really bad.

Aspects of many of them formed characters and incidents in Black Light. Reporters are like magpies, we hoard everything. You never know when a tiny piece of information will be useful. I know now.

In the early noughties, I tracked down a sex worker who had been seriously assaulted by a notorious murderer. The fear in her eyes when she talked about that killer is something I will never forget. That terrified face was the basis for the character of Lucy Fowler. I often think about her. I hope she is safe today.

The scene in the hotel at the start with Rachel Winter is a version of a story I was told years ago. A detective garda on a drugs search had a man jump out of a wardrobe and put a gun in his mouth. The stand-off lasted two hours in real life. Two hours with a gun in your mouth.

John Lazarus was in my head for a long time, well before I wrote this novel. His character and those of all the other officers in *Black Light* are based on myriad cops that I have interacted with over the years. I've taken a personality trait from one, a mannerism from another. There are maybe five real life cops whose personalities have had a major impact on the Lazarus character. They are all passionate police officers who do their best every day to make a difference. Ireland is lucky to have them. I can't name most of them, but I want to thank them all.

There is, however, one who I can identify.

For the record, although the character is entirely fictional, the main inspiration for Lazarus was Detective Sergeant Michael Moran, of An Garda Síochána.

Cop.

Rescuer of children.

Friend.

He has hunted predators for decades in Ireland and abroad.

I interviewed him once when he was working for Interpol in France in a child protection role. It was a grim job, but he did it with an unflinching dedication. He brought me into his office. I noticed huge earphones there. In my naivete, I asked what they were for. He told me he wore them when he was examining child sexual abuse videos. He did not want anyone else to have to listen the children's, or babies', screams.

If you search his name on the internet, one of the million photos of him is of me interviewing him in that office. The headphones are hanging on the wall as he points to the screen of two computers on his desk. We pixilated the screens. You don't want to know what was on them.

But I did shamelessly steal that real life vignette for this novel.

So thanks, Mick.

I hope the screams fade away one day.

Dublin, August 2022.